To Stephen H. Heeney,
with appreciation,
from Leon ??? Galbord

January 1975

???

# UGETSU MONOGATARI

TALES OF MOONLIGHT
AND RAIN

1 Formal portrait of Ueda Akinari, on silk, made in 1786 by Tosa Hidenobu. (Nara, Tenri Central Library.)

# UGETSU MONOGATARI

## TALES OF MOONLIGHT AND RAIN

A Complete English Version of the
Eighteenth-Century Japanese Collection
of Tales of the Supernatural

by UEDA AKINARI
1734–1809

based on the first woodblock edition of 1776
with illustrations and an introduction for
Western readers

Translated and edited by
Leon M. Zolbrod
Professor of Asian Studies
University of British Columbia

London    George Allen & Unwin Ltd
Ruskin House   Museum Street

First published in 1974

ISBN 0 04 823116 9

Not for sale in the United States and Canada. A North
American Edition of this book is published by the University
of British Columbia Press.
This is one of the books assisted by the Asian Literature
Program of the Asia Society, New York, and has been
published with the help of a grant from the Humanities
Research Council of Canada, using funds provided by the
Canada Council.


UNESCO COLLECTION OF REPRESENTATIVE WORKS
JAPANESE SERIES
This book has been accepted in the Japanese Series of
the Translations Collection of the United Nations
Educational, Scientific and Cultural Organisation
(UNESCO)




Printed in Great Britain
in 12 point Barbou type
by W & J Mackay Limited, Chatham

*To Fumiko*

# TRANSLATOR'S FOREWORD

*Ugetsu monogatari*, or 'Tales of Moonlight and Rain,' numbers among the best-loved Japanese classics. These nine illustrated tales of the supernatural from eighteenth-century Osaka combine popular appeal with a high literary standard. The author expressed his complex views on human life and society in simple yet elegant and poetic language. At the same time, he wished to entertain his readers with mystery, ghosts, and otherworldly occurrences in the hope that people might pause for thought at a time when men and their institutions had begun to change at an alarming rate.

Twenty years ago, when I saw Mizoguchi Kenji's movie version, one of the most perfect films in the history of Japanese cinema, I first learned about these tales. Later I lived for a time in northern Japan in a rambling old house, an antiquated blend of Japanese and Victorian architecture. It was said to be haunted by the spirit of a young girl who decades earlier had committed suicide in a third-story tower. Each evening in the winter an old woman would come to my quarters to cook my dinner, and she would spend her idle moments with a paperback version of the tales. 'What are you reading?' I once asked her, and by way of reply, she smiled in embarrassment.

Afterward, I saw a prize-winning film, 'The Bewitching Love of Madame Pai,' which had been inspired by one of these tales. Later, again coming into contact with the author's world, I discovered that Akinari had helped to create a form of narrative prose that reminds one of Gothic romances and the ghostly tales of certain English and American writers, such as Hawthorne and James. At one time, as I studied in a tiny cubicle on the eighth floor in Butler Library, I translated portions of two tales. Then I did a tentative version of yet another. Since 1967, in Vancouver, Tokyo, and Kyoto I have worked sporadically on a complete English edition.

I have done my translation in the belief that we in our world suffer from lack of fantasy. Akinari's universe lies far enough away in time, space, and substance that it will appeal with fresh vigour to modern readers. Experiencing the supernatural as it found expression in an eighteenth-century Japanese collection of tales and discovering how Akinari questioned the prevailing moral values and standards of his age will afford the attentive reader a new dimension in self-understanding. Confrontation with Akinari's tales may suggest an alternative vision of life and help in the search for freedom from the frustrating and smothering effect on human well-being of the combined pressure of a technological society without and a disorganised soul within.

Many persons and institutions have helped me, and I am pleased to thank some of them in public. I am especially grateful to my colleagues, Michael Bullock, William L. Holland, and Stanley E. Read, for reading earlier drafts of the translation and for making various suggestions. I also wish to thank Blake Morgan Young and Michael-Patrick O'Connor for their useful comments. I thank Hamada Keisuke and Sakakura Atsuyoshi, of Kyoto University – the former for sponsoring my most recent extended stay in Japan, for giving hours of pleasant companionship, and for reading and commenting on my introduction – and the latter for sharing his study with me and for offering timely suggestions and advice. I thank Okada Rihei for his help and generosity. He exemplifies the traditions that Akinari upheld. At the age of eighty-one years he travelled to North America to lecture and to learn. Roy E. Teele, editor of *Literature East and West*, published an earlier version of my translation of 'White Peak,' for which I thank him.

Among the institutions that have helped me, I specifically thank the Canada Council, the Dorothy Killam Foundation, and the University of British Columbia for generous financial support. Without their aid I could not have travelled to Japan, nor could I have prepared the illustrations. I also thank the Tenri Central Library, Kadokawa Shoten, Iwanami Shoten, the National Diet Library, the Kaguwashi Shrine, the Saifukuji

Temple, the Suntory Museum of Art, the Tokyo National Museum, the Kyoto National Museum, and the Itsuo Art Museum for their courtesy and cooperation. The Humanities Research Council of Canada has also helped make possible publication of this book.

I am grateful to Mr and Mrs Tomioka Masutarō for housing me in Kyoto and for photographing Tomioka Tessai's caricature of Akinari. I thank Mrs Betty Greig, Mrs Jackie Irwin, Miss Sheena McDonald, and Mrs Lauryn Purych for their help in typing the manuscript, which at one stage was shuttled back and forth by air across the Pacific Ocean. Last of all, I thank my wife. While the work was in progress she has given birth to three children, and she has also typed several draft versions of the manuscript, beginning with the original hand-scrawled copy. I enjoyed our many conversations about the work, and this book is dedicated to her.

Leon M. Zolbrod
Vancouver, British Columbia, and Kyoto, Japan

# CONTENTS

# ILLUSTRATIONS

LINE ILLUSTRATIONS

# INTRODUCTION

Born in the merchant city of Osaka in 1734, Ueda Akinari, the author of *Ugetsu monogatari*, was a creative figure of unique talent in eighteenth-century Japan. He died in 1809, in Kyoto – at that time the capital of the nation. Dissolving the family business, which he inherited, he became a physician and practised this profession until a young girl in his care died and he decided to give up medicine. He studied and wrote *haiku* and *waka* poetry, and he took part in the revival of Japanese scholarship and literature in the late eighteenth century. Although he was closely familiar with Chinese classics, as well as vernacular prose, he remained critical of all manner of pedantry. His preface to the tales dates from 1768, but the book was not published until 1776, jointly in Kyoto and Osaka, and he probably completed his final version around this time.

A meeting of the famous medieval poet, Saigyō, and the ghost of a former emperor who in a remote time predicted an age of war and turmoil begins the collection. A prophecy in the ninth tale that the leadership of the Tokugawa shogun will bring peace to the realm marks the end. All of the tales reflect real and imaginary events ranging from the seventh to the seventeenth century. Connections between the stories may not be obvious on first reading, but upon closer perusal a total form emerges, indistinctly as a mystic scene in a Chinese landscape and as hauntingly as the supernatural itself.

1 *Meaning of the Title*
*U* means 'rain.' *Getsu* means 'moon.' *Monogatari* suggests an elegant kind of fiction, such as that in ancient Japanese court romances. In the twelfth century during a time of war and turmoil the poet Saigyō (1118–90), who was also a Buddhist priest, travelled about the countryside praying and composing verse.

He was remembered for his simple way of life, his belief in art, and his fondness for peace, not war. Besides his poetry, he also wrote a collection of Buddhist tales and sketches designed to instruct and inform as well as to move the heart. The first of Akinari's nine tales begins with a passage taken from one of these sketches, and Saigyō may be thought of as the fictitious narrator. A nō play entitled *Ugetsu* also tells of Saigyō's travels and of an encounter he had with the world of spirits. Therefore, Akinari's title is related first of all to the opening tale and reminds one of the poet Saigyō in real life and in the world of make-believe. But still deeper levels of meaning are also implied, showing further association with all nine of the tales.

Dream and fantasy characterise the nō play, *Ugetsu*. The season is autumn. In a poor hut at Sumiyoshi, on the eastern edge of what is now Osaka Bay, an old man and woman are arguing. She likes the moonlight and wants to let it through the chinks of a board roof. He enjoys the sound of rain on one of straw. But he complains in poetic diction,

> *Shizu ga noki-ba wo*   Thatching the eaves of our poor hut  
> *fuki zo wazurō*   Means too much fuss and bother.

Saigyō appears and asks for a night's lodging. The old man agrees to let him stay on condition that he find a good beginning for the verse. Saigyō replies,

> *Tsuki wa more*   Moonlight may enter,  
> *ame wa tamaredo*   And rain may stand in puddles,  
> *tonikaku-ni*   But at any rate . . .[1]

Thus he meets the challenge and suggests how foolish it is to quarrel over trivial matters. Later, the old man and woman are revealed as messengers of the deity of Sumiyoshi – god of poetry, happiness, travel, the sea, and protector of the nation.

In his preface Akinari writes that he finished the tales late one spring night, when the rain ended and the moon shone faintly by his window. The terms that he uses resemble those in a Chinese collection of supernatural tales of the Ming dynasty, *Ch'ien teng hsin hua* (New Tales for Lamplight),[2] to which Akinari was indebted. Not only does the title conjure memories of Saigyō and evoke the world of the supernatural, but it also shows a taste for the classical prose, poetry, and drama of China as well as Japan.

'Rain' and 'moon' are contrasting qualities. The first implies life, love, youth, passion, and innocence – in Yeats's terms, 'The young with one another in their arms.' The moon, that coolest of heavenly bodies, on the other hand connotes grief and sorrow and stands for wisdom, maturity, and enlightenment. Together, rain and moon suggest a movement from innocence to experience. In the end the idea of moon gains ascendancy, as youthful ardour is mitigated by wisdom. Appropriately for a collection of supernatural tales, the elements of rain and moon – female and male, softness and hardness, feeling and logic – are kept in harmony, with neither a destructive flood nor cold chill prevailing.

Finally, the title alludes to the author's home city of Osaka, where the god of Sumiyoshi was worshipped with special reverence. Both in the tale and in the play, Saigyō travels westward and has a poetic exchange with a miraculous being. By means of art man communicates with the world beyond. A feeling of awe and terror is created within a framework of restrained beauty. Saigyō stands for the archetypal master of magic, whose chants have hypnotic effect and induce a trance-like state. He is seer, prophet, interpreter of the gods, sorcerer, and entertainer. Akinari's title promises not only an enjoyable collection of ghostly tales but also a memorable literary achievement, which reflects man's eternal problems and embodies the finest spirit of an age. Deservedly, *Ugetsu monogatari* is recognised as a great work in the Japanese tradition.

Ghostly tales have always stirred the imagination, and Akinari's collection continues to attract a wide audience. But the work's high reputation as a literary classic comes partly from the author's indebtedness to old Chinese and Japanese literature and to Buddhist philosophy and partly from his involvement with the moral questions of his own time. Besides dealing with spectres, demons, and apparitions, Akinari takes enduring themes, ideas, and metaphors from the Oriental tradition and puts them in fresh new garb, conveying a full measure of human wisdom and understanding and revealing profound connections with earlier works. Still, he avoids the bookish character of many Confucian classics in favour of the gentle persuasiveness associated with Taoism and the Buddhist teachings. As in the best products of Japanese genius, he communicates states of feeling by means of the skillful creation of mood and emotion. He uses not direct assertion, but rather implication and suggestion, thereby inducing a lyrical and romantic tone. Underlying the tales is a subtle response to nature in a world where good and evil co-exist in a delicate balance, easily upset. The tales receive a rich tradition, reinforce it, and transmit it to posterity in a stronger form. While ordinary people have enjoyed the stories for entertainment, readers aware of their literary and historical background have found all the more reason to study and treasure them.

2 *Biographical Sketch of Ueda Akinari*
Of his real mother he had but a shadowy memory. She was a woman of pleasure in the Osaka gay quarter. He never knew his true father's identity. Luckily, he was adopted by a former samurai named Ueda Mosuke, who had prospered as an oil and paper merchant in Osaka and lived with his wife and daughter. But trouble followed in the wake of good fortune, and soon after coming to the Ueda house Akinari fell ill of smallpox. His father and mother prayed to the god of the Kashima Inari Shrine, and Akinari later believed that this deity had saved his life. He himself recovered, but his foster mother died soon afterward. Mosuke remarried, and his new wife proved to be a capable helpmate and a good mother.

Unfortunately, the middle finger of Akinari's right hand was deformed, making it as short as the little one. He thought this to be a result of his childhood illness, but more likely it was a congenital defect caused by venereal disease, a common malady in the gay quarter, where he was born. 'Whenever I took a brush, the finger might as well not have been there,' he later wrote, and because of this deformity he could never become a famous calligrapher or master the art of painting.

Growing up in the Ueda household, he and his step-sister benefited from the new mother's maternal care and the father's stern discipline. To some extent his childhood feelings are suggested in certain of the tales. Perhaps he thought of himself as a lazy, unworthy, and irresponsible son, like Katsushirō, in 'The House Amid the Thickets,' or as a secondary child, like Toyoo, in 'The Lust of the White Serpent' – subordinate and secretly resentful. Just as Toyoo met with scorn from his father and elder brother while his mother and sister-in-law showed sympathy and understanding, perhaps Akinari's father was firm and resolute, and his stepmother tended to be somewhat lax and permissive.

By the standards of the day, he had a good education. He attended a private school primarily for the merchant class, where he did classical studies under Nakai Shūan (1693–1758) and Goi Ranshū (1698–1762). Also, he joined in a *haiku* group over which Takai Kikei (1687–1761) presided, and he remained a lifelong friend of Kikei's son, Kitō (1741–89), a recognised poet in his own right. In time he became familiar with Yosa Buson (1716–84), the most famous *haiku* poet after Bashō and also a master of the literary style of painting. The *haiku* poet and artist Matsumura Gekkei (1752–1811; Goshun was his painting name) was numbered among his acquaintances, and in later years Akinari enjoyed the friendship of Ozawa Roan (1722–1801), one of the outstanding *waka* poets of the age. Therefore, Akinari's circle of acquaintances extended to the fields of *haiku*, *waka*, Chinese poetry, painting, and of course scholarship. He developed a very broad and cultivated range of interests.

During the 1750s, his step-sister fled with a lover. In spite of Akinari's pleas on her behalf, his father disowned the girl, and as a result he held sole responsibility for carrying on the family name and business. Although his father tried to force him into a marriage of convenience, Akinari insisted on wedding a girl from Kyoto, named O'Tama, who had been serving for five or six years at the Ueda house. The fictional scene in 'The Lust of the White Serpent,' where Toyoo fears that he will be disowned if he reveals his love for the unobtainable Manago, may reflect emotions that Akinari experienced before he was married. Afterward, he and O'Tama remained childless, and one wonders if Akinari was sterile by heredity. Still, O'Tama retained her husband's love and devotion, and years later, when she died, Akinari felt heartbroken. He expressed his grief in terms similar to those found in several of his tales, where men confronted deep, personal tragedy.

As a young man he tried his hand at fiction in the manner of the 'floating world,' publishing in 1766 and 1767 two collections of amusing character sketches, mostly about naughty young men and women. But around this time he began to study with Katō Umaki (1722–77), who in turn was a disciple of Kamo Mabuchi (1697–1769), the greatest teacher of ancient Japanese learning. Under Katō's tutelage Akinari discovered new seriousness of purpose. Hereafter he turned in earnest to scholarship and classical literary pursuits and regretted ever having dabbled in the fiction of the floating world. The mature Akinari may be thought of as a poet and scholar who gained wide renown for his works of fiction.

For a period of time after his father's death Akinari managed the family business, though hardly with enthusiasm. Like Samon, in 'Chrysanthemum Tryst,' or Toyoo, he cared more for learning than for practical affairs. His ideas in 'The Caldron of Kibitsu' concerning a former warrior whose degenerate son runs away, abandoning home and family, may have reflected in part his step-sister's similar action or even his own wish to do the same. But just as the fictitious Toyoo eventually reformed and assumed his adult responsibilities, so too did Akinari, at least in some degree.

When home and business were destroyed by fire, early in 1771, he exerted little effort to make up the loss, realising that his talents did not suit him for the world of trade and com-

merce. As he indicated in 'Wealth and Poverty,' he thought
that the wisest course of action was to stop pushing himself in
this direction and instead live a simple and tranquil life, main-
taining his 'purity of heart.' Thus he liquidated his father's
business and decided to become a physician, studying under
Tsuga Teishō (1718?–95?), who was an erudite Confucian
scholar and a popular author, as well as a medical practitioner.
Teishō had previously published two collections of tales inspired largely by Chinese vernacular literature, which was
increasingly in vogue. From him Akinari learned about both
medicine and colloquial Chinese fiction, joining a group of men
who were experimenting with new modes of short-story writing. In 1776, the same year that he began independently to
practice medicine, he published *Ugetsu monogatari*, using the
pen name of Senshi Kijin, which means something like 'The
eccentric Mr Cut-Finger,' an apparent reference to his physical
deformity.

Although he did not openly acknowledge that he was the
author, the appearance of his tales may have been related to his
beginning practice as a physician. Perhaps here was a way to
attract patrons and advertise his skill. One notices the prominent role that illness played in the tales – Soemon's condition
in 'Chrysanthemum Tryst,' the description of Sode's malady in
'The Caldron of Kibitsu.' Travellers stranded far from home took
ill, and owing to the charity of a kind benefactor they recovered.
Akinari believed that sickness was largely psychological, an
idea derived from his studies of classical Japanese, and one
shared by Motoori Norinaga (1730–1801) and other scholars
of the school of national learning. Significantly enough, Sode's
suffering, and indeed her possession by a spirit, was modelled on
that of Lady Aoi, in *The Tale of Genji*.[3] In real life, Akinari
later revealed that a certain man from the Hamlet of Ōka (the
place name itself appeared in 'Bird of Paradise') had once come
to Osaka to study medicine and been stricken ill. Akinari's
acquaintances proved unable to treat him. Then the patient's
elder brother arrived. Asking the doctors to leave, he said to
his brother, 'You've studied medicine for a long time in Kyoto

and Osaka, but you still haven't mastered the art. . . . Now put your trust in me.' He stripped the sick man naked and calmly began fanning him. At intervals he fed him thin porridge and made him drink broth. At last the fever subsided and the man recovered. Akinari was deeply impressed by the incident, and it strengthened his conviction that illness was largely a state of mind.

He expressed his philosophy as a physician in the maxim, 'Enough is already too much.'[4] Forebearance, restraint, and discretion were to him positive ideals. But he also said, 'Not to remain indifferent to what one sees is the essence of being human,'[5] an attitude that reminds Western readers of the Oath of Maimonides, and one that also reflects the Confucian classics. Both as an author and as a medical man, he dedicated himself to relieving people of pain and suffering. Throughout his life he maintained this simple ideal, vowing never to use his profession to gain riches, peddle influence, or amass wordly possessions.

While practicing medicine he kept up his serious study of classical literature, especially early poetry, diaries, and court romances. But increasingly he realised his limitations as a doctor, and he confessed his inadequacy to heal pain and cure disease. 'I knew that I was neither learned nor skillful,' he wrote, 'but I did my best. . . .' Whenever he found an illness that he did not understand, he would inquire after the patient two or three times a day. Even after referring someone to another physician, he would pay daily visits. Once, however, he made an erroneous diagnosis of a young girl's illness, and she died. The father was unaware of the mistake and accepted his loss philosophically, but Akinari continued to feel shame long afterward. Perhaps as a consequence of this incident, he practiced medicine for only eleven years, giving up the profession and retiring with his wife and stepmother to a modest cottage on the outskirts of Osaka. Especially in the years following 1793, when he moved to Kyoto, he prepared lectures and commentaries on the Man'yōshū[6] and other early works and relied on the help of patrons and friends. All the while his reputation as a *waka* poet and scholar of the national learning grew, and his views attracted wide attention.

Throughout his life Akinari enjoyed travel. As a youth he had gone sightseeing in Nara and Yoshino with his father, and some evidence (though admittedly incomplete and ambiguous) indicates that he had visited eastern Japan. During the years when his home was in Osaka he regularly travelled to the Kyoto area, and after moving to the capital he often journeyed to Osaka. On earlier trips to Kyoto he had met the *haiku* poet, Buson, and he remained on friendly terms with other poets and painters, as previously mentioned.

After his wife's death, in 1797, for a time he suffered a degree of blindness. But miraculously he regained his vision, and during the last decade of his life he showed renewed vigour as an author. Except for the years between 1798 and 1803, when he made his home in a quiet district of Kyoto, Akinari repeatedly moved, seldom staying in one place for even a year. A woman who had long served in the Ueda family lived with him briefly until 1799, when she died. Then the widow of an old friend from Osaka, the nun Yuishin, joined his simple household. She found amusement in writing *waka* verse and devoted herself to Akinari, becoming known as his 'adopted daughter.' Among the significant events of his declining years, friends in Osaka in 1803 held a banquet to honour his seventieth birthday according to Japanese reckoning. For the occasion a literary personality and government official, Ōta Nampo (1748–1823), sent a poem from Edo, and congratulatory verses also came from well-wishers in Kyoto, attesting to the high regard in which he was held.

His life fell between the two most fertile periods of cultural revival, or renaissance, of early modern times – that of the Genroku Era at the end of the seventeenth century, and that of the Bunka and Bunsei Eras, in the early nineteenth. His best-known title, *Ugetsu monogatari*, stands out as the most memorable Japanese prose work of the eighteenth century, and Akinari is remembered as the last great early modern author of the Kyoto–Osaka area. Although writing fiction was not his favourite activity, it brought him enduring fame. His first love remained for scholarship and ancient Japanese literature, especially early poetry and court romances such as *The Tale of Genji*. Always aware of the irony of life, he showed much of the satirist's rapier thrust, wounding with a touch that is scarcely seen. Deeply affected by the conflicting currents of thought that swept Japan in the late eighteenth century, he held deep reverence for the past and respected eccentric behaviour in others. More and more he felt dismayed by the shallowness and materialism of Kyoto and Osaka society, and his attitudes made people think of him as an intransigent and anti-social person. In addition, there remained the mystery of his birth and his physical deformity, which affected his character and made him profoundly sensitive about his origins.

A unique mixture of the poet, scholar, and storyteller, he felt indignant at his contemporaries who refused to believe in miracle, fantasy, and the power of the gods. He was at once a traditionalist and a rebel against tradition. No doubt, the most revealing act of his last years was his effort, in 1807, to destroy his manuscripts by throwing them into a well, at which time he wrote,

| | |
|---|---|
| *Nagaki yume* | Long-felt delusions |
| *mi-hatenu hodo ni* | Shall never more disturb me, |
| *waga tama no* | For my soul has gone – |
| *furu i ni ochite* | Cast into an ancient well – |
| *kokoro samushi mo* | And how cold my heart now grows.[7] |

A cool mind in a warm body, he wished to renounce all earthly ties; yet, to the end, he clung precariously to life.

### 3 Reading Books

For Akinari, publishing the tales meant a radical departure from his earlier works, which had been *ukiyo-zōshi*, or sketches of life in the 'floating world.' Beginning with Ihara Saikaku (1642–93) and his successors in the seventeenth century,[8] this form of narrative prose developed partly from earlier modes of the short story, partly from guidebooks that described life and society in the gay quarter, and partly from *haikai* poetry, though to be sure the continuing influence of the theatre left its mark as well. Often satirical or whimsical in tone, the tales of the floating world remained in vogue for nearly a century, diverting readers with caricatures of various types of people. In addition, however, in some of the collections there appeared supernatural tales, stories of famous historical persons, and accounts of samurai vendettas. But *Ugetsu monogatari* represented another kind of prose fiction, known as *yomihon*, or 'reading books,' a form that even more than the fiction of the floating world was intended for the medium of the printed page and for perusal in one's study, rather than for the recital hall, teahouse, or stage. As with the fiction of the floating world, the reading books carried attractive illustrations.

Several features affected literary fashion in the late eighteenth century and distinguished Akinari's tales and other reading books from earlier publications and won for them growing acclaim. First of all, they were not based mainly on incidents from real life gleaned in the market place or on dramatic material taken from the popular stage. Many of the tales boasted of skillful and inventive plots and afforded somewhat fuller development of character than earlier kinds of prose fiction. Also the authors used history and classical scholarship imaginatively to create new stories, and they emphasised the moral purpose of literature. Emerging national consciousness, fresh interest in foreign studies, and especially the growing tide of Chinese vernacular fiction influenced the taste of readers for tales that were at once complex, exotic, romantic, and yet in a sense realistic. Although the style combined elements of Chinese and Japanese and showed characteristics of both literary and colloquial diction, it remained a modified form of classical prose, not significantly different from that of Saikaku. In some of the early reading books the language seemed tortuous and affected, but Akinari managed to combine the suppleness of Heian prose, the delicacy of court poetry, the solidity of classical Chinese, and the familiarity of everyday speech to create an elegant and graceful effect.

Commonly, the reading books appeared in sets of from three to seven thin volumes bound separately with heavy paper covers, coloured like soft *origami*, in shades of beige, amber, peach, blue, or green, sometimes with an embossed pattern or a printed design. Title slips in cursive script were pasted in the upper left-hand corner of each volume. The pages themselves, in imitation of medieval manuscripts, were hand-printed by means of wooden blocks, each one being a unique design, individually carved – a composite product of the author, designer, and engraver. Every volume usually carried at least a pair of illustrations, mostly by artists of the *ukiyoe* school. For purposes of display the bookseller wrapped the sets in attractive paper envelopes, suggestive of the contents. The format of the reading books was modelled after that of the tales of the floating world and popular Chinese works of the Ming and Ch'ing dynasty. Most of the early titles consisted of short stories, and today all of these books are collector's items.

The remote origins of the reading books may be traced to the middle ages, when Zen priests and other travellers brought from China compilations of ghostly tales. Later on, samurai returning from the Korean expeditions of the 1590s imported similar titles along with newer colloquial novels and collections of short stories. Some of these were reprinted in Japan and avidly studied by groups of men as well as by individual scholars. Indeed, fascination with Chinese popular literature accompanied official support for Confucian learning, though most early commentators viewed these works with contempt, treating them not as serious literature but rather as a means to gain new understanding of Chinese social and legal institutions that might be applicable to Japan. Gradually, ordinary readers also learned about such novels as the picaresque romance, *Shui hu chuan* (*Water Margin*, or in Pearl Buck's translation, *All Men Are Brothers*),[9] and about the collections of short stories that were published around the end of the Ming dynasty. Japanese writers adapted Chinese titles, and booksellers readily issued these as new works. The popular author, Saikaku, as well as the shogun's Confucian advisor, Hayashi Razan (1583–1657), contributed to the development of the reading books, which may really be seen as a long and gradual process.[10]

By the middle of the eighteenth century Tsuga Teishō, the Osaka physician from whom Akinari learned medicine, had published a collection of tales in which he combined Chinese plots with Japanese literary traditions and a historical setting. Although they were marred by a stiffness of style and an unnatural idiom similar to that used in Japan for reading classical Chinese, Teishō's short stories in particular foreshadowed Akinari's tales. Teishō and his fellow authors wanted a form of literature that might express their views on life and art in an elegant style and with a neoclassical diction. They hoped that by means of their work they might reach a wider audience and create new interest in foreign literature, classical learning, and public affairs. Therefore, to some degree the reading books were moralistic and instructional. They were written by talented and high-minded men who wished to save the country from internal strife, economic decay, and even foreign invasion.

Quite naturally, Chinese and Japanese influences went hand in hand. Indeed, behind the revival of interest in the *Man'yōshū* around Akinari's time lay not only the efforts of Japanese scholars but also the teachings of their Chinese counterparts, who emphasised the study of ancient classics and the value of historical and textual criticism. Akinari himself was such a scholar. Although Japan still faced another century of isolation, new books and fresh ideas were entering from the outside world; men once again looked beyond the borders, the institutions, and the existing modes of literary expression in Japan. The reading books afforded opportunity to show daring and imagination and suggested signs of a changing intellectual climate.

Later on, the form that Akinari helped to perfect led to a species of historical romance similar to the Gothic novel in the West. Noted artists designed lavish illustrations with heroes in bombastic poses, and the reading books reached a growing audience. Nowadays Akinari's tales and other titles deserve attentive study not only because of their literary merit but also because of their contribution to the modern Japanese novel. In the preface to the tales, for example (which was written in literary Chinese rather than plain Japanese), Akinari revealed his interest in the literature of his own nation and also that of other countries. The Chinese *Water Margin* and the Japanese *Tale of Genji* were placed on the same high level.

To be sure, the reading books are often thought of as classics to study rather than tales to enjoy, but one quickly recognises the lively spirit of these entertaining works, as well as the high moral values for which they stood. Even without years of study one might learn to appreciate the skill with which the Chinese and Japanese elements were blended. The titles themselves were often published for profit, but the samurai, as well as townsmen like Akinari, who wrote the tales, were deeply involved with contemporary life, and they managed to create serious fiction that still compels the reader's attention. The techniques for cladding foreign literature in Japanese guise, which Akinari and others pioneered, provided a model for early-Meiji students of Western literature, foreshadowing the wholesale adoption of modern influences during the past century. Today in the West the introduction of works such as *Ugetsu monogatari* may give readers new awareness of traditional Asian values and make one pause for thought as the age of plastic replaces that of bamboo.

4 *The Romance of Travel and the Poetry of Place*
Within Japan every place is home. Among few people has the spirit of the open road attained more refined expression in art and literature. 'The days and months are the travellers of eternity and so are the passing years,' wrote the *haiku* poet, Matsuo Bashō (1644–94), less than a century before Akinari's time. 'Those who steer boats across the sea or drive horses over the earth till the end of their days make their home wherever their travels take them. Many men of old have died on the road, and I too for long have been stirred by the wind that blows the clouds and filled with a ceaseless desire to wander.'[11] Not only in Akinari's day but during earlier periods as well,

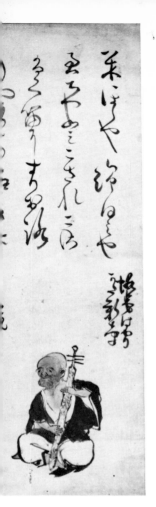

3

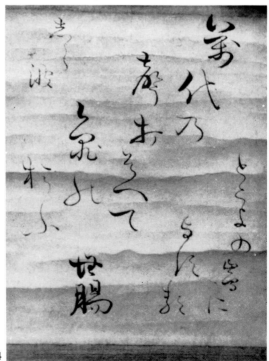

4

[S]elf-caricature of Ueda Akinari,
[inscri]bed with a light verse (*kyōka*).
[Tottori]; photograph courtesy of
[Kado]kawa Shoten.)

[D]etail from caricature of Ueda
[Akin]ari, by Tomioka Tessai (1836–
[1924]; probably inspired by the
[abov]e. (Kyoto, Tomioka Masutarō.)

[A t]*aka* verse, 'All through the
[age]s . . .' in the author's own hand.
[Ōsa]ka, Fuji Fujio.)

5 'Once upon a time . . . I began to journey' (p. 98). Saigyō on his travels, from a picture scroll of the Kamakura period, *Saigyō monogatari emaki*, attributed to Tosa Tsunetaka. (Okayama, Ōhara Museum of Fine Art; National Treasure.)

6

7

6 'I passed through Naniw of the falling reeds' (p.98). Painting by Reisei (or Okada) Tamechika (1823–64), 'Moonlight and Rain.' (Tokyo, Kosaka Junzō; from *Kinsei meiga taikan*; Important Cultural Property.)

7 'Here where one may see only the tracks of the wandering stag' (p. 99). Painting by Matsumura Goshun (1752–1811). (Hyōgo, Itsuō Art Museum

the theme of man as wayfarer found rich expression in Japanese literature. Indeed, the voyage and the pilgrimage have always figured in poetry, diary, and romance. No wonder, then, that travel should play such a large part in Akinari's work, and that it suggested a journey toward enlightenment and an effort to learn the hidden nature of man himself. This theme appears in the opening passage of the first tale and recurs in nearly every story.

By Akinari's day travel was a conventional theme in elegant writing, and allusion to earlier works was an essential element. From the *Man'yōshū*, for instance, Akinari borrowed images such as autumn hillsides bright with yellow foliage and names of specific places like Narumi bay, 'where the plovers leave their tracks on the beach.' Typically, the localities mentioned at the beginning of 'White Peak' and elsewhere were found in earlier essays, diaries, and romances. Similar usage occurred not only in dramatic literature but also in fiction and in prose-poems by *haiku* masters. The technique of weaving the names of renowned scenic spots rhythmically into the text to conjure a series of scenes and vistas calls to mind a thousand years or more of writing about travel. Known as the *michiyuki*, or 'road going,' it imparts a tone of sadness and lends a touch of poetic elegance.

The spirit of earlier travellers haunted Akinari. Time had brought change to many of the places mentioned in the tales, and the two centuries that have passed since they were written have witnessed yet further transformation. But the poetic names survive, as if ghosts of bygone eras. The barrier of Ōsaka, lofty Mt Fuji with its characteristic trail of smoke, the plain of Ukishima, the barrier of Kiyomi, the inlets and bays around Ōiso, the purple grass of Musashino moors, and all the rest bring to mind scenes immortalised by the bards of the *Man'yōshū* and by subsequent generations of poets. The place names of the first tale, for instance, which describe a great arc from Kyoto eastward, northward, and then westward, figure in Saigyō's record of his travels. Bashō later emulated Saigyō, whose terms of description Akinari used virtually without change. On the spot where Saigyō's ghostly audience with the former emperor took place there stands even today a simple earthen mound covered with dried leaves and fallen twigs. The limestone fence that now encloses Sutoku's grave is of recent construction, but the distant view of the islands and bays has altered but little since ancient times, with ships that trade between distant lands or carry people and goods between various provinces reminding one of more than a millennium of history.

Whereas the central action in 'White Peak' takes place overlooking the Inland Sea, that of 'Chrysanthemum Tryst' involves the old post road that linked the home provinces with western Japan. The province of Sanuki stands for travel by sea. The town of Kako represents journey by land, and it appeared in the earliest written records. The legendary first emperor passed by here on his eastward trip to Yamato. A verse in the *Man'yōshū* described how,

> 'While I linger,
> Passing Inabi Plain,
> The Isle of Kako,
> Dear to my heart,
> Appears in sight.'[12]

During Akinari's time crowds of foot travellers stopped nightly at Kako's many inns, and the town was an important place to the weary people who every evening scurried to find lodging. The winding coastline and the nearby beaches of Akashi and Takasago, with white sand and green pines, suggest the quintessence of loveliness. The main character in the tale meets his faithful friend as a result of the vicissitudes of travel, and the latter's need to continue on his way separates the two men. In the end Samon himself, in order to avenge his 'brother's' death, journeys down the high road. Today, however, no one knows where the ancient inns stood, and the town, destroyed in war, is indistinguishable from other cities of similar size. The beauty of the beaches remains only in the mind's eye.

Although the main action in the first two tales carries the

reader to the west of Kyoto, that of 'The House Amid the Thickets' deals with what in those days was the more remote Kantō region in eastern Japan, between the towering Chichibu mountains and the web of rivers and canals that drain into Tokyo Bay and the Pacific Ocean. Places famed in *Man'yōshū* poetry and mentioned in the military chronicles of the middle ages set the scene for a poignant theme – the sorrow of parting and the bittersweet return of the long-lost husband or lover. The precariousness of travel in wartime and the revelation of a ghostly reunion lend an additional measure of fragile beauty. Visitors to the village of Mama, not far from Tokyo, may still find near a neglected temple a well from which the legendary young woman, Tegona, is said to have drawn water. Her restless spirit is still thought to wander in search of salvation.

Surely few authors have described historical and poetic places through the eyes of a painter who has dreamed that he was a fish. 'The Carp That Came to My Dream' is set at Lake Biwa, the largest body of fresh water in Japan – renowned for its natural beauty and for its role in the nation's history. By its shores in the seventh century an emperor briefly held his court. Afterward uncle became pitted against nephew, and the imperial house was divided. Since early times the 'Great Bay of Shiga' and the surrounding mountains and villages have evoked deep sentiment among poets and visitors. From the Mii Temple, where the painter in the tale dwells and where Ernest Fenollosa's ashes were buried, spring the waters with which emperors and empresses were washed at birth.[13] About two centuries before Akinari's time nearly all of the temple had been destroyed in war and then rebuilt. In Akinari's own day and later, popular wood-block prints celebrated the eight famous sights around the lake – 'snow in the evening on Mt Hira,' 'sailboats returning to Yabase,' 'the autumn moon over Ishiyama Temple,' 'dusk at Seta,' 'the evening bells at Mii Temple,' 'wild geese alighting at Katada,' 'sunset at Awazu,' 'rain at night in Karasaki' – many of which were sung in the *nō* plays and mentioned by Bashō and even by Saikaku, as well as Akinari. The passage in the fourth tale that tells of riding 'the waves that rise and fall with the gusts that blow from Mt Nagara,' employs the conventional poetic journey, or *michiyuki*, with unusual daring and imagination and brings visions of the green mountains encircling the lake.

In the fifth and seventh tales, the scene is set to the south of the rich Yamato plain, which nourished early Japanese civilisation. The Yoshino and Kumano area still boasts of such scenic splendours as flowering trees, plummeting waterfalls, deep gorges, and secluded holy spots. It figures often in history, legend, and poetry. 'Bird of Paradise,' the fifth tale and the only one directly involving the author's own period, begins with two travellers, a father and son, who pass through the deepest recesses of Yoshino to view the cherry-blossoms. Footworn from their exertions, they reach the Buddhist citadel of Mt Kōya, sacred peak of the esoteric Shingon sect, which the author himself as a youth had similarly visited with his father and climbed 'with impulsive heart' to spend the night.[14] Besides the story of Kūkai's miraculously founding the temple and the material about Hidetsugu's fateful journey at the end of the sixteenth century, the place name itself evokes memory of drama, tale, and legend, such as that about a son searching in vain for his father, who had retired to the forbidden cloisters of Mt Kōya.

Except for the last, all of the tales similarly involve places famed in earlier literature and history. 'The Caldron of Kibitsu,' for instance, also uses place names from the ubiquitous *Man'yōshū* and the ancient and medieval chronicles. 'The Lust of the White Serpent' conjures up scenes in Kumano, Yoshino, and Yamato. To many of the blossoming mountains, rushing streams, and tide-swept beaches early emperors had made imperial pleasure trips, and virtually every spot that Akinari mentions reveals rich literary and historical associations. Another tale set in the Kantō region is 'The Blue Hood.' Here, a priest in search of religious enlightenment passes through the village of Tonda, below the Daichūji Temple, which once flourished as a great religious institution in the northern Kantō but now languishes as a rural place of worship near the road to Nikkō. Like Saigyō's journey to Sutoku's grave, Kaian's ascent of the mountain is described in terms typical of travel in literature and drama, with overtones of poetry and high romance.

Of course the motif of travel in Akinari's tales brings the reader into contact with earlier history and literature, but it performs other functions as well. First of all, the journey calls to mind the archetypal quest. Akinari's, however, is not epic and directed outward; rather, it represents a search for self-knowledge and for understanding of ones place in time and space. Also, it draws the reader from his private universe to join the author in a make-believe world. But finally, it indicates that his tales are not provincial, dealing only with Osaka and Kyoto, but national – spanning the length and breadth of the land. The sixty-six provinces formed one nation, though not until a century after Akinari completed his preface was it reborn as a modern state.

5  *Historical Background*
Much of the fascination with travel and the lyric beauty of place names in the tales comes from Akinari's sense of history and the passage of time. For over a thousand years the nation had endured, and as a student of its traditions, Akinari knew what changes had taken place in customs, manners, and institutions. Each of his tales was set in times past, mostly during the middle ages, between the twelfth and the late sixteenth century, as the following list shows:

1  'White Peak': late twelfth century.
2  'Chrysanthemum Tryst': late fifteenth century.
3  'The House Amid the Thickets': mid-fifteenth century.
4  'The Carp That Came to My Dream': early tenth century.
5  'Bird of Paradise': seventeenth or eighteenth century.
6  'The Caldron of Kibitsu': early sixteenth century.
7  'The Lust of the White Serpent': unspecified, but apparently the Heian period.

8 'The Blue Hood': late fifteenth century.
9 'Wealth and Poverty': late sixteenth century.

Although the tales were written in an age of peace, a number of them involve warfare and the conflict between an early system of central government and the new feudal institutions that dominated national life after the middle of the twelfth century. The first story, for instance, is set in the days when rule by code of law was yielding to feudal privilege. The clash between old and new, the role of foreign ideas, and the question of sovereignty figures against a background of cataclysmic change. As a twelfth-century historian wrote, 'When the Emperor Toba died, the Japanese nation was plunged into disorder, and subsequently the age of the warrior began.'[15] Court nobles had never before asked provincial warriors for help to settle by force of arms in the capital itself a dispute over succession to the imperial throne. 'White Peak' reflects the collapse of an entire society. It describes the end of an epoch in terms that suggest scattering cherry-blossoms, the waning moon, and nostalgia for bygone days.

Before becoming a Buddhist priest, Saigyō, the narrator, had served Toba. Only one year older than Sutoku, Saigyō knew how vexed the emperor felt at being a mere figurehead while his father remained the power behind the throne. He understood how Sutoku had been forced to abdicate in favour of his younger half-brother, Konoe, and how when the latter died, Sutoku wanted his own son, Prince Shigehito, to be emperor, so that in time he himself might hold power as a retired monarch. But Sutoku's wishes were thwarted. His brother, Go-Shirakawa, was placed on the throne, and after the father passed away, the son rebelled. His forces were defeated and he was banished, but according to popular belief he left a curse that led to a series of national calamities, all of which is described in the first tale from Saigyō's point of view.

Along with other early modern scholars and writers, Akinari wondered why disaster struck the imperial house and what form legitimate government should take. In 'White Peak' he presents this issue as a conflict between the Chinese Confucian point of view and native Japanese ways. Ironically, Sutoku, a descendant of the 'eight hundred myriad gods' supports a foreign institution, while Saigyō, a follower of an alien religion, defends Japanese customs. Political thought and historical fact are combined with fiction in such a manner that Akinari could claim for his tale the respectability long associated with orthodox scholarship. In Japan, as in China, history was thought of as a mirror of truth. The past reflects an image that might help in making decisions for the future. By contrast, fiction was normally scorned as a web of lies. But Akinari's work helped to establish prose fiction as a means of expressing historical criticism and cultural values.

While the background for 'White Peak' and much of Akinari's interpretation of events may be traced to an early military chronicle, the *Hōgen monogatari* (Tales of the Hōgen Era),[16] a similar record[17] also figures in 'Chrysanthemum Tryst,' which is set three centuries later. At this time, during the confused period after the outbreak of the Ōnin Wars, contending forces brought renewed violence and civil discord to the nation, and the ideal of peace and order seemed doomed. Amako Tsunehisa's rise to leadership and his storming of Tomita Castle on the eve of the Japanese New Year typify an age when strong local leaders challenged the authority of distant lords. Just as Tsunehisa went on to become the ruler of many provinces, warriors elsewhere also tried to extend their influence.

Behind Akinari's fascination for this process of change and his nostalgia for what had been lost lies the belief that history has a moral significance and that the past forms a continuous pattern stretching back to antiquity. Men assumed that something had gone wrong, and they believed that by examining certain crucial turning points they might discover why this happened. Then by adjusting national policy one might restore society to normal. Accordingly, the middle ages were thought to be bad, because military authority had been glorified and the strong trampled the weak. Powerful houses had split into rival factions, and it seemed unlikely that a united nation could ever emerge from the chaos. Innocent people, such as Katsushirō and Miyagi, in 'The House Amid the Thickets,' all too often bore the brunt of the misery and suffering of war.

For this tale, as well as for the previous ones, Akinari turns to the military chronicles.[18] When Uesugi Noritada drove Ashikaga Shigeuji from Kamakura, forcing him to take refuge in Shimōsa, life in eastern Japan was upset, much as described in the tale and in Akinari's historical sources. Similarly, the dispute over succession to the leadership of the Hatakeyama house was an actual occurrence.[19] 'The House Amid the Thickets' reminds one how simple people were torn from their roots and forced to endure sorrow and bitterness, owing to the evils of a military system that they themselves had in no way created. Around villages that had once prospered weeds grew tall, and in the words of the Chinese poet, Tu Fu, 'New ghosts are wailing there now with the old,/Loudest in the dark sky of a stormy day.'[20]

To some extent the historical significance of the setting for 'The Carp That Came to My Dream,' around Lake Biwa and the Mii Temple, has already been discussed, but several additional points deserve mention. A priest and painter by the name of Kōgi is said to have lived at the temple in the early ninth century. Also, Shinto places of worship existed here from very early times, associating the place with supernatural powers. The area calls to mind the tragic events of the late seventh century, when the Emperor Tenchi's son was deposed by his uncle, the Emperor Temmu. During the Heian period many court nobles and ladies would visit the famous temples around the southern part of the lake, and according to legend, here Lady Murasaki, inspired by the moon over Ishiyama Temple, wrote *The Tale of Genji*. Awareness of these details adds considerably to the reader's appreciation of Akinari's account of Kōgi's mysterious dream.

Toward the end of the middle ages great barons vied for control of the nation's economic resources, and fierce battles raged between competing leaders. The war cries of massive armies signalled the close of the period. Oda Nobunaga (1534–82) intelligently used new techniques and weapons to bring half of Japan under his rule. Toyotomi Hideyoshi (1536–98), a man of humble birth, skillfully completed the work of unification. After he died, however, his vassals fell to quarrelling, and Tokugawa Ieyasu (1542–1616) emerged as victor. Ieyasu's successors governed Japan peacefully and without serious challenge during the early modern period, and urban centres such as Osaka and Edo prospered and grew. Still, memory of the past lingered on, and the events of the late sixteenth century continued to evoke shock and horror.

These times figure in 'Bird of Paradise,' which is set when 'the land of Peace and Calm had long been true to its name,' in the seventeenth or eighteenth century. Spending a night on Mt Kōya, Muzen and his son are reminded of earlier days. 'The Mound of Beasts,' in Kyoto, which is mentioned at the end of the tale, stands for the way in which the grotesque conflict between Hideyoshi and his nephew, Hidetsugu, still gripped people's imagination.

Hideyoshi, one of the most remarkable autocrats of the time, like Henry VIII, failed not on the battlefield but in the bedroom. He fathered only two children, both born late in life. The first died in infancy, and because there seemed little chance of his having another, he appointed his nephew, Hidetsugu, as heir. To Hideyoshi's chagrin, the young man led a wanton life and killed men for sport, earning a reputation as 'the murdering regent.' When a second son was born, however, Hideyoshi wished him to be his successor, and relations with his nephew quickly deteriorated. In 1595 Hideyoshi ordered his nephew, together with a small retinue of his followers, to retire to Mt Kōya, and he commanded that they die by ritual suicide. Hidetsugu and his young companions disembowelled themselves, with one of their number beheading the others, and Hideyoshi's emissary performed the same service for the last of the condemned men. The nephew's family was then cruelly slain. His wife, ladies-in-waiting, and small children were dressed in their best clothes and dragged through Kyoto to the common execution ground. Here, on a gibbet, Hidetsugu's head was exposed, and the children were killed in front of their mothers' eyes. All were buried at Sanjō in a common grave marked as 'The Mound of Beasts.'[21] Such were the events that Muzen mulled over following his confrontation on Mt Kōya with Hidetsugu's ghostly entourage. In handling this material, moreover, Akinari had to be very circumspect, because it could be regarded as treasonous to write frivolously about events in which the Tokugawa family or other prominent military houses of that time played a part.

Long before Hideyoshi's rise to power, during the period of the fifth Ashikaga shogun, the Akamatsu family of the province of Kibi became embroiled in one of the many succession disputes of the middle ages. This family was descended from a noble line of warriors who had fought with distinction and found great favour with Ashikaga leaders. When the fifth shogun decided in favour of one claimant, he was assassinated by the other – Akamatsu Mitsusuke – who then fled to his home castle. The deceased shogun's supporters besieged him, and seeing that his cause was hopeless, he committed suicide. Izawa Shōtarō, in 'The Caldron of Kibitsu,' though a fictional character, is said to have been descended from a samurai who had survived this siege and escaped to a village, where he lived as a peasant. The story itself has little to do with actual events, but significantly enough, Akinari places it against the background of one of the incidents that undermined the authority of the Ashikaga shogun and led to a century of internecine war, thus paving the way eventually for the rise of the Tokugawa family.

Many famous places figure in 'The Lust of the White Serpent,' making it one of the richest of all the tales in terms of historical geography. The cape of Sano is mentioned in the *Man'yōshū*, as are the mountains of Yoshino. The names of the emperors Jimmu and Nintoku are associated with the Kumano area, to the holy spots of which court nobles and members of the imperial family often made pilgrimage. The Tsuba Market and Hase Temple appear frequently in Heian literature. The

Dōjōji Temple, of Komatsubara, is immortalised in the *nō* and on the *kabuki* stage.[22] Although no date is given, internal evidence shows that the tale was set in the Heian period. In spite of the dearth of names of actual persons and events, 'The Lust of the White Serpent' thus reveals Akinari's sense of history and the passage of time.

Similarly, no specific date is mentioned in 'The Blue Hood.' But the Zen priest, Kaian, was an actual person who lived in the fifteenth century, and the Daichūji Temple is a real place. The Oyamas were descended from the Fujiwara line and had settled on a manor in the vicinity of Tonda, flourishing as one of the strong local families. Such use of historical detail heightens interest in the priest who is fatally attracted to a beautiful boy, his erotic lust for corpses, and the mysterious change that Kaian witnesses.

Oka Sanai, the principal character of 'Wealth and Poverty,' is also a historical personage. His master, Gamō Ujisato, served as one of Hideyoshi's comrades in arms. Both men fought with distinction for Nobunaga, and as a reward Ujisato received one of Nobunaga's daughters in marriage; furthermore, he was baptised as a Christian. Later, Hideyoshi assigned him to Aizu, in the east, and it is recorded that he feared Ujisato and eventually had him poisoned. Historical anecdotes tell how Ujisato's famous retainer, Sanai, loved to display his great wealth, how people criticised him for this, and how he rewarded his follower's frugality in a way that suggests Akinari's treatment in the tale.

But more generally speaking, gold is the main subject of the tale. This metal in ancient Japan was valued chiefly for its decorative qualities. During the middle ages it took on a religious meaning, symbolising the Western Paradise to believers of the Pure Land sect of Buddhism or Zen enlightenment to adherents of this school. Not until the Momoyama period and the introduction of new mining techniques from China did it acquire economic significance as a basis for financial transactions. Even then, gold coins such as those minted at the end of the sixteenth and early seventeenth century, which Sanai gave to his follower, were not very practical as currency and were used primarily as rewards or prizes.²³ In the final passage Akinari cautiously touches upon the political situation of the time and mentions the famous generals of the day. Hideyoshi's period of ascendancy, it is said, would be short, and an auspicious prophecy tells that the Tokugawa family would bring both peace and prosperity to the realm, in a passage perhaps designed to mollify would-be censors.

## 6 *Philosophy and Religion*

Philosophy and religion deal basically with the three questions of where man comes from, where he goes, and how he should spend his life on earth. Traditionally, in Japan Shinto thought and beliefs suggested for the first that the gods gave man life. Buddhism taught regarding the second that when a person died he might attain salvation in paradise. Confucian doctrine, pertaining to the third, urged everyone in moral and ethical terms to live in harmony with his brothers and with the universe. As expressed in a phrase popular in Akinari's day, 'The three teachings are one.' Besides these three main systems of philosophy and religion, the role of Taoism and *Shingaku* deserves mention. Akinari's tales were written for a society in which people felt close to the world of nature and to the gods of the nation. Prayer, music, ritual, and the spiritual life were still valued more highly than the practice of business. Increasingly, however, emphasis on commerce and wealth tended to weaken old traditions, and in a large degree Akinari wished to counteract such developments and strengthen the spiritual quality in national life.

First of all, the vital and emotive side of the tales involved Shinto beliefs. Many able men wished to break away from the constraints of orthodox Confucian teachings. They put renewed faith in native gods, who were chiefly semi-divine and often benevolent local deities and existed in a hierarchy leading up to the imperial family's ancestral spirit. In an unbroken chain, each individual was linked to the rest of society, and time continued from the original creation as if ripples of water from a primordial splash. Life welled and surged without need or plan, in an abundance of forms held together by a throbbing, vital impulse.

The school of national learning served as the scholarly and philosophical arm of Shinto beliefs, and one of the momentous questions of the time involved the matter of sovereignty. Without the crown there would be no England, and without the emperor there would be no Japan. In 'White Peak,' where Akinari deals with the role of the emperor and state, he reaffirms the Japanese idea of 'one line forever,' and he emphasises the divine right of the imperial family. As noted earlier, Sutoku takes the Confucian point of view that government rests on public opinion, whereas Saigyō argues in favour of national customs and traditions that began in the dawn of history and carry magical significance. The unique character of Japan consists in having a sovereign who traces his lineage to divine origins. According to Akinari's belief, the imperial family must be venerated, Shinto ceremonies observed, and the sacred shrines supported. Indeed, after Akinari's time, partly owing to the influence of 'White Peak,' Sutoku's spirit was enshrined in Kyoto in an effort to atone for the suffering that he had endured.

Elsewhere, Akinari touches on Shinto shrines and rituals. In 'The Caldron of Kibitsu,' for instance, he mentions rites involving fire and water. Boiling water was stirred with a wand of dwarf bamboo leaves, and the drops of moisture that rose from the swirling mass were thought to contain the essence of divinity. The singing sound of the caldron was used to prophesy future events. Such caldrons are mentioned in early reports of trial by ordeal, and in shamanistic terms these rituals symbolise a sacred marriage between the god of fire and the goddess of water. Bands of mountain cenobites, known as *yamabushi*, associated the boiling caldron with the mother's womb. To enter it denoted purification by undergoing the pains of hell and achieving rebirth to a higher life. The shrine of the Yamato clan deities figures incidentally in 'The Lust of the White Serpent.'

In contrast to the Shinto aspect of the tales, the Confucian

side deals primarily with morality and ethics. Despite his association with the Shinto movement, which was gaining in power
and influence, Akinari shunned the excesses of the school of
national learning, thinking of himself as an independent scholar.
He upheld the basic virtues of the Confucian classics – loyalty,
honour, duty – much in the samurai tradition of his father. He
stressed such values as stability and frugality. He respected life
and felt deep concern for future generations. He criticised all
forms of selfishness and personal indulgence. But his Confucian
beliefs were tempered by the conviction that the gods and
spirits still flourished and that a man who lacked faith and piety
risked madness or death. To him the Confucian calling entailed
not sterile didacticism but moral intensity, as exemplified by the
ideals that Samon and Soemon share in 'Chrysanthemum
Tryst.' Similarly, the desire to turn over a new leaf, which
Katsushirō, Toyoo, and the aberrant monk of 'The Blue Hood'
possess in common, suggest that a person who resists the forces
of decline and restores his innate purity and goodness might
contribute to the general welfare and help to arrest social decay.
This Confucian quality helped bring about the Meiji Restoration and the modernisation of Japan. One might reshape an
individual or a civilisation without annihilating it.

Traces of Taoist thought and attitudes also appear in the
tales, serving to impart an element of mystery and romance.
Oftentimes, however, it is virtually impossible to distinguish
Taoist ideas from those of Shinto.[24] Akinari extolled the spontaneous man's innate desire to follow nature and transcend the
illusory and unreal distinctions on which all human systems of
morality were based. Travelling as a free spirit, living simply,
acting naturally, and taking things easy combined with a belief
in the irony of life. All living creatures were assumed to be equal.
For instance, part of the basic idea in 'The Carp That Came to
My Dream' may be traced to an anecdote in the Chinese Taoist
classic, *Lieh tzu*, involving a man who was fond of seagulls and
every morning went into the ocean and swam about with them.
Another anecdote from the same text, which tells of a man who
carved a mulberry leaf out of jade and imitated nature so ex-

quisitely that no one could distinguish his artifice from the real object, resembles Akinari's idea at the end of his carp tale.[25] The 'innocent heart,' a term used to describe Katsushirō, in the third tale, is related to the Taoist ideal of simplicity (as well as that of Shintoism), and conveys a sense of uprightness and scrupulous honesty combined with an easy-going nature. All manner of pretence is equally to be shunned. Akinari's disgust for Shōtarō, the deceitful wretch in the sixth tale, and his ambivalence toward Manago, the serpent spirit of the seventh tale, remind the reader that passion throws out a myriad tentacles. It destroys peace and reduces the mind to a state of turmoil. It has to be quelled in order to maintain one's self-control. Whereas Shōtarō fails to curb his natural appetites, Toyoo succeeds, though only at enormous cost.

Akinari's values and standards were also influenced by *Shingaku*, or 'Heart-learning.' This doctrine began among merchants in Osaka and later spread to other areas, gaining adherents among all classes of people.[26] Although basically Confucian in its emphasis on how man ought to live in the present, it embraced Shinto and Buddhist ideas, as well. Virtues such as hard work, thrift, and ambition were emphasised, though men were enjoined to avoid the extremes of greed and avarice. Warfare, however, held little romantic attraction. As Akinari writes in 'Wealth and Poverty,' 'Brave men whose business is with bows and arrows have forgotten that wealth forms the cornerstone of the nation, and they have followed a disgusting policy.' His spirit of gold shows startling resemblance to the God of Wealth, a curious and grotesque folk-deity who holds sheaves of rice, as if to indicate that worldly riches need not be evil. Obviously, then, Akinari's concept of morality, despite its basically Confucian orientation, has little connection with narrowly orthodox views but rather displayed a broad, eclectic spirit.

Buddhist philosophy imparts a universal quality to the tales and contributes much to their subtlety. Akinari's concept of reality shows features of the teachings of the Tendai sect, or T'ien-t'ai, as this distinctively Chinese school that may be related to Taoism was called in the country of its origin. Akinari accepts the Buddhist belief (though to be sure it is shared by the Taoists) that life is but a dream and a shadow. Because people are trapped in the wheel of life and death and endure manifold afflictions, men practice spiritual cultivation – as Priest Kaian in 'The Blue Hood' forces the aberrant monk to do – in order to gain religious salvation and destroy the illusions that cause suffering. Such meditation was based on the doctrine of 'concentration and insight' (*shikan*, or in Chinese, *chih kuan*), and it required one to silence his active thoughts and to reflect on the true nature of matter and phenomena. Mind was thought to dominate over matter. Man might control his destiny by meditation and monastic discipline, as taught in the Chinese commentaries on the Lotus Sutra.[27]

This philosophy permeates Heian literature,[28] medieval poetry, the *nō* theatre, and *haiku*, as well as Akinari's tales. Indeed, at times the Tendai teachings and those of Christianity seem quite parallel. Milton's lines, 'The Mind is its own place, and in itself/ Can make a Heaven of Hell, a Hell of Heaven,' and his idea that 'real and substantial liberty' comes from within rather than from without man's heart,[29] resemble Akinari's assertion that, 'A slothful mind creates a monster, a rigorous one enjoys the fruit of the Buddha.' Akinari believed that without religious discipline, however individualistic a form it might take, man could not survive spiritual crisis, and he accepted the idea that sorrow was inherent in human life, a point of view hardly foreign to the Puritan or Calvinist mind. Although by Akinari's time these ideas were interpreted in Shinto terms and figured prominently in Motoori's writings on classical Japanese literature, they stemmed originally from Buddhist doctrines.

Akinari and other learned men of the eighteenth century agreed that Buddhism as a religion was useless and that the clergy was degenerate. Nevertheless, the underlying themes and imagery of the tales suggest that this faith still dominated the popular imagination. Recurring Buddhist images, such as bells, drums, cymbals, and conch shells, tell of the resonant quality of the universe and indicate auditory and musical harmony. When these reassuring sounds are far away, as in the first, fifth, and eighth tales, one feels an eerie sense of foreboding. The bird of paradise, whose song is Buddha's law, in the fifth tale conveys an apocalyptic sense of miracle. In Akinari's day temples remained powerful landowners and enjoyed political patronage. Those that had been burned at the end of the middle ages, such as the Mii Temple, were rebuilt, and they continued to attract devout pilgrims.

Just as the heavenly bodies revolved, so too might dead souls return to the world of the living, though understandably their form would be altered. The past is never forgotten; the future cannot be ignored. The cosmos itself is constantly changing, and even the soul is subject to metamorphosis. In a Buddhist sense, Miyagi, of 'The House Amid the Thickets,' is both a reincarnation of the legendary Tegona of old and also a separate individual. Owing to the many changes in Japanese society, faith may have been reduced to a vestige of former days, but Buddhism, together with Shinto, Confucian, and other beliefs, still played a role scarcely less impressive than that of the Church in the Western world. Once having separately discerned the main philosophical and religious elements of the tales, however, the reader must let them commingle and re-emerge in a harmonious union of these beliefs, which the tales represented for an age when myth still had magical power over poets and ordinary people.

7 *The Art of Fiction*
In the preface to the tales Akinari briefly expresses his views on the art of fiction. Praising *Water Margin* and *The Tale of Genji* – the most widely known works of Chinese and Japanese narrative prose – as monuments of creative imagination, he suggests that they are true to life because they embody deep feeling and evoke an intimate sense of the past. Without being explicit, he compares his own tales to these older masterpieces, inviting readers to enjoy what he has created. He points out that although his tales are somewhat fanciful in subject matter, they show a degree of unity, and he hopes that people will not be

misled into thinking that his stories are literally true, so that he need not fear being punished, as Lo Kuan-chung and Lady Murasaki had supposedly been, for deceiving people.

The remarks in his preface reveal an interest in the theory of literature and the uses of fiction, one which lasted for the rest of his life. He first wrote of his views on this subject in the 1770s in an essay that does not survive. Later on, in 1793, when editing Kamo Mabuchi's work on the *Ise monogatari* (The Tales of Ise),[30] he told how the art of fiction had flourished in China and Japan. He explained that the objectives were the same both in Chinese narrative prose and in Japanese tales and romances. Writers wishing to lament their personal unhappiness about the world they lived in showed their feelings in the form of nostalgia for times past. In his own words, 'When an author sees the nation flourishing, he knows that it must eventually decay, like the bloom of a fragrant flower. When he considers what happens in the end to leaders of state, he privately laughs at their folly. He points out to people who might seek longevity what finally became of Urashima Tarō's bejewelled box. He makes foolish men who struggle to collect rare treasures feel ashamed of themselves. He tries to avoid the desire for fame, composing his innocent tales about events of the past for which there are no sources.'[31] Akinari believed that literature is a vehicle by which to express in a highly sublimated form one's discontent with society, and his views remind the Western reader of such works as Shelley's 'Defence of Poetry,' Wordsworth's *Preface to the Lyrical Ballads*, and James's *Art of Fiction*.

Nevertheless, no conflict arose between the demands of art for art's sake and art intended primarily as a means of communicating truth. For Akinari the two were inseparable, and he embraced both, believing that Lady Murasaki and Lo Kuan-chung had done likewise. Fiction heightened one's consciousness and carried the soul to a spiritual union with higher reality. In Buddhist terms art was ecstasy, and suggested a mind or heart wonderful and profound beyond human thought. As in Tendai and Zen philosophy, the human heart became its own creator, intuitively forming a mental vision of reality. Accordingly, art did not merely imitate nature; rather, the poet shaped it, as the sculptor did his material or the painter his forms. Artistic excellence depended on the quality of the poet's vision and the level of his spiritual development or awareness. One cut away what was gross, straightened what was crooked, and lightened what was heavy. In the act of literary expression one encompassed truth and knowledge and communicated it concisely and accurately within the limits of one's understanding. Beauty was not subordinate to truth but was an intrinsic part of it. Art was not the handmaiden of religion: the two were as if the wings of a single bird, both of which were needed to fly.

Where did such views come from? On the one hand, Akinari knew of Lady Murasaki's famous passage about the art of fiction, and on the other hand he was familiar with the remarks of the ancient Chinese historian, Ssu-ma Ch'ien. Lady Murasaki herself combined the idea of art for its own sake and art as a medium for conveying truth While stressing the practical value of literature, she wrote of how fiction might deeply move the reader and how the author himself might be stirred by 'an emotion so passionate that he can no longer keep it shut up in his heart.'[32] Behind Lady Murasaki's views on fiction lay Buddhist and Chinese philosophy, as well as earlier Japanese essays such as the *kana* preface to the *Kokinshū*.[33] Just as the lotus flower grows above the turbid waters, so does purity and truth rise above evil. Fiction might deal with 'lies' or describe evil as well as good, but its ultimate aim is to express truth and help people in their spiritual development.

Actually, as Akinari realised, Lady Murasaki's theory of literature does not contradict Ssu-ma Ch'ien's. According to both views art involves morality, and literature has a social function, though to be sure, in practice Lady Murasaki shows an unsurpassed aesthetic awareness. Utilitarian concerns are as important as strong emotions deeply felt. In Ssu-ma Ch'ien's words, authors of great literary works are aggrieved men who, 'Poured forth their anger and dissatisfaction,' because they feel 'a rankling in their hearts.' Being unable to accomplish what they wished, they write about ancient matters 'in order to pass on their thoughts to future generations.'³⁴ The reader is immediately reminded of Lady Murasaki's understanding of literature as the outcry of the passionate heart.

In addition to being directly familiar with Ssu-ma Ch'ien and Lady Murasaki's ideas, Akinari admired a famous preface to the *Water Margin*, which was written by a late-Ming Chinese scholar named Li Cho-wu (1527–1602). Like Akinari, he too stressed the importance of profound feeling and asserted that good authors are always motivated by 'anger and dissatisfaction.' 'To write without deep emotion,' he said 'was the equivalent to shivering without suffering from the cold or groaning without feeling sick.'³⁵ In a flowery passage at the end of his preface, Li explains that a romance should be a serious work, which men must read in order to understand the true significance of life. When vexed and aggrieved, the writer turns to romance and criticises injustice by means of creating an idealised universe. One recalls Dickens's view that the creative faculty must have complete possession of the author or poet and master his whole life.

Deeply influenced by earlier Chinese and Japanese writers, Akinari embodies in almost every tale a typically Confucian moral, a Buddhist concept of fate, and a Shinto belief in the power of the impassioned heart. Virtue must be rewarded and vice punished, in the present as in ages past. If a man is greedy, lustful, or overly ambitious, he might lose what he loves most, suffer great hardship, and experience deep emotional pain. Avarice brings only sorrow and misfortune. Man must also beware of woman's spell, for she might use her charms to destroy him.

Akinari's basic ideas about the art of fiction contrast somewhat with those of Motoori. Whereas Motoori taught that the purpose of the novel, tale, or romance was, 'Not to preach morality but to evoke a certain pattern of emotional sensibility,'³⁶ Akinari tried to balance artistic and utilitarian ends. He believed that the suffering previous authors endured for their art was worthwhile, and he implied that his tales might stand comparison with the best work of his illustrious predecessors. Combining bold assertiveness and defensive humility, Akinari's views on fiction contribute to the moral integrity and the sense of beauty that distinguish his tales from lesser works.

## 8  *World of the Supernatural*

'The music of Heaven. . . . Wordless, it delights the mind,' wrote the Taoist sage, Chuang-tzu.[37] On the one hand Akinari's tales deal with reality and reflect the natural world, but on the other they soar to a loftier realm, where ghosts and spirits freely appear and men encounter inscrutable forces. Out of a precarious balance between the sensory world and the realm of the unknown 'the music of heaven' emerges. To the travelling priest, distraught scholar, wayward husband, artist, pilgrim, or impressionable youth the shadows of the imagination may arise in music and dance. They may be heard and understood, Akinari suggests, by a simple and spontaneous man in a situation highly charged with emotion.

Before all else, the supernatural side of the tales was intended to attract the reader. The original subtitle carried the words *Kinko kaidan*, or 'New and Old Tales of Wonder,' inviting the public to enter a world charged with spectral activity and haunted by gods and spirits. Far from the reassuring notes of bells and trumpets, where Buddhist chants and ringing staves could not be heard, magical sounds fill the air. Matter and energy become fused in a miraculous union of man and shade. Whatever the mind might imagine becomes real, and man gains a sense of mystic vision and illumination, as if the soul suddenly takes light from a supreme being. Like all mystics, Saigyō and the other men in *Ugetsu monogatari* vividly remember their confrontation with spirits that are at once dead and alive. In each tale the climatic action takes place at night, the favourite time for ghosts and apparitions, when the past is turning into the future. The role of the supernatural underscores the belief that Japan was a country rich in gods and spirits.

Although Akinari's ghosts and other worldly creatures show an animal nature that defied control and mastery, they have neither the bleeding skulls nor luminous hands of the spirits of

Gothic novels; nor are they headless apparitions clad in armour or eerie forms extending phosphorescent claws toward the victim's throat. Rather, they are at once more primitive and more modern – to curb their power one needs prayer, meditation, and purity of heart. In spite of certain gloomy or even terrifying details, they leave on one an impression not of ugliness but of beauty. Above all, Akinari believed in his spirits and wished to convince his readers that the gods still lived and that the earth was charged with their elemental force. By evoking the gods and spirits he might illumine what was dark within himself and also within the reader.

Stories of ghosts, genies, demons, miracles, and animals that influence human events have always held universal appeal. In China, despite Confucian exhortation that the spiritual world is not a proper topic for human inquiry, tales and anecdotes about supernatural beings are as old as recorded literature. Indeed, the *ch'i lin*, or 'unicorn,' a benevolent spiritual animal, is said to have appeared as an omen to the mother of Confucius before her son's birth. According to legend, a charioteer later wounded a similar beast, foretelling the sage's death. Marvellous creatures appear freely in Taoist writings. Notices of occult beings occur in early dynastic histories. The oldest separate collection of supernatural tales was compiled around the end of the third century AD. In T'ang times the literary tale of the marvellous attained maturity, and from early times Chinese examples inspired Japanese writers.

Myth and legend in Japan expressed belief in the existence of spirits. Fairies and semi-celestial beings were thought to roam about the woods, mountains, seaside, waterfalls, and lakes, appearing in the spring haze or autumn mist. Great deities might journey in search of a loved one's soul or visit palaces under the sea in quest of a lost talisman. Various powers were attributed to the benevolent gods of heaven and earth and also to malicious spirits. Other mysterious forces were felt too vaguely to be personified. One worshipped the forces of good and used various spells to exorcise those of evil. Omens, divination, dreams, and oracles taught people how to live in a world filled with magical power. A verse in *The Tales of Ise,* which suggested several incidents in Akinari's tales, describes how evil spirits had an affinity for abandoned dwellings:

| | |
|---|---|
| *Mugura oite* | When the weeds grow tall, |
| *Aretaru yado no* | And a tumble-down house |
| *Uretaki wa* | Stands awesomely, |
| *Kari ni mo oni no* | You should beware that demons |
| *Sudaku nari keri* | Are swarming there inside.[38] |

Wherever shadows were deep, spirits and phantoms were sure to lurk, as indicated in a variety of early and medieval works. Some beliefs and stories were of native origin, and others came from China or even India.

As mentioned earlier, three centuries before Akinari's time new collections of Chinese short stories were brought to Japan, giving fresh impetus to the development of the supernatural tale. After the art of landscape painting was perfected, story-tellers tried all the harder to cloak the natural world in a garb of mystery, inviting the reader to exercise his imagination and depicting a universe full of mysterious beings and forces. Consequently, in Akinari's day the Chinese influence in painting and the popularity of the ghostly tale went hand in hand. Japanese collections of supernatural tales were directly inspired by Chinese examples and appeared in several forms of narrative prose, notably the *kana* books, the tales of the floating world, and of course the reading books.

Especially after the appearance of *Otogi bōko* (The Bedside Storyteller) in 1666, a number of similar works were issued, leading eventually to Akinari's tales. *Ugetsu monogatari,* however, differs from earlier collections in a number of ways. One finds an emphasis on the human reaction rather than on the sensational appearance of the phantom or apparition, a tendency already found in *Saikaku shokoku-banashi* (Saikaku's Tales from Various Provinces). Compared to Akinari's, the earlier works are more anecdotal in nature – like the Buddhist narratives and stories of the middle ages. They typically resemble a sutra turned topsy-turvy: the supernatural event comes first and the moral follows, but the instructional feature of the scriptures nevertheless remains. True enough, in Akinari's tales the moral function has by no means disappeared, but the story stands as an independent work of literary art, similar to a well-wrought ghostly tale by Henry James, or other Western masters. Moreover, Akinari strove to add features that appealed to the scholarly interests of readers who had hitherto scorned popular fiction as unworthy of their attention. Still, at the same time that he paid careful attention to literary craft and scholastic respectability, Akinari (like the Christian mystics and the neo-Platonists) believed in the occult, the supernatural, and the transcendental. To appreciate his viewpoint one must put aside rational criticism and transport himself backward in time to a dimly lit world, where moonlight as the main source of nocturnal illumination was intense and pure. Here, as Saikaku said, 'Everyone is a ghost. Anything in the world is possible.'[39] Or, in Akinari's own words, in the darkness, when the flickering oil lamp dies, 'Demons might appear and consort with men, and humans fear not to mingle with spirits.' Then when the light is restored, 'The gods and devils disappear and hide somewhere, leaving no trace. . . .'[40] Until the end of his life Akinari insisted that the power of the supernatural was real, and he based his argument on personal experience as well as on evidence from earlier literature. As with a Japanese garden, which represents not only nature itself but its idealization, the tales embody not only a view of reality but a vision of its essence. Akinari's reader finds himself ineluctably on the edge of a magic circle, ready to be drawn up by unseen powers in a vortex of light and song.

## 9 *Literary Style*

By the early middle ages a literary style that mixed both Chinese characters and Japanese phonetic symbols known as *kana* had become the standard form in narrative prose. Akinari's tales were in this style, which until the modern period was used primarily in novels, short stories, and popular histories. Many of the principal words were written with Chinese characters used according to their meaning, while particles, suffixes, and some semantic elements were expressed phonetically. Known descriptively as the *Wakan konkōbun*, or the 'Chinese Japanese mixed style,' it differed from the form of court poetry and Heian romance in three ways. First of all, being more straightforward, it lacked some of the elegant, poetic, and suggestive qualities of classical poetry and romance. Secondly, it permitted additional Chinese constructions, which allowed for more rigour and precision but which also demanded greater learning for its mastery. Lastly, it admitted as much colloquial grammar and vocabulary as the author fancied. In spite of influence from the spoken language, however, the mixed style remained a literary tool, largely divorced from ordinary speech.

For several reasons this style had begun to change by Akinari's time. First of all, popular drama and the rhetoric of the recital hall had a strong influence on narrative prose. Secondly, the revival in learning led by such scholars as Mabuchi and Motoori, who deliberately reverted to the classical mode of literary composition, led to fresh ideas about appropriateness in style. Yet further impetus came with the study of Chinese language and literature. Consequently, Akinari pursued a dualistic ideal. While aiming at a pure and lucid classical style, he wished to convey a sense of plain speech with a Chinese flavour. The result was a variation of the mixed style, known as *gazoku-bun*, 'elegant and plain style,' or *giko-bun*, 'neoclassical style.'

Akinari realised that overly refined expression often fails to convey human sentiment, whereas simple and plain language might communicate such feelings with directness. He tried to combine the good qualities of elegance and simplicity while resisting the weight of blind tradition and refusing to be a prisoner of archaic forms. In the tales everything is expressed as one might wish to talk, but yet more dignified, attractive, and interesting. The result is a powerful and flexible tool able to impart the subtle message of the human heart and reflect the profound wisdom of the ancient sages. Better than anyone of his generation, Akinari mixed the stateliness of the old with the freshness of the new in a uniquely successful style.

By convention in Akinari's day the beginning of a tale or play was usually noble in taste, musical in tone, and composed with an ear for poetry. Ideally, the introductory section gave the reader a telescoped view of the whole. For instance, the opening passage of 'White Peak' adumbrates not only the theme of the first story but also that of the entire collection – a quest for enlightenment. Likewise, 'Chrysanthemum Tryst' begins with an imitative and sonorous passage that hints at what was to follow. Then in the body of the tale a plainer tone is employed, and at the end a short summary sentence resumes the earlier style. The rhetorical manner of classical Chinese alternates with the simpler rhythms of Japanese poetry and romance, much as the skylark soaring and diving. Akinari often strove for special effects at the beginning in order to enhance the quality of elegance and attain the desired balance.

Nevertheless, elegance in excess leads to frigidity. By capturing the word or phrase that gives the precise effect he wanted, and by adding an occasional light touch or a deft bit of irony, Akinari avoided this fault. In 'Chrysanthemum Tryst,' an old warrior grumbles ironically to his youthful companion about how young people are too timid. Throughout 'The Carp That Came to My Dream' Kōgi is treated with great whimsy. In 'Wealth and Poverty' Sanai's droll tone creates an atmosphere of lightness, despite the heavy nature of the subject. Akinari tried to convey a full measure of the absurdity and vulnerability of human nature.

For the most part, however, the style remains severe, formal, and erudite, largely owing to the way Akinari used his various literary sources and employed his personal feelings and experiences. Beneath the plain surface of the prose an elaborate beauty lies hidden, reminiscent of that in the nō drama or the tea ceremony. The more unwieldy the subject, the more delicately he refined it, as in 'Bird of Paradise.' Here the material is controlled so strictly that the uninformed reader can scarcely imagine the deeds and events that Hidetsugu's apparition represents. The story overshadows real life, as the moon may eclipse the sun.

Certain mechanical aspects of style also add to the total effect. Most of all, one recalls the cursive, calligraphic script of the original edition, which was carved on wooden blocks and printed on double leaves of soft, hand-made paper. Many abbreviations are used, along with a number of extra *kana* symbols that were not officially considered as part of the syllabary. When the text was printed in movable type, all of this became lost. Punctuation in the original consists simply of a small oval sign that serves as a full stop, comma, semi-colon, and question mark. A *waka* verse of five, or a *haiku* of three lines in English takes only a single, slightly indented column in the woodblock text. Because quotation marks are not used, the reader is often free to decide whether a given passage should be dialogue or narrative. To the uninitiated person it is hard to tell where one syllable ends and the next begins or whether a certain symbol is Japanese or Chinese. The hand-printed text represents a work of art, in some ways plain and simple and yet complicated and demanding. The Western reader deserves to see the calligraphic form, even though he may never learn how the script is deciphered.

Usually Akinari's style was clear and lucid, at least as traditional Japanese literary texts go, but some points remain puzzling. Was the opening tale a first- or a third-person narrative? Was Akinari really telling about Saigyō, or for artistic purposes was he assuming the personage of Saigyō? The tale begins with words attributed to the twelfth-century poet, but later the name is used in a manner that might indicate either a personal narrative or an omniscient narrator. After the ghosts of Hidetsugu and his followers appear in 'Bird of Paradise,' a similar change in tone occurs. But some degree of vagueness and lack of explicitness is common in traditional Japanese texts. This adds to the appeal of the work and invites the reader's active participation in recreating it in his own mind.

Concerning how Akinari combined Chinese and Japanese stylistic elements, one recalls how the playwright Chikamatsu

Monzaemon (1653–1725) wrote that with Chinese hair styles people used Japanese combs, and with the native coiffure they did the reverse, so closely were the two cultures mixed. The same is true of Akinari's diction. Far beyond normal needs, he dotted his text with curious and difficult Chinese characters. These are explained in a Japanese gloss written by the right side of each line. Oftentimes, the diction seems fanciful or even outlandish, with archaic expressions from the *Man'yōshū* and colloquialisms found only in Chinese vernacular novels and tales. But Akinari's mastery of syntax pleased and surprised the reader of his day, though demanding of him the patience and concentration needed to read poetry.

The preface, however, being written entirely in one double leaf of literary Chinese, without any gloss at all, presents stylistic problems of its own. Although it may have been common knowledge in Akinari's day, how many people know nowadays who Lo Kuan-chung is or why his children are supposed to have been deaf? Unless one is familiar with Chinese classics, how could he guess that the phrase 'crying pheasants and quarrelling dragons' is derived from such works as *The Book of Changes*? Few Western readers are familiar with the legend that Lady Murasaki was sent to hell. The Chinese style of the preface and the information it contains was intended to give comfort to scholars and gentlemen who might be tempted to read the tales. The technique of using such a preface that embodies allusions to previous works enhances Akinari's style and marks it as part of the mainstream of early modern Japanese literature. The only recourse for the Western reader is to have copious textual notes and steadfast patience.

Of the two contrasting elements of style – the elegant and stately neoclassicism and plain speech tempered with a Chinese flavour – the first prevails over the second. A curious mosaic is the result, rich in rhetorical devices from earlier prose and poetry. The formal cadence of Chinese classics, pillow-words from early Japanese poetry, and expressions that echo *The Tale of Genji* all helped Akinari to achieve the desired combination of lyric and narrative qualities. Frequently, decorative elements form images and metaphors. Many of these are quite natural, as when heavy dew is compared to a steady drizzle of rain (a figure found in *The Tale of Genji*). But others are more difficult and arcane. When Sutoku's life in retirement, for instance, is likened to dwelling 'in the Grove of Jewels, or on faraway Ku-she Mountain,' knowledge of Chinese classics is needed to understand that the emperor had abdicated and continued to live in dignified circumstances. Ordinary images and obscure literary allusions both serve to intensify the mood, the former by adding intimacy and familiarity, the latter by suggesting depth and profundity. In addition, such devices as the rhythmic progression of numbers near the beginning of 'Bird of Paradise' and elsewhere are intended as a decorative technique to afford extra pleasure for the attentive reader. Acrostics, logograms, puzzles, riddles, and all manner of play on words have long been popular in Japan.

At times the cadence breaks into song, in a union of poetry and music. To savour the full effect, the tales must be read aloud. Like a *nō* play or a Gregorian chant, the flow of sound rises and falls in a solemn yet lyrical melody, because the texture of the language more nearly resembles that of traditional drama or poetry than that of modern prose fiction. Indeed, musical elements, such as rhythm, harmony, and symmetry, contribute greatly to the stylistic excellence of the tales. But image, metaphor, and music lead one back to myth and allegory. Akinari's style was ideal for spinning parables around an event and for emphasising the frailties of man. To find the ultimate meaning of the tales one must return to the content.

10 *Chinese Influence*

Just as during the past century the Western influence has been pervasive, so in Akinari's time little remained untouched by the civilisation of China. The Four Books and the Five Classics of the Confucian tradition comprised the basic course of study in the private schools. Such texts were learned by rote and held in respect, much as the family Bible in the West. The wisdom of these classical works went unquestioned, and advanced education was built on its foundation. Quite naturally, Akinari was indebted not only to the basic Confucian texts but also to various other Chinese sources – dynastic histories, T'ang poetry and prose, Ming fiction and essays.

His indebtedness to the Confucian classics shows up in many distinctive expressions scattered throughout the tales. Some of these may have come from his direct knowledge of Chinese sources; yet others were derived indirectly. For instance, 'the crying pheasants and quarrelling dragons' of the preface appear not only in *The Book of Changes* and the *Shu ching*, two pre-Confucian classics, but also in the preface to the Ming collection, *New Tales for Lamplight*, which Akinari admired. Such phrases reflect his broad learning and his taste for classical scholarship, which he shared with other fine minds of the eighteenth century. As one would expect, he was familiar with the *Analects* and *The Book of Mencius*, a pair of texts that until the twentieth century guided men on a path of upright behaviour and taught that human beings are part of a natural order that pervades the entire universe. The laconic words and provocative ideas of Confucius and Mencius helped Akinari to convey a tone of moral urgency, a flavour of folk wisdom, and a touch of popular appeal, aiding him to achieve ready communication with his readers.

After mastering the basic books of the Confucian tradition, students in Akinari's day moved on to refined literature and instructive history. One is therefore hardly surprised to discover in his tales a number of passages indebted to Ssu-ma Ch'ien's *Shih chi* (Records of the Grand Historian of China), as well as other titles of the period of the warring states and the early imperial age. In particular, the scepticism and mysticism of the classical Taoist philosophers met with new popularity around Akinari's time, as previously mentioned. Bashō and other *haiku* poets emulated the unrestrained fancy of the Taoist masters, and the scholars of the national learning also accepted such influence in the formulation of their ideas and the development of their style. Wherever Akinari extolls the beauty of nature or describes mystery and surprise, the *Tao-te-ching*, *Chuang-tzu*, and *Lieh-tzu* are never far removed. A measure of Akinari's wry sense of humour comes from Taoist sources.

The influence of T'ang prose and poetry and that of Ming and Ch'ing painting are also obvious, though they come partly through intermediate sources. In Akinari's day the most widely read anthology of T'ang poets was periodically reprinted and extravagantly admired. The Japanese painters who called themselves *bunjin*, or 'literary men,' some of whom were Akinari's close friends and associates, exemplified the ideals and objectives of Li Po and Tu Fu. Like the artists of his day, Akinari practiced calligraphy, poetry, and antiquarian studies. The same transcendental philosophy that these artists conveyed in purely visual terms may be found in the tales. Love of the simple life away from the noise and tension of the city, pleasant conversation with congenial friends, and a sense of the futility of worldly ambitions characterised Po Chü-i's poetry, Buson's painting, and of course Akinari's tales. Ultimately, the account of Saigyō's ascent of Mt Chigogadake owes as much to poems and paintings of the Yangtze gorges or the mountains of Shensi and Szechuan as to actual descriptions in contemporary guidebooks or earlier literature. The same may be said of Muzen and his son's climb to Mt Kōya and of Kaian's visit to the Daichūji Temple. Largely, the inspiration of T'ang poetry and prose was transmitted through the amateur painters and authors of the Ming dynasty, who worked not to fulfill a patron's wishes but rather to cultivate human character and find personal pleasure.

No doubt the most powerful and direct literary influence, however, remains that of Ming fiction and essays. Every tale shows traces of the language, style, or plots of *New Tales for Lamplight* and the three anthologies of colloquial short stories known as the *San yen*. The long picaresque romance, *Water Margin*, served Akinari not only in his preface but also in his description of the dilapidated temple in 'The Blue Hood.' One particularly unusual Ming source is an early sixteenth-century encyclopedic compilation entitled *Wu tsa tsu* (Five Assorted Offerings), by Hsieh Chao-che, a poet, scholar, official, traveller, and collector of old books and objects of art. Banned in eighteenth-century China, *Wu tsa tsu* was preserved in Japan, where owing to its breadth and scope and highly personal tone, it found special favour among artists and men of letters. Akinari consulted the work frequently in later years, as well as when he was writing the tales.

But how may one analyse the total effect of the Chinese influence on the tales? Above all, Akinari's readers expected a serious author to display his knowledge of recondite classics. They welcomed the Chinese flavour, especially that of relatively fresh and unfamiliar works, such as *Water Margin* and the *San yen*. Therefore, the student of literary history will find one sort of significance. But for the general reader several other points of view come to mind. The first of these is translation. Although one cannot apply this term rigorously to any complete story, owing to the freedom that Akinari takes, some parts of certain tales come very close to being translations. Four of these, 'Chrysanthemum Tryst,' 'The House Amid the Thickets,' 'The Carp That Came to My Dream,' and 'The Lust of the White Serpent,' retain much of the spirit of their Chinese models. Names are changed, scenes reset, and stylistic conventions, imagery, and allusions from classical Japanese literature are added, but these tales remain faithful to the Chinese and give somewhat the impression of a free and poetic translation or adaptation.

All of the four tales mentioned above, and especially 'The Lust of the White Serpent,' nevertheless reveal enough Japanese elements that an uninformed reader might think of them as purely a product of native inspiration. Although the immediate source for 'The Lust of the White Serpent' is a Chinese story about a white snake who appears in the form of a beautiful woman and bewitches a young man, Japanese legends about serpents in human guise also existed from early times. While nearly every situation in the Chinese model has its parallel in Akinari's tale, the setting, characters, and diction are all Japanese. Furthermore, the Chinese version is more loosely constructed and designed to appeal to the ordinary city-dweller. Akinari's treatment reminds the reader of a *nō* play.

The spirit, whether really that of woman or serpent, must be firmly exorcised. Although the sacrifice is great, man achieves maturity and learns to purify his heart.

Akinari's use of Chinese material (as well as that of his Japanese sources), suggests an attitude toward originality that may seem strange to a modern Western audience. Novelty for its own sake carried a low premium. Readers accepted a story more readily if they thought it was old or had come from China. Consequently, imitation was encouraged. For Akinari this act did not mean intellectual poverty or failure of the imagination; rather, it indicated a noble trust in his own strength. Far from abandoning one's creative personality and yielding himself to another author or work, one practiced imitation in order to gain aesthetic merit. By following in the footsteps of the men of old, one hoped to find new worlds. By mastering his sources, one infused them with fresh life. Imitation as an accepted mode of creativity dated back to the practice of early Chinese and Japanese poets. Far better to copy with skill, it was generally held, than to make something that was new but inane.

By understanding how Akinari uses his Chinese sources one may learn to appreciate passages that suggest another author, literary work, or even the manner of an entire period or culture. One discovers how Chinese phrases or metaphors are skillfully adapted to enrich the Japanese language and how Akinari handles the stylistic problems of his Chinese literary sources. In their visual form Chinese characters and phrases might preserve their original meaning. By adding a phonetic gloss, Akinari could suggest a Japanese interpretation and denote specific literary associations. The possibilities were virtually limitless, as if one were to mix French and English poetry with quotations from Latin and Greek classics. Owing to Akinari's ingenuity, a reader could enjoy the visual and semantic associations of the Chinese character with the security and immediacy of the Japanese phonetic script, keeping the best of both worlds. Accordingly, nearly every tale in some degree makes free use of aphorisms, images, metaphors, motifs, and ideas from Chinese texts. The discovery of how this old material is used adds to one's pleasure and enlarges one's understanding, as if a door has opened, leading into an uncharted realm of the human imagination.

11 *Influence of Japanese Classics*
Two streams of narrative prose flourished in Akinari's day. The first was mainly fed by earlier literature and history – Chinese as well as Japanese. The second was inspired by actual life and experience in the everyday world. More often than not, the former was serious and noble in tone and was meant to enlighten or instruct the reader. The latter was intended to be popular, amusing, and primarily for entertainment. Although a tendency to combine the two streams persisted, on the one hand Saikaku's tales of the floating world and the character sketches published by the Hachimonjiya, or 'Figure Eight Shop,' usually belonged to the second category, and, on the other, *Ugetsu monogatari* and the 'reading books' are properly classified with the first. Quite understandably, Akinari's indebtedness to earlier Japanese works extended to nearly every literary form and period.

No doubt the reader has already realised that the lyric impulse of the *Man'yōshū* and court poetry was preeminent among the Japanese influences. Indeed, poetry pervades the entire Japanese tradition. The poet, hot with the blood of life, seized experience and turned it into song, gracing whatever he touched with a startling awareness of human feelings. Concise and melodious, the poetry that resulted was rooted in everyday life, and its basic aim was to free men and women from the restraint of mundane affairs. Whenever a person was possessed by deep emotions about life and love or overcome with sadness and sorrow, whenever he felt a smothering sense of constraint, he might try through poetry to share his feelings with others and thereby find relief from his frustrations. The simplicity of Japanese poetic forms served to further this ideal. Almost anyone might combine words to form a musical pattern with a reasonably clear meaning, though the best poets in addition achieved intimacy, allusiveness, depth of feeling, and a maxi-

mum of content within a minimum of form. Certainly the
attentive reader of the tales will recognise the voice of Japanese
poetry, even without the aid of detailed notes, though their
inclusion may lead one to still fuller appreciation.

Above all, the earliest and greatest anthology, the *Man'-
yōshū*, exerted a conspicuous influence on the tales. Study of this
collection was one of the favourite activities of the scholars of
the national learning. Indeed, Akinari contributed his share to
its explication and to its revival in late eighteenth-century Japan.
In his choice of diction and geographic names and also in the
content of the stories themselves, Akinari showed fondness for
this fountainhead of Japanese poetry. A few points relating to
the influence of the *Man'yōshū* on the tales have already been
discussed, but for a full understanding of its inspiration the
Western reader should consult Japanese commentaries and
studies. Yet other early collections of verse, including the best-
known imperial anthologies, also left their mark. *The Tales of
Ise*, however, deserves special mention. To an early collection
of *waka* verses it is supposed that unknown authors added brief
snatches of narrative prose which told about the circumstances
behind the poems. The resulting work became a classic of
Japanese literature and served as a handbook for young lovers
and a guide for mature men and women who wished to convey
their feelings for one another in poetry. Besides the specific influence of this work on *Ugetsu monogatari*, in later years Akinari
wrote a preface and commentary for *The Tales of Ise*, and the
title as well as the style of his light and amusing sketches on contemporary life and manners – *Kuse monogatari* (*Ise*, a place name,
becoming *Kuse*, meaning 'Faults') – were derived from this
Heian classic.

Traditionally, in Japan, poetry was combined with prose.
The two forms harmonised, as a man and a woman well
matched. The classical romances that Akinari knew and to
which he devoted great energy owe much to both the poet and
the storyteller. Although works such as *The Tale of Genji* deal
with everyday life, they suggest in lyrical prose interspersed
with *waka* verse an unreal world, which one might wind into a

painted scroll, each colourful scene merging with the next.
Without suggesting that Akinari's tales in any way rival *The
Tale of Genji*, which breaks away in volcanic fashion from the
surrounding terrain to form a magnificent peak of its own, both
works suggest a quest, that simplest of all romantic structures.
Neither Lady Murasaki's novel nor Akinari's collection of tales,
however, shows an insatiable craving after absolute knowledge
at whatever cost. Rather, each reveals a Buddhist search for
wisdom – that most pragmatic and adjustable of virtues. The
authors told not of adventure or high romance, but more simply
the search of the soul for understanding and the struggle of man
to achieve a degree of enlightenment in a human world where
people often repeat their old accustomed mistakes. The wisdom
found in Akinari's tales, therefore, teaches one to find happiness
in this life by casting off worldly desire and by curbing ambition.
It represents a Buddhist sense of resignation (though tempered
by Chinese thought and native attitudes toward life), as found
in the poem,

| | |
|---|---|
| *Iro wa nioedo* | Though the blossoms may be fragrant, |
| *chiri nuru wo* | They are doomed to fall, |
| *waga yo tare so* | Just as in this world of ours |
| *tsune naran* | No one lives forever. |

| | |
|---|---|
| *Ui no okuyama* | Today I'll cross the mountains |
| *kyō koete* | Of this mortal world |
| *asaki yume mi shi* | And cast off dreams of vanity |
| *ei mo sezu* | And forget all futile pleasures. |

Indeed, these simple stanzas, which use each phonetic symbol
of the Japanese language one time only, have served for a
thousand years as a sort of alphabet song, and they very nearly
epitomise Akinari's theme.

The literature of the Yamato and Heian periods not only
influenced the tone of Akinari's tales, but it also afforded him
techniques for integrating poetry with prose and furnished him
with his underlying motifs. In another way of expressing the
search for wisdom that *Ugetsu monogatari* shares with the best-

known works of Japanese literature, Akinari's contemporary, Motoori, wrote of *mono no aware*, or 'the awareness of things,' though he was referring specifically to ancient literary classics. Akinari's tales also evince this quality. Like *The Tale of Genji*, they may help make young people aware of the pain of growing old and recall to old people what it was to be young.

Still another kind of earlier literature that left its mark on the tales was the personal narrative, a form that emerged in the Heian period, developed during the middle ages, and maintained its popularity until the present day. Although in the West few such works figure as memorable classics, some of the most highly regarded books in the Japanese tradition consist of diaries, travel sketches, and personal essays. As with the court novel, these works often combined prose and poetry, showing the Japanese preference for mixed forms and demonstrating what a narrow and shifting boundary separate fact from fiction and art from reality. Moreover, these texts had a special impact on the development of taste. When art springs directly from life, then the personal diary, travel sketch, and random notes might furnish not only pleasure for the original writer but also enjoyment for the casual reader. Examples such as Lady Sei's *Makura no sōshi* (The Pillow Book)[41] and Yoshida Kenkō's *Tsurezuregusa* (Essays in Idleness) in a general way influenced Akinari's style and helped to form his attitudes toward life. Kenkō's motto, 'The one thing you can be certain of is the truth that all is uncertainty,' indeed applies to Akinari's tales. Beauty was linked to its perishability, and the most precious thing about life was its constant surprise, a point of view that Lafcadio Hearn called 'the genius of Japanese civilization.'[42]

Besides the forms already discussed, collections of medieval Japanese stories known as *setsuwa* figured prominently in the tales. Oftentimes literary versions of legends handed down by word of mouth and compiled by Buddhist priests, these short narratives, that abound in miracles, contributed greatly to the development of the mixed style during the middle ages. Inspired by Buddhist sermons and scriptures, they reveal an intermingling of oral and written tradition, and because they are often allegorical and instructive, many of them resemble fables. Akinari's diction, metaphor, and handling of the supernatural especially benefited from the example of these medieval short stories. In particular, Akinari learned the storyteller's conventional formulas and transitional phrases from the medieval *setsuwa*, which partly helps to explain why he concludes several of his tales with passages that call to mind the raconteur's matter-of-fact ending.

Certain of the war tales, or military chronicles (the best examples of which set the standard for the mixed style from the middle ages until Akinari's day) left their mark as well. Not only did he reflect a familiarity with widely-known titles, such as the *Heike monogatari* (The Tales of the Heike) and the *Taiheiki*,[43] but Akinari also reveals indebtedness to lesser-known works. Rather than epic descriptions of massed combat or great warriors equal to a thousand men, however, Akinari found in these texts first of all an interpretation of national history, as discussed earlier. But he also derived from the memorable episodes of the medieval chronicles techniques for treating sad and poignant episodes in a touching manner. The war tales abound in examples of religious enlightenment and supernatural incidents. Among the remote precursors of the medieval chronicles, the *Kojiki*[44] and the *Nihon shoki*,[45] which tell of the lineage of the gods, the conquest of unruly deities, and the exploits of the early emperors, similarly figure in both the style and content of *Ugetsu monogatari*. Behind these sources, no matter how indirectly, lay the inspiration of the oral tales of the mountain and forest peoples of Northern and Central Asia and the ancient prototypes of Eastern European and Siberian mythical songs, heroic folk poetry, and fully developed epics.

One more branch of medieval literature that deserves mention is the *nō* drama. This remarkable form of theatre combines the complex literary devices of Japanese poetry, the epic material from the war tales, the philosophical outlook of Buddhism, and new elements such as the conventional *michiyuki*, or 'travel scene.' The *nō* conveys its lyric beauty in both representational and poetic terms. Many of Akinari's ghosts and spirits, for instance, remind the reader of similar creatures in the *nō* – at once beautiful and gentle, in a world impossible to define and yet ultimately real. During Akinari's day the *nō* ranked high among fashionable amusements, and the ethereal quality of its texts influenced much of the popular literature and drama of the time. Both in the *nō* and in Akinari's tales, art and life mingle independently of time and space in a manner that demonstrates the essential oneness of existence, stirring the imagination by means of music and the dance and using travel as a symbolic motif. The structure of the individual tales reveals striking similarities to that of the *nō* plays, with an introductory portion (equivalent to the *jo*, or 'preface,' of the *nō*), a period of development (the *ha*), and a climax (*kyū*, where music, dance, and poetry merge in flowery splendour). But even more intriguing than that of any individual drama was the influence of the *nō* performance on the overall structure of *Ugetsu monogatari*. This matter deserves separate treatment.

By Akinari's time commercial publishing was widespread. Printed books had become ordinary items for purchase, and the practice of copying manuscripts declined. Authors might expect gain or profit from their occupation, rather than chiefly pleasure and self-satisfaction. New forms of imaginative literature matured, including *haiku* poetry, the short story, and the popular novel. Japanese scholars have come to refer to works of narrative prose by a number of special terms, such as *kanazōshi* (books written in the Japanese mixed style, rather than in pure Chinese), *ukiyo-zōshi* (the fiction of the floating world), *yomihon* (reading books), and *kusazōshi* (chapbooks). Nevertheless, the short stories and novels of the time displayed several features in common. They were written primarily in the mixed style, as previously mentioned. They were intended not for a small literary circle but for anyone who had the money to buy or borrow a book and leisure time to read. Each year new titles vied for success, and many authors relied on light wit, satire, and realism to win acceptance. On the one hand, numerous works catered to a perennial interest in the pleasure quarter and the entertainment world, but on the other hand some popular books inculcated a taste for contemplative pursuits, such as the study of national history, classical learning, and the scholarly branches of literature. Yet others fostered the practical virtues of loyalty and filial piety. A few authors, including Akinari, wrote both kinds of books – those for entertainment and also those for enlightenment. Frequently both purposes were combined in a single work, making it hard for the modern reader to set up clearly defined boundaries between what is frivolous and what is not. Nevertheless, Akinari's tales, like the best of the reading books, reflect not so much the ligher strain but rather the serious tendency in the popular literature of the day. As described above, they were part of the mainstream of Japanese literature.

## 12  *Structure*

The masterpieces of traditional Japanese literature include unusually long works such as *The Tale of Genji* and exceptionally brief forms like *haiku*. Sometimes small units were linked to make larger pieces that reveal an artistic unity of their own. Akinari's tales exemplify this point. It will be remembered that a tale about a former emperor who in a remote time had predicted an age of war and turmoil begins the collection. An announcement that the leadership of the Tokugawa shogun would bring peace to the realm marks the end. Although the significance of the arrangement of the nine tales and the overall structure might not be obvious at first, a total form emerges, indistinctly as a mystic scene in a Chinese landscape and hauntingly as the supernatural content of the tales.

To some extent certain familiar technical devices impart a unity of tone. One of these is the repetition of similar themes and patterns. For example, in 'White Peak,' 'Bird of Paradise,' and 'Blue Hood,' a holy man on his travels has a supernatural experience. In 'The House Amid the Thickets,' 'The Caldron of Kibitsu,' and 'The Lust of the White Serpent,' a man is involved with a woman who later takes the form of a ghost or spirit. Conflict between father and son is mentioned in four of the tales. Warfare figures in five of them. In six of them the main

character experiences a physical collapse (reflecting the pos-
sibility that Akinari was a sufferer of epilepsy). Various stylistic
devices also help to impart a sense of harmony to the collection.
Careful use of the well-turned phrase, an occasional ironic or
whimsical touch, and numerous scholarly allusions to Chinese
and Japanese literary sources all serve this purpose. Intriguing
though these qualities are, certain additional elements reinforce
the feeling of psychological unity that marks the tales. The idea
of the continuity of existence – the cycle of growth, illness,
death – is stressed throughout the collection, conveying a sense
of man's journey from the cradle to the grave and describing a
series of acts and events leading from innocence to experience.
Along the way one meets with a fleeting vision of the archetypal female goddess. All of this may be represented by the
image of rain and moon.

Each story forms a unit, with a meaning of its own, but taken
together the tales suggest an organic whole greater than the
sum of its parts, like an imperial anthology of court poetry, a
sequence of linked verse, or a full programme of *nō* (with plays
about gods, warriors, women, ghosts, and a congratulatory
prayer of thanksgiving at the end). Underlying the structural
integrity of *Ugetsu monogatari* are Chinese aesthetic values that
the Japanese had early adopted. During the T'ang and Sung
dynasties poets had begun to write sequences of verse, some of
which, for instance, represented the changes of nature throughout the four seasons. Similarly, painters made landscape scrolls
that unfolded from one scene to the next in a progress from the
fresh new buds of spring to the withering of life in winter,
implying a self-renewing cycle of birth, growth, decay, and
death. Inspired by magical Buddhist figures and diagrams that
symbolise the power and the form of the cosmos, poet and
painter learned to depict an entire universe in visual or verbal
terms. The contemplative man spending a summer night
observing the image of the moon reflected in his garden pool
saw in microcosm the vastness of time and space and the rela-
tive insignificance of the individual.

Landscape painting and the ghostly tale both lead to mystical experience. After viewing hills and valleys clad in mist and clouds, the painter, whose every brushstroke is charged with life, discovers hidden forms that exist only in the mind's eye. When the poet elaborates on such a vision, he creates the ghostly tale. 'The Carp That Came to My Dream,' with a powerful touch of irony suggests how such a poetic vision might take on the dimensions of reality. A painted fish could leap into a real lake. Herein lies one of the links between the world of Akinari's tales and that which his contemporaries who called themselves *bunjin*, or 'literary men,' depicted in their landscapes, portraits, or flower and bird studies. Perhaps partly owing to the deformity of his right hand and his consequent inability to master the art of painting, Akinari was able to create an imaginary world by pouring heart and soul into his ghostly tales.

Most of all, however, the organisation of the tales is reminiscent of the arrangement of pieces in a full programme for the *nō* theatre. First came a play about the gods, because they stood for creation and guarded the nation down through the ages. Secondly came a drama about battle, which conveyed the struggle to protect and sustain life and the desire to commemorate the men who pacified the country with bows and arrows. After warfare came peace and a mysterious calm, which woman by means of love helped to perpetuate. But ghosts and spiritual creatures emerged to challenge man and reprove him, showing that his glory might vanish and that life was like a dream. The weaknesses and shortcomings of mankind, as well as human achievements, were thereby represented to the onlookers, but in the end the vital forces auspiciously prevailed. Man was reminded of his moral duties and of the promise that even after spring had passed, again it shall return.

From the middle ages on, sometimes there might be a different number of pieces in a *nō* performance, but the general principles for arranging the programme were usually followed. Akinari prepared his tales similarly (indeed one recalls that his title was derived from the *nō*). 'White Peak' stands as the equivalent of a play about gods. 'Chrysanthemum Tryst' brings to mind dramas in which the ghost of a warrior appears. 'The

House Amid the Thickets' suggests a 'wig' play, where the principle character is a woman, and it reminds one that love is usually associated with sorrow. 'The Carp That Came to My Dream' and 'Bird of Paradise' show certain characteristics related to the deep and mysterious quality of life in the everyday world. 'The Caldron of Kibitsu,' 'The Lust of the White Serpent,' and 'The Blue Hood' all contain scenes that cautioned the reader what disaster might befall the man who failed to show prudence and circumspection in daily conduct. Last of all, 'Wealth and Poverty,' complementing the opening piece, serves a purpose similar to that of a 'congratulatory' play. In the tales, as in the *nō*, decline is followed by restoration. Peace and prosperity succeed toil and suffering. The tales, therefore, describe a paradigm of life.

Besides calling to mind a full programme of the *nō* theatre, most of the tales, as mentioned earlier, show traces of being organised around the theme of the archetypal quest. Saigyō, searching for enlightenment, meets Sutoku, the rebellious and unrepentant ghost of a former emperor. Samon, a youthful scholar, whose adventures were previously limited to the world of books, takes inspiration from Sōemon's ghost. As a result of confronting the world of real experience, he avenges his friend's murder. Katsushirō leaves home and wife to seek wordly wealth, but in the end what he really achieves is understanding and wisdom. Kōgi's view of the depths of Lake Biwa through the eyes of a fish afford him true knowledge of the impermanence of earthly pleasures and realisation of the fragile quality of life. The experience of Muzen and his son on Mt Kōya has a similar effect on the pair. Katsushirō seeks personal happiness, but he is unprepared to accommodate himself to the demands of home and family. Toyoo at first gives in to temptation, endangering his life, but later he finds maturity, though only at an extreme price. The fatherly mendicant, Kaian, saves a lost soul and in the process discovers a new facet of the human spirit. Lastly, Sanai's ghostly interview with the spirit of gold yields him a vision of a future era of peace.

As with many *nō* dramas, much of the significant action in

the tales involves relations among men. In contrast to the earlier court romances, woman plays a secondary role, reminding one of her subordinate position in a Confucian society. According to Buddhist beliefs, as well, she suffers from various hindrances that make it difficult for her to attain enlightenment without first being reborn as a man. Compared to the men in the tales, the women are less firmly in control of their destiny. Nevertheless, Western readers will likely find the three stories in which women play a central role to be the most memorable of all. Despite her subordinate position, woman in the tales suggests the charm and grace of the archetypal female goddess or the mysterious calm of the natural environment, which man never wholly subdues. In her other guise she shows the demonic quality of the witch or shamaness. In 'The House Amid the Thickets' woman appears in her passive form as a loving but forsaken wife, but in 'The Caldron of Kibitsu' and 'The Lust of the White Serpent' she takes on the more active role of the lamia, the witch, and the vampire. The strength of love might transcend the grave. Overwrought feelings transform a jealous woman into a deadly fury. An excess of fervour creates a beautiful woman from a snake – or perhaps it is the other way around. In general, however, Akinari describes a man's world, where woman is either devoted or dangerous. Ironically enough, an excess of devotion leads to danger, which in Buddhist terms means clinging to desire. Akinari suggests that woman must devote herself to man but that too much of this quality might cause pain and anguish.

During the years while he was working on his tales and trying to find a suitable occupation, Akinari possibly felt that his own wife and his step-mother were painfully devoted to him, and that he was undeserving of their love. As did his hero, Samon, he dabbled in scholarship. Like Katsushirō, he had abandoned his father's business, essentially for selfish reasons, to enter a new line of work that offered no assurance of success. Like Shōtarō, he had philandered in the gay quarter and neglected his family's occupation. He felt himself to be weak, like Toyoo, undeserving of his adoptive father's patronage, and remote from the family trade. Thus the tales reflect phases of his own psychological development.

At the beginning of the tales the Buddhist view finds espousal as the quickest way to wisdom, but in the end an attempt is made to transcend this outlook for a more pragmatic approach, in keeping with a new age. Meantime, throughout the collection Akinari sustains his meditative and detached tone. The lonely hermits and the youths who search for fulfilment and enlightenment emerge as his heroes. Mainly he tends to avoid direct confrontation with tragedy, bloodshed, or suffering. Nevertheless, enough gruesome material finds its way into the tales to reveal an ample glimpse of a demonic vision, with symbols of the prison, the madhouse, and death by torture. Shock and horror, one recalls, must figure in any journey from innocence to experience.

But despite certain unusual features in the overall structure and the influence of early Chinese and Japanese works, Akinari in each tale emphasised a single moment of insight, as have good modern short story writers. As a totality of related parts all of the tales combine to form an integral and unified work of art.

## 13 *Akinari's Legacy*

After the first appearance of the tales in Osaka and Kyoto in 1776, they steadily rose in popularity, and the text passed through several editions. Like other books of the time, *Ugetsu monogatari* circulated mainly through lending libraries in the large urban centres and smaller provincial cities. Relatively few people could afford to buy their own private copy, and some readers even transcribed the text that they borrowed. Scholars as well as casual readers took note of the tales, and Akinari's fame and reputation rose. Motoori Norinaga, doyen of the school of national learning, exchanged views with him on a variety of matters, including Japan's proper role in the world community.[46] By the end of the century Ōta Nampo visited Akinari and called him the outstanding writer of the day.[47] Another Edo author, Takizawa Bakin (1767-1848), tried without success to meet him, but he praised Akinari as a great man of letters and regretted only that he shunned social intercourse and was so retiring by nature.[48]

Meanwhile, the tales began to exert an influence on the literary scene. Itami Chin'en (1751 ?–81 ?) in a reading book entitled *Kinko kaidan miyamagusa* (Deep Mountain Grass: New and Old Tales of Wonder), which came out in Osaka in 1782, used situations from 'The Caldron of Kibitsu' and 'The Lust of the White Serpent.'[49] Other authors, particularly in Edo, the most rapidly growing urban centre in Japan at the time, tried to emulate Akinari's successful combination of a neoclassical style and a popular mode of storytelling. Even authors of chapbooks, such as Tōrai Sanna (1749–1810),[50] borrowed passages from Akinari's tales. Santō Kyōden (1761–1816),[51] realised the significance of Akinari's work and used the same techniques and materials in his historical romances. But above all, Bakin himself perfected the idea of using real or imaginary characters out of the past to create historical novels that appealed to serious readers who were interested in art, scholarship, society, and politics.[52] Bakin several times employed the idea of an interview with the ghost of a famous man, as had Akinari in 'White Peak' and 'Bird of Paradise.'[53]

Many of the same names of people, places, events, and even the classical Chinese metaphors of Akinari's tales appeared in Bakin's novels.[54] The idea of a worthless man who for the sake of another woman neglects his wife and eventually meets a violent death at the hands of her rancorous ghost not only found expression in 'The Caldron of Kibitsu' but also in Bakin's reading book, *Kanzen Tsuneyo no monogatari* (The Story of Tsuneyo).[55] The situation described at the beginning of 'The Lust of the White Serpent' was also imitated by Bakin in *Kinsesetsu bishōnenroku* (Handsome Youths),[56] where a young man similarly meets a woman at a temple during a sudden rain shower and lends her his umbrella. Later in the same episode a mysterious serpent appears. But aside from specific influence on Kyōden and Bakin's plots, Akinari's greatest contribution to later authors was his skilful use of classical metaphor and his treatment of the supernatural world. Without his work Japanese

literature of the nineteenth and twentieth century would have
been much the poorer.

Men such as Nampo, Bakin, and Kyōden helped to preserve
the memory of Akinari's work. The former pair correctly
identified two earlier titles that Akinari refused to admit having
written.[57] Bakin was instrumental in transmitting the posthumous work, *Harusame monogatari* (Tales of Spring Rain).
During Akinari's own lifetime he and his tales became objects
of study. Then not long after his death, a certain Obayashi
Kajō (1782?–1862), a retainer in the Ōban, or 'Guard,' the
military branch of the government service, who was conversant
with Confucian doctrines, as well as the tenets of the school of
national learning, in 1823 edited Akinari's *Kuse monogatari*, adding a variety of notes and comments[58] and attesting to the
growing recognition of his genius.

With the surge of Western influence after 1868, for a time
interest in Akinari and his tales diminished. But by 1890 the
climate had changed, and people began paying more attention
to things Japanese. The tales were mentioned in an early history
of prose fiction.[59] Movable-type editions became available,[60]
and hereafter *Ugetsu monogatari* was often reprinted. Writers
and poets of the Meiji Era – especially those involved with the
Japanese romantic movement – turned to them for inspiration
and found the same enduring qualities that had attracted an
earlier generation. The novelist Kōda Rohan described Saigyō's
journey to the emperor Sutoku's grave in terms that showed
'White Peak' to have been the model. A poet named Takeshima
Hagoromo was influenced by the tales. A poetic version and a
dramatisation of 'The House Amid the Thickets' appeared.[61]
During these years Lafcadio Hearn introduced 'Chrysanthemum Tryst' and 'The Carp That Came to My Dream' to
English-speaking readers, marking the beginning of their
recognition in world literature.[62]

In the twentieth century Akinari's literary reputation has
continued to flourish, and his tales have been acknowledged as
a central work in the Japanese tradition. Suzuki Toshinari's
annotated edition in 1916[63] included a lengthy introductory

essay on such topics as Akinari's views on literature, how the tales came to be written and published, their literary background, the influence of medieval narrative prose, the role of the supernatural, and the impact on later authors. A revised version of Suzuki's work in 1929 boasted of four illustrations by Kaburagi Kiyokata, in which Akinari's themes were represented in pictorial terms.[64] Suzuki's careful and innovative study influenced later scholars, and Kaburagi's drawings demonstrated the hold that the tales exerted on artists as well as poets.

Literary men continued to respond to Akinari's classical style and emotional power. The novelist Tanizaki Jun'ichirō in 1920 prepared a scenario for a motion picture based on 'The Lust of the White Serpent.'[65] In 1924 Satō Haruo (who, incidentally, was born in Shingu, the home of Akinari's fictional hero, Toyoo) published the first of many items he was to write about the tales and their author.[66] Akutagawa Ryūnosuke was an ardent student of the tales. One of Dazai Osamu's first stories, 'Gyofukuki,' which appeared in 1933, was inspired by 'The Carp That Came to My Dream,' and the author wrote that when he first read Akinari's tale as a child, it made him want to become a fish.[67] In the mid-1930s Okamoto Kanoko published an essay on Akinari.[68] As mentioned in the Translator's Foreword, two film versions were produced in the 1950s. Meanwhile, Mishima Yukio in 1949 wrote an appreciative essay that showed the powerful influence Akinari's work had on him during his formative years. To him, Akinari represented 'a marriage of moralist and aesthete,' and Mishima praised the poetry, beauty, irony, and detachment found in the tales. 'White Peak' was his favourite, followed by 'The Carp' and 'Chrysanthemum Tryst.' The romantic quality of Mishima's own writings owes a good deal to Akinari, whom he called 'the Japanese Villiers de L'Isle-Adam.'[69] Literary critics have similarly shared a high opinion of the tales.[70]

Among early twentieth-century scholars, a number of men have helped to make *Ugetsu monogatari* one of the most familiar titles in Japanese literature. Fujii Otoo, for instance, played a special role in Akinari studies. He assisted in editing a collection of the authors representative works; he prepared a separate volume of posthumous writings; he wrote scholarly and critical essays, and he produced a valuable biographical study.[71] Other men in the meantime concentrated on understanding Akinari's indebtedness to earlier literature. Two of the most prominent of these, Yamaguchi Takeshi and Gotō Tanji,[72] have demonstrated the complexity of the Chinese and Japanese literary sources. Tsujimori Shūei published a biographical study.[73] In 1946 an independent monograph on the tales, by Shigetomo Ki, appeared.[74] Maruyama Sueo presented a detailed bibliography of secondary sources, and in 1951 he introduced newly discovered work by Akinari, which enabled readers to grasp more fully the degree of his talent and genius.[75] By the middle of the twentieth century Akinari's tales were sometimes compared in extravagant terms with such works as *The Tale of Genji*, the most remarkable achievement in all of Japanese literature.

More recently, intensive research and analysis has led to new knowledge and understanding. Nakamura Yukihiko, a widely respected scholar of early modern literature, has contributed to a realisation of Akinari's breadth as a literary man.[76] Others, such as Moriyama Shigeo, Sakai Kōichi, Ōba Shunsuke, and Morita Kirō, have published appreciative studies.[77] Takada Mamoru has pieced together all the available details of Akinari's life, and he has also published a well received critical monograph.[78] Until his untimely death, Uzuki Hiroshi was working on an exhaustively thorough annotated text of *Ugetsu monogatari*, which his co-worker, Nakamura Hiroyasu, completed – a monumental effort that all future students of the tales will surely consult.[79] Asano Sampei has prepared a collection of Akinari's *waka* verse with essays and notes on the sources and criticism and discussion of the author's ideas on poetry. More recently he has edited a text of *Tales of Spring Rain*.[80] Yet other well known scholars and critics have written about the tales, reaffirming their value. General anthologies of Japanese literature normally include selections from them, and a person can hardly claim to be well read unless he is conversant with *Ugetsu monogatari*.

Since Lafcadio Hearn's introduction of two of the tales in English, other translators have tried to convey the elusive beauty of the work to the rest of the world. In the 1920s a version of 'The Blue Hood' appeared in an English language periodical in Japan.[81] In the 1930s Wilfred Whitehouse published translations of five of the tales with notes and commentary in *Monumenta Nipponica*,[82] an important journal for Japanese studies. Pierre Humbertclaude in the same journal began an ambitious critical study on Akinari including his early popular works.[83] By the early 1940s all of the tales had been translated at least once. In the 1950s René Seiffert, in Paris, published a complete French translation with notes and commentaries on the individual tales.[84] Meanwhile, other Western scholars of Japanese literature were also attracted to Akinari's work. Carmen Blacker and W. E. Skillend translated 'The Carp That Came to My Dream.'[85] Dale Saunders published new translations of several tales,[86] and Lewis Allen one of 'Chrysanthemum Tryst.'[87] James Araki wrote an essay introducing scholars to recent Japanese studies.[88] Also, during the 1960s a Hungarian translation appeared in Budapest, a Polish one in Warsaw. Kazuya Sakai, of Mexico City, published eight of the nine tales in a Spanish version.[89] An analysis of the tales may be found in a Czechoslovakian doctoral dissertation available in Prague. The author, Libuse Bohackova, has also published a complete translation.[90] Most recently, several young English-speaking scholars have turned their attention to *Tales of Spring Rain*,[91] and Kengi Hamada has published a translation of *Ugetsu monogatari* in book form.[92] Nevertheless, one can hardly claim that the tales have been available in a suitable form for the general public. The present edition should help the reader more readily to appreciate Akinari's accomplishment.

## 14 *The Present Edition*

In Akinari's time there existed a bond between reader and writer unlike that in the West today. If the author sketched the outline and suggested the emotions and the spirit of what he wanted to say, the reader would fill in the rest – as with a

Chinese or Japanese painting. It was acceptable to leave white spaces and even blurred places. Modern English prose, however, demands greater clarity. The translator must often pick one of several possible readings. He needs to put the text into a different focus.

Basically, I wanted the translation to read as if the original were written in common English. To this end I made my own interpretation of the tales, but I did not let the shadows of my imagination obscure the author's original intent. I tried to take the work as an eighteenth-century reader might have done and to recreate the impression that the book left on Japanese readers of long ago – though in a manner that would appeal to the feelings and understanding of a modern Western audience.

Rather than be as colloquial as possible, I have blended elements of spoken English with an occasional literary turn of phrase, so that the reader might better imagine the tone of Akinari's 'mixed-style.' I picked a formal cadence, while keeping in mind that Akinari himself used some of the conventions of the oral storyteller. The style of my translation may slow some readers down, but I hoped to reproduce part of the elegant flavour and the poetic quality of the original. It is well to remember that Akinari – like the Pre-Raphaelites – tried to revive a style that belonged to a period centuries earlier than his own day.

When I had a choice, I used the Japanese order of phrases and images, and I allowed myself a bit of inversion and elegant variation to help suggest the original text. But when English syntax seemed to cry out at being wrenched, I relaxed my grip. To a slight degree I edited the text for the convenience of Western readers. Failure to do so would have meant a clumsy and pedantic translation. With proper names, for example, the *in*, or 'cloistered emperor,' of the first tale, becomes Toba. The *shin-in*, or 'new cloistered emperor,' becomes Sutoku. En'i is Saigyō, and so on.

Nothing, however, can replace the original wood-block text, with its soft, handmade paper, cursive script, and irregular *kana* symbols. Seeing it furthers a love and appreciation of the work and arouses a desire to feel it and to find its sounds. Perhaps a facsimile edition or photographic reproduction of the text may eventually be available, and readers may learn to appreciate its aesthetic qualities and examine it as an example of eighteenth-century wood-block printing. For students the *hentai-gana* script (as the irregular form of the cursive syllabary is known) could serve as practice in reading pre-Meiji texts.

As the basic text for the present translation, I have used the first edition of the tales, which was issued at the booksellers' establishment of Yabaidō, a joint venture by Umemura Hambei, of Kyoto, and Nomura Chōbei, of Osaka. Specimen photographs are provided of the copy in the Tenri Central Library, and I have inserted notes that tell where each page of the wood-block text ends. I have also examined the copies in the National Diet Library and in Kyoto University Library, and in the reprint of that formerly owned by Tomioka Tessai and Mizutani Futō and now in the possession of Mr Matsuura Sadatoshi. Mr Nakamura Hiroyasu in 1967 published this text in a photographic reprint. I also consulted many commentaries and special studies, most notably those by Uzuki Hiroshi and Nakamura Yukihiko.

One of the minor changes that I have made involves the *kanazukai*, or orthography. Akinari used the classical way of representing the sounds of Japanese in written form. But for the reader's convenience, I put all words in their modern form. As a result, *teu* became *chō*; *itau*, *itō*; *jiyaukuhau*, *jōkō*, and so on. Anyone interested in this matter should look at tables in dictionaries such as the *Kōjien* or *Meikai kogo jiten*. For the *nigori*, or voiced consonants – *ga-*, *za-*, *da-*, *ba-*, *pa-*, and their related sounds – I usually followed modern editors rather than the cursive text, but in the notes I have pointed out a number of examples of Akinari's usage. Believing that it was more effective in English (and with the support of Japanese commentaries that refer to the tone of a dramatic monologue), I rendered the opening tale in the first person, though other translators have used the third person narrative. Therefore, the 'I' in 'White Peak' refers not to Akinari, the author, but to Saigyō, the twelfth century poet, who reveals himself in a monologue addressed to the reader.

Although I kept in mind not only the needs of the general reader but also the student who has some knowledge of the Japanese language and who is ready to begin to enjoy traditional Japanese literature, my introduction and notes are more appreciative than critical. I avoided tedious points of grammar. I mentioned only a few of the oddities in Akinari's use of Chinese characters and Japanese diction. I did not exhaustively report all of the literary sources – rather, I was very selective. Students are urged to consult Uzuki or Nakamura's text, both of which are readily available. I tried to avoid giving an impression of esoteric remoteness, hoping rather to arouse new interest in Japanese literature. Indeed, I believe that the tales deserve to be widely read not only by adults in all walks of life but also by young people in the schools wherever the English language is used.

In translating the *waka* verses in the notes, I wanted mainly to show how Akinari's diction and syntax suggested the classical poetry of Japan. I was content to find a plausible reading in English, and I made little effort to discuss the technical devices of Japanese prosody. Anyone who wishes to go more deeply into the form and meaning of the verse should turn to the Japanese texts that I have cited and read Robert Brower and Earl Miner's fine book on Japanese court poetry. Especially for the *Man'yōshū* poems, I tried to be as clear and straightforward as possible, in the belief that simplicity is the outstanding feature of this anthology.

Place names in the notes are usually identified with their modern locations. Thus, the old provinces are given as the present-day prefectures. Tago Bay (see text, note 11), for instance, is said to be in Shizuoka, not in Mikawa (the name of the equivalent province). The word 'city' denotes the modern Japanese *shi*, an administrative unit below the prefectural level with a certain amount of urban development. It is comparable to *gun*, which is a predominantly rural unit called a 'district.'

My choice of editions of works cited in the notes was eclectic. Although they are not often those available to modern readers, I made some effort to deduce what texts of certain Chinese works Akinari may have used, because this is of interest to students of Chinese and Japanese cultural relations. For Japanese titles, I usually picked those in the series *Nihon koten bungaku taikei*, because they are easily obtainable and of high quality. For texts not in this series, I took handy modern reprints, turning to pre-modern editions as a last resort. I thought of using only books that Akinari might have seen, but aside from being an amusing bibliographic exercise, this would have proved maddening to any reader who tried to verify my references only to discover that the few available copies were all preserved in remote libraries in Japan. Wherever possible, I have listed English translations. The notes to the introduction and the text are numbered in two separate series, but I did not repeat full citations in the second series for any work previously listed in the first. More so than the introduction and the transla-tion, my notes reflect the interest of the scholar or student. Still, I hope that the general reader will find occasional pleasure in glancing through them.

A few remarks on the calendar are necessary. In Akinari's time the years were calculated in a sexagenary cycle, using the Chinese zodiac. This consisted of twelve animal signs, also known as 'branches,' and ten other symbols that represented the five elements (wood, fire, earth, metal, and water) each used twice. Years were given era names, which were of various duration as recommended by official astrologers. The seasons were slightly different than now. New Year's day marked the beginning of spring, and it fell on the first, second or even some-times the third new moon after the winter solstice. Therefore, each season came a little earlier than now. The months were adjusted to the lunar cycle – the fifteenth day always coinciding with the full moon. Each month was known by its number, from the first to the twelfth, and also by a poetic designation. The hours of the day were counted by using the twelve animal signs to represent two-hour periods. In addition, the night was measured by five units sometimes called 'watches.' For the names of historical and literary periods, I have tried to follow standard usage. Readers who want fuller information on these matters should see Herschel Webb's handy volume, *Research in Japanese Sources: A Guide*.

Throughout the book I used the Hepburn system to transliterate Japanese words, following the 1931 and 1942 editions of *Kenkyusha's New Japanese-English Dictionary*. The consonants are pronounced as in English, except that the 'g' is always hard, as in 'give.' The vowels are as in Italian. A long vowel (most often *ō*) means that the length of the sound should be twice the usual duration. For Chinese words, I have used the modified Wade-Giles system found in the *Mathews' Chinese-English Dictionary*. With Japanese proper names, that of the family comes first, except when an author originally wrote a book or article in a Western language. In the case of Japanese and Chinese books written before the modern period and also for well-known reference works and series, I adopted the usual practice in Japan and attached primary importance to the title, rather than the author, editor, or compilor.

To help the reader 'see' the text in terms of imagery familiar to Akinari and to people in Japan, I have also added a number of illustrations. For the most part, the modern traveller who visits the actual places mentioned in the tales will be disappointed, because the beauty in the mind's eye far excels that of mundane reality. Everyone looks through lenses of diverse kinds, but most people need assistance to see things in the light of the past. By viewing the world through Akinari's eyes one gains a sharper focus on life. One learns the relativity of all human needs, standards, and beliefs. One finds a new image of himself. Akinari's poetry may lack some of the grandeur of Lady Murasaki, the incisiveness of Lady Sei, the simplicity of Bashō, the wit of Saikaku, or the scale of Bakin, but he still had a powerful vision of reality that compels the modern reader's attention. His tales will add much to any effort to renew a right spirit in the heart of man.

# NOTES ON THE
# INTRODUCTION

1 In *Yōkyoku taikan*, ed. Sanari Kentarō (1930–31; rpt. Tokyo: Meiji Shoin, 1963), vol. 1, p. 332. For this verse see also the *Senjūshō*, a collection of Buddhist short stories attributed to Saigyō, in Iwanami bunko (Tokyo: Iwanami, 1970), p. 151.

2 (Japanese, *Sentō shinwa*) Comp. Ch'ü Yu, in 1378 (Kyoto: Hayashi Shōgorō, 1648), 2, 33b (hereafter, *New Tales for Lamplight*); for other editions, see Kokuyaku Kambun taisei, vol. 13 (1922; rpt. Tokyo: Kokumin Bunko, 1924), p. 70; see also Chou I, ed. (Shanghai: Chung hua shu chü, 1962), p. 55. Also see Shigetomo Ki, *Ugetsu monogatari no kenkyū* (Tokyo: Yaesu Shuppan, 1946), pp. 311–14; and Uzuki Hiroshi, *Ugetsu monogatari hyōshaku*, in Nihon koten hyōshaku zenchūshaku sōsho (Tokyo: Kadokawa, 1969), p. 18.

3 See Arthur Waley, trans., *The Tale of Genji* (1925–33; 1 vol. rpt. London: Allen & Unwin, 1935; 4th impression, 2 vols, 1965); for Japanese text, see *Genji monogatari*, in Nihon koten bungaku taikei, 99 vols (Tokyo: Iwanami, 1957–66), (hereafter, NKBT), vols 14–17.

4 *Yoki hodo to omou wa sugitaru nari.* 'Tandai shōshin roku,' *Ueda Akinari-shū*, ed. Nakamura Yukihiko, in NKBT, vol. 56, pp. 258–9.

5 See 'Chrysanthemum Tryst' and text, note 140.

6 The earliest surviving anthology of Japanese poetry; compiled in the 8th century. See Nihon Gakujutsu Shinkōkai, ed., *One Thousand Poems from the Manyōshū* (1940; rpt. New York: Columbia University Press, 1965) (hereafter, NGSK); also see, NKBT, vols 4–7.

7 In Asano Sampei, ed., *Akinari ʐen-kashū to sono kenkyū* (Tokyo: Ōfūsha, 1969), p. 248.

8 For Saikaku and the *ukiyo-ʐōshi*, see Howard Hibbett, *The Fiction of the Floating World* (London: Oxford University Press, 1957); Ivan Morris, trans., *An Amorous Woman and Other Stories by Ihara Saikaku* (New Haven: New Directions, 1963); and Hasegawa Tsuyoshi, *Ukiyo-ʐōshi no kenkyū: Hachimonjiya-bon wo chūshin to suru* (Tokyo: Ōfūsha, 1969).

9 Pearl Buck, trans., *All Men Are Brothers* (1937; rpt. New York: Grove Press, 1957), 2 vols. As one example of an early printed text that helped make *Water Margin* more accessible in Japan, see *Ritakugo sensei hiten chūgi suikoden* (Chinese, *Li Cho-wu hsien sheng pi tien chung-i shui hu chuan*) (Kyoto: Hayashi Kyūbei, 1728), the first 10 chapters of the 120-chapter version, punctuated for Japanese readers.

10 See Takizawa Bakin, *Kinsei mono-no-hon Edo sakusha burui*, ed. Kimura Miyogo (Nara: Privately published, 1971, for a facsimile reprint of this pioneering study of the development of early modern prose fiction with a meticulously prepared introduction by the editor).

11 See *Oku no hosomichi*, in NKBT, vol. 46, p. 70.

12 NGSK, p. 49; NKBT, vol. 4, pp. 150–1 (no. 253).

13 See William Aston, trans., *Nihongi: Chronicles of Japan from the Earliest Times to A.D. 697* (1896; rpt. 2 vols in 1, London: Allen & Unwin, 1956), II, 293.

14 *Suzuro-gokoro shite*. See 'Iwahashi no ki,' in *Akinari ibun*, ed. Fujii Otoō (1919; rpt. Tokyo: Shūbunkan, 1929), pp. 263–86; and 'Tsuzura-bumi,' in *Ueda Akinari zenshū*, ed. Iwahashi Koyata and Fujii Otoō (1917; rpt. 2 vols in 1, Tokyo: Kokusho Kankōkai, 1923), I, 71–9, N.B. p. 71.

15 *Gukanshō*, comp. the priest Jien, in 1220, in NKBT, vol. 86, p. 206. See also H. Paul Varley, *Imperial Restoration in Medieval Japan*, Studies of the East Asia Institute (New York: Columbia University Press, 1971), pp. 15–21.

16 The edition that commonly circulated in early modern times was the *Kokatsujibon Hōgen monogatari*, in NKBT, vol. 22, pp. 335–99 (hereafter *Hōgen monogatari*). See also William R. Wilson, trans., *Hōgen monogatari: Tale of the Disorder in Hōgen*, A Monumenta Nipponica Monograph (Tokyo: Sophia University, 1971).

17 *Intoku taiheiki*, comp. Kagawa Masanori and Kagetsugu, in the 17th century, in Tsūzoku Nihon zenshi, vols 13–14 (Tokyo: Waseda Daigaku Shuppan-bu, 1913).

18 Especially the *Kamakura ōzōshi*, in Gunsho ruijū, vol. 13 (Tokyo: Keizai Zasshi-sha, 1900), pp. 650–714. This work treats events of the 14th–15th century, beginning with an account of the ambitions of Ashikaga Ujimitsu (1357–98) and ending with a description of the rise to power of Ōta Dōkan (1432–86). Unlike the other titles mentioned so far, the *Kamakura ōzōshi* apparently was not printed and circulated only in manuscript.

19 See Varley, *The Ōnin War: History of Its Origins and Background*, Studies of the East Asia Institute (New York: Columbia University Press, 1967), pp. 88–95.

20 In Witter Bynner, trans., *The Jade Mountain: A Chinese Anthology, Being Three Hundred Poems of the T'ang Dynasty* (1928; rpt. New York: Alfred A. Knopf, 1945), p. 170.

21 Akinari's main source was the *Taikōki*, comp. Kose Hoan, in 1625. See Shiseki shūran, vol. 5 (Tokyo: Kondō Kappansho, 1900). Western readers may wish to consult accounts such those by Sir George Sansom, *A History of Japan, vol. 2: 1334–1615* (London: The Cresset Press, 1961), pp. 364–7, 370; and James Murdoch and Yamagata Isoh, *A History of Japan During the Century of Early Foreign Intercourse (1542–1651)* (Kobe: The Chronicle Office, 1903), pp. 380–4.

**22** See Donald Keene, ed., *Twenty Plays of the Nō Theatre* (New York: Columbia University Press, 1971), pp. 237–52. Also see text, note 490.

**23** See Hayashiya Tatsusaburō, 'Nihon bunka no higashi to nishi,' *Sekai* (Jan. 1971), p. 339.

**24** For the relations between the school of national learning and the Taoist teachings and for Akinari's indebtedness to this branch of Chinese philosophy, see Sakai Kōichi, *Ueda Akinari* (Kyoto: San'ichi Shobō, 1959), pp. 138–49; for the similar interest of one of Akinari's contemporaries, see Keene, *The Japanese Discovery of Europe, 1720–1830*, rev. ed. (Stanford: Stanford University Press, 1969), p. 82.

**25** Lionel Giles, trans., *Taoist Teachings from the Book of Lieh-Tzu . . .*, Wisdom of the East Series (1912; rpt. London: John Murray, 1947), pp. 49, 108.

**26** See Robert N. Bellah, *Tokugawa Religion* (Glencoe: Free Press, 1957); and Ronald Philip Dore, *Education in Tokugawa Japan* (Berkeley: University of California Press, 1965), pp. 230–43.

**27** See Wm. Theodore de Bary, ed., *The Buddhist Tradition in India, China, and Japan*, The Modern Library (New York: Random House, 1969), pp. 155–66; and Morris, *The World of the Shining Prince* (London: Oxford University Press, 1964), p. 103, who refers to the same doctrine as 'calm contemplation.'

**28** Morris, ibid., p. 98.

**29** 'Paradise Lost,' *The Complete Poetical Works of John Milton . . .*, ed., William Vaughn Moody (1899; rpt. Boston: Houghton Mifflin, 1924), p. 105; and 'The Second Defence of The English People,' *Milton's Prose Writings*, ed. K. M. Burton, Everyman's Library, No. 795 (1927; rpt. London: Dent, 1958), p. 345.

**30** *Ise monogatari ko-i*; for Akinari's preface to it, see *Akinari ibun*, pp. 544–6; for complete English translations of this Heian classic, see Helen Craig McCullough, *Tales of Ise: Lyric Episodes from Tenth-Century Japan* (Stanford: Stanford University Press, 1968); and H. Jay Harris, *The Tales of Ise: Translated from the Classical Japanese* (Tokyo: Chas. E. Tuttle Co., 1972).

**31** See 'Yoshiya ashiya,' in *Ueda Akinari zenshū*, II, 408.

**32** *The Tale of Genji*, p. 501; NKBT, vol. 15, p. 432.

**33** An important milestone in the history of Japanese literary criticism, by Ki no Tsurayuki (868?–945?), co-editor of the *Kokinshū*, comp. in AD 905, the first imperial anthology of *waka* poetry. See NKBT, vol. 8, pp. 93–104. See also Makoto Ueda, *Literary and Art Theories in Japan* (Cleveland: The Press of Western Reserve University, 1967).

**34** Letter to Jen Shao-ch'ing, trans., Burton Watson, *Ssu-ma Ch'ien: The Grand Historian of China* (New York: Columbia University Press, 1958), pp. 65–6; found also in the early Chinese anthology, *Wen hsüan*, a text well known to educated people in Lady Murasaki's day and in

Akinari's time. See the Japanese edition, *Monzen bōkun taizen* (Osaka: Ōta Gon'uemon, 1699), 11, 29a–34b.

35 'Tu Chung-i shui hu chuan chü' (Japanese, 'Doku chūgi suikoden jo'), in *Ritakugo sensei hiten chūgi suikoden*, 1, 1a–3b. See also, Chūgoku koten bungaku taikei, vol. 55 (Tokyo: Heibonsha, 1971).

36 Quoted in Ryūsaku Tsunoda, de Bary, Keene, et al., *Sources of Japanese Tradition* (New York: Columbia University Press, 1959), p. 534.

37 Watson, trans., *The Complete Works of Chuang Tzu* (New York: Columbia University Press, 1968), p. 158.

38 NKBT, vol. 9, p. 143.

39 *Hito wa bakemono yo ni nai mono wa nashi.* Preface, *Saikaku shokoku-banashi, Saikaku-bon fukusei*, in Koten bunko, vol. 17 (Tokyo: Koten Bunko, 1953). IV, 4.

40 *Oni mo idete hito ni majiwari, hito mata oni ni majiwarite osorezu;* and *kami mo oni mo izuchi ni hai-kakururu, ato nashi.* 'Me hitotsu no kami,' *Harusame monogatari* (Tales of Spring Rain), Sakurayama Bunko text, ed. Maruyama Sueo, *Ueda Akinari-shū*, in Koten bunko, vols 47–8 (Tokyo: Koten Bunko, 1951), I, 108.

41 For a complete translation, see Morris, *The Pillow Book of Sei Shōnagon*, 2 vols (New York: Columbia University Press, 1967).

42 See Keene, trans., *Essays in Idleness: The Tsurezuregusa of Kenkō* (New York: Columbia University Press, 1967), pp. xviii, 163.

43 For a complete translation of the former, see Arthur Lindsay Sadler, 'The Heike Monogatari,' *Transactions of the Asiatic Society of Japan*, 1st ser., 46, part 2 (1918), i–xiv, 1–278; 49, part 1 (1921), 1–354, 1–11 (rpt. Tokyo: Yushodo, 1965). For a partial translation of the latter, see McCullough, *Taiheiki* (New York: Columbia University Press, 1958).

44 For a recent translation, see Donald Philippi, *Kojiki* (Princeton: University of Princeton Press, 1968).

45 Also called the *Nihongi*. See note 12.

46 See 'Kakaika,' *Ueda Akinari zenshū*, I, 423–64.

47 Recorded in 'Tandai shōshin-roku,' NKBT, vol. 56, p. 316. Ōta Nampo was also known by his pen name, Shokusanjin.

48 See 'Kiryo manroku,' *Nikki kikō-shū* in Yūhōdō bunko (Tokyo: Yūhōdō Shoten, 1913–15), p. 597.

49 I am indebted to Professor Hamada Keisuke of Kyoto University, for calling this to my attention.

50 Mentioned in my '*Kusazōshi*: Chapbooks of Japan,' *Transactions of the Asiatic Society of Japan*, 3rd ser., 10 (1968), 126–7; and James T. Araki, '*Sharebon*: Books for Men of Mode,' *Monumenta Nipponica*, 24 (1969), 39, 41–2.

51 For a summary of Kyōden's literary activities, see my *Takizawa Bakin*, Twayne's World Authors Series, 20 (New York: Twayne, 1967), N.B., pp. 56–99; and Araki, 'Sharebon,' *passim*.

52   See Chapter 3 of my *Takizawa Bakin*.

53   Most notably with Sutoku, in *Chinsetsu yumihari-zuki*; see NKBT, vol. 60, pp. 215–25.

54   As pointed out in Asō Isoji, *Edo bungaku to Chūgoku bungaku* (1946; rpt. Tokyo: Sanseidō, 1957), pp. 661–2.

55   *Kanzen Tsuneyo no monogatari* (Osaka: Kawachiya Tōbei, 1806).

56   See *Kinsesetsu bishōnenroku*, in Teikoku bunko, 2nd ser. (Tokyo: Hakubunkan, 1928–30), vol. 6, pp. 38–9.

57   See Nakamura, ed., *Akinari*, in Nihon koten kanshō kōza, vol. 24 (Tokyo: Kadokawa, 1956), p. 31.

58   First reprinted in Kinko bungei onchi sōsho, vol. 4 (Tokyo: Hakubunkan, 1891), pp. 165–233; more recently, a different text of *Kuse monogatari* has appeared in Maruyama, ed., *Ueda Akinari-shū*, II, 79–197.

59   Sekine Masanao, *Shōsetsu shikō* (Tokyo: Kinkōdō, 1890), N.B., part 2, pp. 29–31.

60   Matsumura Shintarō, ed., *Ugetsu monogatari* (Tokyo, 1893); and the popular series, Teikoku bunko, 50 vols (Tokyo: Hakubunkan, 1893–97), vol. 32.

61   All mentioned in Suzuki Toshinari, *Shinchū ugetsu monogatari hyōshaku*, 2nd ed. (Tokyo: Seibunkan, 1929), pp. 132–4.

62   See 'A Promise Kept,' and 'The Story of Kogi,' *A Japanese Miscellany* (1901), in *The Writings of Lafcadio Hearn* (Boston: Houghton Mifflin, 1922), X, 193–8, 230–7. In addition, readers may find similarities between 'The Caldron of Kibitsu' and Hearn's 'Of a Promise Broken,' pp. 199–207.

63   When the 1st ed. of his *Ugetsu* appeared (see note 61).

64   *Ibid.*, frontispiece, and facing pp. 290, 300, 310.

65   Mentioned in Joseph L. Anderson and Donald Richie, *The Japanese Film: Art and Industry* (Tokyo: Tuttle, 1959), pp. 39–40.

66   Collected in his posthumous *Ueda Akinari* (Tokyo: Tōgensha, 1964).

67   In *Dazai Osamu zenshū*, I (Tokyo: Chikuma Shobō, 1967), 61–70, XII (1968), 383. See also Keene, *Landscapes and Portraits: Appreciations of Japanese Culture* (Tokyo: Kodansha International, 1971), p. 188. Thomas J. Harper, trans., 'Metamorphosis,' *Japan Quarterly*, 17 (1970), 285–8.

68   Okamoto Kanoko, 'Ueda Akinari no bannen,' *Bungakkai* (Oct. 1935), pp. 351–369. This has been reprinted in Kuwabara Shigeo, ed., *Ueda Akinari: Kaii yūkei no bungaku arui wa monogatari no hokkyoku* (Tokyo: Shichōsha, 1972), pp. 300–11.

69   Mishima Yukio, 'Ugetsu monogatari ni tsuite,' *Bungei ōrai* (Sept. 1949), pp. 48–51.

70   See Takada Mamoru, *Ueda Akinari kenkyū josetsu* (Tokyo: Nara Shobō, 1968), p. 8.

71   See note 14. His essays and other work may be found most notably in *Edo bungaku kenkyū* (Kyoto: Naigai Shuppan, 1922); *Edo bungaku sōsetsu* (Tokyo: Iwanami, 1931); and *Kinsei shōsetsu kenkyū* (Osaka: Akitaya, 1947).

72 For Yamaguchi's efforts, see *Edo bungaku kenkyū* (Tokyo: Tōkyōdō, 1933); and 'Kaisetsu,' *Kaidan meisaku-shū*, in Nihon meicho zenshū, vol. 10 (Tokyo: Nihon Meicho Kankōkai, 1927), pp. 1–100; Gotō Tanji's work, more than thirty essays in all, beginning in 1934 appeared in various scholarly journals and collections; these are cited in the detailed bibliography in Uzuki, *Ugetsu*, pp. 713–27, mentioned above (see note 2).

73 *Ueda Akinari no shōgai* (Tokyo: Yūkōsha, 1942).

74 See note 2.

75 'Ueda Akinari kankei shomoku gainen,' *Koten kenkyū*, 4, no. 2 (1939), 76–86; no. 3, 95–104; no. 4, 180–93; and 'Kaisetsu,' in *Ueda Akinari-shū*, I, 5–51; II, 3–7.

76 In addition to editing *Ueda Akinari-shū* and *Akinari* (see notes 4, 57) and other works, he has published numerous essays, all of which are held in high regard.

77 See Moriyama's interpretive essays in various journals and collections; for Sakai, see note 24; for Ōba, see *Akinari no tenkanshō to dēmon* (Tokyo: Ashi Shobō, 1969); for Morita, see *Ueda Akinari*, Kinokuniya shinsho (Tokyo: Kinokuniya, 1970).

78 *Ueda Akinari nempu kōsetsu* (Tokyo: Meizendō, 1964); see also notes 70, 92.

79 Cited above, in note 2.

80 See note 7 and also his *Kōchū harusame monogatari* (Tokyo: Ōfūsha, 1971).

81 Alf. Hansey, trans., 'The Blue Hood,' *The Young East*, 2 (1927), 314–9.

82 'Ugetsu Monogatari: Tales of a Clouded Moon,' *Monumenta Nipponica*, 1, no. 1 (1938), 242–51; no. 2, 257–75; 4, no. 1 (1941), 166–91.

83 'Essai sur la vie et l'oeuvre de Ueda Akinari,' ibid., 3, no. 2 (1940), 98–119; 4, no. 1 (1941), 102–23; no. 2, 128–38; 5, no. 1 (1942), 52–85.

84 *Contes de pluie et de lune* (*Ugetsu-Monogatari*): *Traduction et commentaires* (Paris: Gallimard, 1956).

85 'The Dream Carp,' in *Selections from Japanese Literature (12th to 19th Centuries)*, ed. F. J. Daniels (London: Lund Humphries, 1959), pp. 91–103, 164–71.

86 'Ugetsu Monogatari, or Tales of Moonlight and Rain,' *Monumenta Nipponica*, 21 (1966), 171–95.

87 '"The Chrysanthemum Vow," from the Ugetsu Monogatari (1776) by Ueda Akinari,' *Durham University Journal* (1967?), pp. 108–16. Mr Allen mentions having received a copy of the tales from a Japanese naval officer in Saigon in 1946.

88 'A Critical Approach to the Ugetsu Monogatari,' *Monumenta Nipponica*, 22 (1967), 49–64.

89 Hani Kjoko and Maria Holti, trans., *Esō ēs hold nesei* (Budapest: Kulture Kiado, 1964) (not seen); Kazuya Sakai, *Cuentos de lluvia y de luna*, Enciclopedia Era, 7 (Mexico City: Ediciones Era, 1969); and a translation

by Wieslaw Kotanski, mentioned in Kyrystyna Okazaki, 'Japanese Studies in Poland,' *Bulletin, International House of Japan*, no. 27 (April 1971), p. 12

90 Libuse Bohavkova, 'Ueda Akinari Ugecu monogatari: Rozbor sbírky a jednotlivých povídek a jejich motivických prvků' (The Ugetsu monogatari of Ueda Akinari: An Analysis of the Collection, of the Individual Stories, and of Their Motifs), Diss. Charles University, Prague, 1966–67, mentioned in Frank J. Shulman, *Japan and Korea: An Annotated Bibliography of Doctoral Dissertations in Western Languages, 1877–1969* (Chicago: The American Library Association, 1970), p. 190. Her translation is entitled *Vyprávění za měcíce a děstě* (Prague: Odeon, 1971), 204 pp.

91 See Anthony Chambers, 'Hankai: A Translation from Harusame monogatari, by Ueda Akinari,' *Monumenta Nipponica*, 25 (1970), 371–406; Blake Morgan Young, *The Harvard Journal of Asiatic Studies*, 32 (1972), 150–207.

92 Complete except for the author's preface, *Tales of Moonlight and Rain: Japanese Gothic Tales by Ueda Akinari* (Tokyo: University of Tokyo Press, 1971). Takada Mamoru contributed an essay to this volume, 'Ugetsu Monogatari: A Critical Interpretation.' See pp. xxi–xxix.

# NEW AND OLD SUPERNATURAL STORIES

*Ugetsu monogatari*

Complete in Five Volumes

Published at the Booksellers
Establishment of Yabaidō

From an envelope that originally wrapped the
five thin volumes of the first woodblock edition of
1776, in the National Diet Library, Tokyo

# VOLUME ONE
## PREFACE

Lo Kuan-chung wrote *Water Margin*, and for three generations he begot deaf mutes.[1] For writing *The Tale of Genji*, Lady Murasaki was condemned to hell.[2] Thus were these authors punished for what they had done. But consider their achievement. Each created a rare form, capable of expressing all degrees of truth with infinitely subtle variation and causing a deep note to echo in the reader's sensibility wherewith one can find mirrored realities of a thousand years ago.

By chance, I happened to have some idle tales with which to entertain you, and as they took shape and found expression, with crying pheasants and quarrelling dragons,[3] the stories came to form a slipshod compilation. But you who pick up this book to read must by no means take the stories to be true. I hardly wish for my offspring to have hare lips or missing noses.

Having completed this work one night late in the spring of the Meiwa Era, under the zodiac of earth and the rat,[4] when the rain cleared away and the moon shone faintly by my window, I thereupon gave it to the bookseller, entitling it *Ugetsu monogatari*.

*Signed*: Senshi Kijin[5]

*Sealed by*: Shikyo Kōjin[6]
Yūgi Sammai[7]

# I WHITE PEAK
## (Shiramine)

Once upon a time[8] I got permission from the barrier guards of Ōsaka, and I began to journey. Each sight along the way left its imprint on my heart. Although the yellow leaves of the autumn peaks[9] tempted me to linger, I visited Narumi bay,[10] where the plovers leave their tracks on the beach, and later I saw the smoke curling from lofty Mt Fuji,[11] and I passed the plain of Ukishima, the barrier at Kiyomi,[12] and the many bays around Ōiso and Koiso.[13] I saw the delicate purple grass of Musashino moors,[14] the early morning calm of Shiogama,[15] the rush-thatched huts of Kisagata[16] fishermen, the boat bridge at Sano,[17] and the hanging bridge at Kiso.[18] As I have said, each sight left its imprint on my heart.

Still, I wanted to visit the places in the West made famous in poetry. In the fall of the Third Year of Nin'an,[19] I passed through Naniwa, of the falling reeds,[20] and shivered in the winds of Suma and Akashi[21] bay. Finally, by Hayashi,[22] in Miozaka, in Sanuki, I set aside my bamboo staff for a while – not so much owing to weariness from my long pilgrimage but rather because I desired a hut for spiritual comfort in which to practise ascetic meditation.

Nearby this hamlet,[23] I heard, at a place called Shiramine stood the Emperor Sutoku's[24] tomb mound, and I decided to go there and worship. Early in the Godless Month[25] I climbed the mountain, which was so densely covered with oak and pine trees that even on a day[26] when clouds trailed across the blue sky it felt as dreary as if a steady drizzle of rain were falling. The steep cliffs of Mt Chigogadake loomed above me, and from ravines hundreds of feet below billows of mist arose, making every step a precarious undertaking.

Then, in a small clearing among the trees I saw a high mound of earth atop which three stones had been piled. The entire place was covered with brambles and vines. Sad of heart, I wondered, 'Is this where the emperor rests?'

In the depth of my grief I found it hard to be certain whether I was dreaming or awake. Indeed, when I had seen[27] him with my own eyes deciding on matters of state from his throne in the great halls of the palace,[28] the hundred officials[29] had addressed him as 'Your Exalted Majesty,' and accepted his every command with trembling and awe. After he abdicated in favour of the Emperor Konoe,[30] he lived in retirement as if in the Grove of Jewels or on faraway Ku-she Mountain.[31] Who could have guessed that here where one may see only the tracks of the wandering stag,[32] among the thickets in a mountain recess where no worshippers come to pay their respects, a former emperor should lie entombed. Here was a lord who had commanded ten thousand chariots.[33] Alas, how fearful the way one's deeds from a previous existence pursue the soul and never let it escape from transgression! How vain is the world! Pondering these matters, I could hardly hold back my tears.

'I shall honour his soul throughout the night,' I vowed, and kneeling on a flat rock in front of his grave, I began softly to intone a sutra. Then a verse in his honour occurred to me:

| | |
|---|---|
| *Matsuyama no* | Though these pine-clad hills |
| *nami no keshiki wa* | That overlook the breaking waves |
| *kawaraji wo* | Stand here unchanging |
| *katanaku kimi wa* | You, my lord, have disappeared, |
| *narimasari keri*[34] | And can not come back again. |

With increased devotion I continued my prayers. How wet my sleeves became from the dew!

Soon after sunset an eerie darkness filled the recesses of the mountain. The cold rose from the stone where I sat and penetrated through the leaves that covered me. I felt cleansed in spirit,[35] but a chill struck my bones. An uncanny terror gripped my heart. Although the moon arose, the trunks of the thick forest trees blocked its image as I grieved on through the pitch black night.

Almost in a trance I heard a voice call, 'Saigyō, Saigyō.'[36] I opened my eyes and peered[37] through the darkness, where the strange form of a man loomed, tall of stature and thin as death. It was impossible to distinguish his features or the colour and cut of his garments as he stood before me. But being a priest seeking enlightenment,[38] I replied without fear, 'Who are you?'

'I have come,' he answered, 'to chant for you a response to your verse:

| | |
|---|---|
| *Matsuyama no* | At these pine-clad hills, |
| *nami ni nagarete* | Buffeted by the breakers, |
| *koshi fune no* | My skiff touched shore. |
| *yagate munashiku* | But it was no use, |
| *nari ni keru kana*[39] | And my life soon expired. |

I am very pleased that you have come.'

At once, I knew that I was confronted by the ghost of the Emperor Sutoku. I bowed, with tears in my eyes, and replied, 'But why is your soul still wandering? I came here because I envied the way you left the impure world. Although I worship here tonight for your salvation, I don't know whether to feel joy or sadness at seeing your ghost. Now that you have departed[40] from this world and freed yourself from earthly entanglements, you ought to find repose in the soul of Buddha.'

In spite of my heartfelt remonstration, Sutoku merely gave a provocative laugh.[41] 'Surely, you didn't know,[42] but it's I who've recently caused all the trouble in the world. While I was still living, I began to practise magic and brought about the disturbance of Heiji. Now that I have died, I will put a curse on the imperial family. Beware! Beware! Before long I will throw the whole nation into chaos.'

'What a horrible thing to say,' I replied, my tears ceasing at his words. 'People have always thought you were very intelligent, and you must realise full well a ruler's moral responsibility;[43] so, Your Majesty, I want to ask you whether you believe that your intention to revolt during the Hōgen Era[44] was in accordance with the teachings of the Sun Goddess,[45] or if you were scheming for selfish ends? Please explain your-self.'

Hereupon, his highness grew indignant. 'Listen!' he said. 'The Emperor ranks highest among men. Yet, when someone from above disturbs the course of humanity, he must be punished, in keeping with the will of heaven[46] and following the wishes of the people. During the Eiji Era,[47] though I had done nothing wrong, I obeyed my father's command and abdicated in favour of the Emperor Konoe, who was only three years old.[48] One can hardly say that my action was selfish. But when Konoe died prematurely, both I myself as well as the people believed that my son, Prince Shigehito,[49] should rule the nation. But I was thwarted by Lady Bifukumon'in's[50] jealousy, and can you imagine how humiliated I was at having my line usurped by Goshirakawa,[51] the Fourth Prince? Shigehito had a talent for ruling, whereas Goshirakawa had no such skill. Although my father suffered from such vices as in-ability to appoint good men and tended to seek counsel from the palace ladies, still, as long as he lived I observed filial piety and remained loyal to him. But when he died, my patience gave way, and I moved with courage and decision.

'Once upon a time in China a subject struck down his lord,'[52] he raved wildly in conclusion, 'and because the deed was in accord with heaven and conformed to the wishes of the people, the man founded a line that endured for eight hundred years – the Chou Dynasty. All the more justifiable would it be for a capable heir to replace a ruler during whose reign hens crowed in the morning.[53] You have deserted your family[54] to indulge in Buddhism. From selfish desire to gain future salvation, you have sacrificed human ethics for faith in karma. Can you deny that you have confounded the way of Shakyamuni with the teachings of Yao and Shun?'

'Your Highness takes refuge in arguing about lay affairs,' I began, without shrinking from him,[55] but rather drawing closer. 'Yet, you have failed to free yourself from desire. There is no need to cite examples from faraway China. Long ago Emperor Honda of our imperial line[56] passed over his eldest son, Prince Ōsasagi,[57] and designated his youngest, Prince Uji, to be heir apparent. When the emperor died, each son tried to give way to the other, and neither would ascend to the imperial rank. After three years the matter still remained unsettled, and Prince Uji in an excess of grief said, "Why should I prolong my days and bring trouble to the nation?" and he put an end to his own life. Because of this Prince Ōsasagi had no choice but to ascend the throne.[58] Still, he fulfilled the task of heaven and ruled with brotherly love, he served with devotion and un-selfishness as a true example of the way of Yao and Shun. Prince Uji was the first man in our country to respect the teachings of Confucius and practise the Kingly way, summon-ing Wani, of Kudara,[59] and studying under him. In spirit, these princes, elder and younger brother, equalled the sages of China.

'I have heard people say[60] that in the text known as *The Book of Mencius* it states, "At the beginning of Chou, King Wu, in wrathful indignation, brought peace to the people of the empire.[61] This was not a case of subject slaying sovereign. Rather, it was putting to death a despised creature called Chou, who was an outrage against humanity and righteousness."

'Strange to say, all manner of Chinese books – classics, histories, and poetry – have come to us. But *The Book of Mencius*, alone, has yet to reach Japan.[62] Ships that bear this text, I have heard, invariably encounter typhoons and sink. This is because[63] in our country ever since the Sun Goddess founded it the imperial succession has continued unbroken. Should anyone introduce such a sly doctrine as that found in *Mencius*, a wicked person in later ages might usurp the line of the gods and deny his crime. The eight hundred myriad gods hate the very thought, it is said, and send divine winds to over-turn ships carrying this book. So you see, the teachings of sages from other lands on many occasions do not necessarily fit our realm. Besides, do you recall *The Book of Songs*?

> Brothers may quarrel within the walls,
> But outside they defend one another from insult.[64]

i White Peak: The ghost of the emperor confronts the priest Saigyō

You, however, ignored ties of blood.[65] Then, after the Emperor Toba died,[66] while his body still lay in state,[67] the flesh not yet having grown cold, you started hoisting banners and twanging bows[68] to struggle for the throne. What greater breach of filial piety can one imagine?

'That which lies under heaven is like a holy vessel.[69] He who tampers with it for selfish ends can never succeed. Supposing, for example, that people had urged Prince Shigehito to ascend the throne. Unable to rule with virtue or spread peace, and impaired by being without right moral principles, he would have brought disorder to the world. The people who wanted him the previous day would then suddenly have become his enemies.

'Far from getting what you wanted, you received the cruelest punishment inflicted in all time and were turned to dust in this remote place. At all costs, I beg of you, forget past grudges. I pray and beseech you to show intelligence and return to the land of paradise and find eternal repose.'

'To blame me for my conduct and accuse me of criminal action,' his highness lamented, with a long sigh, 'is not without justice. But how could anyone such as I, banished to an island such as this and tormented in a house such as that of Takatō, in Matsuyama,[70] endure meeting no human beings[71] except the attendant who three times a day brought food?

'When on my pillow in the dead of night I heard the cry of the wild geese soaring across the sky, I longed for the capital, wondering if that was where they were flying. At dawn the plover's call on the beach rent my heart till I thought it would break. Even should a crow's head grow white, I would never get a chance to return to the capital, so certain was I fated to become a ghost by the seaside. Hoping at least for relief in the world to come, I copied the five Mahayana sutras.[72] But it would have been a pity to leave them on this desolate, stony shore,[73] where one cannot hear the sound of bells and trumpets. "At least, please let the work of my brush be permitted to enter the capital," I wrote to the abbot of the Ninnaji Temple, sending him the sutras, to which I had attached the verse,

*Hama chidori*       Plover on the beach –
*ato wa miyako ni*    Although your footprints
*kayoedomo*        Journey to the capital,
*mi wa Matsuyama ni*  You must stay by pine-clad hills,
*ne wo nomi zo naku*[74]  Where your lonely cry resounds.

'The councillor, Shōnagon Shinzei,[75] however, opposed me and convinced the emperor that I meant to lay a curse[76] on the land, and therefore to my chagrin the sutras were sent back. Since antiquity, in Japan as well as China, struggles for the realm have pitted brother against brother. Such cases are by no means rare. But because it struck me what a heinous crime this is, I had copied the sutras[77] in the hope of making up for my ill behaviour. But no matter how much his advisors may have intervened, my brother's disregard of the law under which our relationship should have been considered[78] and his decision not to accept my calligraphy have now made him my bitter enemy.

'Then, I took these sutras and used them to pray for bad ends[79] in an effort to give vent to my rage. Once I made up my mind, I cut my finger and wrote an oath in blood.[80] This, and the sutra, I cast into the sea at Shido.[81] I withdrew from the sight of mankind and begged with all my heart to become a king of Evil.

'That is why the Heiji Rising broke out.[82] First I took advantage of Nobuyori's[83] overweening desire for high rank and led him to plot with Yoshitomo,[84] the enemy who irked me most. During the Hōgen Era his father – Tameyoshi[85] – and all of his brothers had given their lives for my cause. But he alone drew his bow against me. Tametomo's[86] bravery together with Tameyoshi and Tadamasa's[87] strategy had brought victory in sight. Then fire driven on by a southwest gale forced us to flee from the Shirakawa Palace,[88] and on the steep slope of Mt Nyoigatake[89] I injured my leg. Although I tried to find shelter from the rain and dew by hiding underneath a woodcutter's stack of oak kindling, I was eventually captured and banished to this island – all of which torments fell on me because of Yoshitomo's malicious plotting.[90]

'To revenge myself, I placed a curse on Yoshitomo's cruel heart and led him to join Nobuyori's conspiracy. For his treasonous crimes against the gods of the nation he was soundly beaten by Kiyomori,[91] who is hardly clever at the art of war. Finally, retribution for having slain his father, Tameyoshi, came when his own retainer[92] slew him. It marked the fulfilment of the curse of the gods of heaven.

'Shōnagon Shinzei, who always boasted of his learning, had a perverse streak and enjoyed saying "no" to people, and thus I got him to make enemies of Nobuyori and Yoshitomo. In the end he fled from his home and hid in a hillside cave near Uji.[93] After he had been flushed from his refuge and caught, his severed head was exposed by the river bank at Rokujō.[94] Here was fitting punishment for his role in the events that led to the rejection of my sutras.

'But that was not all. In the summer of the Ōhō Era[95] my curse ended Bifukumon'in's life. In the spring of the Chōkan Era[96] I brought about Tadamichi's[97] death. I myself died in the autumn of the same year. But by the flames of vengeance, which were still far from exhausted in their might, I finally became a great king of Evil,[98] head of the more than three hundred kinds of demons. Every time my band sees happiness, they turn it to misery. Whenever they see the country at peace, they cause war.

'Only Kiyomori continues to flourish,' he concluded, his voice rising to an alarming pitch. 'He has placed his entire family and his relatives in high offices,[99] and he rules the country by caprice. Only Shigemori's[100] sense of loyalty and duty keep the time from being right. But you shall see! The Taira Clan shall not long endure. Goshirakawa has injured me till my only recourse lies in revenge.'

'Because you are so involved in an evil karma with the world of demons,' I replied, 'and ten thousand billion leagues separates you from Buddha Land, I have nothing more to say to you,' and I faced him in silence.

Thereupon a tremor shook the mountains and valleys. The wind rose, as if to fell the forest trees. Sand and pebbles flew in

a vortex toward the sky, and as I watched, dumbstruck, a ball of
flame flared up where his highness stood, illuminating the mountains and valleys, as if it were day. In the light I could clearly
see his highness's features. His face[101] flushed crimson. His hair
hung down to his knees, as tangled as if a thorn bush. The pupils
of his eyes were turned up, leaving only the whites exposed,
and his hot breath came in painful gasps. His persimmon-
coloured robes[102] were filthy with soot. His fingernails and toe-
nails had grown as long as a beast's claws. Every detail
betrayed the terrifying and frightful form of a demon king.

'Sagami! Sagami!' his highness screeched,[103] addressing the
sky. A cry came in reply, and a bird-like goblin resembling a
black hawk descended, paid homage to his highness, and
awaited his command.

'Why have you not more quickly taken Shigemori's life and
made Goshirakawa and Kiyomori suffer?' his highness shouted.

'Goshirakawa's good fortune has not yet run out. Shigemori's
loyalty and faith are hard to pervert. But if you wait for the
signs of the zodiac to revolve once,[104] Shigemori's life will
end, and when he dies his family's fortunes will be destroyed.'

Clapping his hands in joy, his highness said, 'These enemies
of mine, to the last man, will perish in the sea before me.'

His voice reverberated from the hills and valleys with an
eerie and indescribable echo, and as I witnessed the debased
nature of such witchcraft, I could no longer repress my tears.
Through one last verse I tried to restore him to his senses:

| | |
|---|---|
| *Yoshi ya kimi* | Even though, My Lord, |
| *mukashi no tama no* | You once lived in jade splendor |
| *toko totemo* | And held a royal throne, |
| *kakaran nochi wa* | Now that you have passed away |
| *ika ni kawasen*[105] | How can you hope to change your lot? |

'Ruler and ruled meet a common fate,'[106] I chanted loudly,
with all my heart. When he heard my words, he showed signs of
pleasure, and his face grew calmer. The ghostly flame gradually

subsided, and then the emperor's form disappeared from sight,[107] and the bird-like goblin also vanished without a trace. The moon of ten-odd days was hidden behind the peaks. Under the dark trees in the black night, I felt as though I was enveloped in a world of dreams.

Before long the sleep-ending light of the dawn sky[108] brought the gay chirruping of the morning birds. Then I chanted a section of the Diamond Sutra[109] in prayer for his majesty and descended the mountain. Back in my hut I pondered over the events of the night before and reviewed each detail in my mind. Beginning with the Heiji Rising, in the facts about persons and in the dates of events, I could detect no mistake. But I kept it all to myself and never uttered a word to anyone.

Nearly thirteen years later, in the autumn of the third year of Jishō,[110] when Taira Shigemori was stricken ill and departed from this world, Taira Kiyomori, Prime Minister of the nation, vented his malice against Goshirakawa, confining him in the imperial villa at Toba.[111] Later he removed him to the temporary capital at Fukuhara[112] and caused him to suffer various indignities. Then Yoritomo[113] arose like the east wind to contend with the Taira, and Yoshinaka[114] swept down like the northern snow to drive them away from the capital. The entire Taira clan was pushed into the Western seas, and finally, by the waters of Sanuki, at Shido and Yashima,[115] many of their brave warriors met their end, entombed in the bellies of turtles and fish.[116] When the survivors were pressed to Akamagaseki, at Dannoura,[117] the infant emperor, Antoku, [118]perished at sea, as did all the commanders of the Heike forces.

His highness was not a dewdrop mistaken, and what he related was as terrifying as it was mysterious. Thereafter people adorned his shrine with jewels, decorated it in vermilion and blue lacquer, and worshipped the august virtue of his majesty.

People who visit the province all offer him spirit festoons[119] and honour him as a powerful god.

# II  CHRYSANTHEMUM TRYST
## (Kikuka no chigiri)

Green, green grows the spring willow.[120] But never plant it in your garden. Never pick a falsehearted man for a friend.

Although the willow may bud early, does it hold up when autumn's first wind blows? A falsehearted man makes friends easily, but he is fickle. Whereas the willow for many springs takes on new colour, a falsehearted man will break off with you and never call again.

In the province of Harima in the town of Kako[121] there dwelt a scholar whose name was Hasebe Samon. He lived a poor but honest life, and except for the books that kept him company[122] he hated being tied down by any possessions. Samon had an aged mother, who was in no way less virtuous than that of Mencius,[123] and she constantly worked at spinning to help her son do as he wished. A younger sister had been brought up in the Sayo household in the same village. This family, which was extremely rich and prosperous, recognised the character of the Hasebe mother and children and took the young girl in marriage. The two families thus became closely related. On one pretext or another, the Sayos would sometimes send food and other presents, but Samon never accepted them, saying, 'Should a man bother others for what his own mouth eats?'

One day Samon went to pay a visit to an acquaintance in the town, and he and his host enjoyed themselves, talking about modern times and olden days. Then, he heard through the wall the anguished voice of a man crying pitifully in pain. Samon inquired about it, and the master of the house replied, 'It seems to be a man from the Western provinces. He said that he fell behind his travelling companions, and he asked me to put him up for the night. Because he carried himself like a warrior and there was nothing common about him, I took the man in. But that night he came down with a severe fever, and he has been unable even to move by himself. These three or four days he has lain in a pitiful state. Still, I don't know exactly where he came from, so I find myself in an awkward situation.[124] You can imagine how disturbed I am!'

'What a melancholy tale!' said Samon. 'I can certainly understand how worried you feel, but it must be all the more distressing for the stricken man to find himself taken with such an illness while passing through a place where he doesn't know a soul. What if I were to go and examine him?'

The master held him back. 'Fevers are infectious,[125] I've heard, so I don't even let my servants go in. You had better not go near him and expose yourself.'

'Life and death depend on heavenly fate,'[126] replied Samon with a laugh. 'How can diseases be transmitted by humans? The idea is fit only for ignorant and common people. We have no need for such beliefs,' and so saying, he pushed open the door and went in to the man.

As Samon's host had said, the invalid was certainly not of the lower classes, and he seemed to be in serious condition. Emaciated,[127] he lay in agony on an old blanket, his face jaundiced, his skin dark. He looked up at Samon beseechingly.

'Please give me a cup of warm water,' he said.

'You mustn't worry,' said Samon drawing nearer. 'I'm sure that I can help you.'

After discussing the matter with his host, Samon chose a medicine, determined the dosage himself, boiled it,[128] and gave it to the sick man. He prepared gruel and cared for him like a brother, for indeed the patient was in no condition to be left unattended.

'Why are you so generous to a wandering traveller?' said the warrior, moved to tears by Samon's warmth and compassion. 'I'll find a way to repay your kindness, even if I die.'

'You mustn't speak in such a fainthearted manner,' advised Samon. 'Generally a fever like yours lasts a certain number of days. Then it's over, and it doesn't stop you from living to an old age. In the meantime, I'll come daily and take care of you.'

Samon did just as he promised and devoted himself to saving the man. As a result, the illness gradually left his body. The sick man regained his strength and profusely thanked the master of the house. He praised Samon for his charity[129] and asked about his occupation, and he also spoke of his own circumstances.

'To begin with, my name is Akana[130] Sōemon. I was born and raised in the village of Matsue,[131] in the province of Izumo. Because I gained some knowledge of the military classics,[132] the lord of Tomita Castle,[133] Enya Kamonnosuke,[134] made me his teacher and studied under my direction. Later, he chose me for a secret mission to Sasaki Ujitsuna,[135] of Ōmi. During my stay in Ujitsuna's residence, the previous lord of Tomita, Amako Tsunehisa,[136] together with the Yamanakas[137] and their supporters stormed the castle by surprise on New Year's Eve.[138] My lord, Kamon, was among those who perished in the battle.

'Because the province of Izumo has been a Sasaki domain since earlier times,' Akana continued, 'and the Enyas were the constable's representatives, I urged Ujitsuna to help Mizawa and Mitoya[139] destroy Tsunehisa. But Ujitsuna was an incompetent general; though he put on a brave front, he was really a coward at heart, and he gave no assistance. Instead, he kept me in his province. It was no use staying there any longer, so I stole away with my bare life, and on the way back to my province I came down with this sickness and had to put you to all this trouble. I owe you more than my life in turn for your kindness. Even if it takes me the rest of my days, I shall certainly repay you.'

'Not to remain indifferent[140] to what one sees,' replied Samon, 'is the essence of being human. I don't deserve any special thanks. Just stay here until you get better.'

Encouraged by Samon's sincerity, Akana in a few days felt almost completely well, and meanwhile Samon discovered that he had found a good friend. In their conversations day and night Akana began to speak somewhat inarticulately of the classical philosophers and their schools, and Samon respected his swift and penetrating insight.[141] Because of Akana's long familiarity with the military arts, here the two men found perfect agreement. Admiring each other and happy to be together, they swore vows of brotherhood. Akana, being the elder by five years, accepted the privilege of being senior.

'I lost my father and mother long ago,' he said. 'But now your aged mother[142] is my own. Please give me the honour of meeting her. Do you think that she would understand such a childish desire?'

Samon was overwhelmed with delight. 'Mother has always been worried about my being so alone. When I tell her of what you've said, she'll feel that years have been added to her life.' Together they visited his home.

'My son has little talent,' said the old mother, happy to meet him. 'Nor are his studies in step with the times. He has lost all chance for a call from the blue clouds. I beg of you, do not leave him; teach him as an elder brother should.'

'A gentleman values honour[143] and gives no thought to fame or wealth,' replied Akana, with a bow. 'Today a mother has honoured me with love. A brother has honoured me with respect. Beyond this, what more could I ask for?' He remained in their home for some time amid joy and happiness.

Yesterday and today[144] they were blooming, but now the blossoms on the summit of Onoe[145] have all fallen. Despite the chilling breeze that blew, and the sweeping waves,[146] one could tell from all the signs that summer was drawing near. 'The reason that I fled from Ōmi,' said Akana to Samon and his mother one day, 'was to find out what's happening in Izumo, so I'll go there and see and then presently return. Though I may slave on peas porridge and water,[147] I'll be sure to repay you for your kindness. For now, please let me depart.'

'If indeed you must leave, brother, when do you think that you'll be back?'

'Time passes so quickly,' said Akana. 'At the most, it won't be later than this autumn.'

'What day then shall I pick to wait?' said Samon. 'By all means, let's name one for our meeting.'

'Let us set the Chrysanthemum Festival, the Ninth Day of

8  'In the hedges the wild chrysanthemums burst into bloom' (p. 113).
Painting by Yosa Buson (1716–1784), 'The Pleasures of Autumn,' from
an album made in 1771, in collaboration with Ike Taiga, 'Ten Con-
veniences and Ten Pleasures' (*Jūben jūgi*). (In the collection of the late
Kawabata Yasunari; from *Buson ihō*; National Treasure.)

9 'He left and hurried
toward the capital' (p.
Painting by Yosa Buso
(Formerly in the collec
of Mutō Sanji; from *Bu
gashū*.)

the Ninth Month,[148] as the date for my return,' said Akana.

'Brother, on that day don't forget me,' said Samon. 'A sprig of chrysanthemums and some thin wine will be ready and waiting for you.' After they exchanged their faithful promises, Akana left to go West.

Each fresh month and day[149] slipped quickly by. The holly berries on the lower branches began to change their colour. In the hedges the wild chrysanthemums burst into bloom, as the Ninth Month arrived. On the Ninth Day Samon arose earlier than usual.[150] He cleaned the matting in the thatched hut, placed two or three stems[151] of yellow and white chrysanthemums in a small vase, and emptied his purse to buy wine and rice.

'The province of Izumo,[152] where he set out from,' said his aged mother, 'lies far beyond the mountains.[153] I have heard that it is a hundred leagues away.[154] You cannot be certain that he will arrive today, and after he appears it will hardly be too late to get things ready.'

'Akana is a warrior[155] true to his word,' replied Samon. 'He would never forget our meeting. I'd be ashamed of what he'd think if he saw me bustling about after his arrival.' The wine was the best, the fish was fresh, and everything was ready in the kitchen as he waited for his friend.

There was not a cloud in the sky, and it was clear for miles around. Travellers, who used the grass for their pillow, spoke to one another as they passed.

'Today is a splendid day for so-and-so to reach the capital,' said one.

'It's a sign that business is bound to be good,' replied his fellow.

A warrior of fifty or more years was talking to one of about twenty, similarly attired. 'Since the day has turned out to be so nice,'[156] he complained, 'if we had caught a boat at Akashi[157] and left on the first sailing this morning,[158] we'd be almost to the stopover at the Ushimado[159] straits. You young people are too timid, and you're always wasting a great deal of money.'

'But when our lord went to the capital,' replied the younger man to console him, 'and crossed from Azukijima[160] to

Murozu,[161] he ran into all kinds of trouble – at least according to what the people in his party said. So when you stop to think about it, ferry crossings around here[162] are always something to avoid. Don't be angry. In Uogahashi[163] I'll treat you to buckwheat noodles.'

A packhorse driver lost his temper, 'Hey, you dead nag! Open your eyes,' and he pushed the packsaddle back into place and drove the beast forward.

Although the afternoon gradually drew to a close, the man Samon was waiting for still had not come. The sun sank in the west. Feeling tense and upset, Samon watched the hurry-scurry of legs hastening to find a lodging place, his eyes constantly fixed on the distance.

His mother called him and said, 'Don't think him fickle, like the autumn sky;[164] after all, the chrysanthemum's deep hue lasts for more than a day. What right would you have to complain so long as he keeps his word and comes back, even though it might be the season for the late autumn rains to begin? Come in and lie down for a while, and then wait again tomorrow.'

Samon found it hard to refuse, but he induced his mother to go to bed first. Hoping against hope, he stepped outside the door and looked about. The Milky Way shimmered[165] with a pale light. The moon's icy wheel shed its glow on him, aggravating his loneliness. A watchdog's bark rang out through the clear air, and the sound of the waves in the bay seemed as if surging round the very place where he stood.[166] The moon presently disappeared behind the mountain peaks, and about to give up, Samon decided to go back in and close the door, when he happened to take a last look.[167] Out of the dim shadows a man emerged, as if mysteriously borne on the wind. It was Akana Sōemon!

Samon's heart leaped for joy. 'I have been waiting for you since early this morning,' he exclaimed. 'True to your promise, you've returned, and how happy I am. Please come in.'

The figure, however, merely nodded and said nothing. Samon led him in, showed Akana to a cushion facing the southern window,[168] and bade him sit down.

ii Chrysanthemum Tryst: In one stroke Samon avenges the death of his brother Sōemon

'You were so late in getting here,' said Samon, 'that mother grew tired of waiting; thinking that you'd come tomorrow, she has gone to bed. Shall I wake her up?'

Akana once again shook his head negatively, still remaining silent.

'After pressing on through the night,' said Samon, 'surely you're worn out, and your legs must be tired. Please relax and let me pour you a cup of wine.' So saying, he warmed the wine, arranged the fish, and invited Akana to eat. But Akana covered his face with his sleeve,[169] as though he were trying to avoid the smell.

'Perhaps my poor efforts[170] are unworthy to entertain you,' said Samon, 'but I have tried my best. Please don't think ill of me.'

Although Akana again made no answer, he breathed a long sigh. Shortly thereafter he spoke saying, 'How could I ever refuse your sincere hospitality?[171] I shall not deceive you. I'll tell you the truth. But you mustn't let yourself be surprised. I am not a being of this mortal world;[172] my ghost has appeared to you in human form.'

'How can you say such a terrible thing?' said Samon in astonishment. 'And yet, I can't be dreaming.'

'After we parted,' said Akana, 'I went back to my province. Most of my countrymen had submitted to Tsunehisa's power, and no one spoke about the good old days under Enya. I have a cousin named Akana Tanji, who was in Tomita Castle. I called on him, and after convincing me of the advantages,[173] he arranged for me to meet Tsunehisa. I pretended to agree with Tsunehisa's views, and I carefully observed his actions. He was an exceedingly brave man, and he trained his troops carefully; still, he was as suspicious as a fox of anyone who showed intelligence, and I found no retainers who were of faithful heart and served as his claws and fangs.[174] Knowing that there was little sense in my staying any longer, I told him of our chrysanthemum tryst, and I was about to leave, when Tsunehisa expressed displeasure at this and ordered Tanji to confine me in the castle,[175] where I remained until today.[176]

'"Should I fail to keep my promise," I thought, feeling utterly despondent, "what would dear brother think of me?" But there was no way to escape. In ancient times someone said, "A man cannot cover[177] a thousand leagues in a day, but a spirit in such a period can easily travel the distance." Yes, this was the answer. I threw myself on my sword, and astride the dark night winds I have come all this way to keep our chrysanthemum tryst. Take pity on my soul.'

As he finished speaking, his eyes grew dim with tears. 'Now we must part forever,' he added. 'Be sure to take care of mother.' He appeared to rise from his seat, and thereupon he vanished, without a trace.

Samon desperately tried to stop him, but a chill wind blinded him for a moment, and he could not tell which way the spirit went. He stumbled and fell on his face and lay there, crying in grief. His mother awoke with a start, and upon looking to see where Samon was, she found that he had collapsed by the alcove, where the wine jar and the plate of fish[178] had been set.

'What happened?' she asked, as she struggled to help him to his feet, but Samon wept convulsively, and he was unable to answer.

'If you're upset because Akana didn't keep his promise,'[179] said the mother, upbraiding him firmly, 'how can you ever apologise if he should come tomorrow? Don't be so childish.'

'He has already come, tonight,' Samon finally replied, 'expressly for our chrysanthemum tryst. I tried to offer him fish and wine, but he kept refusing me. Then he explained that because he had been unable to observe his promise, he had thrown himself on his sword and that his ghost had covered the hundred leagues. Finally, he disappeared. That's what made me disturb your sleep. Please forgive me,' and he began to weep bitterly.

'A man confined in prison,'[180] the mother said, 'even in his dreams thinks of amnesty; a thirsty person dreams of drinking fresh water, as the proverb goes. You were in similar circumstances. Now calm yourself.' Samon shook his head.

'But really, it was no dream or fantasy. He was right here in front of me,' and once again he burst into tears and fell down in lamentation. The mother now ceased to doubt him; she comforted him and mourned with him all through the night.

The next day Samon bowed to his mother saying, 'Ever since I was a boy, I've devoted myself to studying, but I'm known neither for loyalty[181] to my country nor for devotion to my parents. I've spent my life in vain. My brother, Akana, gave his life for the sake of duty. Today I'm going to go to Izumo and at least by gathering his remains try to show my faithfulness. Please take care of yourself and let me leave you for a while.'

'Go, my son,' the mother replied, 'but come back soon and set my old heart at rest. Don't stay long or make this our day of final parting.'

'Life is like a floating bubble,' said Samon. 'Morning and evening, destiny remains uncertain; but I'll do my best to return quickly,' and still in tears, he left the house and went to the Sayos, begging them to look after the mother.

Along the way to the province of Izumo, though he was hungry, he did not think about food; though he was cold, he did not think about clothing. He would spend the night weeping, even when he dozed off, even while he dreamed, and in ten days he reached the great castle of Tomita.

First, he went to Akana Tanji's house and identified himself by name. Tanji received him and said, 'Unless you got the news about my cousin from some winged creature, how could you have learned? It's preposterous.' He questioned him closely, but Samon rebuked him.[182]

'A warrior ought not to show concern for material things.[183] For him loyalty alone counts. My brother, Akana Sōemon, was faithful to his word, and his poor ghost travelled a hundred leagues to keep a promise. The least I could do in return was to push on day and night to come here. There is something in my studies about which I wish to ask you. I pray you, answer me clearly.

'Long ago, when Kung-shu Tso, of Wei,[184] was lying ill in bed, the King of Wei, in person, came to visit him and took his hand, saying, "If anything should happen to you, who could protect the country for me? For my sake, leave me your instructions."

'"Shang Yang[185] may be young," replied Tso,[186] "but he has rare talent. In case your majesty does not wish to use him, you must never permit him to leave the country, even if you have to resort to murder. Should he be allowed to go to another state, misfortune is sure to befall later."'

'After faithfully telling him this, Tso secretly summoned Shang Yang and said, "I recommended you to the king, but he appeared not to accept the idea. I told him, then, that if he would not use you, he should destroy you. This is putting the lord first and the vassal second. You must quickly flee to another country in order to avoid harm!"[187]

'How can one compare this incident with that of you and Sōemon?'

Tanji bowed his head and said nothing. Samon moved closer to him.

'My brother Sōemon, by cherishing his relations with Enya and not serving Amako, acted as a loyal samurai. You, however, by forsaking your former master, Enya, and submitting to Amako, failed to behave as a warrior should. My brother regarded his chrysanthemum tryst as a matter of honour. By giving up his life and travelling a hundred leagues, he showed the height of faithfulness.

'You, however, to curry favour with Amako, tortured a man of your own flesh and blood and caused him to die a violent death. That was hardly the conduct of a comrade in arms. Even though Tsunehisa may have held him by force, you should have remembered your old relations and secretly treated him as Tso did to Shang Yang. To run only after profit and advantage is not customary for a samurai family, though this does seem to be the style of the Amako house. Oh, why did my brother ever return to this country!

'I believe in loyalty and love. That's why I came here. And you. You, for your action, leave a foul name!'

Hardly had Samon finished speaking, when he drew his sword, and attacked the man, and cut him down with one stroke.

Before the retainers could recover from their alarm, Samon fled, leaving no trace.

Amako Tsunehisa,[188] upon hearing of what happened, was so impressed by how deeply faithful the two brothers were, that he ordered no one to pursue Samon.

Ah, indeed, one should not attach himself to a falsehearted man.

# VOLUME TWO

## III THE HOUSE AMID THE THICKETS

*(Asaji ga yado)*[189]

In the province of Shimōsa,[190] district of Katsushika, village of Mama, during the Kyōtoku Era, there once lived a man named Katsushirō. Ever since his grandfather's time the family had dwelled here in prosperity, owning many fields and much rice land. But the youthful Katsushirō was lazy; he disliked working the land and regarded such labour as a dreary task. In consequence, his wealth declined; his relations had less and less to do with him. Eventually he grew ashamed of himself and longed to find some means or other by which he might restore his family's fortunes.

Around this time, a man named Sasabe no Sōji, who travelled each year from the capital to buy Ashikaga dyed silk,[191] happened to make one of his frequent visits to the village of Mama, where his kinsfolk lived. Having met him on previous occasions, Katsushirō asked Sasabe to take him to Kyoto as a merchant. Sasabe agreed quite readily[192] and said, 'We can leave whenever you're ready.'

Because he knew that Sasabe was a reliable man, Katsushirō was pleased at his reply. He soon sold his remaining rice fields, spent the money on bolts of white silk, and prepared to depart for Kyoto. His wife, Miyagi, who was beautiful enough to stop any man's eyes, had always taken good care of Katsushirō, but at this decisive moment she disapproved of his purchase of goods and of his projected journey to Kyoto. She did her best to dissuade him, but in the face of his impetuous nature all her efforts were in vain, and so, though deeply distressed by the uncertainty of her own future,[193] she faithfully helped him to get ready.

'While you're gone I shall have no one to turn to,' said Miyagi on their last night before the painful parting. 'My heart is sure to wander lost among the moors and mountains,[194] and it will be a lonesome time for me. Remember me day and night and hurry back. I shall pray with all my heart for your good health;[195] no one knows what tomorrow may bring. Be resolute, but still, feel pity for me.'

'You know how I shall drift, as if on floating wood,[196] and stay long in unknown provinces,' Katsushirō replied, consoling her, 'but when the leaves begin to turn, in the fall, I'll come back.[197] Please have courage while you wait,'[198] and as dawn broke in the cock-crowing land of Azuma,[199] he left and hurried toward the capital.

In the summer of that year[200] fighting broke out in Kamakura between Lord Shigeuji and Governor Uesugi.[201] After his mansion had been burned to the ground, Shigeuji was forced to withdraw to Shimōsa, where he had strong support, and the entire East was suddenly thrown into turmoil. Young men were conscripted as soldiers, and more and more it became a matter of every person for himself; old people fled to take refuge in the hills, and the word would spread, 'Today the army will burn our village,' or, 'Tomorrow enemy troops are coming,' and women and children ran here and there, crying in consternation and anguish.

Miyagi wondered if she too shouldn't take safety somewhere, but she trusted in her husband's bidding to wait until autumn, and though her heart was filled with anxiety, she remained at home, counting each day. But after the autumn winds came and Miyagi still heard no tidings, she lamented in disappointment, 'He too has grown as fickle as the inconstant world,' and she wrote,[202]

| *Mi no usa wa* | I cannot convey |
| *hito shimo tsugeji* | The bitterness of my sorrow, |
| *Ōsaka no* | But would you point out to him – |

*yū zuke tori yo*    Songbird of evening –
*aki mo kurenu to*[203]  That autumn is almost over.

Still, many provinces separated Miyagi from her husband, and there was no one with whom she could send word.

After the outbreak of war people's ways changed for the worse. A man who from time to time had visited the house and knew of Miyagi's beauty tried to seduce her, but she staunchly kept her moral standards and succeeded in remaining faithful. From then on, she bolted her door and refused to see any visitors.

Meanwhile, her maidservant had left. She used up her small hoard of savings, and though the old year ended, things were still unsettled in the new one. During the previous autumn, Shogun Yoshimasa[204] had ordered Tō no Tsuneyori,[205] Lord of Shimotsuke, who held Gujō, in the province of Mino, to take the imperial banner and go to his domains in Shimotsuke. From here, he made preparations with his clansman, Chiba no Sanetane,[206] to attack Shigeuji, but the latter put up a staunch defence, and no one knew when the war might end. Bands of outlaws everywhere pillaged and burned settlements and built fortifications. No place in the Eight Provinces[207] remained safe, and throughout the wretched world there was great destruction.[208]

Having arrived in Kyoto with Sasabe, Katsushirō soon sold all[209] of his silk, because around this time in the capital there was a great demand for luxuries. He made a good profit and was preparing to return East, when he heard reports that Uesugi's troops had taken the Kamakura Palace and pursued Shigeuji to an area around his home, which had become the centre of a raging battle.[210] 'It's like the crossroads of Cho Lu,'[211] people said. Katsushirō knew that even rumours about local events were often exaggerated, and that there was no telling what had happened in a place as far away as the distant white clouds; but he nevertheless felt uneasy when he left the capital at the beginning of the Eighth Month.

On the all-day climb over lovely Kiso hill,[212] a band of robbers barred his way and stripped him of everything he possessed. In addition, he heard that further east new barriers[213] had been set up here and there and that travellers were forbidden to pass. Now he had no means of sending word to his wife. 'Perhaps,' he thought, 'my home has been lost in the fires of war, and Miyagi is no longer living in this world, and my native village now serves as a dwelling place for demons.' Thereupon, once again he turned toward Kyoto, but when he reached Musa,[214] in the province of Ōmi, he suddenly fell ill, stricken with the fever.

In that village there lived a wealthy man named Kodama Yoshibei,[215] who was Sasabe's father-in-law, and Katsushirō implored his help. Kodama took him in, summoned a physician, and paid for all the medicines. When Katsushirō's fever had at last subsided, he thanked his benefactor profusely; but he was still not well enough to travel, and he had no choice but to stay there until spring. Meantime, because people liked his straightforward nature and his amiable disposition, he began to make friends in the village, and not only Kodama but others as well valued his company. Later he went to Kyoto and called on Sasabe; afterward he returned to Ōmi and took lodging with Kodama, and before he knew it seven years had gone by as if in a dream.

It was now the second year of Kanshō.[216] The Hatakeyama brothers,[217] in the province of Kawachi, near the capital, were engaged in a dispute, and trouble threatened the area around Kyoto. Also, in the spring of the same year plague spread out of control, and corpses lay piled in the streets. People believed that the end of the world was coming, and they grieved at the transience of life. Katsushirō thought, 'How degenerate I've grown! What use have I made of my life? I've done nothing, and here I am in a distant province living[218] off the charity of a stranger. How long can I go on this way? I don't know what has become of my wife, who I left in my native village, and by staying these long years in fields that grow the grass of forgotten love,[219] how can I think of myself as a reliable person! Even though Miyagi may be dead and everything changed, I must at least go and find out and make her a grave mound.'

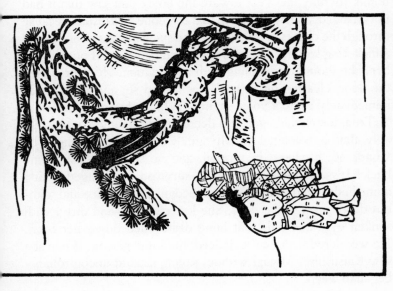

iii  The House Amid the Thickets: Katsushirō and Grandfather Uruma
return to the house amid the thickets to pray for Miyagi's soul

Katsushirō told his friends about his decision, and during a spell of fine weather in the Rainy Month,[220] he took his leave, reaching his native place in little more than ten days. He neared his former home late one day when the sun had already set in the west and rain clouds hung low, almost touching the earth, making the evening unusually dark. But this was, after all, his old familiar village, and as he crossed the summer moorland it scarcely occurred to him that he might lose his way. A bridge that once spanned[221] the rapid stream had now collapsed; to be sure, no sound of horses' hooves could be heard. The fields lay desolate and abandoned, and he could barely tell which way the path led. Although most of the dwellings were gone, in several of those that still stood here and there he noticed some sign of life. Virtually nothing, however, looked at all familiar, and after standing and wondering which house might be his, he retraced his steps about twenty paces. There, by the starlight that shone through a rift in the clouds, he at last recognised the tall pine tree that had been split by lightning[222] – the landmark of his home. Joyfully, he went toward the house and saw that it had not changed, and he could tell that someone was inside, because through the chinks in the old door he spied gleams of light from a flickering lantern. 'What if it's a stranger? Can it possibly be her?' he thought, trembling with anticipation. He approached the door, clearing his throat[223] as he did so, and from inside immediately came a voice saying, 'Who is there?'

True, it sounded aged and decrepit, but he knew unmistakably that it belonged to Miyagi. 'Can I be dreaming?' he wondered, his heart in turmoil, and he shouted, 'I've come back! It's a miracle that you've survived, unchanged, living alone in this wilderness.' Miyagi recognised his voice and without delay opened the door. She looked black and dirty, with sunken eyes and hair that hung dishevelled down her back. He wondered if she were, indeed, the same person. When she saw Katsushirō, Miyagi without saying a word uncontrollably began to weep.

Astonished, Katsushirō, too, was silent for a long time, and at last he whispered, 'Had I thought that you were still alive,

I wouldn't have waited so many years. When I was in Kyoto I heard about the fighting at Kamakura,[224] and how when Shigeuji was defeated he fell back to Shimōsa and that Uesugi kept pressing the attack. At the beginning of the Eighth Month I took leave of Sasabe and set out from Kyoto, but on the Kiso Highway robbers took all my money and clothing, and I barely escaped with my life. Then I learned from villagers that along the Eastern Sea Road and the Eastern Mountain Road new barriers had been set up and travellers were being turned back. I also found out that Tō no Tsuneyori had been sent to help Uesugi fight against Shigeuji. I heard that our province was nothing but scorched earth, and that horses had trampled every foot of ground. You must have passed away to dust and ashes, I thought, or if not that, I imagined, perhaps you had drowned. Eventually I went back to Kyoto where I managed to live for seven years on other people's good will. But recently I found myself wondering more and more about old times, and I decided that the least I could do was to return and pay my respects. Even in my wildest dreams, you see, I never imagined that you might still be alive. Surely, you must be like the cloud of Witches Hill[225] or the apparition at the Palace of Han?'[226] Thus did he try to explain his behaviour.

'Soon after you left,' said Miyagi, holding back her tears,[227] 'before the autumn I begged you to return by,[228] trouble broke loose in the world. The villagers fled[229] from their homes to take to the seas or to find refuge in the mountains, and the few men who stayed mostly behaved like brutes. No doubt feeling bold because I was now living alone, someone tried to trick me with flattering words, but I knew that I would rather die as a broken jewel than go on living as common clay.[230] Many times I had to bear heartache and sorrow. When the Milky Way[231] told of autumn, you had not returned, so I waited through winter. But spring came and there was still no news. I thought of going to Kyoto to find you, but even a strong man could not loosen the barrier locks, and there was no way at all for a woman to get past. I stayed here, like the pine outside the house, waiting with the owls and foxes,[232] until today in vain.

But now that you've come back, I'm delighted, and all my reproaches for you are forgotten. I'm very happy now, but you should know[233] that a woman could die of yearning, and a man can never know her agony.'

Again she broke into weeping, and Katsushirō took her in his arms and comforted her, saying, 'These nights are the shortest of all,' and they lay down together. In the cool darkness the window paper rustled as the breeze whispered through the pines. Exhausted from his travel, Katsushirō fell into a sound sleep. Around the fifth watch,[234] however, when the sky began to grow light,[235] he suddenly became partially aware of the world of the senses. He vaguely knew that he was cold, and groping with his hands, he tried to pull up the covers. But to his surprise leaves rustled beneath his touch, and as he opened his eyes a cold drop of something fell on his face.

He wondered if it were rain coming in, and then he noticed that the roof was gone, as though torn away by the wind, and that it was daybreak, and the pale shining moon of dawn still remained in the sky. All of the shutters to the house were gone, and through spaces in the dilapidated latticework bed[236] there grew high grass and weeds. The morning dew had fallen and soaked his sleeves wringing wet. The walls were covered with ivy and vines, and the garden was buried in tall madder weed. The season was still late summer,[237] but the desolation of the house reminded him of autumn moors.

'Miyagi is not here! Where could she have gone?' he thought, upon finding that she no longer lay with him. 'Have I been bewitched by a fox?'

Although it had been long deserted, the dwelling was without a doubt his old home. He recognised its spacious interior, its walls, and even the storehouse – all of which he had built to suit his own particular tastes. Bewildered and uncertain and scarcely knowing where he stood, he slowly realised that Miyagi was surely dead and that this was now the home of foxes and badgers – and perhaps, too, of fearsome evil spirits who had entered this desolate place and taken the form of his wife. 'Or was it her ghost,' he thought, 'her ghost yearning for love that

10 'I traveled on over mountains and through hamlets until once more I found myself by the shores of the lake' (p. 136). Right half of paired screens by Yosa Buson. (Formerly in the collection of Yokoe Manjirō, Osaka; from *Buson meiga*.)

11  'It is our privilege to grant
you for a time the shape of a
golden carp' (p. 136). A pair of
paintings by Matsumura
Goshun. (Hyōgo, Itsuō.)

came back to meet me?[238] It was just as I remembered her,' and in an excess of grief, he began to weep.

'It is only I, I alone who remain unchanged,'[239] he muttered, as he searched – first here, then there. Finally, in what had been the sleeping quarters he saw her grave, a heaped up mound of earth, which someone had covered by boards removed from the verandah in order to give protection from rain and dew. 'Is this where her ghost came from last night?' he wondered, horrified and yet entranced.

Amid the implements that had been placed there to dispense holy water, he found a crude strip of wood with a slip of old and tattered Nasumo paper.[240] Although patches of the writing had faded away and some of the characters were hard to read, he recognised his wife's hand. No holy name[241] and no date were there, but merely thirty-one syllables that showed sharp awareness of approaching death:

| | |
|---|---|
| *Sari-tomo to* | I have wept in sorrow, |
| *omou kokoro ni* | Longing for him to come back, |
| *hakararete* | But how can I go on living |
| *yo ni mo kyō made* | In this world, till now deceived |
| *ikeru inochi ka* | By vain hopes of his return! |

Recognising for the first time that Miyagi was in fact dead, he flung himself to the ground, weeping bitterly and lamenting how cruel it was not even to have knowledge of the day or the year on which she had perished. At last he stopped weeping, and arose. The sun had climbed high in the sky, and walking to the nearest house,[242] he saw the man who lived there and realised that it was not one of the old residents, but he wondered if he perhaps knew.

'Where are you from?' demanded the other man, before Katsushirō had a chance to speak.

'I used to be the master of the house next door,' Katsushirō replied with a bow, 'but I've spent the past seven years in Kyoto on business and just came back last night, only to find that my place is in ruins[243] and no one lives there. It seems that my wife has died and that someone made a grave, but I wish that I knew just when it all happened. If you by chance have heard, I wonder if you'd please tell me?'

'You must feel terribly upset,' the man said, 'but I haven't lived here for even a year, and I suppose that her death must have taken place quite a while before I came. I don't know much at all about the previous residents, for most everyone who used to inhabit this village fled when the fighting broke out, and a great majority of the people who now make their home here came from elsewhere. Still, there's an old man who seems to have stayed. Sometimes he goes to your house and prays for the salvation of a departed soul. Perhaps he can tell you about your wife.'

'Then, could you please show me where this old man lives?'[244] Katsushirō asked.

'About a hundred paces toward the seashore there are many hemp fields that he has planted,' the man explained, 'and nearby you'll find a small hut where he dwells.'

Feeling a sense of relief, Katsushirō made his way there and discovered an old man of about seventy years of age whose back was piteously bent seated on a round woven mat, sipping tea in front of his open-air fireplace. As soon as he recognised Katsushirō, he asked, 'Why did you take so long to come back?'

Katsushirō then saw that this was Grandfather Uruma, who had long resided in the village, and he greeted the old man politely and described how he had gone to Kyoto and stayed, quite contrary to his original intentions. Katsushirō told him of his strange experience the night before and began to thank him for having said prayers, but he could no longer hold back his tears.

'Soon after you went far away,' Grandfather Uruma explained, 'in the summer, I think it was, raging battle broke out, and the villagers scattered and fled. All of the young men were conscripted, and the mulberry fields quickly changed back into thickets fit for foxes and rabbits. But your brave wife trusted that you would keep your promise to return by fall and refused to desert her home. Because my legs are lame and I have trouble walking even a hundred steps, I too shut myself up tightly[245] and never left. Although tree spirits and other fearsome monsters at one time established themselves in your place, that young woman continued to stay on, though I never in my whole life saw anything more pitiable. Autumn passed; then spring came, and that year on the Tenth Day of the Eighth Month she died. Grieving desperately at her loss, I carried soil with my own decrepit hands and buried her in a coffin. To mark the grave mound I used a verse that she herself had composed before she passed away. I did my best to assemble some things for prayer and for dispensing holy water, but because I never learned how to write even a little, I had no way of recording the date, and the nearest temple is so far away that I could not get a name for her memory. Five years have since passed, but judging from what you've said, no doubt your brave wife's ghost has visited you to tell you of the anguish that she suffered. Let us go back once again and pray with all our heart.'

So saying, the old man took up his staff and led the way. The pair of them knelt in front of the grave, lifting up their voices in lament and chanting prayers all night, until the dawn. As they kept their vigil in the darkness, the old man told Katsushirō a story:

'Long before even my grandfather's grandfather was born, bygone ages ago,[246] there lived in this village a beautiful maiden named Mama no Tegona. Her family was poor, and she wore dresses made of hemp, and collars fixed with blue. Although her hair went uncombed and she walked unshod, her face was as perfect as the moon when at the full, and her smile was like the fragrance of the flowers. Because she surpassed even the ladies of the capital, clad in their rich brocades, she was courted not only by the men of this village but also by guardsmen from the capital and even by men from neighbouring provinces, who conveyed their love and longed for her. But Tegona grew sad and despondent that she could not give her heart to the suitor of her choice, and she cast herself to the waves in the bay. Struck by the way that her fate reflected the sorrow of life, many poets of old wrote verses about her, and the legend has been handed down. When I was a boy and my mother told it to me, I used to listen, enthralled, and filled with pity for the young woman. Yet now I feel that your wife Miyagi's fate was sadder by far even than that of innocent young Tegona of old.'

While speaking, Grandfather Uruma wept profusely, unable to stop, losing control of his emotions as old people so easily do. Katsushirō, upon hearing the story, was also beside himself with grief, and in the clumsy style of a man from the provinces, he made a poem:[247]

| | |
|---|---|
| *Inishie no* | No matter how much |
| *Mama no Tegona wo* | They loved Tegona |
| *kaku bakari* | In that bygone age, |
| *koite shi aran* | I loved my dear wife |
| *Mama no Tegona wo* | Every bit as much. |

Of his true feelings he could scarcely express a small part, but in some ways his plaintive cry may have been more genuine than poems by far more skilful hands.

The story of Miyagi and Katsushirō was brought back by merchants who from time to time have paid visits to that province.

# IV  THE CARP THAT CAME TO MY DREAM
## *(Muō no rigyo)*

Long ago, around the time of Enchō,[248] there lived at the Mii temple[249] a priest by the name of Kōgi. Owing to his skill as an artist, his name was widely known, but instead of doing such subjects as Buddhist portraits, landscapes, or flower-and-bird studies, Kōgi[250] would go out on Lake Biwa in a small boat whenever he was free from temple duties and give money to the fishermen who worked with their nets[251] in order that he could return the fish that they had caught into the water and sketch them while they leaped and played. As the years went by his paintings grew more and more exquisite.[252] Once, after putting all his heart[253] into a drawing, he grew sleepy and dreamed of entering the water and swimming together with many fish. When he awoke Kōgi immediately painted what he had seen and put it on his wall, calling it, 'The Carp That Came to My Dream.'

People admired the delicacy of his paintings and vied with one another to get them, but while Kōgi would readily give away whatever flower-and-bird study or landscape they desired, he was very unwilling to part with his carp pictures.

He would tell everyone in a merry voice, 'A monk can hardly give the fish that he has raised to an ordinary person who takes life or eats seafood.' His paintings and his witty remark both became famous throughout the land.

One year Kōgi was taken ill,[254] and after seven days passed suddenly his eyes closed and his breath stopped, as if he were dead. His disciples and friends gathered together grieving at their loss, but because some slight warmth remained in his chest they stayed by his side, just in case, and watched over him for three days. At the end of this time his arms and legs appeared to stir a bit, and suddenly he sighed, opened his eyes, and as if a person just waking up, he arose and turned to those assembled, saying, 'I have been away from human affairs for a long time. How many days have passed?'

'Master,' replied his disciples,[255] 'three days ago[256] you ceased breathing. Not only the people within the temple but everyone who in the past has enjoyed the pleasure of your company came to pay you homage and to discuss the matter of funeral services. But because your heart still seemed to be warm, we refrained from closing you up in a coffin, and instead we kept watch over you. Now you have come back to life, and how wise that we did not bury you. All of us rejoice.'

Kōgi nodded and said, 'One of you must go to the mansion of our patron,[257] Vice-Governor Taira, and say to him: "The master miraculously lives. My Lord, although you are now enjoying your wine and having your freshly sliced fish prepared, please leave your banquet and come to the temple. You shall hear a strange story." Then note the reaction of those present. All will be exactly as I have related.'

Greatly mystified, a messenger went to the mansion and saw much to his amazement that just as the master had predicted, the Vice-Governor was sitting with his younger brother, Jūrō, and his retainer, Kamori, enjoying his wine. He repeated what he was told, and when the people at the Vice-Governor's mansion heard the message, they were astonished, and setting aside their food, all of them[258] proceeded to the temple.

Raising his head from his pillow, Kōgi apologised for putting them to so much trouble. The Vice-Governor expressed his joy at Kōgi's recovery.

'Would you please oblige me by answering a question?' Kōgi then asked. 'Did you order some fish from Bunshi, the fisherman?'

'To be sure, I did,' replied the Vice-Governor in surprise. 'How do you happen to know?'

'That fisherman,' said Kōgi, 'brought to your house in a basket a fish more than three feet long.[259] You and your brother were seated in the south room playing *go*.[260] Kamori sat nearby, eating a large peach as he watched the game develop. Delighted when the fisherman carried in the large specimen, you gave him one of the peaches that was placed on a tall dish.[261] Also, you offered him a cup of wine and treated him to several rounds of drinks, while the cook[262] proudly took the fish and began to slice it. Everything I have said, down to the last point, is completely correct, isn't it?'

Upon hearing what Kōgi related, the Vice-Governor and his companions were dumbfounded and knew not what to think.

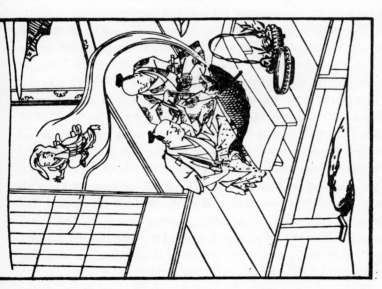

iv  The Carp That Came to My Dream: Kōgi's spirit departs from the golden carp

They asked how he possessed this detailed knowledge of what had happened.

'I was in such pain from my illness,' Kōgi replied, 'that I could bear it no longer. Unaware that I had died, I wished to cool my burning fever a little,[263] so I took up my walking stick and went out through the gate. Somehow, I seemed to forget my sickness, and I felt like a caged bird released into the sky. I travelled on over mountains and through hamlets until once more I found myself by the shores of the lake. As soon as I saw the jade green liquid I wanted to enter it, and without further thought I cast aside my clothing and sprang with all my might, plunging deeply into the water. I found while swimming around here and there that I could do anything I desired, though from childhood on I had never been used to the water. Whatever my situation may have been then, it is true that a man swimming in the water can never enjoy it as much as a fish; when I began to envy the way they were gliding about, a large one nearby said, "Master, I can easily fulfil your wish. Please wait here for me." So saying, he disappeared far into the depths.

'Presently a man wearing a crown and court dress rose up astride the same fish followed by many other creatures of the deep. He said to me, "The God of the Sea[264] speaks. You, old priest, by previously freeing living creatures,[265] have accrued great merit. Now, having entered the water, you want to swim like a fish, and it is our privilege to grant you for a time the shape of a golden carp[266] and to let you enjoy the pleasures of our watery domain.[267] But you must take care not to be blinded by the sweetness of bait and get caught on a hook and lose your life." Thereupon he left me and disappeared from sight. With great wonder, I looked around at my body. Unawares, I had been adorned with fish scales, gleaming like gold, and I had assumed the form of a carp. I flapped my tail, moved my fins, and swam everywhere to my heart's desire, without thinking it the least bit strange.

'At first I rode upon the waves that rise and fall with the gusts that blow from Mt Nagara,[268] and then I swam about the Great Bay of Shiga.[269] But people on foot[270] trailing their skirts in the tide as they walked to and fro startled me, and I plunged far down into the deep waters that reflect the lofty peaks of Hira.[271] I wanted to hide,[272] but couldn't, for the fishing fires of Katada lured me, uncontrollably. With the inexorable approach of evening, and after the pure black night fell,[273] the moon lodged in the sky above the Bay of Yonaka, gleaming on the top of Mirror Mountain[274] and shining on the countless inlets of Yaso Harbour.[275] To my delight no place was left untouched by the beauty. I felt astonished at seeing the mountain on Oki Island[276] and at viewing the red fences of Chikubushima[277] reflected on the waves. As morning drew near and the famous wind[278] rose off Mt Ibuki, the boats of Asazuma set out, waking me from my dreams among the reeds. I dodged the ferryman's deft boat pole at the Yabase[279] Crossing, and time and again the keeper of the Seta[280] Bridge forced me to turn back. When the sun was warm,[281] I floated. When storm winds blew, I swam to the bottom, a thousand fathoms below.

'Suddenly, I felt hungry and I knew that I needed something to eat. Searching here and there but finding nothing, I grew ever more frantic, until I came to the hook and line that Bunshi had cast. His bait looked very tempting. Still, in my heart I realised that I must obey the Sea God's warning. I was a disciple of Buddha. Even if for the present I were unable to find food, how could I stoop so low as to take fish bait? I went away.

'But after a while my hunger grew more intense, and once again I thought it over, and I could bear it no longer. Supposing I took the bait – Would I be so foolish as to get caught? Bunshi and I were old acquaintances, so there was no need for me to hesitate, I decided. I swallowed the bait. Bunshi quickly pulled at the line and caught me.

'"What are you doing?" I shouted. But he handled me as though he had heard nothing, and he strung a cord through my jaw, moored his boat among the reeds, and throwing me into a basket, he went to your door. You and your brother were playing *go* in the south room. Kamori was seated nearby, eating some fruit. When you saw what a large fish[282] Bunshi had brought, you and your companions admired it greatly. '"Gentlemen! Can't you tell? I'm Kōgi," I screamed at all of you as loudly as I could. "Let me go. Take me back to the temple," I kept shouting. But you acted as if nothing were the matter and merely clapped your hands in delight.

'Presently, your cook jabbed the fingers of his left hand into my eyes and grabbed me firmly while with his right he took a well-sharpened blade. Laying me on a chopping board, he started to cut me, and I cried out in desperate pain, "How can you cause injury to a disciple of Buddha! Help, save me!" But he ignored my words, and finally, just as I could feel him cutting me I awoke from my dream.'

Everyone was greatly surprised, and the Vice-Governor said, 'Now that we've heard your story, we realise that the fish's mouth moved each time, but it emitted no sound whatsoever. How strange that such an event should take place before our very eyes!' Immediately, he sent a servant back to the house with orders to cast the chopped fish into the lake.

Thereafter, Kōgi recovered from his illness, and much later, having lived out his natural span, he passed away. When his end drew near, he took a number of scrolls bearing the likenesses of carp[283] and threw them in the lake, whereupon the painted fish emerged from the paper and silk and swam about in the water. For this reason, Kōgi's paintings have not been handed down. A disciple, however, by the name of Narimitsu,[284] inherited Kōgi's mastery and gained great renown. After he painted a cock on a panel in the Kan'in Palace,[285] a real rooster that saw it is said to have scratched at the likeness.

This story may be found in an old collection of tales.

# VOLUME THREE

## V  BIRD OF PARADISE
### (Buppōsō)[286]

Japan, the Land of Peace and Calm,[287] had long been true to
its name. Its people rejoiced in their labour and still found time
to relax underneath the cherry-blossoms in spring and to visit
the many-coloured groves of trees in autumn. Those who wished
might take long trips by sea with the tiller as their pillow[288] and
visit the strange shores of Tsukushi.[289] Yet others could set
their hearts on the pleasure of climbing such peaks as Mt Fuji
and Tsukuba.[290]

In Ise, in the hamlet of Ōka,[291] there lived a man whose
name was Hayashi. He retired early from his occupation in
order to make way for his son, and he took the tonsure and
called himself Muzen, though he did not actually become a
priest.[292] He had always been a healthy man, and he liked
travelling to various places as he grew on in years. When his
younger son, Sakunoji, began to mature, Muzen worried lest
the boy be too countrified, and wishing to show him how people
in the capital live, he took him to spend about a month at his
establishment in Kyoto, in the Second Ward. Toward the end
of the Third Month they went to view the cherry-blossoms in
the deepest recesses of Yoshino.[293]

After enjoying themselves for seven days or so at a temple
where he was known, Muzen told the boy that they had never
been to Mt Kōya,[294] and that since they were so near they
ought to pay a visit. Thus they made their way through the
thick, green foliage of early summer, passing by a place known
as Tennokawa[295] and then climbing the Mountain of Mani.[296]
As they toiled up the steep path, the sun began to set before
they noticed it.

They prayed at the central halls[297] and the famous buildings, and also at the shrine of the founder, and then they tried to ask for lodging at the various cloisters, but no one would respond. Finally they inquired of a passerby about the local custom.

'People who have no connections with one of the temples or priests' dwellings,' replied the man, 'must go down the mountain and wait for dawn. Nowhere on this peak can anyone put up a stranger for the night.'

Upon hearing this news, Muzen felt tired and exhausted, and he was at a loss what to do, particularly after having dragged his aged body up the steep mountain path.

'It's dark now, and our feet are sore,' said Sakunoji. 'How can we ever manage to climb down such a long way? I'm young and don't mind sleeping on the grass, but it would be terrible should you become ill.'

'It's just this sort of thing,' said Muzen, 'that brings out the sorrow of travel. Even though we might exhaust ourselves and ruin our feet going down the mountain to spend the night, it still wouldn't be the same as sleeping at home.[298] Besides, we don't know how far we'll have to walk tomorrow. This mountain is the most sacred place in Japan.[299] Kūkai was one of our greatest religious leaders. Certainly after coming here it ought to be worthwhile spending a night praying for our life in the afterworld. Since we have such a good chance, let us pass the hours meditating at the shrine of the founder.'

Thereupon, they followed along a dark path flanked by cedars until they reached the shrine. They climbed onto the wooden verandah around the lantern hall[300] in front of the shrine and spread out their rain garments to sit on. While quietly intoning praise to the Buddha, they forlornly awaited the deepening of night.

An area of twenty acres had been landscaped, and the groves of trees did not appear the least bit sinister. Every last pebble had been swept from the hallowed ground. Nevertheless, the cloisters were far away, and the sound of chants, bells, and ringing staves could not be heard. The thick foliage that sheltered the pair from the clouds grew green and luxuriant.

The sound of water flowing in a thin trickle beside the path penetrated to the depth of their being and brought poignant thoughts to mind. His senses alert, Muzen began to speak,

'You see, when Kūkai became a deity,[301] even the rocks and trees attained a spirit. Now, over eight hundred years later, his power is even more evident and revered. Among the many places where his deeds are remembered,[302] this mountain remains the holiest one of all. Long ago, when he was still alive, Kūkai crossed over to distant China, and finding great inspiration he said, "Wherever my trident[303] rests, that site shall be hallowed land for the practice of my teachings."

'Gazing up toward the heavens, he threw the instrument, and strange to say, it came to rest on this mountain. The Pine Tree of the Trident, which stands in front of the central halls, grows on the very spot where the relic is supposed to have fallen. All of the grass, trees, rocks, and springs on this mountain, with no exception whatsoever, are believed to have spirits. How strange it is that you and I are spending the night here. It must have been ordained by fate. Although you are yet young, you must never let your faith fail.'

Muzen spoke quietly, but the sound carried mysteriously through the night.

'Buppan! Buppan!'

Seemingly from within the woods behind the shrine came the cry of a bird, and then, somewhat closer, the sound of an echo.

'How remarkable!' exclaimed Muzen, his attention diverted. 'That call just now must be a bird of paradise.[304] I've been told that they lived on this mountain, but no one has ever been certain of hearing it before.[305] Surely it's a sign that because we are spending the night here Buddha will forgive us our sins and grant us salvation. After all, that bird is said to nest only in sacred places like Mt Kashō[306] in the province of Kōzuke, Mt Futara[307] in the province of Shimotsuke, the Daigo Ridge[308] in Yamashiro, and Mt Shinaga[309] in Kawachi. That it's found on this mountain is well known to many from Kūkai's poem,

Alone in a cold grove I prayed,
As dawn came to my hut,
And with the song of one bird
I heard the call of the three treasures.

Each feathered creature has its voice,
Every man has his own heart,
And music fills the clouds and streams
With hallowed resonance.[310]

'And there is another ancient verse,

| | |
|---|---|
| *Matsunoo no* | By Matsuo Shrine, |
| *mine shizuka naru* | On the ridge, abiding in silence |
| *akebono ni* | In the early dawn, |
| *aogite kikeba* | I lift up my head and hear |
| *buppōsō naku*[311] | The bird of paradise cry. |

'It is handed down in legend that long ago, when High
Priest Enrō,[312] of the Saifukuji Temple, was the outstanding
master of the Lotus Sutra, the deities of Matsuo ordered this
bird to serve him always, and ever since then it is supposed to
have nested in the precincts of their shrine. We have already
heard the first of tonight's mysteries – the cry of the bird. Being
on this spot how can I resist the inspiration!'[313]

He cocked his head to one side for a moment, and in seven-
teen syllables of the *haikai* mode,[314] which was one of his
perennial pleasures, he recited,

| | |
|---|---|
| *Tori no ne mo* | Even a bird's call |
| *himitsu no yama no* | Tells how the sacred mountain |
| *shigemi ka na*[315] | Has flourished and grown. |

Taking out his travelling ink stone,[316] Muzen recorded the
verse by the light from the lantern hall. He strained his ears,
hoping to catch the bird's cry once more, but to his surprise,
from a long way off in the direction of the cloisters he heard

v  Bird of Paradise: At Mt Kōya the samurai announces the approach of
Toyotomi Hidetsugu and his party

instead a solemn shout to clear the way. Gradually the voice drew nearer.

'What sort of person could be coming to worship this late at night?' Muzen exclaimed in fear and wonder. Father and son exchanged glances, and afraid even to breathe, they fixed their gaze in the direction of the voice.

At last, a young samurai herald stamped noisily across the wooden bridge and advanced toward them. Terrified, they crouched down and hid by the right side of the hall, but the warrior quickly found them.

'You, there! Who are you?' he said. 'His Highness approaches. Get down immediately.'

They scurried down from the veranda and bowed low, huddling to the ground. Presently, they heard the echo of many feet and the loud reverberation of shoes.[317] A nobleman wearing linen cap and court dress ascended to the hall, and four or five warriors who were with him seated themselves to his right and left.

'Why haven't the others come?' the nobleman asked, turning to his companions.

'No doubt they will soon be here,' came the reply.

Thereupon, more footsteps sounded, and a warrior of distinguished bearing, surrounded by Buddhist acolytes with shaven heads, made his obeisance and mounted to the hall. The nobleman, turning to the warrior who had just arrived, addressed him, saying:

'Hitachi,[318] why are you so late?'

'Two samurai, Shirae[319] and Kumagae,[320] wished to prepare some wine for your lordship,' he replied, 'and since they were so thoughtful, I decided to try to fix you a dish of fresh fish, and that is why we lagged behind the rest of the party.'

As soon as they had brought out the food and drink, the nobleman called, 'Mansaku,[321] pour my wine.'

In response, a handsome young samurai slid forward on his knees and did the honours. The wine was passed around to everyone, and great merriment ensued. Then once again the nobleman spoke:

12 'Let us pass the hours meditating at the shrine of the founder' (p. 140). Facing the Lantern Hall, behind which the actual shrine is situated.

13 'When Muzen was crossing the Sanjō Bridge, he remembered about the Mound of Beasts' (p. 149). An eighteenth century view of the area. The Zuisenji temple in the far left is also shown in detail. (From *Miyako meisho zue*.)

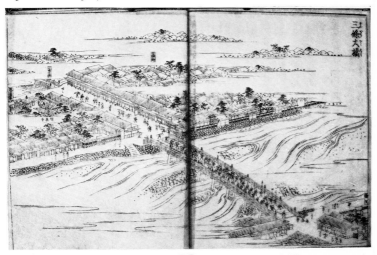

14 'The men plowed in the spring and reaped in the autumn, and their household grew prosperous' (p. 150). Painting by Yosa Buson, 'Planting and Harvesting in the Countryside,' paired screens made during the years 1754–57. (Kyoto Prefecture, Yano Nirō; from *Buson ihō*.)

15 The Kibitsu Caldron (p. 151). (Okayama, photograph courtesy of Kadokawa.)

'We haven't enjoyed Jōha's conversation lately.³²² Call him.'

The summons was relayed, and from behind the place where Muzen and his son had prostrated themselves³²³ a priest of huge build, broad of face and with vivacious features, straightened his priestly robes and advanced to the edge of the assemblage. When the nobleman asked him to explain a variety of points about classical matters, the priest gave a detailed reply to each question, after which his inquirer, enormously pleased, said, 'Let him be rewarded.'

Then a warrior addressed Jōha, saying, 'This mountain was opened by a person of great virtue, was it not? I've heard that although every single rock and tree here has its own spirit, the waters of the Brook of Jewels³²⁴ nevertheless contain poison, and whenever people drink it they drop dead; so Kūkai wrote,

| | |
|---|---|
| *Wasuretemo* | In case you forget, |
| *kumi ya shitsuran* | And partake of these waters – |
| *tabibito no* | Travellers who ascend |
| *Takano no oku no* | Into the high recesses, |
| *Tamagawa no mizu*³²⁵ | Where the Brook of Jewels begins. |

'At least this is how it has been handed down. In spite of his great virtue, why couldn't Kūkai make this poisonous stream dry up? How can you explain such a disturbing contradiction?'

'Your verse,' Jōha replied with a smile, 'is preserved in the imperial anthology, *Fūgashū*. An introductory note says, "Along the path to the inner cloister of Mt Kōya, there is a stream called the Brook of Jewels, on the surface of which³²⁶ dwell numerous poisonous insects, and in order to keep people from drinking these waters, Kūkai left the following poem for posterity." This is how it is interpreted, and the verse is just as you remembered it. Yes, one can easily understand why you should harbour doubt, because Kūkai possessed such bountiful supernatural powers. He could employ invisible deities to make paths where none had been before. He penetrated rock as easily as a normal man digs through earth. He subjugated great serpents. He tamed fabulous birds. When one recalls all the exploits for which everyone under heaven admires him, the note in front of this verse obviously fails to ring true. Since ancient times in various provinces[327] there have been streams called the "River of Jewels," and all the verses written about them praise their pure water. So, the Brook of Jewels here can hardly be poisonous. Rather, the idea of the verse is more likely that a brook of such famous name also exists on this mountain, and even though people who come here to worship may have forgotten about it, charmed by the clear running water, they will scoop it up with their hands. One may conclude that the note in front of the verse was most likely derived from some later person's mistaken report about the presence of poison. Besides, should one pursue his doubts more deeply,[328] he will find that the tone of this verse is not in the style of the time when the capital was moved to Kyoto.[329]

'But also, in the classical language of our country expressions such as "garland of jewels,"[330] "jewel-bedecked curtains,"[331] and "bejeweled finery"[332] were used in praise of purity or beauty. "Clear water" was called "jewel water," "jewel springs," or "jewel brook." Why would anyone attach the prefix "jewel-" to a stream that was contaminated? A person who devotes himself to Buddhism[333] does not necessarily understand poetry and can very easily make such mistakes. Your suspicions about the meaning of this verse show that you are very perceptive, even though you yourself do not write poetry.'

Thus did Jōha warmly praise the warrior, and the nobleman as well as all the others in the assemblage most heartily approved of the explanation.

From behind the hall came the cry, *'Buppan! Buppan!'* It sounded nearby. The nobleman raised his winecup aloft and said,

'This bird sings but rarely. How glorious that it does so for our drinking party tonight. Jōha! Let us have a poem.'

'My short verses,'[334] the priest replied politely, 'must sound rather hackneyed to your lordship's ear. There is a traveller spending the night here, and he can write poetry in the *haikai* style[335] that is now so popular. It may seem fresh to your lordship, so I suggest that you call on him for a stanza.'

'Then send for the man,' came the reply.

A young samurai went to where Muzen knelt and said, 'You have been summoned. Go to his lordship.'

Unable to decide whether he was dreaming or awake and hardly able to control his fear, Muzen crept up to where Hidetsugu sat. The priest turned to Muzen and said,

'Recite to his lordship the verse that you composed a short while ago.'

'I'm sorry, but I can't remember what I wrote,' said Muzen, in fear and trembling. 'I only beg of you, forgive me.'

Thereupon Jōha said, 'Did you not record something about the sacred mountain? His Lordship wishes to hear it. Quickly, recite it for him.'

Even more afraid, Muzen replied, 'Please tell me who this nobleman may be, that you address him in such manner and hold for him in this mountain recess a nocturnal banquet. I feel that something most strange has taken place.'

'I wish to inform you,' responded the priest, 'that his lordship is the chancellor,[336] Hidetsugu. The remaining gentlemen are Kimura Hitachi-no-suke, Sasabe Awaji,[337] Shirae Bingo, Kumagae Daizen, Awano Moku,[338] Hibino Shimotsuke,[339] Yamaguchi Shōun,[340] Marumo Fushin,[341] the Lay Priest Ryūsai,[342] Yamamoto Tonomo,[343] Yamada Sanjūrō,[344] Fuwa Mansaku, and myself, Jōha,[345] Transmitter of the Law. You stand here on miraculous trial. Quickly now. Recite what you earlier wrote.'

Indeed, if he had had any hair on his head, it surely would have stood on end, so frightened was Muzen, and he felt as though his very heart and soul were about to ascend the heavens. Trembling desperately, he removed from his pilgrim's bag a sheet of fresh paper. He wrote on it with a shaky brush and held out the document.

Yamamoto Tonomo took it and recited in a clear voice,

| | |
|---|---|
| *Tori no ne mo* | Even a bird's call |
| *himitsu no yama no* | Tells how the sacred mountain |
| *shigemi ka na* | Has flourished and grown. |

'Quite a fine verse,' said the nobleman. 'Now let us have someone to compose the last two lines.'

Whereupon, Yamada Sanjūrō drew himself slightly forward and said, 'Let me try my hand at it.'

After pausing briefly to collect his thoughts, he wrote:

*Keshi taki akasu*    With burnt offerings we wait
*mijika yo no yuka*[346]  For the brief night to end with dawn.

'How is this?' he asked, handing the verse to Jōha.

'It's very good,' said Jōha, and he gave it to Hidetsugu.

'Not bad at all,' said Hidetsugu by way of compliment,[347] and he had the wine cup passed around once more.

Suddenly the face of the gentleman named Awaji changed colour, and he screamed, 'Now it's time to join battle. I hear the demons from the Hell of Fighting Beasts[348] coming for us. Arise, my lord!'

Every man assembled there grew as red as if bathed in blood. They all leaped to their feet and danced, crying out, 'Tonight again we'll smash Ishida, Masuda, and all the rest.'[349]

'We've shown ourselves to these good for nothing rascals, here,' said Hidetsugu to Kimura. 'Drag the pair of them along to the battle.'

'It is not yet time for them to die,' said several of the old retainers, who interposed themselves and forbade such action. 'You'd better refrain from your customary evil tricks,' and with these words, the forms of all the men seemed to vanish into the distant clouds.

Father and son fell into a faint and for a time lay as if dead. The first signs of dawn[350] broke across the eastern sky, and the falling dew, cold and wet against their skin, restored them to consciousness. But their fright remained unabated until it was fully light, and with all their heart they prayed in the name of Kūkai. When at last the sun arose, they hurried down the mountain and went on to Kyoto, where they employed medicine and acupuncture to recover their health.

One day, when Muzen was crossing the Sanjō Bridge, he

remembered about the Mound of Beasts,[351] and gazing toward the Zuisenji Temple, he thought, 'Even here in broad daylight, how ghastly it all seems!'

Muzen told his story to people in the capital, and that is how the tale has come to be recorded.

# VI  THE CALDRON OF KIBITSU
## (Kibitsu no Kama)[352]

'You may hate the clamours of a jealous wife,[353] but when you grow old you'll learn her true worth.' Who was it that uttered those words? Even if a jealous wife does not cause you great misfortune, she will interfere with your business affairs, destroy your possessions, and bring down on you your neighbours' criticism. And if she does cause you genuine calamity, you might lose your home, ruin your country, or become an object of ridicule for the whole world. Since ancient times the poison of jealousy has stricken untold multitudes of men.

When a jealous woman dies, she may become a serpent. She can wreak her fury with a thunderbolt.[354] Even if you should cut the flesh of a vengeful woman into mincemeat,[355] it wouldn't help. True, these are extreme examples, and if a husband watches closely over his own conduct and educates his wife, he can surely avoid such disasters. Nonetheless, if a man is overcome by some capricious whim and arouses his wife's jealous nature,[356] he may end up by doing harm to himself. 'To tame a bird it takes determination; to tame a wife it requires a husband's native manliness.' This saying is certainly true.

In the province of Kibi,[357] in the district of Kaya, in the village of Niise, there lived a man named Izawa Shōdayū. His grandfather had served the Akamatsu of Harima,[358] but after the war in the first year of Kakitsu the old man fled from the Akamatsu castle and settled in Niise. Down to Shōdayū's time three generations had passed; the men plowed in the spring and reaped in the autumn, and their household grew prosperous. But Shōdayū's only son, Shōtarō, hated farming. He was drunken and dissipated, and he abandoned himself to lust, ignoring his father's admonitions. Because Shōtarō's conduct upset them, his parents often discussed the problem with one another.

'Surely,' they decided, 'if we can marry him to a lovely girl from a good family, he will straighten out of his own accord.' They asked people to search everywhere throughout the province, and fortunately a matchmaker came and said,

'The head priest of the Kibitsu Shrine, Kasada Miki, has a daughter named Isora, whom nature has blessed with great beauty. Even more, she serves her parents well, is clever at verse, and can play the zitheren. Her family descends from the Kamowake of Kibi[359] and is therefore of good lineage; so, should she become connected with your house, it would be a good omen, and I ardently wish for such a union to take place. Now, sir, how do you feel about the proposition?'

'It sounds like a splendid idea,' said Shōdayū, greatly pleased. 'The match would be the opportunity of a thousand years for us. But the Kasadas are nobility in this province, and we are nameless peasants. And since our house hardly compares with theirs,[360] I don't see how they could ever accept the offer.'

'You mustn't depreciate yourself so much!' laughed the old matchmaker. 'I assure you that we'll raise a song in celebration.'

Thereupon, the matchmaker went and talked to Kasada, who was also pleased, and when he told his wife, she encouraged the idea.

'Our daughter is already in her seventeenth year,' she said. 'Morning and evening I've been praying that we can find her a good husband, and the problem has been on my mind. Let us quickly pick a day and send the Izawas our betrothal gifts.'

So earnestly did she entreat her husband, that they decided immediately upon the marriage and prepared a response. With joy the betrothal gifts were made ready and dispatched. An auspicious day was chosen, and plans were set in order for the wedding ceremony.

Now, people who worshipped[361] at the Kibitsu Shrine customarily made an offering of various kinds of grain and prepared boiling water to seek an omen for good or ill. When the vestal virgins completed their prayers and the water came to a boil, if the omen were good the caldron sang with a sound like that of lowing oxen. If the omen were bad, the caldron remained silent. This was known as the test of the Kibitsu Caldron. Hoping that the gods meant to grant good fortune, Kasada summoned together vestal virgins and shrine attendants. The water was set to boil, but when Kasada performed the rite – perhaps because the gods disapproved of the marriage – there arose not even the chirping sound of an insect crying in an autumn field. Kasada felt upset and told his wife what had happened.

'The caldron most likely gave no sound,' she replied, with self-assurance, 'because the attendants failed to purify themselves. We've already exchanged betrothal gifts, and once the scarlet cord is tied,[362] you know, though the couple come from enemy houses or from different countries, nothing may be changed. Besides, the Izawas are descended from a long line of warriors, and we know they keep a strict household. Even if we tried to call the whole thing off, they would never stand for it. Isora has heard that her fiancé is an elegant gentleman, and she has been counting each day – she can hardly wait.[363] If we were to tell her now that something has gone wrong, there's no predicting what she might do. Then no matter how sorry we were, it would be too late.'

How like a woman it is to inveigle a husband into agreeing. Kasada, himself, having originally favoured the idea of marriage, harboured no deep doubts. He followed his wife's wishes and continued to prepare for the wedding. Both of the families gathered with all their relatives to sing of the thousand years of the crane and the myriad ages of the tortoise[364] and to wish the couple eternal happiness.

When Isora went to her new home, she arose early[365] each morning and went to bed late every night. She seldom left her father- and mother-in-law's side, and she made herself wise in her husband's ways, putting heart and soul into serving him. The older Izawas admired her filial virtues and enjoyed her companionship. Shōtarō also appreciated her efforts, and the couple lived in harmony.

But there remained his old habit of playing around with women,[366] and in due course Shōtarō fell in love with a courtesan named Sode from the port of Tomo.[367] Eventually he ransomed her and set up a separate household in a nearby village, where he spent most of his days, rarely returning home. Vexed by his behaviour, Isora once tried to remind her husband that he was making his parents angry, and she accused him of being an unreliable fellow,[368] but no good came of it. In fact afterward Shōtarō stayed away from home for several months.

His father, however, was unable to stand by and watch Isora's constancy and devotion any longer, so he disciplined Shōtarō and placed him in confinement.[369] Isora felt sorry for her husband and served him attentively morning and evening. She also quietly sent things over to Sode's place and made every effort to do what she could. One day, while the father was away from home, Shōtarō used all of his wiles on Isora, saying, 'When I see the sweetness and goodness that there is in you, it makes me realise at last just how rotten I've been. I ought to have sent Sode back where she came from and tried to patch things up with father, but, you see, she is from Inamino,[370] in Harima, and her parents have died, leaving her with absolutely no prospects at all, so I felt sorry for her and took her in. If I abandoned her now, surely she would become a common whore in some port town. Although the outlook for her might not seem much better there, I've heard that in the capital one can find understanding people. I would like to send Sode to

Kyoto, where she can seek a position with a person of quality. But in my predicament I can't do anything. How can we get[371] the money to put clothes on her back and send her away? You must help somehow and obtain for her what she needs.' Hearing him speak so sincerely, Isora responded with delight.

'Don't worry about a thing,' she replied, and secretly she sold her own clothing and personal belongings and also went back to her mother to request money, all of which she gave to Shōtarō.

After getting the money Shōtarō stole away from home, taking Sode with him, and fled toward the capital. When Isora learned how Shōtarō had tricked her, she fell into grief and rage and ultimately became ill. The Izawas and the Kasadas condemned Shōtarō and pitied Isora, but although they tried everything that medicine could do, day after day she even refused to eat. Nothing seemed to be of any avail.

Meantime, in the province of Harima, in the district of Inami, in the hamlet of Arai[372] there lived a man named Hikoroku. Because he and Sode were close relatives, the fugitives first called on him and for a while rested their feet.

'Even in the capital,' Hikoroku suggested to Shōtarō, 'you can't simply turn to anyone. You should stay here. You can share my food, and we'll find a way to make a living together.'[373]

Shōtarō felt relieved at such comforting words, and he decided that it would be best to settle down there. Hikoroku rented a dilapidated house next to his own dwelling and helped the couple move in, feeling pleased that he seemed to have found two friends. Sode, however, within a few days of their arrival complained of feeling a draught, and for no apparent reason she suffered agonies and became deranged, as though possessed. Owing to the misery that she suffered from her condition, Shōtarō even forgot his meals. He embraced her and comforted her, but she lay[374] perpetually weeping. Painful seizures of the chest would render her unconscious, and when she awoke her state remained unchanged. Shōtarō felt great anxiety, wondering whether the cause lay in a living demon and perhaps had some connection with Isora, whom he had left in his native village.

'Why should it be anything of that sort?' said Hikoroku, in disagreement. 'I've seen many cases of people who get what's known as "the plague." When her fever goes down a bit, it'll all seem like a dream.' The casual way that he spoke reassured Shōtarō. But by the seventh day, inexorably, and without the least sign of improvement, all had been in vain.

Filled with anguish, Shōtarō lamented to the heavens and beat upon the earth, swearing that he would follow Sode in death.[375] Hikoroku tried to calm him, pointing out that they could hardly let the body lie as is. Finally, Sode's remains turned to smoke on a wild moor, and Shōtarō gathered the ashes, constructed a mound, and placed a marker there. He called in a priest and devoutly prayed for the salvation of Sode's soul.

Although Shōtarō now prostrated himself and tried to communicate beyond the grave, he had no means for summoning Sode's spirit.[376] When he looked up and thought of his native hamlet, he realised that it was even further away than Hell. Behind him his familial ties were severed and before him loomed oblivion. Each moment of the day[377] he lay in grief, and as he went night after night to pray at Sode's grave, grass began to grow on the mound, and the occasional chirping of insects added to his melancholy.

While Shōtarō was lost in the reveries brought on by this lonely autumn,[378] he saw that a similar sorrow existed under the heavens,[379] when a fresh grave appeared next to Sode's. A woman in mourning came here to pray, and Shōtarō noticed that she offered flowers and sprinkled water.

'How unfortunate,' he said, 'a young woman like you frequenting this wild, deserted moor!'

'Yes, I have been coming here each evening to worship,'[380] replied the woman, turning to him. 'But you are already praying when I arrive. You must be lamenting for a loved one from whom you have been parted. I can well imagine your terrible grief,' and she broke into tears.

'Just ten days ago,' Shōtarō explained, 'my beloved wife passed away, and being left in this world with no one to turn to, I find that my visits here bring me at least some solace. I'm sure that the same must be true of you.'

'I come to pray,' replied the woman, 'for the memory of the master who employed me and who was recently laid to rest here. My mistress is so sad that she has fallen ill and must remain at home, and I've been bringing incense and flowers here in her behalf.'

'I can readily understand that she[381] should fall ill,' said Shōtarō. 'Who, may I ask, was the deceased man, and where does his family live?'

'My master was once an important person in this province,' the woman explained, 'but owing to slanderous remarks, he lost his lands and was forced to endure a life of poverty on the edge of the moors.[382] My mistress used to be renowned for her beauty[383] as far away as the next province, and it was on her account that my master forfeited his house and estate.'

Trying to sound as though he were not too curious, Shōtarō said, 'If your mistress is living nearby, I might pay her a visit and console her by talking about our similar misfortunes. Please show me the way.'

'The house lies a short distance from the path you usually use,' replied the woman. 'Since my mistress has no one to comfort her, by all means drop in when you have the time. Meanwhile, I'm sure that she'll be anxiously waiting for me to return.' Thereupon, the woman arose and departed.

Shōtarō followed along the narrow path for about two hundred paces and turned in, walking for another hundred steps, and there by a shadowy grove[384] stood a small thatched hut. On the wretched looking bamboo doorway the moon, slightly more than half full, cast its light unimpeded. Shōtarō noticed a small garden, which had been left to neglect.[385] Through the paper in the window the rays of a dim lamp shone, adding to the desolation of the scene.

'Please wait here,' said the woman, as she entered. Shōtarō, standing by an old well covered with moss, tried to peer into the house,[386] and through a small opening in the Chinese paper he caught a glimpse of flickering lamplight and a gleaming black lacquer cupboard,[387] which made him want to see more.

At last the woman reappeared, saying, 'I have told my mistress that you wished to call on her, and she has asked me to show you in and to set up a partition so that she may speak with you. She has now come to the outer wall. Allow me to take you to her.' She led him through the front garden and around to the rear. The door was barely open, and within the tiny, makeshift reception room stood a low screen at the edge of which a piece of shabby bedding was visible. Behind this the mistress of the house sat concealed.

'I heard of your tragedy and how it led to your being afflicted with an illness,' said Shōtarō, facing toward the screen. 'I have lost a dearly beloved wife, myself, and though it may seem rather sudden, I wanted to pay you a visit, so that we might share each other's sorrow.'

'What a surprise to meet you here!' said the mistress, opening the screen a trifle. 'Let me show you how bitter my revenge can be.' Shōtarō was astonished to see the figure of Isora, whom he had left in his native village. Her face had grown pallid and spectre-thin, and her listless eyes held a vacant stare. She pointed at him with a thin, blue finger[388] that struck terror into his heart, and Shōtarō, screaming in horror, fell as if dead.

Later, as he came to his senses and opened his eyes, hesitantly at first, he saw that what had appeared to be the house was in reality a small meditation hall containing a blackened Buddhist image, which had always stood there on the deserted moor. The bark of a dog in the distant village restored his courage, and Shōtarō hurried home to tell Hikoroku what had happened.

'What sort of fox did you let yourself get tricked by?' said Hikoroku. 'When you are swayed by fear, you'll always feel the torment of spirits that can lead you astray. When a person grows timid, as you have done, and sinks into such misfortune, he should pray to the Gods and Buddhas and calm his mind. In the hamlet of Toda[389] there is a famous soothsayer.[390] Purify

vi The Caldron of Kibitsu: Shōtarō unexpectedly meets Isora's vengeful spirit

yourself and ask him to give you a charm.' Later he led Shōtarō to the diviner's place, informing the holy man of all that had come to pass and requesting him to foretell the future.

'Calamity has already closed in around you,' the priest explained to Shōtarō, after performing divination. 'You cannot afford to relax. The ghost has snatched away a woman's life, and its anger remains unabated. Your very existence is in constant danger. Because it left the world seven days ago, for the next forty-two,[391] counting from today, you must stay in confinement and keep yourself pure and clean. By paying heed to my warning, you may be able to avoid almost certain death and save yourself. But if you make even the slightest mistake, all will be lost.'

Leaving nothing to chance, he took his brush, and over Shōtarō's entire back and then his arms and legs the holy man wrote characters in the style of ancient seals.[392] In addition, he gave him slips of paper with spells inscribed on them in vermilion ink.[393] 'Place these charms on each door,' he instructed, 'and pray to the Gods and Buddhas. Don't do anything wrong, or you'll surely die.'

With fear and hope conjoined, Shōtarō returned home, affixed the vermilion charms to his door and windows and shut himself up in complete seclusion. That night, at about the time of the third watch,[394] a horrible voice moaned, 'Oh, how hateful! Someone has put a sacred charm here.' Afterward, there was silence. Shōtarō passed the long hours of darkness filled with anxiety. As soon as the light of dawn began to show, he felt a sense of relief and pounded on the wall facing Hikoroku's place and told his companion what had happened.

Hikoroku for the first time took seriously what the priest had said, and he stayed up the following night with Shōtarō to wait for the third watch. Wind howled through the pine trees as if to topple the very trunks,[395] and rain fell, adding to the eerie atmosphere, while the two men separated by thin walls reassured one another until the fourth watch began. Then, on the paper window of the smaller hut a beam of red light flashed through the pitch black darkness, and a voice resounded with an unearthly ring, 'Oh, how hateful! There is a sacred charm here too.' The hair on Hikoroku's head and body all stood on end, and for a time he lost consciousness.

When daybreak came the two men talked of what had happened during the night. Every evening they longed for the dawn, and the forty-two days seemed more than a thousand years in passing.[396] Meanwhile, each night the demon prowled around the house or perched on the rooftop screaming, its doleful cry every time more terrible than the last. Eventually, the forty-second evening came. Hoping only to get through one more night, Shōtarō took particular care after darkness had fallen, and at last, during the fifth watch, he perceived in the sky the first traces of light. Like a man awakening from a long dream, he immediately called Hikoroku, and through the wall came the reply,

'What is it?'

'My long period of isolation has finally ended,' said Shōtarō. 'Not once have I seen your face. For old time's sake do what you can to console me after the dreary and terrifying ordeal I've just endured. Get up and let's go outside.'

'Nothing can happen now,' replied Hikoroku, being an imprudent fellow.[397] 'Come over to my place.' But before he could open the door halfway, from the adjoining hut there arose a scream of bloodcurdling intensity, and Hikoroku was swept from his feet.

Realizing that his friend's life was in danger, Hikoroku grabbed an axe and rushed out to the front path. What Shōtarō had taken for the first signs of daybreak proved to be premature. The moon shone high in the sky, pale and wan, and the wind carried a cold sting. Shōtarō's door, he discovered, stood open, and his companion was nowhere to be seen. Thinking that perhaps he had fled back into the house, Hikoroku went inside to look. But it was hardly the sort of dwelling in which one could hide. He searched along the road, in case his friend had fallen there. Still, he found nothing by the wayside. At a loss as to what could have happened, Hikoroku was struck by the mystery of it, and also by fear.

Holding a torch aloft, he explored everywhere, until finally, on the wall next to the outside of the open door, he noticed fresh warm blood trickling down toward the ground. No body and no bones, however, were to be found. By the light of the moon he spied an object on the edge of the eaves. Upon raising his torch to see what it was, he discovered hanging there nothing else than a bleeding head, torn and mangled.[398] This was the only trace of Shōtarō that remained.

The futility of it, and the terror, can scarcely be recorded by the brush. When the night was at last over, Hikoroku hunted throughout the nearby moors and mountains, but being unable to find any further sign, he abandoned the search. He told the Izawas of what had befallen their son, and they, in tears, reported it to the Kasadas. Meantime, the way in which the diviner's miraculous prophesy and the caldron's ill omen were both completely fulfilled serves to show the power of the supernatural. Thus, the story has been handed down.

16 'Once upon a time . . . in the province of Kii, by the cape of Miwa' (p. 161). Scene from a long landscape scroll by Gion Nankai (1677–1751), 'Pilgrimage to the Three Immortal Shrines.' (Tokyo National Museum; photograph courtesy of Suntory Museum, Tokyo.)

17 'At Miwa's rugged cape,/ And by the Sano Crossing/ No cottage appears in sight' (p. 163). (Photograph courtesy of Kadokawa.)

18 'Leaving only . . . a skeleton lying in the weeds' (p. 193). Painting by Itō Jakuchū (1716–1800). (Hyōgo, Saifukuji temple; photograph courtesy of Tokyo National Museum.)

19 'So how, indeed, can Hideyoshi last?' (p. 203). Sketch for a portrait made by Kanō Sanraku (1559–1635). (Hyōgo, Itsuō; Important Cultural Property.)

# VOLUME FOUR

## VII  THE LUST OF THE WHITE SERPENT
### *(Jasei no in)*[399]

Once upon a time, though it matters not exactly when,[400] in the province of Kii, by the cape of Miwa,[401] there lived a fisherman named Ōya[402] no Takesuke. He was rich in the luck of the sea[403] and took care of many other fishermen who caught all sorts of things, broad of fin and narrow of fin, thus enabling his house to prosper. Takesuke had two sons and one daughter. His first son, Tarō, was a simple but hard-working man, and his second child, a girl, had married someone from the province of Yamato, where she now lived. The third child, named Toyoo, grew to be a gentle young lad, especially fond of polite accomplishments but with little practical sense.

'If I gave him his share of the inheritance,' the father lamented, 'it would soon pass into other hands. Even should another family adopt him to continue their line, I would eventually grow ill from hearing uncomplimentary reports. The best thing to do would be to let him develop in his own way and become a scholar[404] or a priest, if he pleases, and for the rest of his life Tarō could look after his needs.' From then on he made no effort to restrain his son.

Toyoo had a teacher who was a priest at the Shingū Shrine.[405] His name was Abe no Yumimaro, and Toyoo visited him regularly. On one of these trips, around the end of the Ninth Month,[406] when the sea was especially calm, clouds suddenly arose from the southeast,[407] and a light drizzle began to fall.[408] Therefore, as he set out from his master's home Toyoo borrowed a large umbrella, but by the time he came in sight of the Asuka Shrine,⁴⁰⁹ the rain had grown so heavy that he decided to seek shelter at a nearby fisherman's hut.

'Oh, it's the master's younger son,' said the old man who came to the door. 'Your visit is indeed an honour for such a humble place as mine. Please come in and sit down.' He took out a shabby round cushion from which he shook the dust and offered it to Toyoo.

'The rain will surely stop soon, and I'll be all right, so please don't put yourself out for me,' Toyoo protested as he accepted the old man's hospitality.

Then, strange to relate, a sweet voice came from outside saying, 'Please give me some shelter for a little while,' and a young lady entered. She seemed to be not yet in her twentieth year. She was very beautiful⁴¹⁰ and she had lovely long hair and was dressed in an elegant kimono printed with a pattern representing distant mountains.⁴¹¹ A pretty maid fourteen or fifteen years old carrying a bundle wrapped in cloth accompanied her, and the pair looked drenched and bedraggled.⁴¹² When the young woman saw Toyoo, her face flushed with embarrassment, betraying her fine breeding.

Toyoo felt an impulsive stir of excitement, and he thought to himself, 'I've never heard of such a splendid lady living nearby. I suppose she has come from the capital on a journey to the Three Holy Places⁴¹³ and has decided to visit this area in order to enjoy the seaside. But it's certainly unusual that she has no man to accompany her.' He said, 'By all means, make yourself comfortable,' stepping back as he spoke. 'The rain should stop soon.'

'I hope you won't mind the intrusion,' said the young lady, and it being a small hut, the pair sat facing one another. The more Toyoo gazed on her, the more he was struck by her ethereal beauty.

'You appear to be of noble birth,' said Toyoo, utterly bewitched. 'Are you on a pilgrimage to the Three Holy Places, or on your way to the Minenoyu Hot Springs?⁴¹⁴ What can you find to admire by a barren coast such as this? After all, a poet of bygone days wrote:

| | |
|---|---|
| *Kurushikumo* | How painful it is, |
| *furi kuru ame ka* | This rain that pelts on me |
| *Miwa ga saki* | At Miwa's rugged cape, |
| *Sano no watari ni* | And by the Sano Crossing |
| *ie mo aranaku ni*[415] | No cottage appears in sight. |

That day must have been as dreary as this one. Even though this is a lowly hut, the master is indebted to my father, so rest yourself until the rain is over. Meantime, do you mind if I ask where you plan to stay tonight? It might appear improper for me to escort you, but you may certainly borrow my umbrella.'

'How generous of you,' the young lady replied. 'Your thoughtfulness makes me feel as if I were already dry.[416] I'm not from the capital, however. I have lived nearby for quite a while, and thinking that it was a splendid day, I went to Nachi[417] to pray. On my way home in my fright at this sudden shower I had no idea where I might seek shelter, and I inexplicably found myself here. My home isn't far away, and now that the downpour has let up somewhat, I must be going.'

'Do take the umbrella,' Toyoo urged, 'since the rain hasn't completely stopped. I'll get it sometime later. Please tell me where you live,[418] and I may send someone for it.'

'Around Shingū just ask anyone for Agata no Manago's house,' replied the young lady. 'It's growing dark, and I shall take advantage of your kindness and use this on my way.' Accepting the umbrella, she departed as Toyoo watched anxiously. He then borrowed a straw raincoat from his host and returned home.

Toyoo found himself unable to forget even the slightest detail of Manago's appearance. After a fitful night's sleep, toward dawn he dreamed of visiting her house. The entrance and the dwelling itself looked large and grand, with the shutters tightly drawn and the screens lowered, as though she lived in comfort and elegance. Manago emerged to greet him, saying, 'I couldn't forget your kindness, and I was hoping that you might come. Please enter,' and leading him inside, she served him wine and various fruits until he felt pleasantly intoxicated.

She furnished him a pillow, and they lay down together. When Toyoo awoke from his dream, he found that it was morning.

'If only it were true!' he thought, and completely forgetting about breakfast, he went out, disturbed and agitated, and he walked to the village of Shingū, where he repeatedly inquired for Agata no Manago's palace. No one, however, knew where it was, and afternoon came[419] while he was still searching laboriously. Then he noticed Manago's young maidservant walking toward him from the east.

'Where does your mistress live?' Toyoo asked, rejoicing to see her. 'I thought that I'd come by for the umbrella.'

'How kind of you,' replied the maid, with a smile. 'Please follow this way,' and presently she led him to an imposing gate in front of a spacious dwelling and said to him, 'here is where we live.' The building corresponded in every detail, down to the tightened shutters and the lowered screens, to the palace he had seen in his dream, and he marvelled at this as he entered.

'The gentleman who lent us the umbrella has called, and I have brought him here,' the maid announced, hurrying inside.

'Where is he? Show him in,' said Manago, as she appeared.

'I'm sorry to bother you,' said Toyoo, 'but I was on my way to visit Master Abe, who has been my teacher for several years, and thinking that I might pick up the umbrella and return it to him, I decided to stop by. Now that I know where you live, I'll call again sometime,' and he seemed determined to withdraw.

Manago, however, demanded that he remain and said, 'Maroya, don't let him go.'

'Didn't you urge us to take the umbrella?' said the maid, blocking Toyoo's way.[420] 'Now in exchange we insist that you stay here,' and she took him to the southern front room,[421] where floor mats had been arranged. The curtains,[422] the articles in the cabinet,[423] and the design on the drapery[424] were all of the best quality and classical fashion and marked the owner of the house as no commoner.

'It so happens that my husband has died,' said Manago, reappearing, 'and therefore I can't entertain you with a proper feast, but at least let me offer you a cup of poor wine.'

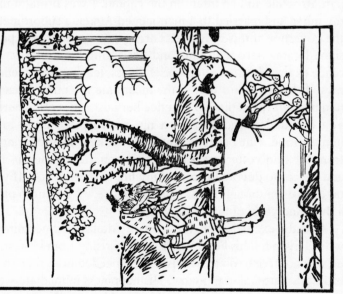

vii The Lust of the White Serpent: (1) Manago and Maroya in their
human form leap into the cascade and disappear

Tall dishes and flat dishes of exquisite taste, each filled with delicacies from the sea and the mountains, and ceramic cups with a jar of wine were all set before him, after which Maroya began to serve the food and drink. Toyoo was beside himself with wonder and could hardly believe all that was taking place. Guest and host alike became flushed with wine, and as Manago raised her cup to Toyoo, her features looked as lovely as a garland of cherry blossoms[425] reflected in the water; a smile rippled on her lips like a spring breeze, and her voice sounded as sweet as a nightingale soaring and flitting among the trees.[426]

'Although it embarrasses me very much, there is something that I must tell you,'[427] she proceeded to say. 'After all, if I were not truthful and consequently fell ill, what innocent god might have to endure unjust accusations?[428] Even though I frankly reveal my feelings towards you, you mustn't take me to be inconstant in my affections[429] – on the contrary. I lost both of my parents while still an infant in the capital. I was brought up by my nurse and married to a man named Agata, a subordinate to the governor of this province. Three years have already passed since I came here with him, and this spring before his term of office expired he died after a brief illness, leaving me to fend for myself. I have heard that in the meantime my nurse became a nun and left the capital to practice her austerities elsewhere, so you can understand that even my native place is no longer home to me. But because you were so kind in sheltering me from the rain yesterday, I know that you are a generous man, and I want to devote the rest of my life to serving you. If you'll take me even though I was married before,[430] I want to pledge a thousand years of love with you.'

Already excited with the idea of Manago's becoming his wife, Toyoo felt his heart stir as if a bird rising from its nest. But he was not free to do as he wished: he needed his father and his brother's permission to marry. His happiness immediately gave way to sorrow, and he said nothing to Manago.[431]

Obviously upset, Manago hurriedly added, 'I'm ashamed that I can't take back what I said. I shouldn't have shown what foolish ideas I have in my poor heart. It was a terrible mistake of me to cause you so much distress, and I wish that I could call on the sea to rise and cover me.[432] Although I meant everything I said, think of it as the result of the wine's heat. Let us forget about the whole matter.'

'I thought from the start,' Toyoo replied, 'that you came from a good family in the capital, and now I see that I was right. It's unbelievable that someone raised as I was along the lonely seashore visited mainly by whales should ever receive such an attractive proposal. But I couldn't answer you directly, because I'm dependent on my father and elder brother, and except for my skin and bones there is nothing that I can call my own. I have no prospects or resources to support you with, and I possess no special talent – all of which causes me great regret. But if you are willing to accept someone like me and suffer come what may, I shall love and cherish you forever. When one stumbles on the hill of love, as did even Confucius,[433] he forgets about both filial piety and his very life itself.'

'I'm delighted that you should make such a promise,' she said. 'In spite of my inadequacies, please come often and stay with me. Meantime, here is something that my former husband prized as a matchless treasure.[434] Keep it with you, always,' and she gave him a precious antique sword ornamented with gold and silver. Feeling that it would be unlucky to refuse such a gift at the beginning, Toyoo accepted the object.

'Tonight you must stay here with me,'[435] Manago implored, but Toyoo replied,

'My father would punish me if I spent the night away without his permission. Tomorrow evening I'll find some pretext for coming,' and he took his leave. Toyoo again found himself unable to fall asleep before dawn.

Early in the morning when Tarō arose to oversee the fishermen[436] and passed by the partly open door to Toyoo's bedroom, he happened to glance inside. By the glow of the fading lamplight he caught a glimpse of the sword, which Toyoo had placed next to his pillow while he slept. 'How strange,' thought Tarō, with considerable apprehension, 'where did he ever get such a thing?' At the sound of his noisily opening the door all the way, Toyoo awoke.

'Did you call me?' he asked, seeing his brother.

'Why do you have that sword by your pillow?' Tarō said. 'It's improper to keep such an extravagant thing in a fisherman's house. If father finds out, you know what he'll say.'

'But I wasted no money on it. I didn't buy it,' protested Toyoo. 'Someone gave it to me yesterday,[437] and I merely brought it home.'

'How would anyone around here ever present you a treasure like this?' replied Tarō. 'In the past you've even wasted money on bothersome Chinese books, but because father rarely says anything to you, up till now I haven't complained either. If you expect to wear this sword on parade in the great shrine festival,[438] you must be out of your mind!' he shouted, raising his voice so loudly that their father heard.

'What has the wastrel done this time?' said the father. 'Tarō, send him in to me.'

'I don't know where on earth he got it,' Tarō replied, 'but Toyoo bought a shiny sword, such as a general might have, and that's no good. You should ask him about it and get to the bottom of things. I'll go and see that the fishermen aren't idle,' and so saying, he departed.

Then the mother called Toyoo and said, 'Why did you buy such a thing? All of our rice and money belongs to Tarō. What do you have that you can call your own? Every day we allow you to do as you wish, but if you continue to make Tarō angry, where under the sun could you ever find a place to live? As someone who has had the benefit of education, why can't you understand that much?'

'But really,[439] mother, I didn't buy it,' Toyoo said. 'A certain person gave it to me, for a reason, and when Tarō saw it, he falsely accused me.'

'What did you do, then,' the father shouted, 'that someone should give you such a treasure? That makes the matter even worse. You'd better tell me all about it immediately.'

'But to explain it just now would be very embarrassing. I'd rather speak to someone else.'

'To whom can you tell anything that you won't say to your elder brother or to me ?' said the father, with irritation.

At this point, Tarō's wife, who was also present, restored the calm by taking Toyoo aside, reassuring him, 'Although I may not be able to help, come and explain things to me.'

'Even before Tarō found the sword and raised a fuss,' said Toyoo to his sister-in-law, 'I had wanted to talk to you privately and tell you about what happened, but meantime I'm already in trouble. Actually, I got the blade from a young lady who is living alone and has asked me if I would look after her. But I'm completely at a loss, because I have no experience, and if I became involved without permission, I'd be mercilessly disowned. Please try to understand.'

His sister-in-law smiled at him and said, 'I've always thought it a pity that you aren't married, and I'm happy for your sake. Although it may be beyond my power,440 I'll try to convey your feelings to the others.'

That night when she explained the situation to Tarō she said, 'Don't you agree that this is good news ? I hope that you'll do your best to convince father.'

'I don't like the idea,' replied Tarō, obviously upset. 'I've never heard of anyone by the name of Agata in the service of the governor of this province, and we should certainly have learned of such a person's death, considering that father is the headman of the village. But first of all, go and bring me the sword.' She immediately carried it in, and after examining it carefully, Tarō sighed and said in a worried voice, 'This is terrible. Recently, a great minister in the capital offered prayers and donated many valuable objects to our shrine, but it seems that these sacred treasures have suddenly disappeared from the storehouse, and the head priest has reported the theft to the governor of the province. In order to find the thief the governor has commanded his deputy, Bunya no Hiroyuki, to go to the head priest's mansion, and I know that they've been working hard on the case. This sword is certainly not the sort of

object a petty official would use. We must show it to father.'
Taking the weapon to his father,[441] he explained matters and
said, 'In such a horrifying predicament, have you anything to
suggest?'

'What a dreadful thing to happen!' said the father, his face
turning pale. 'Up till now Toyoo has never stolen so much as a
single hair.[442] Through what sin of ours should he turn to such
evil?[443] But if anyone else reports him, it will mean the end of
our entire house. For the sake of our ancestors and descendants,
we can't be sentimental over an unfilial son. Turn him in tomorrow.'[444]

First thing in the morning, Tarō went to the head priest's
mansion to tell what had happened and present the sword for
examination. The head priest said in amazement, 'Yes, this is
the same blade that the nobleman gave to us.'

'We must question him about the other lost goods,' said the
governor's deputy when he was informed, 'so arrest the suspect,'
and dispatching ten warriors, he had Tarō show them the way.
Meanwhile, unaware of these events, Toyoo was reading when
the warriors burst in to take him away.

'What have I done?' he protested, though in vain, as they
placed him in bonds, while the father, the mother, Tarō, and
the sister-in-law stood by in confusion and sorrow over such
misfortune.

'The court has summoned you,' said one of the warriors.
'Hurry up, move,' and forming a cordon around the prisoner,
they escorted him to the head priest's mansion,[445] where the
deputy glared at Toyoo.

'By stealing a sacred treasure,' he said, 'you have committed
a terrible crime. Now confess in full where you have hidden the
remainder of your loot.'

'I haven't stolen anything!' Toyoo sobbed, as he began to
understand the reason for the inquiry. 'The widow of a man
named Agata gave me the sword, saying that it had belonged
to her deceased husband. Please summon her, and she will
explain that it's all a mistake.'

'There has been no one in our service by the name of Agata,' said the deputy, growing more angry. 'Lying will only make your punishment harsher.'

'When you've arrested me and have me at your mercy,' said Toyoo, 'how can I lie? I beg of you, please call the woman and ask her.'

Turning to the warriors, the deputy sputtered, 'Where is this Agata no Manago's house? Make the prisoner show you, and arrest the woman.'

The warriors acknowledged the command and forced Toyoo to lead them to Manago's palace, but when the troop arrived there, Toyoo discovered that the once-imposing pillars of the entrance[446] were rotted, and most of the tiling had fallen and lay smashed, and from the eaves dense *shinobu* grass hung down, altogether lending the place an appearance of being deserted. Toyoo stood utterly dumbfounded[447] at the sight, while warriors ran about rounding up the people in the immediate neighbourhood, and presently an old woodcutter, a rice-pounder, and others assembled, bowing down in fear.

'Who lives in this house?' the captain demanded of them. 'Is it true that this dwelling belongs to the wife of a man by the name of Agata?'

'I have never heard of a person by such a name,' replied an old smith, coming forward and kneeling. 'Until three years ago a man named Suguri used to reside here in very prosperous circumstances, and then he sailed to Tsukushi[448] with a shipload of merchandise. The vessel was lost, and his family, which he had left behind in the house, were scattered, and since then no one has lived here. But yesterday the man accompanying you entered the property and stayed there for quite a while, as the old lacquer-maker told me, thinking it very suspicious.'

'In that case,' said the captain, 'search the house thoroughly, so we can report to the deputy.' Pushing the gate open, the warriors entered, and proceeding inside they found that the dwelling itself was in even greater ruin than the exterior. They advanced to the main quarters, and in the spacious garden, once magnificently landscaped, they saw a dried-up pond with a few withered water plants, and in the tangled thickets, which had grown wild, a large pine tree lay sprawled,[449] toppled by the wind – a most desolate sight. As the warriors opened the shutters to the main hall, a foul stench came forth, overcoming all who were present and causing them to fall back in horror. Toyoo watched, speechless and with heavy heart.

Among the warriors, one named Kose no Kumagashi, a brave and robust soul, shouted, 'Come men, follow me!' and tramping with a loud clatter across the floor boards, he charged forward. A full inch of dust lay accumulated, and rat feces were scattered everywhere. Amid the ruins there hung curtains behind which sat a young lady, as still and lovely as a lotus-blossom.

'The governor of the province summons you,' said Kumagashi, facing the woman. 'Come at once!'

She gave no answer, and just as he advanced nearer, intending to seize her, a clap of thunder resounded; before they had any chance to move, everyone was suddenly thrown to the ground as if the earth were rent. No sooner had this happened than the woman vanished without a trace. On the floor lay a glittering heap, which the warriors approached with the utmost caution and examined. They found it to contain objects such as Korean brocades, Chinese damask, twill bands, shields, halberds, quivers, and hoes – all part of the sacred treasure stolen from the shrine. After the warriors had taken these things back[450] with them and explained in detail about the strange happenings, both the deputy and the head priest realised that this was the work of the supernatural. They therefore sentenced Toyoo leniently, though he could not avoid being charged with the actual crime. He was remanded to the provincial office and cast into jail, but Tarō and his father were able to purchase his freedom, and following one hundred day's confinement, Toyoo was released. 'After what has happened, I'm ashamed to be seen around home,' he said to his father. 'May I visit elder sister in Yamato and stay at her place for a while?'

'Yes,' replied the father. 'Having gone through such a dreadful ordeal, there's some danger of your falling seriously ill. Go, and stay for several months,' and he provided him with an escort.

Toyoo's sister lived in the town of Tsuba[451] Market, where she had married a merchant named Tanabe no Kanetada. The couple welcomed Toyoo's visit and were sympathetic about his recent experience. 'Remain with us just as long as you wish,' Tanabe said, treating him with warm hospitality. The New Year came, and then the Second Month.[452]

Near Tsuba Market stood the Hase temple.[453] Among the various Buddhist deities[454] in Japan, the Goddess of Mercy of Hase had worked so many miracles that her renown had spread abroad to China.[455] From the capital, as well as the countryside, many pilgrims journeyed to the temple. In the spring they were especially numerous, and these worshippers always sought lodging in Tsuba Market. Therefore, the town boasted of many inns to accommodate these travellers, and because the Tanabes' house sold such items as incense, holy lamps, and wicks, their shop always bustled with people coming and going. One day, a beautiful lady and her maidservant appeared among the patrons. They were dressed as though on an incognito pilgrimage from the capital. 'Look, our master is here!' said the maid, noticing Toyoo. Stunned with surprise, Toyoo saw that it was Manago and Maroya, and uttering a cry of terror, he fled inside to conceal himself.

'What's the matter?' asked Kanetada and his wife.

'Those demons have followed me here. Don't go near them!' he said, frantically trying to find a place to hide, as everyone got excited and began asking, 'Where?'

'Please, there is nothing to grow alarmed at,' said Manago as she entered. 'Don't be afraid, husband dear. It pained me bitterly to discover that I was responsible for your being accused of a crime, and I tried to find out where you had gone, so that I might explain things and put your mind at ease.[456] I searched everywhere, and now that at last I've found you, I'm very happy. Listen to me, and think about what I say. If there were anything odd about me, do you imagine that I would appear in such a crowd of people and on such a lovely, calm day? My clothing has seams, and when I stand in the sunlight I have a shadow. Think it all over and decide for yourself – but you must, I beg of you.'

'I still can't believe that you're human,' said Toyoo, gradually regaining control over himself. 'After I was arrested and the warriors took me to your place, it was utterly changed. You sat amid the broken-down and dilapidated ruins – the sort of lair one would expect a goblin to inhabit – until the warriors tried to capture you, and then suddenly thunder came from out of the clear blue sky and you vanished without a trace. I saw it with my own eyes. Now you have followed me here. What are you going to do? Get out of here, at once!'

'I can understand why you feel this way,' said Manago, beginning to weep. 'But first you should listen to my side of the story, too. After I heard that the authorities had summoned you, I talked the matter over with an old man who lived nearby and for whom I had earlier done some favours, and he soon made the house look dilapidated and abandoned.[457] Maroya suggested the device of a thunderous noise when I was about to be arrested.

'Afterward, I found a ship and fled to Naniwa, but I wanted to learn what became of you and decided to place my trust in this temple. Here, where the twin fir trees[458] stand, to my great joy we have miraculously met as if carried by the same swift waters. No doubt it was owing to the great power and compassion of the Goddess of Mercy of Hase. As for the sacred treasures, how could a woman possibly steal such things? Most likely, it was an evil deed that my former husband did. Please think it over and try to understand just a little bit how much I love you,' and as she finished speaking, she broke down and wept inconsolably.

Toyoo was still suspicious, but he felt pity for her and lacked the strength to press the matter any further. Moreover, Kanetada and his wife were impressed by the sense of Manago's argument, and seeing how truly feminine her manner was, they harboured no doubts at all.

'When we heard Toyoo's story, we thought of what fearful things can happen in this world,' they said to Manago, 'but we

believe that in our day and age supernatural incidents are unlikely to occur. Because of your patient search and long vigil[459]
in looking for Toyoo we are happy to let you stay with us, even
though he may refuse to believe you,' and they gave her lodging. During the next day or two Manago endeared herself to
the Tanabes and did her best to get them to intercede with
Toyoo. The couple was so warmly delighted at her strength of
character that they finally persuaded Toyoo to consummate his
marriage.

Day by day, Toyoo's feelings toward Manago grew warmer,
and he came to love her and to admire her beauty as much as
before. He promised eternal devotion and was sorry only that
to enjoy their love they had to wait like the clouds[460] that
nightly form on Katsuragi's peaks and Mt Takama and with the
morning bells of Hase Temple release their rain.

Presently, the Third Month[461] arrived, and Kanetada
turned to Toyoo and his bride saying, 'Come, and let us make
an excursion! Although going to Yoshino might not be as
pleasant as visiting the capital, most people prefer it to the Kii
area. "Yoshino of lovely name,"[462] is magnificent in spring-
time. Mt Mifune[463] and the Natsumi River[464] offer endless
variety, and I'm sure you'll agree that it's the best season.

'I'd like to,' answered Manago with a smile. 'It's the place
about which they say,

When the good men of old,
Beheld it and saw it well . . .[465]

And I've heard that even people from the capital regret it[466]
when they can't visit Yoshino. But ever since I was a small girl,
being in crowded places or attempting long journeys on foot
has always made me ill; so, much though it saddens me I'm
afraid that I had better not go with you. I'd be grateful enough
if you'd bring me back a souvenir from the mountains.'

'No doubt it's the walking that makes you so ill,' protested
Kanetada and his wife. 'True, we have no carriage, but still we
shall by no means even let you step on the ground. If you were
to stay here, think of how much Toyoo would worry.'

'After brother and sister have spoken so persuasively,' Toyoo added, 'you must try to go, even though you don't feel up to it.'

Despite Manago's reluctance, the party set out, and although they saw many splendid people nothing could compare with Manago's exceptional beauty. Because Kanetada and his wife had close connections with a certain temple,[467] they went there to pray. The abbot welcomed them, saying, 'This spring you are late in coming to worship. Cherry-blossom season is more than half over and the nightingale's song may have lost some of its clear tone, but never mind – I'll find a good man to escort you about.' He set for them a frugal evening meal.[468]

On the next morning a heavy mist covered the sky, and as it began to clear one could look down from the high ground where the temple was situated and make out a number of scattered hermitages. The chirruping of the mountain birds sounded muffled and dim. Flowers and blooming trees abounded in great variety. The atmosphere in the mountain hamlet had an invigorating freshness. 'People on their first visit,' said the guide, 'usually enjoy the area around the cascades[469] most, because it offers the greatest number of interesting sights,' and he invited them to set out in that direction, descending a winding path into the valley. In ancient times an emperor's pleasure-palace[470] had stood here, and now they watched the young fish swim upstream[471] as the waters dashed through a gorge amid the rock-strewn rapids; they were delighted with the beauty of the fishes' dappled forms.

The party spread out their boxed lunches and were enjoying themselves as they ate. Then, walking over the rocks there appeared an old man with hair that looked as if it were tangled hempen yarn. Nevertheless, he moved his limbs in a lithe and agile stride. Pausing beneath the cascade, he trained a penetrating stare on the picnickers, and noticing him, Manago and Maroya turned to avoid his gaze. But the old man continued to glare at them.

'How strange,'[472] he said. 'You evil demons! Why must you bewitch people? How dare you remain right in front of my eyes?'

Upon his uttering these words, Manago and Maroya suddenly arose and leaped into the cascade.[473] A spout of water ascended, as if to the sky, and the two women disappeared. Clouds engulfed the party and as though spilling black India ink brought down a torrential deluge of rain, while the old man led the shocked and confused people back to the hamlet. They crouched under the eaves of a poor hut, feeling more dead than alive, and the old man turned to Toyoo and said, 'When I looked carefully at your face, I saw that those supernatural creatures were tormenting you, and if I hadn't rescued you, it would surely have cost you your life. In future you must be more cautious.'

Toyoo, stricken with fear, respectfully bowed his head to the ground and explained from the beginning what had happened, pleading, 'I beg you to save me.'

'Yes, I understand,' said the old man. 'These evil creatures are aged serpents.[474] Their nature is governed by lust. It is said that when they mate with a bull, they give birth to a unicorn, and when they cohabit with horses they produce dragon steeds. No doubt, they tricked you and began this dalliance because they found you fair to look upon. But in any case, since they have proven to be so stubborn,[475] I am afraid that you may still lose your life should you fail to take proper precautions.'

Hereupon, Toyoo and his companions felt all the more confused and frightened, and making obeisance to the old man, they said, 'You must be a living god.'

'I am no god, to be sure,' said the old man with a smile. 'I am a priest of the Yamato Shrine,[476] and my name is Tagima no Kibito. I shall be pleased to escort you back. Let us go,' and so saying he set out, with the others following behind.

The next day, Toyoo went to the village of Yamato to thank the old priest for his kindness, taking with him three rolls of Mino silk and two bales of Tsukushi cotton. 'Please free me from possession by these spirits,' he begged.

After accepting the gift, the old priest distributed the goods to the shrine attendants, without keeping any for himself, and he said to Toyoo, 'Those creatures took advantage of your fair looks and tempted you. But you, yourself, owing to a lack of courage and spirit,[477] fell victim to their temporary form. From now on if you act like a man and try to attain a more tranquil heart you will not need to depend on my power in order to get rid of such evil spirits. With all your might make your heart peaceful.' The old man's sincerity left a deep impression on Toyoo, who felt as if awakening from a dream,[478] and after profusely expressing his gratitude to the priest, he returned.

'Because I have failed to be true to my own self, I have allowed beasts to deceive me,' Toyoo said to Kanetada. 'I must learn my duty to my father and elder brother and stop taking advantage of your hospitality. I am grateful for all that you have done in my behalf, and I shall visit you again.' Thereafter, he went back to the province of Kii.

When they heard of the frightful events that had passed, his father, mother, Tarō, and his sister-in-law felt that Toyoo was not really to blame. But they were disturbed at the evil spirit's obstinacy. 'The trouble is probably that we have let you remain unmarried,' they said, coming to a decision. 'We shall find you a wife.'

In the hamlet of Shiba[479] there lived a man known as Shiba no Shōji,[480] head of the local manor. He had an only daughter, named Tomiko, who served as a palace girl at the Court, and requesting that she be excused from her employment, Shiba sent a matchmaker to the Ōya house and proposed that Toyoo become his son-in-law. Negotiations went well, and the betrothal date was set. In due course a messenger was dispatched to the capital to escort Tomiko home, and she returned with much joy.

Accustomed to serving in the great palace, where she had spent several years, Tomiko's manners were impeccable, her appearance splendid to behold,[481] and when Toyoo moved to the Shibas' home and saw her, he felt satisfied in every way with her remarkable charm. But there was something about her that reminded him of his previous love for Manago. The first night passed without any event. On the second night, however, after Toyoo became slightly intoxicated, he said, 'Now that you have spent several years in service at the palace, we country folk must strike you as decidedly boorish. While you were in the capital what captains, imperial advisors, and the like did you sleep with? It's very disconcerting to think about!'

Although Toyoo had spoken playfully, Tomiko suddenly straightened up and replied, 'You, who have forgotten your old promises[482] and have stooped to toy with a worthless common creature! It is your behaviour, on the contrary, that's disgusting.' Her appearance changed. The voice was unmistakably that of Manago.

Astonished to hear her, Toyoo was so struck with fear that his hair stood on end, and he knew not what to do. Noticing his consternation, Manago smiled and said, 'My dear, you mustn't be afraid. We have vowed to the oceans. We have pledged to the mountains. How can you forget so quickly, when it was ordained by fate that we should meet again. If you believe[483] what other people say and recklessly try to abandon me, I shall seek vengeance, and tall though the peaks of the mountains of the Kii High Road may be, your blood will drain from the ridges into the valleys. You must not be so rash as to throw away your life in vain.'

Toyoo trembled uncontrollably, as a man confronted with the prospect of immediate death.

'My lord,' came a voice from behind the screen, 'why are you so upset? This should be an occasion for rejoicing,' and so saying, Maroya appeared.

Upon seeing her, Toyoo fell into a swoon. His eyes closed, and he lay face downward. Manago and Maroya tried cajolery. They tried threats. They tried to bring him around by speaking in turns, but he remained unconscious until the night ended.

Presently, he escaped from the sleeping chamber and went to his father-in-law, saying in a low voice for fear of being overheard, 'Something terrible has happened,' and after explaining he pleaded, 'What can we do about it? Please think of something.'

Shiba and his wife turned pale and lamented, 'But what can we do? There is, however, a priest from the Kurama temple,[484] outside the capital, who ever year makes a pilgrimage to Kumano, and since yesterday he has been staying at a cloister on a nearby mountain. He is a holy man who knows many kinds of exorcism[485] and whose prayers have been eminently successful against plagues, locusts, and evil influence; people around here show him great respect. Let us consult with him.' Shiba lost no time in sending word, and the priest soon arrived.

After learning of what had come to pass, the priest, who was quite confident of himself, said, 'To capture these creatures that resort to witchcraft presents little difficulty. There's no need at all for you to worry.' He made it sound so simple that everyone felt relieved.

First, the priest asked for some sulphur. Then he mixed it with medicine water and placed the solution in a small flask. As he moved toward the sleeping chamber everyone recoiled in horror, but the priest laughed at them and said, 'All of you, old and young alike, wait here, and I'll catch the serpents and show them to you.'

No sooner did he open the door of the sleeping chamber, than a demon thrust its head out at the priest. The projecting extremity was so huge that it filled the doorway, gleaming even whiter than newly fallen snow, with eyes like mirrors and horns like the bare boughs of a tree. The creature opened its mouth more than three feet wide; its crimson tongue darted, as if to swallow the priest in a single gulp.

'Horror!' cried the holy man, as he dropped the flask[486] that he held in his hand. His legs no longer able to support him, he fell over backwards and crawled away, barely managing to escape.

'It's awful. The creature is a god of evil; my prayers are useless. If I hadn't got away on hands and knees, I'd surely have lost my life,' he said, losing consciousness. Shiba and the others tried to help him regain his senses, but poisonous vapours[487] seemed to have attacked him. His face and body were mottled red and black, as though he were stained with dye, and he felt as hot to touch as a bonfire. Later, his eyes alone had power to move, and although it looked as if he wished to speak, he was

viii  The Lust of the White Serpent: (2) Toyoo becomes slightly intoxicated and discovers that the serpent's jealous spirit has entered Tomiko's
body

unable to utter a sound. They kept sponging him with water, but in the end he died. Each of those who saw the priest pass away wailed in confusion and felt as if his own soul might depart from his body.

Toyoo eventually managed to pull himself together enough to say, 'Even the prayers of this most eminent priest have failed. Because the beasts pursue me with such tenacity, they'll seek me out as long as I remain flesh and blood. There is no use causing pain to others for the sake of my life alone. From now on I'll speak to you no more of this matter, and you mustn't worry,' and so saying, he went toward the sleeping chamber.

'Has the demon caused you to lose your mind?'488 asked his father- and mother-in-law. But paying no heed to them, Toyoo approached the room. Quietly, he entered. Manago and Maroya sat facing one another. There was no sign of anything unusual.

'Whatever possessed you to ask someone to try to seize me?' said Manago, turning to Toyoo. 'If you ever again spitefully seek to get rid of us, not only will you give up your life, but I will also make certain that every person in this community shall come to grief. Be thankful rather over our constancy to you and, really, don't ever again behave in such a fickle way.'

Although Toyoo was now repelled by her affectionate tone, he replied, 'I have heard tell of a proverb that says, "Even if a man does not intend to injure a tiger, the beast may still attack the man." Your heart is not human. You've trapped me and brought me trouble again and again. It's frightful that our passing affair should lead you to be so vindictive. I understand that you love me the way a real person would, but why should we stay here and cause other people grief? You must at least spare Tomiko's life.489 Then you may take me anywhere.' Full of joy at hearing such words, Manago nodded in assent.

Arising and withdrawing from the room, Toyoo said to his father-in-law, 'The dreadful creatures will continue to follow me, and it would be heartless of me to remain here and bring you additional suffering. If you will let me go, I think that you will no longer find your daughter's life to be in danger.'

Shiba, however, was adamant in his refusal, saying, 'My

ancestors were warriors, I'll have you know, and I'd be ashamed of what your father's family would think, should I act so spinelessly. I have a better idea. In Komatsubara,[490] at the Dōjōji temple, there lives a revered and venerated priest named Abbot Hōkai. I've heard that old age[491] prevents him from going abroad, but should I ask him, he won't let me down,' and the father-in-law hurried off at once on horseback.

Owing to the long way, it was already the middle of the night before Shiba reached the temple. The old abbot crawled out of the monastery's sleeping quarters, and after listening to the story, he said, 'Yes, it does sound dreadful. I am now rather forgetful – I hardly remember how to work my cures, but I could never ignore a misfortune in your house! You go back now, and I'll come later.' He brought out a monk's robe, which had been saturated in mustard-seed incense,[492] and gave it to Shiba, saying, 'Gently lure one of the beasts to you. Then take this cloak and throw it swiftly over her head and hold the garment down with all your might. If you show the slightest weakness, they are quite likely to escape. Keep your wits about you,' he concluded, 'and do your task well.'

Shiba was delighted as he mounted his horse and galloped home. Secretly, he called Toyoo and gave him the monk's robe and said, 'Carefully do as Abbot Hōkai instructed.' Hiding the garment inside his clothing, Toyoo went to the sleeping chamber.

'Father has given us permission to leave. Come, let us depart at once,' he said, and taking advantage of Managō's pleasure over the idea, he drew out the monk's robe, cast it over her and held it down with all his strength.

'Stop! You're hurting me,' Managō shouted. 'How can you be so heartless. Let me go!' But Toyoo pressed down even harder, exerting his full power, and soon afterward Abbot Hōkai arrived by palanquin. The servants helped him to alight and showed him to the chamber, where he intoned prayers in a solemn chant. At last, he told Toyoo to step back.

Abbot Hōkai removed the robe, and there lay Tomiko, unconscious, with a white serpent more than three feet in length[493] coiled motionlessly on her breast. The old abbot picked up the snake and put it in an iron urn, which his disciple held. He recited additional prayers, and from behind the screen there crawled a small serpent about a foot long, which he also placed in the urn. Thereupon, he took the incensed robe, fastened it tightly around the urn, and departed in his palanquin as everyone clasped hands and wept profusely, paying their respects to the holy man.

After returning to the temple, Abbot Hōkai ordered a deep pit to be dug in front of the main hall, and he commanded that the urn be buried for all time[494] to prevent the spirits' further appearance on earth. It is said that the serpents' mound remains to this day.

According to tradition, Shiba's daughter, Tomiko, never recovered and eventually died, but Toyoo lived on in good health.

# VOLUME FIVE
## VIII THE BLUE HOOD
### (Aozukin)[495]

I

Long ago there lived a holy man of great virtue whose name was Kaian Zenji.[496] While still young he studied the principles of Zen Buddhism,[497] and he always loved to travel with the clouds and the water. One summer after fulfilling his devotions[498] at the Ryūtaiji temple[499] in the province of Mino, Kaian set out on a journey, deciding to spend autumn in the far north. He passed through the province of Shimotsuke along the way, and one evening he found himself in the hamlet of Tomita.[500] He approached a large and obviously affluent house and intended to seek lodging for the night, when some men returning from the fields saw him in the gathering darkness.

'Look! The mountain demon has come. Rise up everybody!' they cried in alarm.

The house was immediately filled with tumult and shouting. The women and children screamed and wailed, falling over one another as they sought to hide. The master of the house took up a heavy staff[501] and came running out, whereupon he saw the old mendicant, Kaian, who was almost in his fiftieth year, wearing on his head a blue-dyed hood. He was clothed in tattered black robes, and he carried a pack on his back.

'Oh, patron of Buddha,'[502] said Kaian, greeting the master with his Zen rod, 'why have you armed yourself thus? I am a wandering priest, and I was expecting someone to appear so that I might beg for a night's lodging, but it's quite a surprise for me to find myself such an object of suspicion. A skinny teacher of the law is hardly apt to turn to banditry. You have no need to fear.'

The master threw aside his staff, clapped his hands, and laughed, 'I threatened so holy a guest only because those peasants foolishly mistook you for someone else. I shall be happy to put you up for the night to make up for what I did.' He apologised, and welcomed Kaian into the house, graciously offering him food and showering him with hospitality.

'Earlier, when the peasants saw you and grew frightened, saying that you were a devil,' the master of the house explained, 'they did so with good reason. Although it involves a horrifying story, I might as well tell it to you.

'On the mountain above this village[503] there stands a temple that used to be the family chapel of the Oyama[504] house, and for generations priests of great merit dwelt in it. The most recent abbot was the adopted son of an important person, and he had a wide reputation for being highly learned and virtuous. The people of this province took him incense and candles and showed their faith and trust; he was even a frequent visitor at my house, and his behaviour was always proper – that is until last spring, when he was invited to be the presiding priest at a baptism[505] in Koshi.[506] After staying there for more than a hundred days, he brought back with him as his companion day and night a young lad in his twelfth or thirteenth year. Because the youth was so good-looking, the abbot fell deeply in love with him, and as time went on he began to neglect his regular duties.

'Then in about the Fourth Month of this year the boy came down with a minor illness. Within several days, however, his condition grew serious, and the distressed abbot summoned an eminent court physician from the provincial capital. It was useless – the boy finally died.[507] The jewel of the abbot's heart had been snatched away, and he felt like a man whose headdress has been shorn of its flowers by the wind. He wept until tears failed him, and he wailed until his voice gave out. So great was his grief that instead of having the body cremated or interred he pressed himself to it day after day, cheek against cheek, hand intertwined with hand.

'In the end he went mad. He played with the boy just as he

ix   The Blue Hood: Men returning from the fields flee from the sight of
the demon monk

had done while the youth was alive. Then, refusing to allow the body to rot and decay, he sucked the flesh and licked the bones until he utterly devoured it. "The abbot has turned into a devil," the people in the temple said, and they all fled. From that time on the abbot began to terrorise the people by coming down night after night to dig up graves in search of fresh cadavers, which he eats. I've heard the old stories about demons, but just think of the problem that we are actually facing. As matters stand, every house is tightly boarded up at sundown, and word has already spread throughout the province. People are unwilling to venture this way. Now you can see why[508] we mistook you for him. What can we do to stop him?'

'Such strange things that happen in this world' exclaimed Kaian, upon hearing this story. 'Some creatures though born as human beings never learn the greatness of the teachings of the Buddhas and Bodhisattvas and dwell to the end of their days in malice and ignorance. Their salvation is prevented through personal greed and spite, and they assume forms from a previous existence. They then try to spend their fury by becoming demons or serpents or by placing curses on people. Since time immemorial there have been so many such instances that they are beyond count. There is no doubt that a person who is still living can indeed change into a demon. A lady in waiting to the King of Ch'u[509] turned into a snake. Wang Han's mother became a ghoul and Squire Wu's wife, a moth.

'Also, there was once a monk who stopped for the night in a lowly peasant's hut. It was raining and the wind howled while he lay awake without even a lamp to comfort him in his loneliness. As the night deepened he thought that he heard the bleating of a sheep, and soon afterwards something kept sniffing at him as if to test whether he was asleep. Disquieted, he took his Zen rod,[510] which he had placed by his pillow, and struck hard, whereupon the creature screamed and fell on the spot. Because of the fuss the old mistress of the house lit a lamp and came to see what had happened, and they found a young woman lying there unconscious. The old woman, weeping, begged him to spare the girl. What could he do? He left and went on his way, but later, when he again chanced to pass through the same village, many people were gathered in the fields to watch something. "What's going on?" asked the monk, advancing closer. "They've taken a woman who has turned into a witch," replied a villager, and they're about to bury her alive."

'So goes the tale. But all of these cases are about women. Probably because of the malice in their nature females readily turn into vicious demons. I've never heard of any example involving a man. To be sure, there was Ma Shu-mou,[511] minister to Yang Ti of Sui, who liked the flesh of children and secretly kidnapped youngsters in order to have them steamed and served as food. But his behaviour, however barbaric it was, differed from what you have described. In any case, if your monk has turned into a ghoul, it must be owing to his past karma. After all, his constant piety,[512] his devotion, and his service to the Buddhas were the epitome of reverence, so he would certainly have been an ideal priest had he not taken in the youth. Quite likely, once he descended into the sinful path[513] of lust and covetousness, he was changed into a demon, and he fell victim to the flames of the fires in the hell of delusion. This probably came to pass because of his self-righteous and arrogant nature. There is a saying, "A slothful mind creates a monster, a rigorous one enjoys the fruit of the Buddha."[514] This monk is an example. If I could transform his spirit and bring the man back to his original self,' Kaian concluded with a fitting resolution, 'it might be an appropriate way to repay you for tonight's hospitality.'

'If you were to do that,' said the master of the house, bowing his head low on the floor and weeping tears of joy, 'it would mean the salvation of the people of this province.' No bells or trumpets could be heard in the dwelling in the mountain village, and as the moon, which had passed its twentieth night, rose and shone through the crannies in the old door, Kaian's host realised how late it had grown. 'It is time to say goodnight,' he said, withdrawing to his room.[515]

## II

At the mountain cloister there remained no sign of habitation. The towering gate was smothered with brambles and thorns.[516] The sutra hall stood empty and covered with moss. Spiders had spread their webs across the Buddhist statuary, and the altar, where burnt offerings had once been made was overlaid with swallow droppings. The main chamber and the living quarters exuded an eerie sense of desolation. As the sun sank, around the hour of the monkey,[517] Kaian Zenji entered the temple and knocked with his staff.

'Please lend a night's lodging to a monk on a pilgrimage,' he shouted repeatedly. But there came no reply. Then from the sleeping chamber a shrivelled monk emerged and advanced feebly.

'Where are you on your way to, that you have come here?' croaked the monk in a hoarse murmur. 'There is a reason why this temple has fallen into decay. It is now deserted, and I have no food[518] whatsoever to give you to eat. Neither can I furnish you with a night's lodging. Return quickly to the village.'

'I've come from the province of Mino,' replied Kaian, 'and I am travelling to Michinoku.[519] As I passed through the village below, the charm of the mountains and the cascading water caught my fancy, and before I knew it here I was. The sun is already sinking and to go back now[520] would take a long time. I beg of you, let me stay for the night.'

'In desolate places like this evil things sometimes happen,' said the monk. 'I can't force you to remain. Nor can I compel you to leave. You may do as you please,' and he spoke no more.

Kaian likewise asked no further questions, and he seated himself beside the monk. Presently, the sun set. Then the darkest part of the night came. Without a lamp it was impossible to distinguish even nearby objects, and the roar of the stream in the valley sounded close at hand. The local monk retired to his sleeping room, making no further sound.

As night deepened, the moon arose and shone with a pure, gem-like brightness that penetrated everywhere. At what Kaian took to be about half past the hour of the rat,[521] the monk appeared from his room and frantically began to shout for his visitor. When he received no reply, he screamed in desperation, 'Baldpate! Where are you hiding? You were right here before.'

He repeatedly ran past the spot where Kaian was seated, but he was apparently unable to see him. The monk then dashed off, as if toward the main hall, but he stopped in the garden.[522] He circled there frantically until he collapsed, as if in exhaustion from a dance, unable to rise.

When daybreak came and the morning sun rose, the monk awoke as if from a drunken stupor. Seeing Kaian in the very place he left him, the monk was overcome with astonishment. He leaned against a pillar and gave a deep sigh, unable to speak.

'What is grieving you?' said Kaian, as he approached him. 'If you are hungry, use my flesh to fill your stomach.'

'Do you mean to tell me that you have been here all night?' the monk finally asked.

'I stayed here, and I did not sleep,' replied Kaian.

'Disgraceful though it is to say,' said the monk, 'I devour human flesh. But I have never touched a Buddha's body, and you are in truth a Buddha. With the dim eyes of a fiendish beast, how natural it was that I could not see you or recognise the coming of a living Buddha. I am struck with awe.' He lowered his head and stood there in silence.

'According to what I have heard from the villagers,' said Kaian, 'one encounter with lust was enough to poison your heart and make you fall into the ways of demons and beasts. Your condition is disgraceful[523] and lamentable and points to an evil fate of unusual magnitude. Because you have gone down to the village night after night and caused the people harm, no one in the local community feels safe. I learned what was going on, and feeling obliged to do something, I came here to persuade you to try to change back to your former self. Will you pay attention to my instructions or not?'

'You are in truth a living Buddha,' said the monk. 'Teach me without delay how I can escape my horrible fate.'

'If you want to listen, then come here,' said Kaian.

He made the abbot sit on a flat rock in front of the veranda, and he removed the blue-dyed hood that he himself wore, placing it over the monk's head. From *The Songs of Experience* he gave him the following stanza:

> Upon the bay the moonlight glows,
> Among the pines the breezes sough.
> Through the night pure darkness flows,
> And who among us can tell how?[524]

'Without leaving this spot you must meditate quietly,' he said, and when you have the meaning of the verse, you will of your own accord rediscover the true mind of a Buddha.' And after he had thus gently instructed the monk, Kaian went down the mountain.

From this time on, the villagers, it may be said, were free from serious misfortune. They remained suspicious and afraid, however, because no one knew whether the monk was living or dead,[525] and they forbade anyone to climb the mountain.

One year soon elapsed, and during the following winter, at the beginning of the Godless Month,[526] Kaian again passed by, this time on his return from the far north. He called at the house where he had previously received a night's lodging and asked for news about the monk.

'Because of your great virtue,' the master said, rejoicing to see him again, 'the devil no longer comes down here, and we all feel as though we have been reborn in paradise. Nevertheless, we are still afraid to go up the mountain, and no one so much as tries it; we really don't know what has happened. But surely, he can't be still alive. While you're staying here tonight, please pray for the salvation of his soul, and all of us will join you.'

'In the event that the monk has been transfigured and gained salvation for himself,' said Kaian, 'I must respect him as a master who has preceded me in finding enlightenment. On the other hand, as long as he lives, he remains one of my disciples. I must find out what has happened.'

So Kaian once again climbed the mountain. Every sign marked[527] the way as untravelled, and he could hardly believe that this was the same route he had followed the year before. Within the temple grounds the grass and weeds stood taller than Kaian himself, and the dew drenched him as though autumn rains were falling.[528] It was impossible to tell which way the path led,[529] and here and there doors had been blown from the buildings and lay broken. Along the veranda that encircled the scullery and the monks' quarters, water had formed puddles, pieces of floorboard had begun to rot, and moss was growing.

When he looked by the side of the veranda where he had ordered the abbot to sit, Kaian saw the shadow-like wraith of a man, so covered with unkempt beard and tangled hair that one could scarcely tell if he were priest or layman. Motionless amid the clumps of burdock and grass that bent beneath him, the man was murmuring in a thin voice, no louder than the buzzing of a mosquito, almost inaudibly, but Kaian could intermittently recognise the chant:

> Upon the bay the moonlight glows,
> Among the pines the breezes sough.
> Through the night pure darkness flows,
> And who among us can tell how?

Kaian watched for a while, and then grasping his Zen rod firmly, he shouted,

'Well, can you tell how?' And with a gutteral cry, he struck the monk on the head.

Suddenly, as frost that meets the morning sun,[530] the figure vanished, leaving only the blue hood and a skeleton lying in the weeds. At this instant the monk probably overcame his stubborn attachment to evil. Surely a divine principle was in operation.

Afterward, Kaian's great power became known beyond the clouds and over the seas. 'The spirit of the founder[531] still endures,' people sang in praise. The villagers gathered together, cleaned up the temple, and had it restored. They entreated

Kaian to establish himself there, after which he changed its former affiliation with the Shingon sect[532] and founded a holy place of Sōtō[533] Zen. This temple still stands today, prosperous and venerated.

# IX   WEALTH AND POVERTY
## *(Himpuku-ron)*

In the province of Mutsu[534] in the retinue of Gamō Ujisato[535] there served a warrior by the name of Oka Sanai.[536] His stipend was large. He was widely respected, and his bravery was renowned everywhere east of the barrier.[537] But this samurai behaved indecorously in one detail.[538] His ambition for wealth and rank far exceeded that of the normal military man. Frugality was his guiding principle, and since he made it the watchword of his household he grew rich with the passing years. Whenever he earned a brief respite from his military duties, he found pleasure not in the tea ceremony or burning incense, but rather in his council chamber, where he would spread out many pieces of gold. The satisfaction that he gained from its display exceeded the joy that most people got from moon-viewing parties and picnics under the cherry-blossoms. People frowned on Sanai's behaviour and thought him miserly and boorish. They looked on him with scorn and shunned his company.

Once having heard that a man who had long been employed in his house secretly kept a bar of gold, Sanai summoned him and said,

'In an age of disorder even a jewel from the Kunlun Mountain[539] is worth little more than a tile or a stone. For a person born in times like ours, when one must live by bow and arrow, a T'ang-hsi or Mo-yang blade[540] would certainly be a treasure worth possessing. Still, even with a good sword one warrior can hardly face a host of a thousand men. But the power of money allows a man to control all the people of the empire. A warrior, therefore, must not use money irresponsibly, but rather he ought to save it. Your accumulating wealth beyond the expectations of a man of humble position[541] is a fine achievement. You shall be rewarded.'

Sanai gave him ten *ryō*[542] in gold, bestowed on him a sword, and took him into his personal service.

As word of this incident spread, people changed their minds and said, 'Sanai isn't the sort of fellow who hoards money from greed or lust. He's merely eccentric.'

The same night that he rewarded his servant, Sanai awoke at the sound of someone near his bedside, and he found by the foot of his lamp a dwarfed old man, smiling as he stood there. Sanai propped himself high on his pillow and without betraying the least sign of alarm said:

'Who are you? If you come to "borrow" supplies from me, you had better have a troop of strong men with you. But when a doddering old specimen like you appears to break my sleep, there is either a fox or a badger at work. What tricks do you know? Show me something to amuse me on this long autumn night.'

'I come to you,' the figure replied, 'as neither an evil spirit nor a human being. I am the apparition of the gold that you have accumulated, and in gratitude[543] for the kindness with which you have treated me through the years, I wish to talk with you tonight. That is why I have appeared.

'I was pleased that you rewarded your servant today, and thinking that I might be able to entertain you with my thoughts, I've assumed a temporary form. Even if most of what I say is tedious prattle, long silence has made me feel somewhat bombastic, so I decided to reveal myself to you and disturb your sleep.

'To be sure, the great sage, Confucius, taught us that the rich need not be haughty.[544] Really, prejudiced remarks such as,

"Wealthy men are always stingy and almost invariably stupid,"[545] only apply to those like Shih Ch'ung of Chin and Wang Yüan-pao of T'ang,[546] who, admittedly did behave like beasts or reptiles. Affluent men of old[547] earned their wealth in a natural way – through timely action. They wisely attended to heaven's chances and earth's opportunities. When the Grand Duke Wang was enfeoffed in Ch'i[548] and trained the citizens in various occupations, people from the seaside rushed to his court to share in the benefits. Kuan Chung nine times called conferences of the feudal lords,[549] and though he was only a court minister himself, his wealth exceeded that of the ruler of a great state. Men such as Fan Li, Tzu-kung, and Po Kuei[550] traded in commodities and worked for profit,[551] amassing a fortune in gold. Ssu-ma Ch'ien wrote of these men in his "Biographies of the Money-Lenders,"[552] but later scholars contemptuously reproached him.[553] These men however, showed little understanding of the way things really are.

'Without a steady livelihood no man can feel satisfied.[554] Farmers work to grow grain. Artisans help them by making useful objects. Merchants strive to distribute their products. Everyone practices his occupation to increase the wealth of his house, to venerate his ancestors, and to provide for his descendants. What more can one ask of a person? Consider some of the sayings: "A man with a thousand weights of gold does not die in the market place."[555] "The rich man and the king enjoy the same pleasures."[556] No one can deny that fish are plentiful in deep pools and animals abundant on great mountains.[557] It's the natural way of heaven.

'But one also comes across phrases such as, "cheerful though poor."[558] Scholars, statesmen, and poets have easily been led to confusion. In our own day, for example, brave men whose business is with bows and arrows have forgotten that wealth forms the cornerstone of the nation, and they have followed a disgusting policy. By killing and maiming people[559] they have sacrificed their own virtue and murdered their own descendants. Their error has been to put too little value on fortune and too much emphasis on fame.

'Do you realise that there need be no contradiction between the pursuit of fame and the quest for fortune? People who become bound by empty words and who underestimate the power of money often repeat cant about "purity" and speak of the wisdom of hermits who take up farming and withdraw from society. Even though they who retire from public life may be wise, their action hardly constitutes wisdom. Gold, you see, is the most precious of the seven treasures. Buried in the earth, it causes mysterious springs to gush forth. It sweeps away impurity. It stores within itself a melodious sound. That a substance of such great purity may only be accumulated by people who are stupid or miserly seems incredible – Oh, it feels wonderful tonight to release my years of frustration and express my deepest feelings.'

'Yes, just as you have indicated,' said Sanai in amusement, as he drew nearer, 'seeking wealth is a lofty aim, and your views are not a bit different from those that I have always held. But there is still a question to which – though you may think it foolish – I would appreciate your giving me a full reply.[560] Now, you have explained that it is almost criminal not to recognise the great power of money and the significance of wealth. But there's some point in what the bookworms say. Practically all of the people who have gained riches in our day are miserly and ruthless men. They enjoy ample wealth themselves, but they make no effort to rescue from poverty either their brothers and relations or those who have faithfully served them since the days of their ancestors. When a man loses his luck and has nowhere to turn for help, then his rich neighbour will even try to beat down the price of his fields and use intimidation to make the land his own. Nowadays even though a wealthy person is respected as village elder, he's often negligent about returning things that he borrowed from people long ago. When a courteous person yields a seat to someone who is rich, the latter will look down upon the kind man as though he were his slave. When an old acquaintance happens to visit a wealthy man to pay his respects during the summer or winter season, he will be suspected of coming to borrow money, and the rich man has his servant tell the caller that the master isn't at home. You can find many such cases.

'On the other hand,' Sanai continued, 'there are people who give complete loyalty to their lord,[561] are known to honour their parents, pay respect where it is due, and willingly help those in need. But these people are forced to sleep with one blanket even in the cold winter months. During the midsummer heat they have no time to rinse out their only summer garment. Even in bountiful years for breakfast and dinner they must make do with a single bowl of porridge. Such people rarely receive visits from their friends. Even their family and relations will have nothing to do with them. Ignored, these people have no one they can complain to; they get no rest till the end of their days.

'Lest one suspect that such people who live in poverty are inattentive to their work,' Sanai said, 'it must be stated that they usually arise early and retire late, pouring heart and soul into their labour, running about east and west always keeping busy. And they are not dull-witted – they simply remain unsuccessful in spite of their talent. Such people are like Yen-tzu, who scarcely knew the taste of a single gourd.[562]

'The Buddhists explain that one's destiny is a consequence of a previous karma,' Sanai also added, 'and the Confucianists teach that fate is decreed by heaven. Now, if one believed in a future life and assumed that the virtuous acts and good deeds performed in this world[563] would assist one in the next, then he might not feel so angry over injustice. Therefore, doesn't it seem that the Buddhist doctrines explain the vagaries of wealth and poverty, while the Confucian teachings are poppycock? Spirit, no doubt you subscribe to the Buddhist beliefs, don't you? If otherwise, tell me your views.'

'Since ancient times your question has never been adequately answered,' replied the spirit. 'In the Buddhist canon, to be sure, it's said that wealth and poverty depend on good and evil in a previous existence. That's how things are supposed to go. But suppose a person in his previous life had completely conquered his own selfishness, had revealed the quality of mercy, and had

x  Wealth and Poverty: The spirit of gold comes in the night to discourse
with Sanai

treated his fellow human beings with decency, and as a result
in his present life had been reborn to a family with wealth and
position. What if he now shows a barbaric disposition, taking
advantage of his treasures, bullying other men, and arbitrarily
flaunting his authority? By what sort of karma[564] could the
man's goodness in his former life have become so diminished?
We're told that the Buddhas and Boddhisattvas disdain fame
and personal gain; so how can one expect to get any ideas from
them regarding wealth and poverty? In my opinion, to explain
that money and position come from good deeds in a previous
existence and to call poverty and misery a person's just deserts
is merely a half-witted idea to soften up old biddies.

'If a man works hard to do good and doesn't worry about
wealth or poverty,' the spirit continued, 'he will earn good
fortune for his progeny, even though the labour may not benefit
himself. The saying, "His ancestors received it, and his
descendants preserved it,"[565] admirably expresses this principle.
Still it's hardly proper to do good with the expectation of reap-
ing the profits for oneself. But I have my own ideas about
whether a mean and curmudgeonly man always grows rich and
prosperous, enjoys life, and comes to a happy end. Listen, while
I explain. As I've said, this is only a temporary form in which
I have appeared; I'm neither a God nor a Buddha, being originally a thing without feeling whose responses are unlike those of
people.

'Affluent men of old accumulated wealth and grew rich by
acting in harmony with heaven and by understanding the
principles of earth.[566] It was a matter of course that these men
should prosper, because they followed the natural way of
heaven. On the other hand, whenever cheap and miserly people
see gold or silver, they run after it as if it were their father or
mother, forgoing proper food, forsaking warm clothing, and
not even sparing their irreplaceable lives. While sleeping and
waking, misers continually brood over wealth, and therefore
getting it becomes for them a matter of urgency.

'But because I'm neither a God nor a Buddha but basically an
object devoid of feeling,' he added, 'I have no responsibility to

judge for people what is right or wrong. It's for Heaven, the Gods, and the Buddhas to praise good and condemn evil. These three make up religion. Their prerogatives are not mine. You must remember that wealth only accumulates where people treat money with respect, because though gold has a spirit its soul differs from that of man. For example consider the case of a wealthy person who for love of his fellow human beings bestows his largess[567] on someone without seeking proper security. If he fails to see when he gives aid that the borrower is a bad risk, then no matter how good his intentions are, his capital will in the end surely be lost. This amounts to knowing the power of money but misunderstanding its essence. When one treats money with disrespect, he may therefore lose his wealth.

'Consider, on the other hand,' he said, 'a person who is born without the heavenly endowment of good fortune. His conduct may be impeccable, and he may be devoted to the welfare of mankind even though he dwells in poverty with scarcely any chance of breaking out of his rut. No matter how hard he tries to exert himself, he may all his life fail in his quest for wealth and position. So you see, the wise men of old searched for wealth and when they found it they took it, but when they could not get it they stopped seeking.[568] Then they did as they pleased in the mountains and forests and forsook the world, living out their days in tranquility. People envied them for their great purity of heart.

'The truth is that the way to wealth and position remains an art. A man who masters its skills can make money more easily than a dolt can pound tiles into dust. So, although I associate myself with people's business affairs, I do not depend on a permanent master.[569] Just when you think I've gathered[570] in one place, I may suddenly run off somewhere else, according to how my master treats me. I'm like water flowing downward.[571] Night and day, moving ceaselessly, I never stop. If a man is idle, he can in time consume even Mt T'ai.[572] In the end he can drink dry even the rivers and oceans.

'A vicious man acquires wealth by competing for it,' the

spirit concluded, 'whereas this is not so with a gentleman.[573] He will try to use his opportunities, and then by austere living, careful budgeting, and hard work his house will naturally flourish, and other men will show him respect. So you see, I recognise neither the Buddhist doctrine of karma nor the Confucian concept of destiny imposed by heaven. I move in a different sphere.'

'Spirit, I find your views in every way remarkable,' said Sanai, growing all the more intrigued. 'Tonight you've managed to dispel many of my persistent doubts. But there is one thing more that I want to ask. At present, Hideyoshi's power prevails over the Four Seas, and it might seem as though the Five Provinces and the Seven Marches[574] are calm. Yet here and there[575] loyal samurai who have lost their master remain in hiding. Under the protection of the lords of great fiefs some of these samurai are watching for a change in the situation and are actively plotting to seize power for themselves. The people, likewise, because they're living in an age of warring states, have exchanged their hoes for spears and are reluctant to work at farming. It's impossible for any samurai to sleep peacefully on his pillow. As matters stand now, the government seems unlikely to endure. Can anyone bring unity and give the people peace ? To whom would you lend your cooperation ?'

'What you ask again concerns the ways of men,' said the spirit, 'and it's not the sort of thing about which I have knowledge. I can speak only from the point of view of wealth. As a strategist, Shingen[576] was absolutely brilliant, but he never controlled more than three provinces, though his renown as a great general is unanimously acclaimed. His dying words are said to have been, "At present Nobunaga[577] is the most fortunate of generals. I always underrated him and neglected to put him down, but now I lie stricken ill. My descendants will surely be destroyed by his hand."

'Kenshin[578] was a brave general, and after Shingen's death no one under heaven was his equal. It's too bad that he had to die so soon. Nobunaga possessed outstanding skill,[579] but he lacked Shingen's wisdom and was inferior to Kenshin in courage. Nevertheless, he acquired wealth, and for a time the whole empire fell under his sway. But considering that he lost his life because he once shamed someone in whom he had placed his trust, you can hardly say that he mastered both the civil and the military arts.

'Even Hideyoshi's great ambition did not aim for the whole world at first. He merely envied Shibata[580] and Niwa's[581] rank and wealth, as one may recall from his having made up the surname of Hashiba.[582] It would seem that he's now like a dragon who upon climbing into the wide heavens forgets how it was to be inside the pond. Although Hideyoshi has changed into a dragon, he belongs to the "serpent" class, and it is said that when dragons develop from snakes, they rarely live longer than three years.[583] So how, indeed, can Hideyoshi last? It is clear that from the oldest times an age of extravagance has never endured. People must practise austerity. But excessive austerity can give rise to venality. One must always try to be frugal without being mean. Nevertheless, though the present Toyotomi government may not last, before long the myriads of people will dwell in harmony, and in every household they will sing "The Dance of the Thousand Autumns."[584] It shall be as you wish,' and so saying, he chanted a Chinese verse of eight characters:

'When the Ming grass of Yao[585] grew green each day,
The hundred names could depend on their home.'[586]

With this utterance, the spirit's exuberance abated, and the distant temple bell tolled the fifth watch.

'The night has already passed,' the apparition said. 'We must part. My long ramblings have robbed you of your sleep.'

With these words he seemed about to leave, when suddenly he disappeared.

Sanai pondered over the events of the night, and when he thought of the verse and understood the general sense of the phrase concerning the hundred names depending on home, he felt a deep faith well up within him. This was certainly an omen of the auspicious grass.

*The Fifth Year of An'ei [1776],*
*Under the Cyclical Sign of Fire and Monkey,*
*On the first day of the summer,*
*By the booksellers*
*Of Kyoto and Osaka*
*Teramachi Dōri and Gojō-Agaru,*
*UMEMURA HAMBEI,*
*and*
*1 chōme Kōraibashi-Suji,*
*NOMURA CHŌBEI*

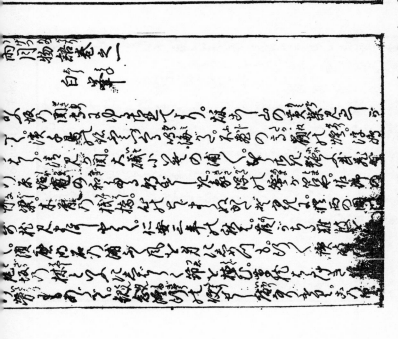

xi Volume One, page 1*b*–2*c*: Portion of the Preface and the first half-leaf of "White Peak."

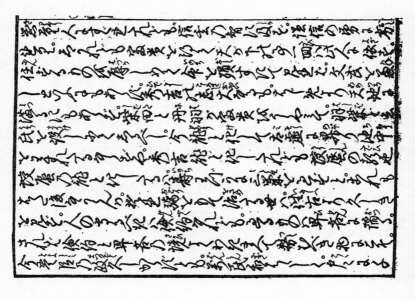

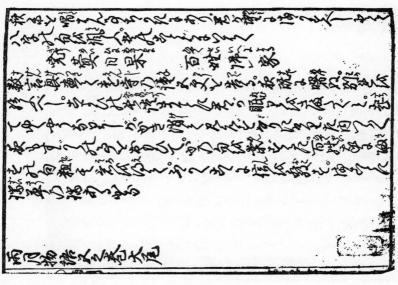

xii Volume Five, page 16b–17a: Final leaf of text of "Wealth and

# NOTES ON THE TEXT

*Note*: Full citations for works previously mentioned in the introduction have not been repeated. The figures in brackets indicate the page numbers of the wood-block edition of 1776.

## *Preface*

1 'For three generations he begot deaf mutes' *San sei aji wo umi*: Lo Kuan-chung's punishment for having written extravagant romances. See Introduction.

2 'For writing *The Tale of Genji* Lady Murasaki was condemned to hell' *Shi-en wa Gengo wo arawashite ittan akushu ni da-suru*: according to a legend found in the *Ima monogatari*, a 13th-century collection of Buddhist anecdotes and tales. This legend also figures in the *nō* play, *Genji kuyō*, where in the end it is revealed that Lady Murasaki is actually Kannon, the Buddhist Goddess of Mercy.

3 'With crying pheasants and quarrelling dragons' *Kiji naki ryū tatakau*: metaphorically, the world of the supernatural. See the Chinese classics, *Shu ching* and *I ching*, as well as the preface to the Ming collection, *New Tales for Lamplight*, 1, 1b, and the Japanese *kanazōshi*, *Otogi bōko*. A crying pheasant represents an ill omen and requires that a worthy minister lecture the ruler on his faults. Quarrelling dragons, their blood flowing black and yellow, tell of danger. Darkness has ended, but the principle of night advances from the realm of moral indifference and battles with the power that gives light; as a result, both elements suffer harm. Cf. James Legge, trans., *The Chinese Classics . . .* (1861–72; rpt. Hong Kong: Hong Kong University Press, 1961), III, 264–5; and Richard Wilhelm, trans., *The I Ching or Book of Changes*, rendered into English by Cary F. Baynes (London: Routledge and Kegan Paul, 1951), II, 25; Japanese preface to *Otogi bōko*, in *Kaii shōsetsu shū*, Kindai Nihon bungaku taikei (Tokyo: Kokumin Tosho, 1927), vol. 13, p. 93.

4 'Late in the spring of the Meiwa Era, under the zodiac of earth and rat' *Meiwa tsuchinoe-ne no ban-shun*: the 3rd month of Meiwa 5 (1768, by the Western calendar) and the 25th year of the 60-year sexagenary cycle used in China and Japan.

5 'Signed: Senshi Kijin' *Senshi Kijin sho-su*: literally, 'the eccentric man with split fingers,' a reference to Akinari's deformity. It may also carry the idea of a quibbler or obscurantist. For his identity as Akinari, see Takizawa Bakin, *Kinseil mono-no-hon Edo sakusha burui*, p. 125; and Kimura Mokurō, Keisetsu sakusha-kō,' in *Zoku-enseki jisshū* (Tokyo: Kokusho Kankōkai, 1908), vol. 1, pp. 273–4.

6 Shikyo Kōjin (first seal) literally, 'a descendant of Tzu Hsü,' an eccentric but fictitious envoy of the ancient Chinese state of Ch'u. He was the subject of the prose-poem 'Tzu-Hsü fu,' by Ssu-ma Hsiang-ju, in the *Wen hsüan*. See *Monzen bōkun taizen*, 2, 35b–38a.

7 Yūgi Sammai: (second seal) literally, 'emersing oneself in pleasure.' See the late Ming work, *Wu tsa tsu*, comp. Hsieh Chao-che (Kyoto, 1661), 15, 36a, 'In writing novels, plays, or light fiction one must necessarily mix truth and falsehood, thereby emersing oneself in pleasure.' Not only does Hsieh's passage touch on a widely-held view of fiction, but Akinari's use of such a fanciful name was typical of Chinese and Japanese authors in early modern times.

1 *White Peak*

8 'Once upon a time,' etc. *Ōsaka no seki-mori ni yurusarete yori*, etc.: cf. *Senjūshō*, p. 69 for this and all the place names mentioned through note 18. Akinari follows his source very closely. 'I' refers not to Akinari but to the 12th century priest Saigyō. See Introduction.

*Ōsaka no seki-mori*, or the 'barrier guards of Osaka,' were formerly placed at the checkpoint between the provinces of Yamashiro and Ōmi (the prefectures of Kyoto and Shiga). Here travellers to the east were supposed to show their credentials. The guards, however, were anachronistic even in Saigyō's day, and the phrase was employed for its poetic associations.

9 'Yellow leaves of the autumn peaks' *Aki koshi yama no momiji*: Chinese characters for 'yellow leaves' with a Japanese *kana* gloss for *momiji*, or 'crimson leaves.' Cf., *Man'yōshū*,

| | |
|---|---|
| Akiyama no | On the autumn peaks |
| konoha wo miteba | When we see the trees all clad |
| momiji wo ba | In their yellow leaves, |
| torite zo shinubu | Who can keep from picking them? |

NKBT, vol. 4, p. 14 (no. 16). Similar Chinese usage occurs in the opening passage of 'Wei tang ch'i yü chi,' in *New Tales for Lamplight*, 2, 34b; and *Kokuyaku Kambun taisei*, p. 71.

10 'I visited Narumi bay,' etc. *Hama-chidori no ato fumi-tsukuru Narumi-gata*: a poetic place name in present-day Nagoya. Formerly it was one of the fifty-three stations on the Tōkaidō Post Road.

11 'Smoke curling from lofty Mt. Fuji,' etc. *Fuji no takane no keburi, Ukishima ga hara*: the wood-block text reads *kefuri*; Mt. Fuji, with Chinese characters meaning 'the inexhaustible.'

The plain of Ukishima, literally, 'floating island,' a belt-shaped strip of low coastal land along Tago Bay, in Shizuoka Prefecture. Cf. Saigyō's verse in the *Sankashū*,

| *Itsu to naki* | All through the night |
| *omoi wa Fuji no* | My thoughts dwelt on Mt. Fuji, |
| *keburi ni te* | With its curling smoke, |
| *uchi-fusu toko ya* | As I lay down to sleep |
| *Ukishima ga hara* | On the plain of Ukishima. |

NKBT, vol. 29, p. 226 (no. 1307).

**12** 'The barrier at Kiyomi' *Kiyomi ga seki*: Shizuoka Prefecture, near the town of Okitsu and the Seikenji temple, famed in Oliver Statler, *The Japanese Inn* (New York: Random House, 1961). From here one could view Miho no Matsubara – a famous strand of pine trees – across the bay. For a discussion of barriers and place names in Japanese literature, see Morris, *Pillow Book*, I, 123, II, 97–9.

**13** 'The many bays around Ōiso and Koiso' *Ōiso Koiso no ura ura*: the Shōnan beaches of Sagami, in Kanagawa.

**14** 'Purple grass of Musashino moors' *Murasaki niou Musashino no hara*: *murasaki*, a grass-like herb belonging to a family that includes the forget-me-not; from its root a dye of the same name was extracted. The province of Musashino (now, Tokyo) used to be renowned for this plant. See *Kokinshū*,

| *Murasaki no* | The purple grasses |
| *hitomoto yue ni* | That bloom in solitary stems |
| *Musashino no* | On Musashino moors – |
| *kusa wa minagara* | How I like to look at them, |
| *aware to ẓo miru* | So delicate and beautiful! |

NKBT, vol. 8, p. 275 (no. 867).

**15** Shiogama: in Miyagi, not far from Sendai. The name, which represents the area of Ōu in northern Honshū, appears among the famous bays in the *Pillow Book* (see Morris, I, 187), as well as the *Kokinshū*, *Tales of Ise*, and *Oku no hosomichi*. Ōu was made up of the former provinces of Mutsu and Dewa (now, the prefectures of Fukushima, Miyagi, Iwate, Aomori, Akita, and Yamagata).

**16** Kisagata: by the Sea of Japan, in southern Akita and northern Yamagata, at the foot of Mt Chōkai. Its lovely islands and inlets formed a famous landscape until an earthquake of 1861 destroyed it, and the bay was turned into dry land. See *Shinkokinshū*,

| *Sasurōru* | As I wandered, |
| *waga mi ni shi areba* | Here was where I find myself – |
| *Kisagata ya* | At Kisagata Bay, |
| *ama no tomaya ni* | And in the rush-thatched fisher huts |
| *amata tabi-ne nu* | I stayed for many a night. |

NKBT, vol. 28, p. 214 (no. 972).

**17** Sano: a village, part of the city of Takasaki, in Gumma, once famed for its floating bridge of boats over which travellers on the Nakasendō, or 'Central Mountain Post Road,' crossed the Tone River. This highway linked the Kyoto–Osaka area with the regions of Kantō (see note 207) and Hokuriku (see note 506).

18 'Hanging bridge at Kiso' *Kiso no kake-hashi*: one of the famous sights of the Nakasendō. Here the highway descended to the Kiso valley from the uplands of Nagano. For Bashō's visit to this place, see Keene, *Landscapes and Portraits*, pp. 109–30.

19 'The fall of the Third Year of Nin'an' *Nin'an san-nen no aki wa*: AD 1168; the *Senjūshō*, p. 46, states simply 'during the Nin'an Era,' but the *Hōgen monogatari*, p. 395, assigns Saigyō's visit to the 3rd year of the era. See also Wilson, *Hōgen*, pp. 99, 149.

20 'Of the falling reeds' *Ashi ga chiru*: a *makura kotoba*, or 'pillow-word,' for Naniwa, which is now Osaka.

21 Suma and Akashi: south of Kobe, where the former post road paralleled the beach. Readers of *The Tale of Genji* will remember these names as the scene of Genji's exile. The place was also famous for its beautiful view of the moon.

22 Hayashi, etc.: Ōkoshi-chō, in the city of Sakaide, in Kagawa, on the island of Shikoku.

23 'Nearby this hamlet,' etc. *Kono sato* [see wood-block text, 1, 1b] *chikaki Shiramine to iu tokoro ni*: Shiramine, name of a Buddhist temple of the Shingon sect. It was founded in the ninth century by Kūkai (see 'Bird of Paradise,' and N.B. notes 294, 303) and is situated on a mountain overlooking the Inland Sea.

24 'Emperor Sutoku' *Shin-in*: (1119–64) literally, 'the new cloistered emperor.' His father was the *in*, or 'cloistered emperor.' Eldest son of Toba (see note 66) and 75th sovereign of Japan, he reigned from 1123–41, when he was forced to abdicate in favour of his half-brother, Konoe (see note 30). At the latter's death, in 1155, Sutoku wished his own son, Shigehito (see note 49), to become emperor, hoping that he himself might become an influential retired monarch like his father and his great grandfather. His main supporters were Minamoto Tameyoshi (see note 85) – along with his sons – and Fujiwara Yorinaga (see note 97). His chief opponents were Goshirakawa (who was his own brother; see note 51), Lady Bifukumon'in (see note 50), Fujiwara Michinori (Shōnagon Shinzei in the tale, note 75), Fujiwara Tadamichi (note 97), and Taira Kiyomori (note 91), all of whom figure in the tale. See Varley, *Imperial Restoration*, pp. 10–11. Also see Introduction and Appendix, Imperial Succession in Twelfth Century Japan.

25 'Godless Month' *Kaminazuki*: Chinese characters for the 10th month and the Japanese poetic name in the *kana* gloss; so-called because at this time all of the deities were said to congregate at the Izumo Shrine, leaving the rest of the nation temporarily bereft. For the names of the months in pre-modern Japan, see Morris, *Pillow Book*, II, 1–2.

26 'Even on a day,' etc. *Ao-gumo no tanabiku hi sura kosame sobo furu ga*

*gotoshi*: cf. *Man'yōshū*, NKBT, vol. 4, pp. 94 (no. 161); vol. 7, pp. 162–3 (no. 3383); and *NGSK*, p. 18.

**27** 'Indeed, when I had seen,' etc. *Geni ma no atari ni mi narishi wa*, etc.: cf. *Senjūshō*, pp. 46–7; Wilson, *Hōgen*, p. 149.

**28** 'Great halls of the palace' *Shishin seiryō*: literally, 'Hall of the Purple Apartment,' where ceremonies and festivities were held, and 'Hall of the Clear Cool,' where the emperor had his private residence.

**29** 'The hundred officials' *Momo no tsukasa*: figuratively for all the court officials. See *Senjūshō*, p. 47; and Uzuki, *Ugetsu*, p. 36.

**30** Emperor Konoe: (1139–55) the 76th sovereign of Japan, he reigned from 1141–55. At the insistence of his mother, the Lady Bifukumon'in (see note 50), he was placed on the throne when less than two years of age by Western reckoning. Here he remained until his untimely death, which followed closely by his father's in the next year became one of the causes of the Hōgen Insurrection. Konoe's personal name is given in the tale as Toshihito, but Narihito is now the preferred reading. See Introduction and Appendix, Imperial Succession.

**31** 'In the Grove of Jewels or on faraway Ku-she Mountain' *Hakoya no yama no tama no hayashi ni*: *Tama no hayashi*, 'The Grove of Jewels'; a Chinese imperial garden in the Sung dynasty, on the outskirts of the city of Kaifeng.

*Hakoya no yama* (Miao Ku-she, in Chinese); a mountain mentioned in the *Chuang tzu*. Here a holy man lived by sucking the wind and drinking the dew. For enjoyment he climbed on the clouds and mist and rode a flying dragon.

Both names were used as euphemisms for a retired emperor's palace. 'The Mistress of Hakoya' was the title of an old Japanese story, and a posthumous work by Akinari was called 'Hakoya no yama.' See Watson, *Chuang Tzu*, p. 33; *The Tale of Genji*, p. 310; NKBT, vol. 15, pp. 141, 453; and *Akinari ibun*, pp. 382–8.

**32** 'Only the tracks of the wandering stag' *Biroku no kayou ato nomi* [1, 2a] *miete*.

**33** 'Lord who had commanded ten thousand chariots' *Banjō no kimi*: said metaphorically of the emperor; see *The Book of Mencius*; cf. also *Senjūshō*, p. 47, *banjō no aruji*; and Wilson, *Hōgen*, p. 150.

**34** Verse: from the *Sankashū*, with only a minor variation. *Matsuyama*, literally, 'pine clad hills.' *Kata-*, in *katanaku*, is an *engo*, or 'related word,' poetically associated with *nami*, 'wave.' It means 'shape,' or 'form.' Therefore, *katanaku*, means, 'Your form has gone,' or more freely, 'You have died.' *Naku* also means 'to weep,' implying further that Saigyō weeps or mourns for Sutoku. See NKBT, vol. 29, p. 233 (no. 1354).

**35** 'I felt cleansed in spirit, but a chill struck my bones' *Shin sumi hone hie*: similar to an expression in 'T'ien t'ai fang yin lu,' *New Tales for Lamplight*, 2, 11a; and *Kokuyaku*, p. 49.

36 Saigyō: the text uses En'i, another name for Saigyō, by which he was known in his later years. I have preferred the designation more familiar to Western readers. See Introduction.

37 'I opened my eyes and peered' *Me wo hirakite sukashi* [1, 2b] *mireba*.

38 'Being a priest seeking enlightenment' *Saigyō motoyori dōshin no hōshi nareba*: This may be interpreted in either the first or third person. I have chosen the former, partly for the sake of English style. See Introduction.

39 Verse: The *Sankashū* gives an explanatory note, 'I went to worship in Sanuki, and at Matsuyama I visited the cloistered emperor's place, but I was unable to meet him.' In the Kotohira-bon text of the *Hōgen monogatari*, however, this verse is attributed to Sutoku's ghost. See Wilson, *Hōgen*, p. 154; NKBT, vol. 29, p. 232 (no. 1353), and vol. 31, p. 183. The expression *koshi fune*, or *koshi-bune*, is somewhat puzzling, but Suzuki, *Ugetsu*, p. 150, explains it as 'boat that came.'

40 'Now that you have departed,' etc. *Kyakushō sokumō shite*, etc.: cf. *Senjūshō*, p. 48.

41 'Sutoku merely gave a provocative laugh' *Shin'in karakara to warawase tamai* [1, 3a].

42 'Surely you didn't know,' etc. *Nanji shirazu*, etc.: Sutoku's ghost is prophesying the Gempei wars between the Taira and the Minamoto and also the events and institutional changes that took place during the middle ages. (See Introduction, and also notes 79–82, 98, and 348).

43 'Ruler's moral responsibility' *Ōdō no kotowari*: wood-block text reads, *ōtō*. As expressed in early modern Japanese interpretations of the writings of Confucius and Mencius. See Hershel Webb, *The Japanese Imperial Institution in the Tokugawa Period* (New York: Columbia University Press, 1968), p. 172.

44 'Revolt during the Hōgen Era' *Hōgen no go-muhon*: the period from the 27th day 4th month of 1156 to the 20th day 4th month of 1159. The insurrection took place in 1156, when Sutoku and his supporters tried to depose Goshirakawa from the throne in an abortive *coup d'etat*.

45 'In accordance with the teachings of the Sun Goddess' *Ame no kami no oshie-tamō kotowari*: cf. *Hōgen monogatari*, p. 352.

46 'Will of heaven' *Ten no mei*: the doctrine of revolution, as found in *The Book of Mencius*.

47 Eiji Era: the period from the 10th day 7th month of 1141 to the 28th day 4th month of 1142.

48 'Emperor Konoe, who was only three years old' *Sansai no Toshihito*: see note 30.

49 'My son, Prince Shigehito' *Waga* [1, 4b] *miko no Shigehito*: (1140–62) Sutoku's only son. Although Goshirakawa (see note 51) was appointed emperor when Konoe died in 1155, the actual enthronement was delayed. Meantime, Sutoku and his backers wanted Shigehito to become emperor. But in the 7th month of 1156, immediately after the failure of his father's

coup, Shigehito became a Buddhist priest, and he lived in seclusion until his death, which preceded that of Sutoku.

50 Bifukumon'in: (1117–60) daughter of Fujiwara no Nagazane; 3rd wife of Toba; mother of Konoe. Her personal name was Tokuko. She had Toba make her son, Konoe, emperor, and after his death in 1155 she urged that Goshirakawa, rather than Sutoku's son, Shigehito, should occupy the throne, thus contributing to the events that led to the Hōgen Insurrection.

51 'Goshirakawa, the Fourth Prince' *Yon no miya no Masahito*: (1127–92) the 77th emperor of Japan; a younger son of Toba (see note 66) by the same mother as Sutoku; reigned from 1155–58. Goshirakawa had been passed over in favour of Konoe, but after the latter's death he was chosen emperor instead of his nephew, Shigehito (see note 49). See also, Introduction, and Appendix, Imperial Succession.

52 'Once upon a time, in China, a subject struck down his lord' *Shin to shite kun wo utsu*: referring to King Wu's act against the last ruler of the Shang dynasty, which gave precedent to the idea of deposing a ruler who fails to act in the interests of the people.

53 'To replace a ruler during whose reign hens crowed in the morning *Hinkei no ashita suru yo wo totte kawaran ni*: criticizing Bifukumon'in's political activities in terms of imagery from the *Shu ching*; when a hen crows in the morning, the realm was said to be in danger. Also see *Hōgen monogatari*, p. 391; and Wilson, *Hōgen*, p. 91.

54 'You have deserted your family,' etc. *Nanji ie wo idete*, etc.: the orthodox Chinese Confucian point of view. A man who followed the Buddhist religion was thought to forsake home, family, and state – the institutions that the sage emperors, Yao and Shun, represented.

55 'I began, without shrinking from him' *Saigyō iyoyo* [1, 5a] *osoruru iro mo naku*.

56 Long ago Emporer Honda of our imperial line,' etc. *Kōchō no mukashi Honda no tennō*, etc. better known as Ōjin, the 15th emperor of Japan. Cf. Aston, *Nihongi*, I, 272–7; and NKBT, vol. 67, pp. 380–9.

57 'Prince Ōsasagi: Ōsazaki, in the wood-block text; Nintoku, 16th in the imperial line.

58 'Had no choice but to ascend the throne' *Yangoto nakute ani no miko mi-kurai ni tsukase tamō*: as described in the *Nihon shoki*, cited above.

59 Kudara: the Korean kingdom of Paikche. See Aston, *Nihongi*, I, 261–3; NKBT, vol. 67, pp. 372–6. This marked the traditional beginning of Confucianism in Japan.

60 'I have heard people say,' etc. *Mata Shū no hajime*, etc.: cf. de Bary, ed., *Sources of Chinese Tradition* (New York: Columbia University Press, 1960), p. 111.

61 'Brought peace to the people of the empire' *Tenka no tami wo yasuku* [1, 5b] *su*.

**62** 'But *The Book of Mencius*, alone, has yet to reach Japan,' etc. *Kano Mōji no sho bakari imada Nihon ni kitarazu*, etc.: as found in the 1661 Japanese ed. of *Wu tsa tsu*, 4, 52a, and also in the Ming printed edition. The passage was deleted from later Japanese reprints of this encyclopedic work. The full text reads, 'The Japanese value Confucian books and believe in Buddhism. They will pay high prices for all of the Chinese classics, except for *The Book of Mencius*. They say that ships carrying this book will capsize and sink. How strange this is!'

**63** 'This is because,' etc.: *Waga kuni wa*, etc.: cf. *Hōgen monogatari*, p. 391.

**64** Verse: cf. the *Shih ching*, or the Chinese classic of poetry, Waley, trans., *The Book of Songs* (London: Allen & Unwin, 1937), p. 202.

**65** 'Ties of blood' *Kotsu niku no ai*: metaphor derived from the Chinese classic, *Li chi* (*The Book of Rites*).

**66** 'After the Emperor Toba died,' etc. *Ichi in kamigakure tamaite*: cf. *Hōgen monogatari*, p. 352.

Toba (1103–56), the 74th sovereign of Japan; reigned 1107–23. After his grandfather's death in 1129, he became in effect the ruler of the nation, though he himself six years earlier had abdicated the throne. Around this time the retired monarch (usually known as the *in*, or cloistered emperor) held actual power, and the reigning emperor (often but a child) served as a mere figurehead. See Varley, *Imperial Restoration*, p. 39.

**67** 'While his body still lay in state,' etc. *Mogari no miya ni mihadae* [1, 6a]: *mogari no miya*, in ancient Japan the place of temporary interment; also known as *araki no miya*. See *Man'yōshū*, NKBT, vol. 4, pp. 96–7 (no. 167), and NGSK, p. 34.

**68** 'Hoisting banners and twanging bows' *Mihata nabikase yuzue furitate*: cf. *Man'yōshū*, where 'banners swayed' with the sound of 'the bowstring's clang,' NKBT, vol. 4, pp. 108–9 (no. 199); and NGSK, p. 40. The wood-block text reads *yusue*.

**69** 'That which lies under heaven is like a holy vessel' *Tenka wa jinki nari*: according to the Taoist philosopher, Lao-tzu, a nation is a spiritual entity, and anyone who acts on it may harm it; he who tries to hold on to it may lose it. In politics, to do nothing is often the wisest course. See Wing-tsit Chan, trans., *The Way of Lao Tzu (Tao-te ching)* (Indianapolis: Bobbs-Merrill, 1963), p. 29.

**70** 'Takatō, in Matsuyama,' etc.: the name of the official in Matsuyama at whose house Sutoku was confined; *Hōgen monogatari*, pp. 393–4.

**71** 'Meeting no human being' *Mairi-tsukōru mono mo nashi* [1, 6b].

**72** 'The five Mahayana sutras' *Gobu no Daijōgyō*: the principle holy books of the Northern branch of Buddhism, as revered especially in the Tendai sect. Sutoku was supposed to have devoted three years to the task of copying them, a feat mentioned in both the *Hōgen monogatari* and the *Gempei seisuiki*. See Wilson, *Hōgen*, pp. 96–7, 157–8.

NOTES ON THE TEXT 215

**73** 'Desolate, stony shore' *Ariso*: see *Man'yōshū*, NKBT, vol. 4, pp. 100–1 (no. 181), and NGSK, p. 70.

**74** 'Verse: cf. *Hōgen monogatari*, p. 394; Wilson, *Hōgen*, p. 85.

**75** Shōnagon Shinzei: (1106?–59) the popular name for Fujiwara Michinori, one of the principal participants in the events of 1156 and 1159–60. He served under five emperors – Toba, Sutoku, Konoe, Goshirakawa, and Nijō – and he was the leader of an influential faction at court. Shinzei urged administrative measures to restore the authority of the throne, and most notably, after Sutoku's revolt in 1156 he recommended that certain of the participants be given capital punishment, in spite of three-century's suspension of such measures. Although the position of *shōnagon*, or 'minor counsellor,' designated a functionary who was only supposed to handle rescripts and memorials on insignificant matters, Shinzei used his closeness to the emperor to gain great power.

**76** 'Curse' *Juso*: in the wood-block text, *shuso*; found not in *Hōgen monogatari* but in *Shiramine-dera engi*, another of Akinari's sources. Cf. text in Gunsho ruijū, vol. 15 (Tokyo: Keizai Zasshisha, 1901), p. 644.

**77** 'Copied the sutras' *Utsushinuru o-kyō naru wo* [1, 7a].

**78** 'Law under which our relationship should have been considered' *Shitashiki wo hakaru beki nori*: according to the Chinese law code of the T'ang dynasty (after which Japanese legal institutions of Saigyō's day had been modelled), persons related to the reigning emperor in the fifth degree or closer might receive lightened punishments for their crimes.

**79** 'Bad ends' *Madō*: literally, 'the way of Mara,' an evil deity in India, who murders people, destroys property, assumes monstrous forms, and inspires wicked men.

**80** 'Cut my finger and wrote an oath in blood' *Yubi wo yaburi chi wo mote gammon wo utsushi*: cf. *Gempei seisuiki*, in Kōchū Nihon bungaku taikei, vol. 15 (Tokyo: Kokumin Tosho, 1927), pp. 275–81, and especially p. 277, where he was said to have cut his tongue. See also Wilson, *Hōgen*, p. 158.

**81** 'Sea at Shido' *Shido no umi*: *Shito* in the wood-block text. This is puzzling, because Sutoku had no connections with the town of Shido or the nearby sea. The *Shiramine-dera engi*, p. 644, however, states that Sutoku placed the sutras in a box 'to present to the Palace of the Dragon,' and cast them in the sea at Shiito. Flames then arose from the water, and a youth emerged, performed a dance, and received the sutras. Likely, Shiito was confused with the town of Shido, near Yashima, where the Taira forces met with defeat in 1185.

**82** 'That is why the Heiji Rising broke out' *Hata Heiji no midare zo idekinuru*: as suggested in *Hōgen monogatari*, p. 394. Heiji is the era name for the period from the 20th day 4th month of 1159 to the 10th day 1st month of 1160.

**83** Nobuyori: Fujiwara Nobuyori (1133–59). He rose to the position of *chūnagon* or 'middle counsellor,' and found favour with Goshirakawa, who himself had abdicated in 1158 and became a cloistered emperor. Shōnagon Shinzei, however, blocked him from advancing further. In 1159 Nobuyori sought the backing of Minamoto Yoshitomo (see note 84) and rose up against Goshirakawa, Shōnagon Shinzei, and their Taira supporters in an unsuccessful revolt known at the Heiji Rising, which Taira Kiyomori (see note 91) put down in 1160. Nobuyori was beheaded by the river bank at Rokujō (see note 94).

**84** Yoshitomo: Minamoto Yoshitomo (1123–60); eldest son of Tameyoshi (see note 85), and the only member of his family who did not support Sutoku's cause in 1156. Rather, he joined the forces that backed Goshirakawa, and he was responsible for the death of his own father and brothers. Later he fell out with Taira Kiyomori and conspired with Fujiwara Nobuyori.

**85** Tameyoshi: Minamoto Tameyoshi (1096–1156); leader of the Minamoto family and Sutoku's staunchest supporter. He was captured in defence of the Shirakawa Palace (see note 88) and beheaded by his own son, Yoshitomo.

**86** Tametomo: Minamoto Tametomo (1139–70); the youngest of Tameyoshi's sons; famous in popular literature as an archetypal tragic hero. He was renowned for his skill as an archer and for his legendary exploits, which were celebrated in Takizawa Bakin's *Chinsetsu yumihari-ɀuki.*

**87** Tadamasa: Taira Tadamasa (d. 1156); a member of the Taira family who supported Sutoku. He was slain by his own nephew, Kiyomori.

**88** 'Shirakawa Palace' *Shirakawa no miya*: built earlier by the emperor Shirakawa (1053–1129) and used by Sutoku's supporters as their base.

**89** 'Mt Nyoigatake' *Nioigamine*: a mountain lying between Kyoto and Ōtsu. I have used the modern name.

**90** 'Yoshitomo's malicious plotting' *Yoshitomo ga kadamashiki tabakari ni* [1, 7b].

**91** 'Kiyomori: Taira Kiyomori (1118–81); head of the Taira family. In 1156 he supported Goshirakawa against Sutoku. Later he defeated Minamoto Yoshitomo's forces in 1159–60 and became the most powerful man in the nation. He relegated Goshirakawa to the role of a puppet, and he gave his daughter in marriage to Takakura (the 80th emperor). Antoku (the 81st emperor, see note 118) was his grandson. Kiyomori assumed the traditional prerogatives of the Fujiwara family and the power of the cloistered emperor, but soon after his death his family's fortunes declined.

**92** 'His own retainer' *Ie no ko*: after he and his raggle-taggle band fled east through the winter snows, hoping to regroup and collect a new force.

**93** Uji: southeast of the capital; now the name of a city in Kyoto Prefecture.

**94** 'River bank at Rokujō' *Rokujō kawara*: the traditional execution ground, at the intersection of Rokujō (the sixth east-west street below the imperial palace), and the dry bed of the Kamo River.

**95** 'Summer of the Ōhō Era,' etc. *Ōhō no natsu*, etc.: in 1161; actually, Bifukumon'in's death had taken place late in the previous year.

**96** Chōkan Era: from the 29th day 3rd month of 1163 to the 5th day 6th month of 1165.

**97** Tadamichi: Fujiwara Tadamichi (1097–1164); son of Tadazane; elder brother of Yorinaga. After his father retired, Tadamichi became the *kampaku*, or 'chancellor,' and the titular head of his family, but during Konoe's reign he and Yorinaga quarrelled over the leadership of the family, and his father made Yorinaga heir. With Lady Bifukumon'in's assistance, however, Tadamichi won Toba's support, and in 1156 he got rid of Yorinaga. Once more the head of his family, he had his son made *kampaku*, but at this time the post carried little power.

Fujiwara Yorinaga (1120–56); also known as *aku safu*, 'evil lord of the left,' and *Uji safu*, after the place of his residence. Following his and Tadamichi's quarrel over the leadership of their family and which of their respective daughters should be married to Konoe, he supported Sutoku's bid for power in 1156 and persuaded Tameyoshi to join his cause, while Tadamichi similarly urged Kiyomori to support Goshirakawa.

**98** 'Great king of Evil' *Dai-maō*: for this belief and the idea that the war and turmoil of the middle ages stemmed from Sutoku's curse, see the *Taiheiki*, NKBT, vol. 36, p. 60 (also see note 348).

**99** 'Entire family and his relatives in high offices' *Ukara yakara koto-gotoku taka-* [1, 8a] *ki kan'i ni*. In the wood-block text, *kotokotoku*.

**100** Shigemori: Taira Shigemori (1138–79); Kiyomori's eldest son. He far exceeded his father in ability and emerged as the most talented leader of his family. A *kabuki* play, *Shigemori kangen*, presents him as a representative loyal son who does his best to correct his father's excesses.

**101** 'Face' *Mi-omote*: literally, 'dragon countenance,' with Chinese characters of this meaning and the Japanese gloss, *mi-* (an honourific prefix) and *omote*, 'face,' used metaphorically for the emperor.

**102** 'Persimmon-coloured robes' *Koromo wa kaki-iro no*: Garments of this colour were worn by several sects of Tantric Buddhists who practiced spells and charms in the mountains.

**103** 'His highness screeched' *Yobase* [1, 8b] *tamō*.

**104** 'Signs of the zodiac to revolve once' *Eto ichi-meguri*: here meaning not the 60-year cycle but only the twelve signs or branches, listed in Morris, *Pillow Book*, II, 204. Saigyō's visit took place in 1167, and Shigemori's death occurred in 1179, twelve years later.

**105** Verse: found in *Sankashū*, p. 233 (no. 1355), as well as in *Hōgen monogatari*.

**106** 'Ruler and ruled meet a common fate' *Setsuri mo shuda mo kawaranu* *mono wo*: *setsuri*, from Sanscrit *sudra*, the cast of farmers and cultivators. Cf. *Hōgen monogatari*, p. 348.

**107** 'Disappeared from sight,' etc. *Kaki-kechitaru gotoku* [1, 9a].

**108** 'The sleep-ending light of the dawn sky' *Ina-no-me no ake yuku sora ni*: *Ina-no-me no*, perhaps meaning 'the bud of the rice,' or 'the eyes of sleep,' is a pillow-word used with *aku*, 'to open,' as in the *Man'yōshū*, NKBT, vol. 6, pp. 92–3 (no. 2022). For *ake yuku sora*, 'morning sky' or 'dawn sky,' cf. *The Tale of Genji*, p. 90; and NKBT, vol. 14, p. 196.

**109** 'Diamond sutra' *Kongōkyō*: part of the *Daihanyakyō* or *Kongō hanya paramikyō*, which in turn is one of the five Mahayana texts mentioned above (see note 72).

**110** Third year of Jishō: AD 1179. *Chishō*, in the wood-block text.

**111** Toba: now part of Fushimi-ku, Kyoto.

**112** 'Temporary capital at Fukuhara' *Fukuhara no kaya no miya*: literally, 'The Palace of Miscanthus,' established in 1180 in what is now Hyōgo-ku, Kobe, when Kyoto was abandoned to the advancing Minamoto forces. Here Goshirakawa was imprisoned in a tiny wooden cell.

**113** Yoritomo: Minamoto Yoritomo (1147–99); grandson of Tameyoshi and son of Yoshitomo. He was banished to Izu after his father's death, but in 1180 one of Goshirakawa's sons granted him a patent to overthrow Kiyomori. With his younger brother, Yoshitsune, and his cousin, Yoshinaka, Yoritomo defeated the Taira forces and afterward established the tradition of rule by military families. See Introduction and Varley, *Imperial Restoration*, pp. 11–12.

**114** Yoshinaka: Minamoto Yoshinaka (1154–84); grandson of Tameyoshi and cousin of Yoritomo. After his father's death in 1156, he was taken to the mountains of Kiso (see note 18), where he grew to manhood. In 1180 he answered the call to arms against Kiyomori, raised troops, and seized Kyoto, forcing the Taira supporters to retreat to the Inland Sea.

**115** 'The waters of Sanuki, at Shido and Yashima' *Sanuki no umi Shido Yashima*: referring to the Inland Sea around the city of Takamatsu, where in the 3rd month of 1185 the Taira forces met with a severe defeat.

**116** 'Bellies of turtles and fish,' *Kōgyo no hara ni* [1, 9b].

**117** Akamagaseki, at Dannoura: now, Shimonoseki, at the extreme southern tip of Honshū.

**118** 'Infant emperor, Antoku' *Yōshu*: (1178–85) 81st emperor of Japan; reigned 1180–85; son of Takakura by a daughter of Kiyomori. After becoming a prisoner of the Minamoto forces, the mother's life was spared, and she became a nun. Her brief meeting with Goshirakawa years later is a poignant episode in the *Heike monogatari* and the subject of the nō play, *Ohara gokō*.

**119** 'Spirit festoons' *Nusa*: symbolic offerings to the Japanese gods, traditionally made of braided white paper, cotton cloth, or silk.

## 2 *Chrysanthemum Tryst*

**120** 'Green, green grows the spring willow,' etc. *Sei sei taru haru no yanagi*, etc.: cf. the Ming tale, 'Fan Chü-ch'ing chi shu ssu sheng chiao' ('Fan Chü-ch'ing's Eternal Friendship'), in the *Ku chin hsiao shuo*, trans., John Lyman Bishop. *The Colloquial Short Story in China: A study of the San Yen Collections* (Cambridge: Harvard University Press, 1956), pp. 88–103.

**121** 'Province of Harima in the town of Kako' *Harima no kuni Kako no umaya*: now, the city of Kakogawa, in Hyōgo Prefecture, near Suma and Akashi, midway between Kobe and Himeji.

**122** 'Except for the books that kept him company' *Tomo to suru fumi no* [1, 10a] *hoka*.

**123** 'In no way less virtuous than that of Mencius' *Mōshi no misao ni yuzurazu*: in the wood-block text, *yuzurasu*. Her legendary devotion to the sage's upbringing and education is described in such Chinese texts as the *Lieh nü chuan* and the *Meng ch'iu*.

**124** 'I find myself in an awkward situation' *Omoigakenu ayamari shi* [1, 10b] *idete*. Ordinary people were not supposed to take in travellers without reporting it to the local authorities.

**125** 'Fevers are infectious' *Ombyō wa hito wo ayamatsu mono*: cf. Bishop, *Colloquial*, p. 88.

**126** 'Life and death depend on heavenly fate' *Shi sei mei ari*: following the *Ku chin hsiao shuo* and also echoing a well-known passage in the Confucian *Analects*. See de Bary, *Sources of Chinese Tradition*, p. 29.

**127** 'Emaciated,' etc. *Omote wa ki ni, hadae kuroku yase*: cf. Bishop, *Colloquial*, p. 89, 'yellow and emaciated,' and Akinari's Japanese source, *Intoku taiheiki*, I, 35, 'Amako Tsunahisa risshin no koto,' where darkness of skin is combined with thinness to describe grave illness.

**128** 'Boiled it' *Nite* [1, 11a].

**129** 'Charity' *Intoku*: a good deed that one performs secretly and with no thought of reward.

**130** Akana: for this surname and most of those that follow, see *Intoku taiheiki*, I, 37, '*Tsunehisa Misawa wo tabakaru koto*.'

**131** 'Village of Matsue, in the province of Izumo' *Izumo no kuni Matsue no sato*: now the principal city of Shimane Prefecture, in southwestern Honshu, on the Sea of Japan. Lafcadio Hearn once lived here, perhaps partly explaining why he chose to adapt this tale into English. See Introduction.

**132** 'Military classics' *Heisho*: the Chinese writings on the art of war, which young samurai studied; usually given as the *Sun-tzu, Wu-tzu, Ssu-ma fa, Ch'eng liao-tzu, San lüeh, Liu t'ao*, and *T'ang T'ai-tsung Li Wei-kung wen tui*.

**133** 'Tomita Castle' *Tomita no jō-*: Tonda, in the *Intoku taiheiki*: also called Tsukiyama-jō, or 'Moon Mountain Castle'; near Matsue, in the town of Hirose, district of Nōgi, in Shimane.

**134** Enya Kamonnosuke: (d. 1486) responsible to the Kyōgoku branch of the Sasaki family for preserving law and order in Izumo. See Varley, *Ōnin War*, pp. 131, 159.

**135** Sasaki Ujitsuna: elder brother of Sasaki Sadayori, who is remembered chiefly for his later efforts to restore the fortunes of Ashikaga Yoshizumi's son and heir, Yoshiharu, in the early 16th century.

**136** Amako Tsunehisa: (1458–1541) Sasaki Sadayori had dismissed him for insubordination, whereupon he plotted with the Yamanaka family and regained power. Cf. *Intoku taiheiki*, I, 35–6. The Enyas and the Amakos were both related to the Sasaki family.

**137** 'Yama- [1, 11b] naka.'

**138** 'New Year's Eve' *Ōmisoka no yo*: 4 Feb. 1486, by the Western calendar.

**139** Mizawa and Mitoya: two of the families who formed the backbone of samurai strength in the province.

**140** 'Not to remain indifferent,' etc. *Miru tokoro wo shinobizaru wa*, etc.: paraphrased from a famous passage in *The Book of Mencius*.

**141** 'Swift and penetrating insight' *Toi wakimōru* [1, 12a] *kokoro*.

**142** 'Your aged mother' *Kentei ga rōbo*: literally, 'Sagacious younger brother's aged mother.' Such honourific circumlocutions were characteristic of colloquial Chinese short stories and novels and became a stylistic feature not only of Akinari's tales but those of Tsuga Teishō and others as well.

**143** 'A gentleman values honour,' etc. *Masurao wa gi wo omoshi to su*, etc.: cf. Bishop, *Colloquial*, p. 89.

**144** 'Yesterday and today' *Ki-* [1, 12b] *nō kyō*.

**145** 'The blossoms on the summit of Onoe' *Onoe no hana mo chirihatete*: cf. *Shinshūishū*.

| | |
|---|---|
| *Hatsuse yama* | At Hase Temple |
| *Onoe no hana wa* | The blossoms on the summit |
| *chiri-hatete* | Have already fallen, |
| *irai no kane ni* | And the evening bell proclaims |
| *haru zo kurenuru* | That spring is nearly gone. |

*Kokka taikan*, p. 587 (no. 189). Uzuki, *Ugetsu*, p. 130, points out that *Onoe* may denote not only 'summit,' but also a place name in Kako. I have followed his interpretation.

**146** 'Despite the chilling breeze that blew, and the sweeping waves' *Suzushiki kaze ni yoru nami ni*: poetic diction suggestive of *Shinchokusenshū* (no. 202) and *Fūyōshū* (no. 395). See *Kokka taikan*, pp. 215, 499.

**147** 'Slave on peas porridge and water' *Shukusui no tsubune*: cf. *Li chi* (*The Book of Rites*), where Confucius said, 'Though one sips only peas porridge and drinks water, he should make his parents happy. This is what I call filial love.'

**148** 'Chrysanthemum Festival, the Ninth Day of the Ninth Month'

*Kokonuka no kasetsu*: one of the principal festivities in China; also observed in Japan. Ever since the T'ang dynasty its celebration has been associated with thoughts of dear friends from whom one is parted. It is observed by climbing to a high place, drinking chrysanthemum wine, and placing sprigs of holly berries in ones hair or tucking them in ones belt. See Bishop, *Colloquial*, p. 100, n. 4; *Wu tsa tsu*, 2, 18b; and Morris, *Pillow Book*, II, 12, n. 54.

**149** 'Each fresh month and day' *Aratama no tsukihi*: *aratama*, literally, 'newly bejeweled,' a pillow-word used since the days of the *Man'yōshū* with expressions of time.

**150** 'On the Ninth Day Samon arose earlier than usual' *Kokonuka wa itsu yori mo hayaku*: cf. Bishop, *Colloquial*, pp. 89–90.

**151** 'Two or three stems' *Ni eda* [1, 13a] *san eda*.

**152** 'The province of Izumo' *Yakumo tatsu kuni*: *yakumo tatsu*, originally a pillow-word for Izumo; later a poetic name for the place. See the *Kojiki*, NKBT, vol. 1, pp. 88, 89; note that Lafcadio Hearn's Japanese name, *Koizumi Yakumo*, reveals an assocation with his place of residence.

**153** 'Far beyond the mountains' *Yama-gita no hate ni*: literally, 'at the end of the shade of the mountains.' The *kana* gloss reads *kita*, 'north,' while the Chinese characters refer to the *San'in*, one of the administrative divisions of ancient Japan, which included the province of Izumo.

**154** 'Hundred leagues away' *Hyaku ri*: cf. Bishop, *Colloquial*, p. 91, where the distance is given as a thousand *li*. Akinari typically changed such quantitative expressions to fit the Japanese scene or to avoid fanciful exaggeration (e.g., see note 256).

**155** 'Akana is a warrior,' etc. *Akana wa*, etc.: cf. Bishop, *Colloquial*, p. 91.

**156** 'The day has turned out to be so nice' *Niwa wa kabakari yokarishi*: *niwa*, defined as 'clear day,' in Ikenaga Hadara and Ueda Akinari, *Man'yōshū miyasu hosei* (Osaka: Katsuragi Chōbei, 1809), 3, 32a. This glossary of terms found in the *Man'yōshū*, which affords valuable insight to the diction of *Ugetsu monogatari*, was compiled by a young disciple of Akinari who died in 1796, and it was later edited for publication by Akinari, himself.

**157** Akashi: See note 21.

**158** 'First sailing this morning' *Asabiraki*: as defined by Akinari, himself, in a commentary of selected verses from the *Man'yōshū*, entitled 'Kinsa.' See *Ueda Akinari zenshū*, II, 65. This and the above-listed text exemplify his scholarly work on the *Man'yōshū*, which is mentioned in the introduction.

**159** Ushimado: in the district of Oku, in Okayama Prefecture, on a promonotory facing Shōdo Island. For an illustration of this port in Akinari's day, see John Whitney Hall, *Government and Local Power in Japan, 500 to 1700: A Study Based on Bizen Province* (Princeton: Princeton University Press, 1966), Plate 43, facing p. 331.

**160** Azukijima: popular name for Shōdo Island, in the Inland Sea.

**161** Murozu: once the chief port of the province of Harima; the town of Ozu, district of Ibo, in Hyōgo.

**162** 'Around here' *Kono* [1, 13b] *hotori*.

**163** Uogahashi: formerly a post stop slightly northwest of Kako; now, Amida-chō, in the city of Takasago, in Hyōgo.

**164** 'Don't think him fickle, like the autumn sky' *Hito no kokoro no aki ni wa arazu to mo*: metaphorical of an irresponsible person who easily changes his mind, as in *Shinkokinshū*,

| | |
|---|---|
| *Iro kawaru* | Just as the colour |
| *hagi no shita-ha wo* | Of the leaves and shrubs |
| *mite no mazu* | Changes in season, |
| *hito no kokoro no* | A man's heart may also prove |
| *aki zo shiraruru.* | As fickle as the autumn. |

NKBT, vol. 28, p. 282 (no. 1352). The *hagi*, usually translated as 'bush clover,' is not green all the year around. Therefore, I have rendered it in more general terms. Cf. note 197, *kuzu no ura-ha no*, 'when the leaves begin to turn.'

**165** 'The Milky Way shimmered,' etc. *Ginga kage kiegie ni*, etc.: see note 231 and Bishop, *Colloquial*, p. 91.

**166** 'The sound of the waves in the bay seemed as if surging round the very place where he stood' *Ura nami no oto zo koko moto ni tachi kuru yō nari*: cf. *The Tale of Genji*, p. 246; and NKBT, vol. 15, p. 38.

**167** 'Take a last look' *Tada* [1, 14a] *miru*.

**168** 'Southern window' *Minami no mado*: the place of honour for guests. See also note 421.

**169** 'Covered his face with his sleeve' *Sode wo mote omote wo ōi*: cf. Bishop, *Colloquial*, pp. 92, 101, n. 7–8.

**170** 'My poor efforts' *Seikyū no tsutome*: a Chinese expression referring to the preparation of food; cf. 'Ai-ch'ing chuan,' in *New Tales for Lamplight*, 3, 21b, and *Kokuyaku*, p. 101; derived ultimately from the dynastic history, *Hou han shu*. See Uzuki, *Ugetsu*, p. 151.

**171** 'Your sincere hospitality' *Kentei ga makoto aru aruji-buri wo* [1, 15b].

**172** 'I am not a being of this mortal world' *Ware wa utsusemi no hito ni arazu*: cf. Bishop, *Colloquial*, p. 92. But the Japanese gloss, *utsusemi*, may be traced to verses in the imperial anthologies and the *Man'yōshū* (e.g., no. 24). See Akinari, 'Kinsa,' *Zenshū*, II, 60.

**173** 'Convincing me of the advantages' *Rigai wo tokite*: interpreted according to a Japanese commentary on *Water Margin*, published in 1757. See Nakamura, NKBT, vol. 56, p. 55, n. 22.

**174** 'Retainers who were of faithful heart and served as his claws and fangs' *Fukushin sōga no ie no ko*: from the *Shih Ching*; cf. Waley, *The Book of Songs*, pp. 110, 118.

**175** 'The castle' *Ōgi*: archaic gloss inspired by examples such as *ōgi no*

*yama*, *Man'yōshū*, NKBT, vol. 5, pp. 298–9 (no. 1474). See also Uzuki, *Ugetsu*, pp. 156, 165.

**176** 'Remained until today' *Kyō ni itarashi-* [1, 16a] *mu*.

**177** 'A man cannot cover,' etc. *Hito ichi nichi ni*, etc.: cf. Bishop, *Colloquial*, p. 92.

**178** 'Plate of fish' *Namori*: *na* was the word for fish as a food; *uo* meant fish in the river or sea, as Motoori Norinaga pointed out in *Kojikiden*, in *Motoori Norinaga zenshū* (Tokyo: Chikuma Shobō, 1968), X, 136.

**179** 'Didn't keep his promise' *Chikai no tagō* [1, 16b] *wo*.

**180** 'A man confined in prison,' etc. *Rōri ni tsunagaruru hito*, etc.: cf. Bishop, *Colloquial*, p. 93.

**181** 'Known neither for loyalty,' etc. *Chūgi no kikoe* [1, 17a] *naku*, etc.: cf. ibid., p. 94.

**182** 'Samon rebuked him' *Samon* [1, 17b] *iu*.

**183** 'A warrior ought not to show concern for material things' *Shi taru mono wa fūki shōsoku no koto tomo ni ronzu bekarazu*: more literally, ' . . . ought not give thought to matters of wealth and position or disappearance and appearance,' echoing Akana's remark on p. 112. (See note 143).

**184** 'Kung-shu Tso, of Wei' *Gi no Kōshukuza*: in the wood-block text, Koshukusa; chief minister to King Liang, of the state of Wei, in China, during the Period of Warring States. His biography appears in the *Shih chi* (*Records of the Grand Historian*).

**185** 'Shang Yang' *Shōō*: famous legalist philosopher; also known as Lord Shang. He later served as the chief minister of the State of Ch'in, and his ideas and policies contributed greatly to the conquest of the other kingdoms and to the unification of China.

**186** 'Replied Tso' *Shukuza iu*: Kung-shu is a compound surname, which Akinari apparently did not understand. I have taken editor's liberty.

**187** 'Avoid harm' *Gai* [1, 18a] *wo nogaru*.

**188** 'Amako [1, 18b] Tsunehisa.'

## 3   *The House Amid the Thickets*

**189** Title: In the wood-block text, *Asachi ga yado*. The title calls to mind especially *The Tale of Genji*. After the death of his mother, the infant Genji was taken to live with his grandmother. Aged and sunk in despair, she did nothing to her home, and 'everywhere the weeds grew high,' and the wild autumn gales added to the melancholy. 'Great clumps of mugwort grew so thick that only the moonlight could penetrate them,' and here young Genji spent his early years. The emperor, remembering the grandmother 'in the house amid the thickets' and lamenting that the youngster remained in such a sorry place, hoped to find some means of bringing the boy to court, and he wrote,

| *Kumo no ue mo* | They who live at court |
| *namida ni kururu* | Themselves may break into tears |
| *aki no tsuki* | At sight of the autumn moon, |
| *ikade sumuran* | But what of someone who dwells |
| *asaji fu no yado* | In the house amid the thickets? |

The motif for Akinari's tale may be found most specifically in a passage in 'The Palace in the Tangled Woods': 'Do you suppose, young man, that if she were not waiting day and night for this famous prince of yours, she would still be living in this wilderness?' Akinari's treatment of the universal theme of the forsaken wife also bears close comparison with 'Ai-ch'ing chuan,' in *New Tales for Lamplight*, and its early modern Japanese adaptations in *kanazōshi, ukiyo-zōshi*, and *yomihon* literature. See *The Tale of Genji*, pp. 11–14, 318; and NKBT, vols 14, p. 41 and 15, p. 154. See also, *New Tales for Lamplight*, 3, 14a–23b; and *Kokuyaku*, pp. 94–103.

**190** Shimōsa, etc.: near the Guhōji temple, in the city of Ichikawa, in Chiba. The place name appears in what may be called the Mama poems in the *Man'yōshū*, which figure in the final section of the tale and are found in NKBT, vols 4, pp. 206, 207 (no. 431–3); 5, pp. 416, 417 (no. 1807–8); 6, pp. 416, 417 (nos. 3386–7); see also NGSK, pp. 190–1, 223–4, 278–9.

**191** 'Ashikaga dyed silk' *Ashikaga some no kinu*: a product for which the vicinity around Ashikaga, in southwestern Tochigi Prefecture, had long been famous; mentioned, for instance, in the *Tsurezuregusa*. See Keene, *Essays in Idleness*, p. 177; and NKBT, vol. 30, p. 363.

**192** 'Sasabe agreed quite readily' *Sasabe ito* [2, 1b] *yasuku ukegaite*.

**193** 'Though deeply distressed by the uncertainty of her own future' *Azusa-yumi sue no tazuki no kokoro-bosoki ni*: *azusa-yumi*, literally, 'birch-wood bow,' a pillow-word for a number of related expressions, including *sue*, 'end,' or 'outcome.' The word *tazuki* means 'livelihood.' N.B. *Man'-yōshū*, NKBT, vol. 6, pp. 284–5 (no. 2985).

**194** 'My heart is sure to wander lost among the moors and mountains' *Kokoro no, no ni mo yama ni mo madou bakari*: *hakari*, in the wood-block text; cf. *Kokinshū*,

| *Izuku ni ka* | No matter where I go |
| *yo wo ba itowan* | To get away from it all, |
| *kokoro koso* | My weary heart |
| *no ni mo yama ni mo* | Is sure to wander lost |
| *madou beranare* | Among the moors and mountains. |

NKBT, vol. 8, p. 293 (no. 947).

**195** 'I shall pray with all my heart for your good health' *Inochi dani to wa omou mono*: cf. *Kokinshū*,

| *Inochi dani* | I shall pray |
| *kokoro ni kanō* | With all my heart |
| *mono naraba* | For your good health – |

| | |
|---|---|
| *nani ka wakare no* | And then what fear will parting bring |
| *kanashi karamashi* | And what grief need we suffer? |

NKBT, vol. 8, p. 197 (no. 387).

**196** 'Drift, as if on floating wood' *Ukigi ni noritsu mo*: cf.

| | |
|---|---|
| *Iku kaeri* | Now how many times |
| *yuki kō aki wo* | Can it be I've come and gone, |
| *sugushi tsutsu* | Like the autumns that pass, |
| *ukigi ni norite* | And drifting as on floating wood, |
| *ware kaeruran* | Shall I ever come back again? |

*The Tale of Genji*, p. 348 (my translation); and NKBT, vol. 15, p. 199.

**197** 'When the leaves begin to turn, in the fall, I'll come back' *Kuzu no ura-ha no kaeru wa kono aki naru beshi*: in the wood-block text, *kusu*; the phrase, *kuzu no ura-ha no*, is a *joshi*, or poetic introduction, for *kaeru*, which means both 'to turn,' as the leaves, and 'to return,' as a husband or lover. Cf. note 164, *hagi no shita-ha wo*, 'Of the leaves and shrubs.'

**198** 'Please have courage while you wait' *Kokoro-zuyoku machi* [2, 2a] *tamae*.

**199** 'Cock-crowing land of Azuma' *Tori ga naku Azuma*: wood-block, *Atsuma*; *Azuma*, ancient name for the eastern part of Japan, and *tori ga naku*, a pillow-word for it; both appear frequently in the *Man'yōshū*, e.g., see note 246.

**200** 'In the summer of that year,' etc. *Kotoshi Kyōtoku no natsu*: according to Western chronology, AD 1455.

**201** 'Lord Shigeuji and Governor Uesugi' *Shigeuji Ason, Kanrei no Uesugi*: Ashikaga Shigeuji (1434–97) and Uesugi Norizane (1411–66), who were bitter enemies and shared power in the Kantō area. In 1454 Shigeuji killed Norizane's son, and consequently the shogun permitted the Uesugi family with appropriate reinforcements to attack Shigeuji. This they did, as described in the tale, forcing him to withdraw eastward and set up a new base. See *Kamakura ōzōshi*, pp. 695–705; and *Go-taiheiki*, in *Tsūzoku Nihon zenshi*, vol. 6, pp. 252–4.

**202** 'She wrote,' etc. *To* [2, 2b] *kaku yomeredomo*.

**203** Verse: cf. *Kokinshū*,

| | |
|---|---|
| *Ōsaka no* | At Ōsaka Barrier |
| *yū-zuke tori mo* | The songbird of evening |
| *waga gotoku* | Must also be in love, |
| *hito ya koishiki* | And just as I myself now grieve, |
| *ne nomi nakuran* | Must weep and cry in vain. |

NKBT, vol. 8, p. 210 (no. 536).

**204** 'Shogun Yoshimasa' *Kyōke*: literally, 'the Kyoto house'; Ashikaga Yoshimasa (1435–90), during whose administration the disastrous Ōnin Wars took place. He is remembered not for valour or political skill but for his patronage of art and his taste for luxury, and especially for the Ginka-kuji, or 'Silver Pavillion,' his hermitage in the eastern hills of Kyoto.

205 Tō no Tsuneyori, etc.: (1401–94) warrior and poet descended from the Chiba family of Shimōsa, where his ancestors held the Tō manor (in the district of Katori).
Shimotsuke is the present-day Tochigi. Gujō (in the province of Mino), is now the name of a district in Gifu Prefecture. See *Kamakura ōzōshi*, pp. 702–3.

206 Chiba no Sanetane: a member of the branch of his family that remained loyal to the Ashikaga shogun during these disturbances. With Tsuneyori, he helped oppose Shigeuji's bid for power in the Kantō region.

207 'Eight Provinces' *Hasshū*: those of the ancient Kantō region, namely Sagami, Musashino, Awa, Kazusa, Shimōsa, Hitachi, Kōzuke, and Shimotsuke (prefectures of Kanagawa, Tokyo, Saitama, Chiba, Ibaragi, Tochigi, and Gumma).

208 'Throughout the wretched world there was great destruction' *Asamashiki yo no tsuie nari keri*: as described in *Kamakura ōzōshi*, p. 703.

209 'Soon sold all' *Nokori-naku kōeki* [2, 3a] *seshi*.

210 'Centre of a raging battle' *Kanka michimichite*: an expression found in 'Ai-ch'ing chuan,' in *New Tales for Lamplight*, 3, 20a; and *Kokuyaku*, p. 101.

211 'Cho Lu' *Takuroku*: scene of a famous battle in ancient China during the age of the legendary Yellow Emperor, described in the *Records of the Grand Historian*.

212 'Lovely Kiso hill' *Kiso no misaka*: where the Nakasendō post road passed through the high mountains between Gifu and Nagano (see note 18). *Mi-* is a poetic prefix meaning 'lovely,' or 'beautiful,' as in *Man'-yōshū*, NKBT, vol. 6, pp. 414–5 (no. 3371).

213 'New barriers had been set up here and there,' etc. *Tokoro-dokoro ni shin-seki wo suete*, etc.: cf. similarity in wording and situation to the tale 'Yūjo Miyagino,' in *Otogi bōko*, p. 200.

214 'Musa, in the province of Ōmi': now, the city of Ōmi-Hachiman, in Shiga. This area is famous for its Ōmi merchants, who in Akinari's day assiduously travelled about the country selling cloth and other goods and accumulating great wealth.

215 Kodama [2, 4b] Yoshibei; wood-block, Kotama.

216 'Second year of Kanshō' *Kanshō ninen*: the year 1461 in the Western world.

217 'The Hatakeyama brothers,' etc. *Kinai Kawachi no kuni ni Hata-keyama ga dōkon no arasoi*: In 1460 Hatakeyama Mochikuni's real son, Yoshinari, and his adoptive son, Masanaga, began a war of succession, and other powerful families became involved. Around this time when one dog barked, ten thousand others joined in, and before a semblance of order was restored, warriors from many provinces participated in the fighting. See Varley, *Ōnin War*, pp. 88–95, N.B. p. 91; and *Go-taiheiki*, pp. 255–7.

218 'Here I am . . . living' *Mi no nani wo ta-* [2, 5a] *nomi*.

**219** 'Fields that grow the grass of forgotten love' *Wasuregusa oinuru nobe ni*: cf. *Kokinshū*,

| | |
|---|---|
| Sumiyoshi to | It's a good place to live, |
| ama wa tsugu to mo | The fishermaids may tell you. |
| naga-i su na | But do not tarry long, |
| hito wasuregusa | For here there is supposed to grow |
| ou to iu nari | The grass of forgotten love. |

NKBT, vol. 8, p. 286 (no. 917).

**220** 'Rainy Month' *Samidare*: the 5th month of the lunar calendar.

**221** 'A bridge that once spanned,' etc. *Inishie no tsugihashi mo*, etc.' see *Man'yōshū*,

| | |
|---|---|
| Ano oto sezu | If there were a horse |
| yukan koma mo ga | That could gallop with silent hooves, |
| Katsushika no | In Katsushika |
| Mama no tsugihashi | Across the wooden bridge of Mama |
| yamazu kayowan | I would come to you every night. |

NKBT, vol. 6, pp. 416-7 (no. 3387). In Akinari's 'Kinsa,' *tsugihashi* is defined as a wooden bridge constructed at a river crossing. See *Zenshu*, II, 102.

**222** 'Split by lightning' *Rai ni kudakareshi* [2, 5b]: Readers of *The Tale of Genji* will notice a general similarity between this description and that in 'The Palace in the Tangled Woods,' pp. 317-8 (see also notes 384 and 528).

**223** 'Clearing his throat' *Shiwabuki sureba*: a customary way of announcing ones arrival, found in *The Tale of Genji* and other texts.

**224** 'Heard about the fighting at Kamakura' *Kamakura no heiran wo kiki* [2, 6a].

**225** 'Cloud of Witches Hill' *Fuzan no kumo*: mentioned in the 'Kao-t'ang fu,' by Sung Yü, in the *Wen hsüan*, which relates how a woman once appeared to a former king in a dream and told him that she was the spirit of *Wu shan*, or 'Witches Hill,' and that in the morning she changed into a cloud and that in the evening she caused the rain to fall. See *Monzen bōkun taizen*, 5, 18b; and Waley, *The Temple and Other Poems . . .* (London: Allen & Unwin, 1923), pp. 65-6. See also note 460.

**226** 'Apparition at the Palace of Han' *Kankyū no maboroshi*: The Emperor Wu of the Former Han dynasty lost his beloved consort, the Lady Li, and he held a seance, hoping that they might be reunited. She appeared to him, but when he tried to embrace her, she vanished. See *Han shu*, ch. 67.

**227** 'Miyagi, holding back her tears' *Tsuma* [2, 6b] *namida wo todomete*.

**228** 'Autumn I begged you to return by' *Tanomu no aki*: meaning both *tanomu*, 'to ask,' 'to beg,' or 'to request,' and also *tanomu no sekku*, the first day of the 8th lunar month, when festivities for the new harvest took place.

**229** 'Villagers fled,' etc. *Sato-bito wa mina ie wo sutete umi ni tadayoi yama ni komoreba*: cf. the *Hōjōki* (An Account of My Hut), trans. Keene, *Anthology of Japanese Literature* (New York: Grove Press, 1955), p. 201; and NKBT, vol. 30, p. 27.

**230** 'Rather die as a broken jewel than go on living as common clay' *Tama to kudakete mo kawara no mataki ni wa narawaji mono wo*: woodblock, *narawashi*; metaphorical expression found in a commentary on 'Ai-ch'ing chuan,' in *New Tales for Lamplight*, 3, 20b, which cites the Chinese dynastic history, *Pei-ch'i shu*. See Uzuki, *Ugetsu*, p. 235, and cf. *Kokuyaku*, p. 101.

**231** 'Milky Way' *Ginga*: associated with the Tanabata Festival of the 7th day, 7th month, which is celebrated especially by lovers. On this day the herdboy star is permitted to cross the Milky Way and meet for one night only with the weavermaid. The 7th month by the lunar calendar also marks the beginning of autumn, so in a more general sense the Milky Way also stands for the season.

**232** 'Owls and foxes' *Kitsune fukurō*: associated with deserted houses in Chinese and Japanese literature. See, for example, *The Tale of Genji*, p. 308; NKBT, vol. 15, p. 138; Po Chü-i's verse, 'Hsiung chai shih,' in *Po shih Ch'ang-ch'ing chi*, 1, 3b–4a; 'Ai-ch'ing chuan,' and 'T'ai hsü ssu fa chuan,' in *New Tales for Lamplight*, 3, 18a; 4, 13b; and *Kokuyaku*, pp. 98, 129.

**233** 'But you should know,' etc. *Au wo matsu ma ni koi shinan wa hito shiranu urami naru beshi*: cf. *Goshūishū*,

| | |
|---|---|
| *Hito shirezu* | But you should know |
| *au wo matsu ma ni* | That while I wait for you |
| *koi shinaba* | I may die of yearning, |
| *nani ni kaetaru* | And how could I ever get back |
| *inochi to ka iwan* | This precious gift of life? |

*Kokka taikan*, p. 98 (no. 656).

**234** 'Fifth watch' *Gokō*: the last of the five periods of the night, beginning about 4:00 a.m., depending on the season of the year.

**235** 'Began to grow light' *Ake yuku* [2, 7a] *koro*.

**236** 'Latticework bed' *Sugaki*: coarsely-woven matting made from reeds or bamboo and used for beds before the more finely woven grass mats known as *tatami* came to be employed.

**237** 'Still late summer,' etc. *Aki naranedomo*, etc.: cf. *Kokinshū*,

| | |
|---|---|
| *Sato wa arete* | The place is desolate, |
| *hito wa furi ni shi* | And mother is growing old |
| *yado nare ya* | In my poor cottage, |
| *niwa mo magaki mo* | And both the garden and the hedge |
| *aki no nora naru* | Will remind you of autumn moors. |

NKBT, vol. 8, p. 150 (no. 248).

**238** 'Came back to meet me' *Kae-* [2, 7b] *ri kitarite*.

**239** 'It is only I, I alone who remain unchanged' *Waga mi hitotsu wa moto no mi ni shite*: cf. *Kokinshū*,

| | |
|---|---|
| *Tsuki ya aranu* | The moon is not the same, |
| *haru ya mukashi no* | And spring is not the spring |

*haru naranu* Of olden days –
*waga mi hitotsu wa* It is only I,
*moto no mi ni shite* I alone, who remain unchanged.

NKBT, vol. 8, p. 250 (no. 747); also in *Tales of Ise*.

**240** 'Nasuno paper' *Nasuno-gami*: wood-block, *-kami*; made in the area of Mt Karasuyama, in the Nasu highlands of Ibaragi.

**241** 'Holy name' *Hōmyō*: posthumous name, given to a person at death and usually inscribed on a grave marker or tombstone.

**242** 'Nearest house' *Chikaki ie* [2, 8a].

**243** 'In ruins,' etc. *Are-susamite*, etc.: cf. 'Ai-ch'ing chuan,' in *New Tales for Lamplight*, 3, 18a; and *Kokuyaku*, p. 98.

**244** 'Where this old man lives' *Ie wa izube* [2, 8b] *nite*.

**245** 'Shut myself up tightly' *Fukaku* [2, 9a] *tate-komorite*.

**246** 'Bygone ages ago,' etc. *Inishie no koto yo* [2, 9b], etc.: cf. *Man-yōshū*,

*Tori ga naku* Where the cock crows,
*Azuma no kuni ni* In the land of Azuma,
*inishie ni* Bygone ages ago
*arikeru koto to* In Katsushika,
*ima made ni* There lived a beautiful maiden
*taezu iikuru* Named Mama no Tegona.
*Katsushika no* (So goes the story
*Mama no Tegona ga* That has been handed down.)
*Asa kinu ni* She wore dresses made of hemp
*aokube tsuke* And collars fixed with blue,
*hitasao wo* But in her simple clothes,
*mo ni wa ori-kite* All unadorned –
*kami dani mo* Her hair
*kaki wa kezurazu* Uncombed,
*kutsu wo dani* Her feet
*hakazu kikedomo* Unshod –
*nishiki aya no* Even pampered ladies
*naki ni tsutsumeru* Dressed in rich brocades
*itsuki-go mo* Could not compare
*imo ni shikameya* With this country girl,
*mochizuki no* Whose face was as perfect
*mitsuru omowa ni* As the moon when at the full,
*hana no goto* And whose smile
*emito tatereba* Was like the cherry-blossoms.
*Natsu mushi no* But as summer insects
*hi ni iru ga goto* Are attracted by the flame,
*minato iri ni* And boats always row
*fune kogu gotoku* Hastening into harbour,
*iki kagure* Many suitors came
*hito no iu toki* And pleaded for Tegona's love,

| | |
|---|---|
| *ikubaku mo* | And she in time grew sad |
| *ikeraji mono wo* | That she could not give her heart |
| *nani su to ka* | In the way that she wished, |
| *mi wo tana shirite* | And she threw herself |
| *nami no to no* | Into the surf |
| *sawagu minato no* | That pounds the shore, |
| *okutsuki ni* | And found a watery grave. |
| *Imo ga koyaseru* | Though it was long ago |
| *tōki yo ni* | When Tegona |
| *arikeru koto wo* | Laid herself to rest, |
| *kinō shimo* | It seems like yesterday |
| *miken ga goto mo* | That I last gazed |
| *Omōyuru ka mo* | Upon her lovely face. |
| *Banka* | Envoy |
| *Katsushika no* | In Katsushika, |
| *Mama no i wo mireba* | When I see the well at Mama, |
| *tachi narashi* | I think of her, |
| *mizu kumashiken* | Standing there and drawing water – |
| *Tegona shi omōyu* | Tegona of old. |

NKBT, vol. 5, pp. 416, 417 (no. 1807–8).

**247** 'Made a poem' *To yomi* [2, 10b] *keru*.


## 4  *The Carp That Came to My Dream*

**248** Enchō: era name for the period 923–30.

**249** Mii temple: also known as the Onjōji; founded in 858 by the priest Enchin. The temple, which overlooks Lake Biwa, has stood in perpetual rivalry with the Enryakuji, on nearby Mt Hiei. See Introduction.

**250** Kōgi: mentioned as the name of an actual person in a collection of anecdotes and tales, the *Kokon chomonshū*, compiled in 1254, by Tachibana no Narisue, in NKBT, vol. 84, p. 312.

**251** 'Fishermen who worked with their nets' *Abiki tsuri suru ama ni*: cf. *Man'yōshū*, NKBT, vol. 4, pp. 144–5 (no. 238); vol. 5, pp. 144–5 (no. 1167) and, 222, 228 (no. 1187).

**252** 'Exquisite' *Kuwashiki*: defined as 'surpassingly beautiful' (*bishō ue naki*) in *Man'yōshū miyasu hosei*, 3, 23b. See also *Man'yōshū*, NKBT, vol. 6, pp. 394–5 (no. 3331), and note 425.

**253** 'Putting all his heart' *Kokoro wo* [2, 11b] *korashite*.

**254** 'One year Kōgi was taken ill,' etc. *Hito tose yami ni kakarite*, etc.: cf. the T'ang tale about Hsüeh Wei, who similarly dreamed that he was a fish, in *T'ai p'ing kuang chi*, ch. 471, and an expanded Ming version entitled, 'Hsüeh lu-shih yü fu cheng hsien,' in *Hsing shih heng yen* (Peking: Jen Min Wen Hsüeh, 1957), pp. 522–43, one of the *san yen* tales. For a rather free translation of the former, see Lin Yutang, *Famous Chinese Short Stories* (New York: John Day, 1952).

**255** 'Replied his disciples' *Shūtei-ra iu* [2, 12a].

**256** 'Three days ago' *Mikka saki ni*: compared with 20 days in *T'ai p'ing kuang chi*, p. 37b, and 25 days in *Hsing shih heng yen*, p. 537.

**257** 'Patron' *Danka*: Buddhist expression from the Sanscrit *dana*, possibly belonging to an inherited group of words that includes the Latin *dare*, Italian *donāre*, and French *donner*. See Carl Darling Buck, *A Dictionary of Selected Synonyms in the Principal Indo-European Languages* (Chicago: University of Chicago Press, 1949), pp. 749–50. See also note 502, below.

**258** 'All of them' *Jūrō Kamori wo mo* [2, 12b].

**259** 'More than three feet long' *Mi take amari*: as in *Hsing shih heng yen*, pp. 530, 534, 537, but not *T'ai p'ing kuang chi*.

**260** *Go*: a game introduced from China and played with black and white counters on a board marked into 361 squares.

**261** 'Tall dish' *Takatsuki*: a tray-like utensil, variously round or rectangular, with a single, supporting leg; see *Man'yōshū*, NKBT, vol. 7, pp. 162–3 (no. 3880); and NGSK, p. 275, 'Put it in a tall dish,/ Set it on a table.'

**262** 'Cook' *Kashiwabito*: with the same Chinese characters as in *T'ai p'ing kuang chi*, p. 38b, but with a Japanese gloss meaning literally 'oak-man,' as found in ancient and medieval texts, perhaps reflecting the custom of serving a variety of foods on the leaves of the oak or other trees. Certain sweets, such as *kashiwa-mochi*, are still so prepared.

**263** 'Wished to cool my burning fever a little' *Atsuki kokochi sukoshi samasan* [2, 13a] *mono wo to*.

**264** 'God of the Sea' *Watazumi*: in *Nihon shoki* and other early texts with this meaning; alternatively, the term is used as a poetic word for the sea.

**265** 'By previously freeing living creatures,' etc. *Kanete hōjō no kudoku ōshi*: *hōjō*, a Buddhist term meaning 'to release living cratures as a work of merit,' and *kudoku*, 'achievement,' 'virtue,' and so on.

**266** 'Golden carp' *Kinri*: as described in *Hsing shih heng yen*, pp. 528, 530, 534.

**267** 'Let you enjoy the pleasures of our watery domain' *Suifu no tano-shimi wo sesase tamō* [2, 13b]: *suifu*, or 'watery domain,' see 'Lung t'ang ling hui lu,' *New Tales for Lamplight*, 4, 2b and commentary; also in *Kokuyaku*, p. 118, but without commentary.

In the wood-block text two different *kana* symbols are used for *se*, in *sesase*. The second is the *se* of *Ise*, a form rarely found in early modern texts. See Introduction, on style.

**268** 'Gusts that blow from Mt Nagara,' etc. *Nagara no yama-oroshi*, etc.: wood-block, Nakara; name of the hill on which the Miidera is built. It is famed in *waka* poetry for its gusty winds and blowing snow in winter. See *Senzaishū*, and *Shokushūishū*, in *Kokka taikan*, pp. 151 (no. 461), 312 (no. 463).

Akinari here departs from his Chinese models to introduce a lyrical passage with famous place names from Japanese history and literature. See Introduction.

**269** 'Great Bay of Shiga' *Shiga no ōwada*: poetic name for Lake Biwa, and especially the area around Karasaki, which served as port of entry for the capital in the late 7th century. See Kakinomoto no Hitomaro's elegy, 'On Passing the Ruined Capital of Ōmi,' in the *Man'yōshū*, NKBT, vol. 4, pp. 26–7 (no. 29); and NGSK, pp. 27–8.

**270** 'People on foot,' etc. *Kachibito no mo no suso nurasu yuki-kai ni*: Sometimes they would accidentally get their clothing wet, unlike those mentioned in the verse in the *Shokukokinshū*,

| | |
|---|---|
| *Kachibito no* | The people who stroll |
| *migiwa no kōri* | On the ice by the shore |
| *fumi narashi* | Walk all around, |
| *wataredo nurenu* | And still they stay dry as they cross |
| *Shiga no Ōwada* | The Great Bay of Shiga. |

*Kokka taikan*, p. 278 (no. 641).

**271** Hira: the range of mountains rising on the west bank of Lake Biwa; also known as the Ōmi alps.

**272** 'I wanted to hide,' etc. *Kakure Katada no isaribi ni yoru ʐo utsutsu-naki*: *Katada* (wood-block, Katata), with the meaning *kakure-katata*, 'hard to hide,' and also *Katada no isaribi*, 'fishing fires of Katada,' another place name on the west bank of the lake, north of Karasaki. *Yoru*, meaning first, 'to approach,' and secondly, 'night,' is used as a *kakekotoba*, or 'pivot-word,' with the double function of *isaribi ni yoru*, 'to approach the fishing fires,' and *yoru ʐo utsutsu-naki*, 'inexorable . . . evening.' *Utsutsu-naki* refers both to Kōgi, or the fish's, reactions and to the advancing darkness.

**273** 'Pure black night fell,' etc. *Nubatama no Yonaka no gata ni yadoru tsuki wa*: *nubatama no*, a pillow-word for night, as in 'jet-black night.' *Yonaka* means both 'night,' and the *Yonaka-no-gata*, 'Bay of Yonaka,' as in *Man'yōshū miyasu hosei*, 4, 27b; and *Man'yōshū*, NKBT, vol. 5, pp. 370–1 (no. 1691). *Yadoru*, meaning 'lodged,' is an *engo*, poetically associated with the moon, the night, the stars, and also the Bay of Yonaka.

**274** 'Mirror Mountain' *Kagami no yama*: a prominent peak on the eastern side of the lake, mentioned in *waka* verse. See *Shinshokukokinshū*, in *Kokka taikan*, p. 661 (no. 460).

**275** 'Yaso Harbour' *Yaso no minato*: literally, 'eighty inlets,' or 'every inlet,' as in the *Man'yōshū*, NKBT, vol. 4, 156–7 (no. 273); and NGSK, p. 63, but Akinari uses it as a place name, to designate the scenery along the eastern shore of the lake in the present-day districts of Yasu and Gamō.

**276** 'Oki Island' Okitsushima: the largest island in the lake; now, Oki-no-shima.

**277** Chikubushima: near the northern end of the lake, where there is a shrine to Benten, the goddess of music, art, and dance. It is well known for its red fences. The reflection on the water is mentioned in a lyrical passage from the *nō* play, *Chikubujima*.

**278** 'The famous wind,' etc. *Ibuki no yama-kaze ni, Asazuma-bune mo kogi izureba*: wood-block, koki; Mt Ibuki, to the east of the lake, is a high peak between Shiga and Gifu. Ever since early times it has figured in story and verse. According to the *Kojiki*, a deity who lived on the mountain assumed the form of a huge, white boar and defeated the legendary hero known as The Brave of Yamato.

*Asazuma*, lit., 'morning place,' or alternatively, 'morning wife' (a woman with whom one spends only a single night), is a place name on the eastern shore of the lake. Here it is used as a prelude to morning, as in Saigyō's verse in the *Sankashū*,

| *Obotsukana* | How fearsome is the wind |
| *Ibuki oroshi no* | That blows down from Mt Ibuki |
| *kaza-saki ni* | And drives ahead of it |
| *Asazuma-bune wa* | The morning boats of Asazuma, |
| *ai ya shinuran* | Which sail together from the shore. |

NKBT, vol. 29, p. 175 (no. 1005).

**279** Yabase: in the district of Kurimoto, on the southeastern shore of the lake.

**280** Seta: at the southern extremity of the lake; famous for its bridge over the Seta River, which further downstream becomes the Uji River.

**281** 'When the sun was warm' *Hi atata-* [2, 14a] *ka nareba*.

**282** 'When you saw what a large fish' *Mana wo mite* [2, 14b].

**283** 'Bearing the likenesses of carp' *Egaku tokoro no rigyo* [2, 15a].

**284** Narimitsu: for this artist's name and the legend that follows see *Kokon chomonshū*, NKBT, vol. 84, p. 312.

**285** 'Kan'in Palace' *Kan'in no tono*: built as the personal mansion of Fujiwara no Fuyutsugu (775–826) and later used as an unofficial imperial residence. It formerly stood on a site slightly southwest of Nijō and Saitōin-dōri, in Kyoto.

## 5 Bird of Paradise

**286** Title: In 'The Festival of Red Leaves,' in *The Tale of Genji*, p. 129, as Genji danced, 'There was a wonderful moment when the rays of the setting sun fell upon him and the music grew suddenly louder. Never had the onlookers seen feet tread so delicately nor head so exquisitely poised; and in the song which follows the first movement of the dance his voice was sweet as that of Kalavinka whose music is Buddha's Law.' See NKBT, vol. 14, p. 271.

Although the *buppōsō* – the name of the sacred bird from which the title comes – is hardly as exotic as the Kalavinka, its cry was similarly associated with the three treasures of Buddhism, one of these being Buddha's law. I have translated the title somewhat freely.

**287** 'Japan, the Land of Peace and Calm' *Urayasu no kuni*: a poetic epithet for the nation. According to the *Nihon shoki*, the god Izanagi in naming the country said that Yamato is the Land of Urayasu. *Ura* is explained as 'in one's heart,' and *yasu* means 'peace' or 'tranquillity.' See Aston, *Nihongi*, I, 135; NKBT, vol. 67, pp. 214–5; and *Man'yōshū miyasu hosei*, 1, 44a.

**288** 'Tiller as their pillow' *Kaji-makura*: poetic metaphor for travel by sea or for sleeping on board ship.

**289** 'Strange shores of Tsukushi' *Shiranui no Tsukushi*: *Shiranui no*; in the *Man'yōshū* used as a pillow-word for Tsukushi, the old name for the island of Kyushu. Although its origin and meaning are not clear, one explanation is the 'Unknown Land of Hi' – namely, the provinces of *Hizen* and *Higo*. According to another explanation, *hi*, or 'fire,' refers to the mysterious lights that guided the Emperor Keikō safely to shore when he went to conquer the Kumaso people. Indeed, late in the summer around the inlets and bays of the Sea of Yatsushiro, in southwestern Kyushu, lights from phosphorescent insects are said to appear.

**290** Tsukuba: a prominent mountain in Ibaragi rising above the Kantō plain. The name is associated with the art of linked verse, because here The Brave of Yamato made an inquiry of an old man, and his words took the form of the upper half of a *waka*. The old man in turn couched his reply in the form of the lower half of a verse. Use of the place name foreshadows how linked verse figures later in the tale.

**291** Ōka: a town in the district of Taki, in Mie Prefecture; home of a physician and acquaintance of Akinari. See Introduction.

**292** 'Though he did not actually become a priest' *Imu koto mo naku*: a common practice in early modern times. For a similar instance in real life, see my *Takizawa Bakin*, p. 101. *Imu koto*, lit., 'to mourn,' also means 'to take Buddhist orders.'

**293** Yoshino: a town in the district of the same name in Nara Prefecture. Since early times the region has been famous for the splendour of its cherry-blossoms and its mountain scenery. Places like Hitome Sembon ('A-Thousand-Trees-at-a-Single-Glance') and Oku Sembon and historical shrines such as the tomb of Emperor Godaigo, among many others, have perennially attracted visitors. For Akinari's journal of his own visit, see 'Iwahashi no ki,' in *Akinari ibun* (see Introduction, note 14; and text, notes 462–5).

**294** 'Never been to Mt Kōya *Imada* [3, 1b] *Kōya-san wo mizu*: Kōya, in the district of Ito, Wakayama Prefecture; the holiest place of Shingon Buddhism; site of a great temple and a sacred shrine to Kūkai (or Kōbō Daishi, 774–835), who introduced the Shingon teachings into Japan.

**295** Tennokawa: a village in the district of Yoshino; also the name of a river that rises in the heart of the Yoshino mountains. Here, at a remote shrine, antique *nō* masks are preserved, some dating from the middle ages, and a circuitous route approaches Mt Kōya to the west.

**296** 'Mountain of Mani' *Mani no mi-yama*: poetic epithet for Mt Kōya, derived from a Sanscrit word, *mani-*, 'jewel.' For the prefix *mi-*, see note 212.

**297** 'Central halls,' etc. *Danjō shodō mitamaya*: referring to the area around the Kongōbuji temple and also to the vicinity of the inner shrine. These two places are known as the 'two platforms,' the first representing the Diamond World, or 'wisdom,' and the second the Realm of the Womb, or 'heart.' See Uzuki, *Ugetsu*, pp. 337-8.

**298** 'Wouldn't be the same as sleeping at home' *Ono ga furusato ni mo arazu* [3, 2a].

**299** 'Japan' *Fusō*: a literary name for the country, derived from the Chinese *fu sang*, a sacred tree thought to grow in the Eastern seas, and by extension the land where the tree was found. For Bashō's use of the name in *Oku no hosomichi*, see Keene, *Anthology*, p. 367, '. . . The most beautiful place in Japan'; and NKBT, vol. 46, p. 82.

**300** 'Lantern hall' *Tōrōdō*: a large structure in front of the park-like enclosure consecrated to Kūkai's spirit. This passage shows the influence of 'Miyakata on-ryō roppon sugi ni kai-suru koto' ('The Meeting with the Ghost of the Emperor Godaigo'), in the *Taiheiki*, NKBT, vol. 35, pp. 447-8; see also Uzuki, *Ugetsu*, pp. 333-6.

**301** 'When Kūkai became a deity' *Daishi no jinka*: Commentators are divided over interpretation of this passage, with Uzuki, *Ugetsu*, p. 344, for instance, stating, 'As if he were a deity.' I have more nearly followed Suzuki, *Ugetsu*, p. 246.

**302** 'Spots where his deeds are remembered' *Ihō rekisō* [3, 2b].

**303** 'Trident' *Sanko*: religious implement commonly used in Shingon rites. Its form was derived from an ancient Indian weapon, and its three prongs represent the three divisions of the Realm of the Womb: namely the Buddha part (which stands for spirit), the Lotus part (growth), and the Diamond part (intelligence).

Among the various legends about Kūkai, one tells of his meeting with the god who lived on Mt Kōya. The deity informed Kūkai that his trident happened to land here, and that thereafter the mountain would be reserved for his holy purposes. See *Sangoku denki*, comp. Gentō, around the end of the 14th century (Kyoto: Murakami Kambei, 1656), 3, 8b-9a. For other editions, see Dai-Nihon Bukkyō zensho, vol. 12 (Tokyo: Bussho Kankōkai, 1912); and Koten shiryō, vol. 3 (in 3 parts) (Tokyo: Sumiya Shobō, 1969). As with the *Senjūshō* (see Introduction, note 1, and Text, notes 8, 19, 27, 33, and 40), this little-known collection of Buddhist short stories and anecdotes is deserving of further study.

**304** 'Bird of paradise' *Buppōsō*: Akinari wrote that he had actually heard the bird on Mt Kōya, though he was unable to see its form. See 'Tandai shōshin-roku,' NKBT, vol. 56, p. 281. The *buppōsō* is a migratory bird about the size of a robin with brilliant blue-green markings, legs and bill of red, and a bluish-white patch under its wings, which is especially noticeable when it flies. It lives in the high branches of cedars and cypresses in the forests of southern Honshū. But the bird whose cry is identified with the three treasures of Buddhism (*butsu*, 'the Buddha,' *hō*, 'the law,' and *sō*, 'the monastic order,' read together *buppōsō*), is now known really to be a species of owl called the *Konohazuku*. See Uzuki, *Ugetsu*, pp. 327–8.

**305** 'Hearing it before' *Kikishi to iu hito* [3, 3a]. Literally, 'People who had heard it before.'

**306** Mt Kashō: north of Numata, in the district of Tone, in Gumma; site of the Ryūgeiin temple, said to have been founded by Ennin (794–864), who is best remembered for the diary of his travels to T'ang China. See Uzuki, *Ugetsu*, p. 350.

**307** Mt Futara: another name for Nantai-zan, which overlooks Lake Chūzenji, in Nikkō National Park. Since early times this peak has been identified as a sacred mountain associated primarily with the worship of the deity Ōkuninushi.

**308** Daigo Ridge: in Daigo-Garan-machi, Fushimi-ku, Kyoto. The Daigo-ji temple was founded here in the year 847, and prayers for rain were traditionally conducted at this site.

**309** Mt Shinaga: in the district of Minami-Kawachi, Osaka Prefecture, bordering Nara Prefecture. On the eastern slope, in the district of Kita-Katsuragi, is the Taima temple. Nearby are the tombs of the emperors Bidatsu, Yōmei, and Kōtoku, as well as those of Prince Shōtoku and the Empress Suiko. See also note 460.

**310** 'Verse' *Shige*: *shi-*, the Chinese *shih*, 'poetry,' and *-ge*, derived from the Sanscrit *gatha*, scriptural writing in poetic form, usually in four line stanzas. Romanised, the verse reads,

*Kanrin doku za sōdō no akatsuki*
*sambō no koe wo itchō ni kiku*
*itchō koe ari hito kokoro ari*
*seishin un-sui tomo ni ryō-ryō.*

Rendered in Chinese, the verse has a rhyme scheme of AABA.

**311** Verse: by Fujiwara Mitsutoshi (1210–76); found in several collections, including the *Fuboku waka-shō*, in Kōchū kokka taikei, vol. 22, p. 292, where it appears with three other poems on the subject of the *buppōsō*.

Matsunoo: now Matsuo, in Arashiyama Miyanomae-chō, Ukyō-ku, Kyoto; site of a shrine to the deities Ōyamakui-no-mikoto and Nakatsushima-hime-no-mikoto.

**312** Enrō: (1130–1208) a priest of the Tendai sect, who rebuilt the Saifukuji on this location. The temple was destroyed in the 14th century, but a deity of the mountain is described as showing favour for the Lotus Sutra. See *Sangoku denki*, 6, 31b–32b.

**313** 'How can I resist the inspiration' *Kokoro nakaran ya* [3, 4b].

**314** '*Haikai* mode' *Haikai-buri*: here designates linked verse in a lighter style than that of the ordinary *renga*. It is related to what is now called *haiku* poetry.

**315** 'Sacred mountain/ Has flourished and grown' *Himitsu no yama no shigemi*: *himitsu no yama*; referring to Mt Kōya, headquarters of the esoteric Shingon sect in Japan. *Shigemi*, 'flourishing,' a *kigo*, or poetic 'season word,' for summer, referring both to the occasion and to the prominence of the temple.

**316** 'Travelling ink stone' *Tabi-suzuri*: smaller than the usual receptacle of carved stone in which caked ink and water are mixed to use for writing with a brush.

**317** 'Loud reverberation of shoes' *Kutsu oto takaku hibikite* [3, 5a]. An unusual kind of footgear in Japan before the modern age, worn only with formal court dress when out-of-doors.

**318** Hitachi: Kimura Hitachi-no-suke; follower of Toyotomi Hidetsugu; committed suicide at the Daimonji temple, in the village of Ishikawa, district of Mishima, Osaka Prefecture. See *Taikōki*, in Shiseki shūran, vol. 6, p. 419; see also Introduction.

**319** Shirae: Shirae Bingo-no-kami; retainer of Hidetsugu; committed suicide at the Jōanji temple (now, the Daiun'in), at Teramachi Shijō-Sagaru, Shimokyō-ku, Kyoto. Ibid.

**320** Kumagae: Kumagae Daizennosuke; retainer of Hidetsugu; committed suicide at the Nison'in temple, present-day Saga-Nison'in Mommae, Ukyō-ku, Kyoto. Ibid., p. 420. These three men, who did not accompany Hidetsugu to Mt Kōya, may be thought to have joined their companions later.

**321** Mansaku: Fuwa Mansaku; page of Hidetsugu; a youth in his eighteenth year; he preceded his lord in death on Mt Kōya. Ibid., p. 418.

**322** 'We haven't enjoyed Jōha's conversation lately' *Taete Jōha ga monogatari wo kikazu* [3, 5b]: Satomura Jōha (1524-1602; the generation's most widely acclaimed master of linked verse. Suspected of being in sympathy with Hidetsugu, he was ordered into confiement at the Mii temple. An early *haikai* master, Matsunaga Teitoku (1571-1653), described him in terms similar to those Akinari uses. See *Taionki*, in NKBT, vol. 95, p. 67; see also Keene, 'Matsunaga Teitoku and the Beginning of *Haikai* Poetry,' *Landscapes and Portraits*, pp. 71-93.

**323** 'Muzen and his son had prostrated themselves' *Waga usuzumarishi*; here the narrative shifts from the third to the first person. Note that the reverse change takes place in 'White Peak.' See note 38 and Introduction.

**324** 'Brook of Jewels' *Tamagawa*: name of the stream that flows under the wooden bridge in front of the Tōrōdō.

**325** Verse: as in the *Fūgashū*, with the warning that the Brook of Jewels is contaminated by poisonous insects. See *Kokka taikan*, p. 524 (no. 1778);

and also Akinari's discussion in 'Tandai shōshin-roku,' NKBT, vol. 56, pp. 281–2.

326 'On the surface of which' *Kawa no minakami* [3, 6a] *ni*.

327 'In various provinces' *Kuniguni ni arite*: these are known as the Roku-Tamagawa, or Mu-Tamagawa, 'Six Jewel-Rivers,'

1 *Ide no Tamagawa*: in the town of Ide, district of Tsuzuki, Kyoto Prefecture (between Kyoto and Nara).

2 *Noji no Tamagawa*, or *Hagi no Tamagawa*; in Noji-chō, city of Kusatsu, in Shiga, near the southern end of Lake Biwa.

3 *Tamagawa no sato*, or the 'Hamlet of Tamagawa,' mentioned in the *Man'yōshū* and identified with present-day Mishimae-chō, city of Takatsuki, Osaka Prefecture (on the Yodo River between Kyoto and Osaka).

4 *Kōya no Tamagawa*, or *Takano no Tamagawa*, which I have translated as the Brook of Jewels.

5 *Chōfu no Tamagawa*, rising in the Chichibu mountains west of Tokyo and flowing along the southern edge of the city into Tokyo Bay to form a boundary with the city of Kawasaki.

6 *Noda no Tamagawa*, or *Chidori Tamagawa*, east of the town of Tagajō, district of Miyagi, Miyagi Prefecture, near Shiogama. All of these names are famed in ancient poetry, and not long after the publication of Akinari's tales the verses were combined into a musical composition, *Roku*[or *Mu-*] *Tamagawa no kyoku*, 'Melody of the Six Jewel Rivers.'

328 'Should one pursue his doubts more deeply' *Mata fukaku* [3, 6b] *utagau toki ni wa*.

329 'When the capital was moved to Kyoto' *Ima no miyako no hajime*; in AD 794.

330 'Garland of jewels' *Tamakazura*: The prefix *tama-* (imparting a decorative or poetic quality to the word it modifies), and *kazura* (a poetic variation of *kuzu*, or *tsurukusa*, an ivy-like vine) – first of all means an ornament for the hair. The expression is also used as a pillow-word for *kaku*, 'to hang,' *kage*, 'image,' or *omokage*, 'form,' 'face,' 'shape,' 'demeanor.' Lastly, Tamakazura is the name of one of the memorable women in *The Tale of Genji*.

331 'Jewel-bedecked curtains' *Tamadare*: wood-block, *tamatare*; variously, an elegant synonym for *sudare* ('bamboo curtains or screens'), for a palace, or for a kind of confection; e.g., *Man'yōshū*,

| | |
|---|---|
| *Tamadare no* | Though it may have shone |
| *osu no ma tōshi* | Through the jewel-bedecked curtains, |
| *hitori ite* | Where I sit alone, |
| *miru shirushi naki* | It has brought no sign of you – |
| *yū-zuku yo ka mo* | The moon now fading in the sky. |

NKBT, vol. 5, pp. 200–1 (no. 1073).

332 'Bejeweled finery' *Tamaginu*: literally, a jewel-bedecked robe; used metaphorically for beautiful clothing; e.g., *Man'yōshū*,

| | |
|---|---|
| *Tamaginu no* | Silk and finery, |
| *sai-sai shizumi* | Her gowns rustled quietly – |
| *ie no imo ni* | Though the girl that I love |
| *mono iwazu kite* | Is now far away, |
| *omoi kanetsu mo* | I think of her all the time. |

NKBT, vol. 4, pp. 246–7 (no. 503).

**333** 'A person who devotes himself to Buddhism' *Hotoke wo tōtomu hito*: namely, Emperor Hanazono (1297–1348), who became a Buddhist priest before compiling the *Fūgashū*, where the note in question first appeared.

**334** 'My short verses' *Soregashi ga tanku*: *tanku*, here meaning the *hokku*, the first, or opening part of a *renga*, 'linked verse,' sequence. He is saying in effect that Hidetsugu is quite familiar with his style and might enjoy a little change.

**335** 'He can write poetry in the *haikai* style' *Haikai-buri wo mōshi-* [3, 7a] *te haberu*.

**336** 'Chancellor' *Kampaku*: wood-block, *Kambaku*; official title of Toyotomi Hidetsugu (see note 97). The post was created during the Heian period for members of the Fujiwara family, who exercised *de facto* rule in the emperor's name. Hideyoshi had prepared a geneology that showed him to be descended from the Fujiwara and therefore entitled to occupy this position. After he formally retired in Hidetsugu's behalf, the title was passed on to his nephew.

**337** Sasabe Awaji: When Hidetsugu was forced to commit suicide by *seppuku* on Mt Kōya, Sasabe, Lord of Awaji, served as his second and afterward followed his master in death. See *Taikōki*, p. 419.

**338** Awano Moku: retainer of Hidetsugu; upon hearing word of his lord's fate, he committed suicide at his home in the vicinity of Awataguchi-chō, Sakyō-ku, Kyoto. Ibid., p. 420.

**339** Hibino Shimotsuke: Lord of Shimotsuke; father of Hidetsugu's concubine, O'Ako; he committed suicide in the vicinity of Kitano, near the Kinkakuji temple. Ibid.

**340** Yamaguchi Shōun: father of another concubine, O'Tatsu; committed suicide in the Kitano area. Ibid.

**341** Marumo Fushin: retainer of Hidetsugu; saying that he was too old for *seppuku*, he asked that he be beheaded. This was done in front of the gate of the Sōkokuji temple, Kamikyō-ku, Kyoto. Ibid.

**342** Lay Priest Ryūsai: retainer of Hidetsugu, whom he preceded in death on Mt Kōya. Hidetsugu, himself, acted as his attendant. Ibid., p. 418.

**343** Yamamoto Tonomo: a young retainer; first of the party on Mt Kōya to commit suicide. Ibid.

**344** Yamada Sanjūrō: second on Mt Kōya to commit suicide; still a youth in his eighteenth year. Ibid. The mass suicide of Hidetsugu and his party was without precedent at Mt Kōya. The monks were loath to permit the orders to be carried out, but they feared that Hideyoshi might completely destroy their temple, as Nobunaga had the Enryakuji on Mt Hiei some three decades earlier.

**345** 'And myself, Jōha' *Kaku iu wa Jōha* [3, 7b].

**346** *Keshi taki*: literally, 'burning mustard seed.' Owing to its hardness and its bitter taste, it is used in esoteric Buddhist rites to overcome demons and to destroy illusions.

**347** 'Said . . . by way of compliment' Kyō-ji tamaite [2, 8a].

**348** 'Demons from the Hell of Fighting Beasts' *Ashuradomo*: from the Sanscrit *ashura* or *sura*, demons who war with Indra. They are the titanic enemies of the *dévas*, and in Buddhist thought they represent one of the eight classes of sentient creatures. People who in a previous existence suffered from pride or jealousy or took pleasure at gaining victory over others entered this category of existence after death and were forced to endure the constant torment of warfare or competition.

In Japan the idea of a hell for power-hungry men or overly ambitious rulers may be traced to such medieval texts as the *Hōgen monogatari*, *Gempei seisuiki*, *Taiheiki*, and *Shasekishū*. Emperors like Sutoku, Gotoba, and Godaigo, who tried to assert themselves and who died harbouring resentment, were said to have entered this hell. Here they were forced to drink molten metal three times a day and to endure various other torments. Nevertheless, they retained the spiritual power to effect curses and assume the form of *tengu*, or demons, who dwelt on famous mountain peaks in many provinces. Shaped something like persons but with a long nose, a beak, and wings like a bird, these demons appeared in the world as a portent of disaster. Sometimes they carried away haughty and prideful persons and pecked them to death or hung them from the branches of trees. See Nakamura, in NKBT, vol. 56, p. 384, n. 8.

**349** 'Ishida, Masuda, and all the rest' *Ishida Masuda ga tomogara*: Ishida Mitsunari (1560–1600); native of Ōmi; famous warrior of the Azuchi-Momoyama period, and one of Hideyoshi's most trusted advisors. After Hideyoshi's death, he supported Hideyori against Ieyasu and was defeated at the Battle of Sekigahara, in 1600, and beheaded in Kyoto.

Masuda Nagamori (1546–1615), native of Owari; lord of Kōriyama Castle, in Yamato, and trusted advisor to Hideyoshi. At Sekigahara he fought against Ieyasu, and consequently his lands were reduced. During the Seige of Osaka, in 1615, he again supported Hideyori's cause, and in defeat he committed suicide. See *Taikōki*, p. 423.

**350** 'The first signs of dawn' *Shino-no-me no*: literally, 'shoots of thin bamboo,' a pillow-word for *aku*, 'to open,' or 'to grow light.'

**351** 'The Mound of Beasts' *Akugyaku-* [3, 8b] *zuka*: The common grave of the victims of Hideyoshi's purge against his nephew, his family, and his followers. A marker still stands at the Zuisenji temple, near Kawaramachi Sanjō, in Kyoto.

## 6   The Caldron of Kibitsu

**352** Title: The Kibitsu Shrine is in the town of Magane, district of Kibitsu, Okayama Prefecture, on the Hakubi rail line, west of the city of Okayama. The principal deity of the shrine is Ōkibitsuhiko-no-mikoto, identified as the Emperor Kōrei's son, who was responsible for subjugating the land of Kibi. Especially venerated during the Heian period, and experiencing a revival of its fortunes in the 15th century, when Akinari's tale is set, the shrine's importance declined in early modern times. After the Meiji Restoration, however, it once again benefited from imperial patronage. It is famed for two sacred kettles, one of which is the singing caldron that figures in the tale.

Among Akinari's literary sources, 'The Chronicles of Ingyō,' in the *Nihon shoki*, deserves special mention. First of all, it contains the central idea of Akinari's tale – the eternal triangle and the suffering it causes when a man takes a wife and later falls victim to the charms of another woman, thereby arousing his mate's jealousy. Ingyō, the emperor, much to the empress's vexation, took the maid Otohime, just as Shōtarō established Sode in a new household. Secondly, the same chronicle also mentions the use of caldrons with boiling water, though here they are used with trial by ordeal. Also, a number of points in Akinari's diction reveal considerable indebtedness. See Aston, *Nihongi*, I, 317, 318–22; and NKBT, vol. 67, pp. 438–9, 440–6.

**353** 'You may hate the clamours of a jealous wife,' etc. *Tofu no yashinai-gataki mo*, etc.: from *Wu tsa tsu*, 8, 7b–12a; cf. Howard Levy, *Warm-Soft Village: Chinese Stories, Sketches and Essays* (Tokyo: Dai Nippon Insatsu, 1964), pp. 10–4.

**354** 'She can wreak her fury with a thunderbolt' *Hatatagami wo furūte urami wo mukuu*: Among the various sources, the idea for the tale also appears in a story about a certain high official in the Chinese state of Shu, where there were many singing girls. While the official's wife was alive he dared not cast a glance at them, but as soon as she died he summoned one of them for his pleasure. A great thunderbolt struck the place where the pair slept and frightened them so that they took ill and finally lost their lives. See *Wu tsa tsu*, 8, 11b.

**355** 'Mincemeat' *Shishibishio*: wood-block, *shishibishi*, a misprint. The first emperor of the Ming dynasty did this to the wife of one of his generals. He ordered that her body be dismembered, salted, and dried. Ibid., p. 12a; Levy, *Warm-Soft*, p. 13; and also the *Ming shih*, biography of Ch'ang Yü-ch'un.

**356** 'His wife's jealous nature' *Onna no kadamashi-* [3, 9a] *ki saga*.

**357** 'Province of Kibi,' etc. *Kibi no kuni Kaya no kōri Niise no sato*: the modern Niwase, now the name of a railroad station and a part of the town of Kibi, district of Tsukubo, in Okayama, between the cities of Okayama and Kurashiki.

358 Harima: now part of Hyōgo Prefecture. For the Akamatsu family, which was descended from the Murakami Genji, see Introduction, and also the medieval chronicle, *Kakitsu-ki*, in Gunsho ruijū, vol. 13, pp. 308–17. See also Varley, *Imperial Restoration*, pp. 88, 123.

359 'Kamowake of Kibi' *Kibi no Kamowake* [3, 9b]: one of the oldest families in the region. When the Emperor Ōjin went to Kibi, Mitomowake, together with his brothers, his children, and his grandchildren, entertained him and afforded him great pleasure. As a reward, the emperor granted the lands of the province to the family. One of the younger brothers, known as Kamowake, was the founder of the Kasada line. See Aston, *Nihongi*, I, 155, 267; and NKBT, vol. 67, pp. 243, 374–7, 626, n. 21.

360 'Our house hardly compares with theirs' *Monko teki subekaraneba*: cf. 'Ts'ui-ts'ui chuan,' in *New Tales for Lamplight*, 3, 24b; and *Kokuyaku*, p. 105.

361 'Now, people who worshipped' *Nao saiwai wo kami ni* [3, 10a] *inoru to te*.

362 'Once the scarlet cord is tied,' etc. *Kano sekijō ni tsunagite wa* etc.: from a Chinese tale of the T'ang dynasty about a person named Wei Ko, who when travelling met an old man reading a book under the moonlight. The old man revealed that he was the god of marriage, and that when he bound a couple's legs with the scarlet cord that he carried in his purse, they could never be parted, even though their families were enemies or they came from different countries.

363 'She can hardly wait' *Machi waburu mono* [3, 10b] *wo*.

364 'Thousand years of the crane and the myriad ages of the tortoise' *Tsuru no chitose, kame no yorozu yo*: proverbial of long life. The literary source may be traced ultimately to a Chinese Taoist work, the *Huai nan tzu*. See also the *nō* play, *Tsurukame*.

365 'Arose early,' etc. *Tsuto ni oki, osoku fushite*: as a dutiful member of the family should, according to the teachings of the *Hsiao ching*, or Confucian classic of filial piety.

366 'Habit of playing around with women' *Tawaketaru saga*: reflecting the diction of 'The Chronicles of Ingyō,' Aston, *Nihongi*, I, 324 ('illicit intercourse'); and NKBT, vol. 67, pp. 448–9.

367 'Port of Tomo' *Tomo no tsu*: mentioned in the *Man'yōshū*, NKBT, vol. 5, pp. 220, 221 (no. 1182), and identified with present-day Tomoe-chō, in the city of Fukuyama, Hiroshima Prefecture, about twenty miles south of the urban centre.

368 'She accused him of being an unreliable fellow' *Ada naru kokoro wo urami kakotedomo* [3, 11a].

369 'Confinement' *Oshikome*: a type of punishment during early modern times, consisting of imprisonment for a set period in one's quarters or in a certain room.

370 Inamino: the strip of coast between Akashi and Takasago, from the

mouth of the Akashi River to that of the Kako River, in Hyōgo; a place name appearing in *Man'yōshū*, NKBT, vol. 5, pp. 220–1 (nos. 1178, 1179).

**371** 'How can we get' *Ta ga hakarigoto* [3, 11b] *shite ataen*: wood-block, *hakarikoto*.

**372** 'Arai' Arai-chō, in the city of Takasago.

**373** 'Make a living together' *Tomo* [3, 12a] *ni watarai*.

**374** 'She lay,' etc. *Tada ne wo nomi nakite, mune semari taegatage ni*: cf. *The Tale of Genji*, p. 162; and NKBT, vol. 14, p. 329, where Lady Aoi's fits of weeping are described in similar terms, as she suffers from possession by the jealous spirit of the Lady Rokujō, with whom Genji has had an affair.

**375** 'Swearing that he would follow Sode in death' *Tomo ni mo to mono-kuruwashiki wo* [3, 12b].

**376** 'He had no means for summoning Sode's spirit' *Chōkon no hō wo mo motomuru sube naku*: Ritual invocations to the dead might be carried out by a variety of means, such as hiring a shaman to call the soul and coax it back with descriptions of the pleasures that awaited it on earth. See Keene, *Essays in Idleness*, p. 174; NKBT, vol. 30, p. 259; and also David Hawkes, *Ch'u T'zu: The Songs of the South, An Ancient Chinese Anthology* (Oxford: Clarendon Press, 1959), pp. 101–9.

**377** 'Each moment of the day,' etc. *Hiru wa shimira ni*: cf. the verse on jealousy in the *Man'yōshū*, 'Each moment of the whole long day,/ Each moment of the darkest night,/ I weep and wait . . .,' NGSK, p. 309; NKBT, vol. 6, pp. 360–1 (no. 3270); and also *Man'yōshū miyasu hosei*, 2, 50b.

**378** 'Lost in the reveries brought on by this lonely autumn' *Kono aki no wabishiki wa waga mi hitotsu zo*; cf. *Kokinshū*, NKBT, vol. 8, p. 140 (no. 193).

**379** 'A similar sorrow existed under the heavens' *Amakumo no yoso ni mo onaji nageki arite*: cf. McCullough, *The Tales of Ise*, p. 83; and NKBT, vol. 9, p. 123, *Amakumo no yoso ni mo hito no. . . .*

**380** 'Coming here each evening to worship' *Yoi-yoi goto ni mōde* [3, 13a] *haberu*.

**381** 'She' *Toji*: literally, 'ladyship'; see *Man'yōshū miyasu hosei*, 3, 22b, where a Chinese expression from 'The Chronicles of Ingyō' is cited. The commentary explains that *toji* is the proper reading and that it means the lady or mistress of a house.

**382** 'On the edge of the moors' *Kono no no* [3, 14b] *kuma ni*.

**383** 'Renowned for her beauty' *Kao-yo-bito naru*: perhaps coined by analogy with 'The Chronicles of Ingyō,' NKBT, vol. 67, p. 445, *kao-yoki-onna wo etari*.

**384** 'By a shadowy grove,' etc. *Oguraki hayashi no uchi ni*, etc.: This and the following description are particularly indebted to *The Tale of Genji*, pp. 63–78, 317–21, passim; and NKBT, vols 14, pp. 139–71, 15, pp. 151–8 (see also notes 222 and 528).

385 'A small garden, which had been left to neglect' *Hodo naki niwa no aretaru sae miyu*: cf. *Genji*, p. 63, and NKBT, vol. 14, p. 140.

386 'Peer into the house' *Mi-iru ni* [3, 15a].

387 'Black lacquer cupboard' *Kurotana*; used mainly for decoration and for displaying such items as incense burners and other small objects. Similar to *zushi* (see note 423).

388 'Thin, blue finger' *Te no aoku ho-* [3, 15b] *soritaru*.

389 Hamlet of Toda: perhaps the Kokurinji temple, of the Tendai sect, in Kakogawa. This institution is also known as Toda-san.

390 'Soothsayer' *On'yōji*: formerly an official of the On'yōryō, or Bureau of Divination; later, any person skilled in matters of astronomy, the calendar, fortune telling, divination, and spells.

391 'For the next forty-two' *Yonjū-ni nichi ga aida* [3, 16a]: According to Buddhist belief, the spirit wanders in a purgatory-like state for forty-nine days; forty-two of these are yet to pass.

392 'Characters in the style of ancient seals' *Tenchū no gotoki moji*; wood-block, *tenryū*; the ancient form of Chinese characters dating from the Chou and Ch'in dynasties, which were traditionally used on seals.

393 'Slips of paper with spells inscribed on them in vermillion ink' *Shufu amata kami ni shirushite*: cf. 'Mu t'an teng chi,' in *New Tales for Lamplight*, 2, 29a; and *Kokuyaku*, p. 65. In China a *fu* was originally a bamboo tally slip, the two halves of which were matched for verification. Later, soothsayers used similar slips, on which they wrote charms with vermilion ink, and the word *shufu* came to mean an amulet or spell. For the early use of such seals and charms among Taoists and Buddhists and on their role in the development of the art of printing, see Thomas Francis Carter and L. Carrington Goodrich, *The Invention of Printing in China and Its Spread Westward*, 2nd ed. (New York: Ronald Press, 1955), pp. 12–18, 48–9, 202.

394 'Third watch' *Sankō*: see note 234. This episode takes place in autumn, when there were 'long hours of darkness.'

395 'Wind howled through the pine trees, as if to topple the very trunks' *Matsu fuku kaze mono wo taosu ga gotoku* [3, 16b]: cf. *The Tale of Genji*, p. 69; and NKBT, vol. 14, p. 151, where a violent storm sweeps through the pine trees around the deserted mansion to which Genji has taken Yugao. Akinari's passage also reveals indebtedness to 'Mu t'an teng chi,' and 'Yung chou yeh miao chi,' *New Tales for Lamplight*, 2, 33b; 3, 8b; and *Kokuyaku*, pp. 70, 87.

396 'Seemed more than a thousand years in passing' *Chitose wo suguru yori mo hisashi*: cf. *The Tale of Genji*, p. 69, 'It seemed to him that this night was lasting a thousand years,' and NKBT, vol. 14, p. 151, *Chiyo wo sugusan kokochi*.

397 'Imprudent fellow' *Yōi* [3, 17a] *naki otoko*.

398 'Nothing else than a bleeding head, torn and mangled' *Otoko no kam ino motodori bakari kaka-* [3, 17b] *rite*.

## 7 *The Lust of the White Serpent*

**399** Title: This is the longest tale in the collection, and it is the most complex in terms of structure and style. For the most part, Akinari remains faithful to a Chinese story set in the famous West Lake region of Hang-chou, entitled, 'Pai Niang-tzu yung chen Lei-feng-ta' ('Madam White Is Forever Buried at Thunder-Peak Pagoda'), in the *Ching shih t'ung yen*, one of the *San yen* collections. But Akinari's 'White Serpent' also reveals his close familiarity with classical Japanese texts, such as the *Kojiki*, the *Man'yōshū*, and *The Tale of Genji*. The legend of Anchin and Kiyohime, immortalised in the *nō* drama, *Dōjōji*, similarly figures in the tale. The result is a literary mosaic dealing with the archetypal idea of a serpent who assumes the guise of a beautiful woman and tries to tempt a man.

**400** 'Once upon a time, though it matters not exactly when' *Itsu no tokiyo nari ken*: cf. opening passage of *The Tale of Genji*, p. 7; and NKBT, vol. 14, p. 27, *izure no on-toki ni ka*.

**401** 'Cape of Miwa' *Miwa ga saki*: at the southern tip of the Kii Peninsula in Wakayama Prefecture; now part of the city of Shingu. This area was formerly known as Kumano, and it is situated south of the Yoshino region of Nara Prefecture.

**402** Ōya: a variation of a surname appearing in the *Shinsen shōjiroku*, compiled in AD 815, a genealogical record of 1,182 surnames from the time of the Emperor Jimmu to that of Saga.

**403** 'Rich in the luck of the sea,' etc. *Umi no sachi arite*, etc.: cf. Philippi, *Kojiki*, p. 148; and NKBT, vol. 1, pp. 134–5.

**404** 'Become a scholar' *Hakase ni mo nare* [4, 1b] *kashi*.

**405** Shingu Shrine: popular name for the Kumano Hayatama Jinja, in Shingu; one of the three holy places of Kumano. Ever since ancient times pilgrims worshipped at the holy spots of the Kumano Nimasu Jinja (Kumano Hongu) and the Kumano Nachi Jinja (Nachi Gongen) before proceeding to the Shingu shrine, the deities of which early Japanese emperors had revered.

**406** 'Around the end of the Ninth Month' *Nagazuki suetsukata*: Japanese gloss meaning the 'Long Month,' with the Chinese characters for 9th month, last 10 days. *Nagazuki* is a poetic designation for the month, and *suetsukata*, literally, 'last part,' is an elegant but archaic word appearing in such works at *The Tale of Genji*.

**407** 'Southeast' *Tatsumi*: Japanese gloss, meaning the direction of the dragon and the snake, with the Chinese characters for 'southeast' – the locality noted for producing especially severe storms.

**408** 'A light drizzle began to fall' *Kosame sobo furi kuru*: wood-block, *soho furi*; cf. *Man'yōshū*, NKBT, vol. 7, pp. 162–3 (no. 3883), *kosame sobo furu*.

**409** Asuka Shrine: in present-day Kami-Kumano, in Shingu.

**410** 'Very beautiful' *Ito nioiyaka-* [4, 2a] *ni.*

**411** 'A pattern representing distant mountains' *Tōyama-ʐuri no*: typical of autumn; this particular design is mentioned in several of the imperial anthologies of *waka* verse.

**412** 'The pair looked drenched and bedraggled' *Shitodo-ni nurete wabishige-naru ga*: wood-block, *Shitoto-ni;* cf. McCullough, *Tales of Ise,* p. 142; and NKBT, vol. 9, 174, *shitodo-ni nurete madoi ki ni keri.*

**413** 'Three Holy Places' *Mitsu yama*; see note 405.

**414** 'On your way to the Minenoyu Hot Springs' *Minenoyu ni ya ide tachi tamōran* [4, 2b]: Yunomine Hot Springs, in the town of Hongu, district of Higashi-muro, where pilgrims often used to bath and rest.

**415** Verse: from the *Man'yōshū*; see NKBT, vol. 4, 154-5 (no. 265) Miwagasaki is now part of Shingu.

**416** 'Your thoughtfulness makes me feel as if I were already dry' *Sono mi-omoi ni hoshite mairi nan*: *i*, of *omoi* (*hi*, in the traditional *kana* orthography), is an *engo*, poetically associated with 'flame' or 'fire.' It therefore leads to *hosu*, 'to dry.' Cf. McCullough, *Tales of Ise,* p. 148; and NKBT, vol. 9, p. 179.

**417** Nachi: see note 405.

**418** 'Please tell me where you live' *Sate* [4, 3a] *mi-sumai wa iʐube ʐo.*

**419** 'Afternoon came' *Hiru katabuku made* [4, 4b]: wood-block, *katafuku*; literally, 'until the sun slanted.'

**420** 'Blocking Toyoo's way' *Tachi-fusagarite* [4, 5a].

**421** 'Southern front room' *Minami omote no tokoro*; the main room of the house, which traditionally faces south in Japanese architecture (cf. note 168).

**422** 'Curtains' *Kichō*; to seclude the place where a person of nobility sat. A pair of vertical poles with a horizontal rod was attached to a stand, and silk curtains in the style of the season were then hung.

**423** 'The articles in the cabinet' *Miʐuchi no kaʐari*; the honorific *mi-* with *ʐushi* (cf. note 387).

**424** 'Drapery' *Kabeshiro*; silk or damask tapestry used to divide the portion of a room reserved for sleeping from the space needed for other activities.

**425** 'Lovely as a garland of cherry-blossoms' *Hana-guwashi sakura*; traditional metaphor for a beautiful woman, as in 'The Chronicles of Ingyō,'

| | |
|---|---|
| *Hana-guwashi* | She was as lovely |
| *sakura no mede* | As the cherry-blossoms, |
| *koto mede wa* | That girl whom I loved, |
| *hayaku wa medeʐu* | And though I had no business loving her, |
| *waga meʐuru ko ra* | I loved her all the same. |

Also cf. *Man'yōshū,*

| | |
|---|---|
| *Hana-guwashi* | Beyond a reed fence |

| | |
|---|---|
| *ashi-kaki-goshi ni* | I first caught a glimpse of her, |
| *tada hitome* | As lovely as the cherry-blossoms; |
| *aimishi ko yue* | Though it was but a single glance, |
| *chitabi nagehitsu* | I sighed for her a thousand times. |

NKBT, vol. 6, pp. 200–1 (no. 2565); vol. 67, pp. 444–5 (also see note 252 and cf. note 462, *na-guwashi no*).

**426** 'Soaring and flitting among the trees' *Koʒue tachi-guku*: cf. *Man'yōshū*,

| | |
|---|---|
| *Ashibiki no* | In a forest grove |
| *ko no ma tachi-guku* | Soaring and flitting among the trees, |
| *hototogisu* | The cuckoo bird sang; |
| *kaku kikisomete* | That was when I heard it first, |
| *nochi koimu kamo* | And that is why I love it so. |

NKBT, vol. 5, pp. 304–5 (no. 1495).

**427** 'Something that I must tell you,' etc. *Iwade yami nan mo; yamu* wood-block, *iwate*; has the double meaning of 'to stop' and 'to fall ill.' The passage means both, 'I can't stop myself from telling you,' and 'If I don't tell you, perhaps I'll fall ill.'

**428** 'What innocent god might have to endure unjust accusations' *Iʒure no kami ni naki na ōu suran kashi*: cf. McCullough, *Tales of Ise*, p. 132; and NKBT, vol. 9, p. 165.

**429** 'You mustn't take me to be inconstant in my affections' *Yume ada-* [4, 5b] *naru koto*.

**430** 'I was married before' *Kitanaki mono ni*: literally, 'I am a thing defiled,' owing to her previous marriage.

**431** 'Said nothing to Manago' *Kotō beki* [4, 6a] *kotoba naki wo*.

**432** 'Sea to rise and cover me' *Umi ni mo ira de*: cf. *The Tale of Genji*, p. 83; and NKBT, vol. 14, p. 181. Notice the similarity of imagery in 'Chrysanthemum Tryst.' See note 166.

**433** 'Stumbles on the hill of love, as did even Confucius' *Kushi sae taoruru koi no yama*: cf. *The Tale of Genji*, pp. 484–5; and NKBT, vol. 15, p. 403.

**434** 'Prized as a matchless treasure' *Futatsu naki takara ni mede* [4, 6b] *tamō*.

**435** 'Tonight you must stay here with me' *Koyoi wa koko ni akasase tamae*: If he had, presumably they would have been man and wife. See William H. McCullough, 'Japanese Marriage Institutions in the Heian Period,' *Harvard Journal of Asiatic Studies*, 27 (1967), 103–67.

**436** 'Oversee the fishermen' *Ago totonōru*: cf. *Man'yōshū*, NKBT, vol. 4, pp. 144–5 (no. 238); and NGSK, p. 61.

**437** 'Someone gave it to me yesterday' *Kinō hito no esa-* [4, 7a] *seshi wo*.

**438** 'Great shrine festival' *Ōmiya no matsuri*: traditionally held at the Shingu shrine on the 15th day of the 9th month, and now on 15 October.

**439** 'But really' *Makoto-* [4, 7b] *ni*.

**440** 'Although it may be beyond my power' *Oroka nari* [4, 8a] *to mo*.

**441** 'Taking the weapon to his father' *Mimae ni mochi-* [4, 8b] *ikite*.

**442** 'Has never stolen so much as a single hair' *Ichimō wo mo nukazaru*: conventional metaphor for honesty, found in *The Book of Mencius*.

**443** 'Through what sin of ours should he turn to such evil' *Nan no mukui ni te kō yokaranu kokoro ya ide-kinuran*: reflecting the Buddhist idea of retribution and implying that he may be caught in a web of misfortune beyond his control.

**444** 'Turn him in tomorrow' *Asu wa uttae-ideyo*: stealing property from a large shrine was classified as a crime the punishment for which extended to the entire family. See Nakamura, NKBT, vol. 56, p. 106, n. 18.

**445** 'Escorted him to the head priest's mansion' *Tachi ni ōi mote* [4, 9a] *yuku.*

**446** 'Pillars of the entrance,' etc. *Mon no hashira*, etc.: cf. *The Tale of Genji*, p. 64; and NKBT, vol. 14, p. 142.

**447** 'Utterly dumbfounded' *Tada akire ni* [4, 9b] *akire.*

**448** Tsukushi: see note 289.

**449** 'Large pine tree lay sprawled' *Ōki-naru matsu no fuki-* [4, 10a] *taoretaru*: cf. *The Tale of Genji*, p. 69; and NKBT, vol. 14, p. 151 (see also note 395).

**450** 'Warriors had taken these things back' *Monofu-ra kore wo* [4, 10b] *tori-motasete*: alternatively, 'After the warriors made Toyoo carry these things back, they explained. . . .'

**451** Tsuba: now part of the city of Sakurai, in Nara Prefecture, south of the city of Nara. Sei Shōnagon called this market the most noteworthy in all of Yamato province, because everyone on their way to Hase temple stopped there, and its connections with the image of the Goddess of Mercy at Hase distinguished it from other places of its kind (see Morris, *Pillow Book*, I, 14). It is also mentioned in the *Kagerō nikki* (The Gossamer Years) and other Heian texts. Akinari, himself, wrote a brief sketch on the subject of travelling to Hase, in which he mentioned the bustling nature of Tsuba market and the goods and products sold there.

The episode that follows bears comparison with the portion of *The Tale of Genji* where Tamakatsura's visit to Hase temple and reunion with her childhood nurse are described. See pp. 444-54; NKBT, vol. 15, pp. 343-54; and 'Hatsuse mōde,' in *Akinari ibun*, pp. 388-90.

**452** 'Second Month' *Kisaragi*: wood-block, *Kisaraki*; Chinese characters for 2nd month, with Japanese gloss meaning, 'the month of new buds.'

**453** Hase temple: slightly to the east of the urban centre of Sakurai. Known variously as the Hatsuse-dera, the Chōkokuji, and the Kagura-in, it was first built during the Nara period, and later it came to be associated with the Shingon sect. The eleven-headed image of the Goddess of Mercy enshrined here was especially popular in the Heian period. The temple has been destroyed several times by fire, including once at the end of the middle ages, when Hideyoshi ordered it put to flames, but it has always been rebuilt, most recently in the 18th century.

**454** 'Among the various Buddhist deities' *Hotoke no* [4, 11a] *on-naka.*

**455** 'Renown had spread abroad to China' *Morokoshi made mo kikoetaru to te*: According to a legend found in one of the manuscript versions of *The Tale of Genji*, the T'ang emperor, Hsi Tsung, had a wife who was very ugly. On the advice of a Taoist sage, he prayed to the Goddess of Mercy of the Hase temple. Then he dreamed that a priest came from the east riding on a purple cloud and washed the empress's face with a jar of water that he carried with him. Suddenly she became very beautiful. See p. 444; and NKBT, vol. 15, p. 343.

For Lady Sarashina's description of a pilgrimage to Hase temple, see Morris, *As I Crossed a Bridge of Dreams: Recollections of a Woman in Eleventh-Century Japan* (New York: The Dial Press, 1971), pp. 98–107.

**456** 'Put your mind at ease' *Mikokoro yari-sesase* [4, 11b] *tatematsuran.*

**457** 'Soon made the house look dilapidated and abandoned' *Tomi-ni* [4, 12a] *nora-naru yado no sama wo koshiraeshi.*

**458** 'The twin fir trees' *Futamoto no sugi*: among the objects of worship at Hase temple. They are mentioned in a *sedōka*, or verse in two stanzas of 5-7-7, in the *Kokinshū*,

| | |
|---|---|
| *Hatsuse-gawa* | On Hatsuse River |
| *Furukawa nobe ni* | Not far from the Ancient Stream |
| *futa-moto aru sugi* | By the twin fir trees standing there, |
| *Toshi wo hete* | I hope that in future years |
| *mata mo ai min* | Once more we shall meet |
| *futamoto aru sugi* | By the twin fir trees standing there. |

These trees fell from heaven, it was believed, and had the power to bring together people in love. See NKBT, vol. 8, p. 313 (no. 1009); *The Tale of Genji*, p. 453; NKBT, vol. 15, p. 354; and Robert Brower and Earl Miner, *Fujiwara Teika's Superior Poems of Our Time* (Stanford: Stanford University Press, 1967), pp. 94–5.

**459** 'Your patient search and long vigil' *On-kokoro-ne no itōshi-* [4, 12b] *ki ni.*

**460** 'The clouds,' etc. *Katsuragi ya Takama no yama ni*, etc.: wood-block, *Kazuraki*; Katsuragi refers to the ridge of mountains in the districts of Kita-Katsuragi and Minami-Katsuragi, between the prefectures of Nara and Osaka, and it denotes especially the group of peaks around Mt Kongōsen, for which Mt Takama is another name. Katsuragi and Takama appear in the earliest poetry and chronicles, and Akinari's diction calls to mind especially Emperor Godaigo's verse in the *Shinshūishū*,

| | |
|---|---|
| *Katsuragi ya* | The billows of cloud |
| *Takama no yama ni* | That form on Katsuragi's peaks |
| *iru kumo no* | And on Mt Takama |
| *yoso ni mo shiruki* | Elsewhere sometimes leave their mark |
| *yūdachi no sora* | In showers of evening rain. |

See also the *Shinkokinshū*,

| *Toshi mo henu* | Year after year has passed, |
| *inoru chigiri wa* | As I pray to meet my love |
| *Hatsuse yama* | At Hase temple, |
| *onoe no kane no* | But the bell that echoes on the ridge |
| *yoso no yūgure* | Tells of someone else's evening tryst. |

See also notes 225 and 309. *Kokka taikan*, p. 589 (no. 289); and NKBT, vol. 28, p. 243 (no. 1142).

**461** 'Third Month' *Yayoi*: the Japanese name, used as a gloss for the Chinese characters, is thought to come from *iya oi*, meaning the time for the buds to grow.

**462** 'Of lovely name' *Na-guwashi no*: pillow-word for Yoshino. See *Man'yōshū*, NKBT, vol. 4, pp. 38–9 (no. 52); and NGSK, p. 69 (see also note 293 and cf. note 425, *hana-guwashi*).

**463** Mt Mifune: a steep slope near Miyataki (where the Yoshino River forms a series of rapids); found in early poetry, e.g., *Man'yōshū*, NKBT, vol. 4, pp. 146–7 (no. 242).

**464** Natsumi River: name of a part of the south bank of the Yoshino River around Miyataki, so-called for its fame as a place to pluck (*tsumu*) fresh green shoots (*na*) in the early spring. Cf. Tanizaki Jun'ichirō (1886–1965), 'Yoshino kuzu' (1931), for a modern story in which these same historical places figure in the narrative.

**465** Verse: ascribed to Emperor Temmu, in the *Man'yōshū*,

| *Yoki hito no* | When the good men of old, |
| *yoshi to yoku mite* | Beheld it and saw it well, |
| *yoshi to ii shi* | They pronounced it good; |
| *Yoshino yoku mi yo* | Look well now at Yoshino, |
| *yoki hito yoku mi* | You poets, now sing you well. |

NKBT, vol. 4, pp. 24–5 (no. 27).

**466** 'Even people from the capital regret it' *Miyako no hito mo minu* [4, 13a] *wo urami*.

**467** 'Close connections with a certain temple,' etc. *Nanigashi no in wa kanete*, etc.: cf. *The Tale of Genji*, pp. 81–2, 90; and NKBT, vol. 14, pp. 177–8, 196 (see note 484) where Genji, recuperating from an ague after his disastrous affair with Yugao, calls on a wise priest in the Northern Hills.

**468** 'Set for them a frugal evening meal' *Yūge ito kiyoku shite kuwase* [4, 13b] *keru*.

**469** 'Area around the cascades' *Taki aru hō*: present-day Miyataki (see note 463).

**470** 'Emperor's pleasure-palace' *Idemashi no miya*: see *Man'yōshū*, NKBT, vol. 4, pp. 28–9 (no. 36); 168–9 (no. 315); and NGSK, pp. 28, 116. Kakinomoto no Hitomaro's verse, 'On an Imperial Visit to the Pleasure Palace of Yoshinu,' is especially well known.

**471** 'Young fish swim upstream' *Chiisaki ayu-domo no miẓu ni sakō*: *ayu*;

a hard-boned game fish common to Japan. The adults spawn in the sea, and the young fish climb upstream in the spring to feed and grow in the swift, fresh waters of the mountains.

**472** 'How strange' *Ayashi* [4, 14a].

**473** 'Arose and leaped into the cascade' *Odori-tachite taki ni tobi-iru to mishi*: In early modern times skilled swimmers would dive from the rocks and let themselves be carried downstream, and Akinari's idea may have come partly from this practice. See Uzuki, *Ugetsu*, p. 529, quoting from a guidebook of the Tokugawa period, *Yamato meisho zue*.

**474** 'These evil creatures are aged serpents,' etc. *Kono ashiki kami wa toshi hetaru orochi nari*, etc.: cf. *Wu tsa tsu*, 9, 1b, 'The nature of the dragon is the most lustful of all. When it mates with a bull it gives birth to a unicorn; when it mates with a pig it gives birth to an elephant, and when it mates with a horse it produces a dragon steed. Should a woman happen to meet with one, she is very likely to become defiled.' See also Takizawa Bakin, *Nansō Satomi Hakkenden*, Iwanami bunko (Tokyo: Iwanami, 1935), I, 26, who shows indebtedness to both *Ugetsu monogatari* and *Wu tsa tsu*.

**475** 'So stubborn' *Kaku made shūneki wo* [4, 14b].

**476** Yamato Shrine: also called Ōyamato-no-jinja; in the city of Tenri, Nara Prefecture, near Nagara Station on the Nara rail line. Formerly venerated as one of the most powerful Shinto shrines in Japan, it is worshipped as the home of a god of the harvest, a Yamato clan deity, and a deity charged with protecting the nation against calamity and disaster.

**477** 'Courage and spirit' *Masurao kokoro*: or, the qualities of a 'manly heart.' These may be thought to derive from a 'tranquil heart.' See Introduction.

**478** 'As if awakening from a dream' *Yume no same-* [4, 15a] *taru kokochi*.

**479** 'Hamlet of Shiba' *Shiba no sato*: a place name that has puzzled commentators. See Uzuki, *Ugetsu*, pp. 538–9, who supposes it to be the present-day town of Nakahechi, district of Nishimuro, Wakayama Prefecture, on the Kumano Kaidō highway, west of the city of Tanabe. Uzuki cites an early nineteenth-century travel journal, *Kumano yuki*, in which the name Shiba-mura is associated with this location. Nearby the town of Nakahechi was the home of the forsaken and vengeful Kiyohime, of the Dōjōji legend, who owing to the excess of her passion was turned into a serpent (see note 490).

**480** Shōji: referring to his position as head of the manor of Shiba; cf. the *nō* play, *Dōjōji*, where Kiyohime's father is called Masago no Shōji.

**481** 'Splendid to behold' *Hanayagi masari* [4, 15b] *keri*.

**482** 'You, who have forgotten your old promises,' etc. *Furuki chigiri wo wasure tamaite*, etc.: cf. *The Tale of Genji*, p. 67; and NKBT, vol. 14, p. 146, where Lady Rokujo's jealous spirit appears to Genji in a nightmare or hallucination.

**483** 'If you believe' *Makotoshiku o-* [4, 16a] *boshite*.

484  Kurama temple: founded in the late 8th century on a mountainside in Sakyō-ku, Kyoto; now affiliated with the Tendai sect. Old commentaries on *The Tale of Genji* identify this institution with the 'certain temple on the Northern Hills,' where Genji went to rest (see note 467).

485  'Holy man who knows many kinds of exorcism' *Ito mo gen-naru hōshi nite* [4, 17b]: For a pertinent discussion of belief in evil spirits, ghostly possession, and their treatment, see Morris, *World of the Shining Prince*, pp. 135–9.

486  'Dropped the flask' *Kogame wo mo soko ni* [4, 18a] *uchi-sutete*.

487  'Poisonous vapors' *Ashiki iki*: cf. the *Nihon shoki*, which tells of a giant water snake that lived by a river and killed many people with its poison. A hero challenged the serpent, which changed itself into a deer and fled. The hero then pursued it into a cave under the water and slew it and all of its fellows, causing the river to flow red with blood. Aston, *Nihongi*, I, 299; and NKBT, vol. 67, pp. 414–15.

488  'Has the demon caused you to lose your mind?' *Ko wa mono ni* [4, 18b] *kurui tamō ka*.

489  'You must at least spare Tomiko's life' *Kono Tomiko ga inochi hitotsu* [4, 19a] *tasuke yokashi*: Manago has assumed Tomiko's form, and they are as if two souls sharing the same body.

490  'In Komatsubara, at the Dōjōji temple' *Komatsubara no Dōjōji*; a Buddhist temple of the Tendai sect, founded in the early 8th century; in the town of Kawabe, district of Hidaka, Wakayama Prefecture. The Dōjōji temple is famous for the legend of Kiyohime, who fell in love with a handsome priest named Anchin, when he spent the night at her father's house on his way to visit the holy spots of Kumano. Anchin promised to return to Kiyohime, but he failed to do so. She grew enraged and changed into a serpent and pursued Anchin to the Dōjōji temple. The monks hid Anchin inside a huge temple bell, but Kiyohime in her serpent form coiled herself around the bell, and the heat of her anger burned Anchin, leaving only his ashes. Cf. versions in *Konjaku monogatari*, NKBT, vol. 24, pp. 277–80; and the *nō*, NKBT, vol. 41, pp. 129–42. A *kabuki* version, *Hidaka-gawa iriai-zakura* (On Hidaka River Cherry-Blossoms Fall with the Evening Bells), was performed in Osaka in 1759. See also, U. A. Casal, 'Magic Vengeance in Old Japan,' *Asiatische studien*, 10 (1956), 114–29.

491  'I've heard that old age,' etc. *Ima wa ōite*, etc.: cf. *The Tale of Genji*, p. 81; and NKBT, vol. 14, p. 177.

492  'Mustard-seed incense' *Keshi no ka* [4, 19b]: see note 346.

493  'A white serpent more than three feet in length' *Shiroki orochi no mitake* [4, 20a] *amari naru*.

494  'For all time' *Yōgō ga aida*: defined in Buddhist terms as a measure of cyclic time; the period between the creation and the recreation of a world or universe.

## 8 *The Blue Hood*

**495** Title: A blue hood suggests an inexpensive flaxen cloth used as a head covering, especially by Buddhist priests of the Sōtō Zen sect.

**496** Kaian Zenji: Kaian is his religious name, and Zenji means Zen priest. He was an actual person and belonged to the Sōtō sect of Zen; he died in 1493, in his 72nd year by Japanese reckoning.

**497** 'Principles of Zen Buddhism' *Kyōgai no mune*: The Japanese text means literally studies outside the normal sects or schools. These were the intuitive doctrines of Zen.

**498** 'Devotions' *Ichige*: an ancient practice that began in India of spending the rainy season in religious exercises at a monastery. These lasted for ninety days from the 16th day of the 4th month to the 15th day of the 7th month.

**499** Ryūtaiji temple: of the Sōtō Zen sect; founded in the late 14th or early 15th century in the mountains near Shimōchi, in the city of Seki, Gifu Prefecture.

**500** 'Hamlet of Tomita' *Tomita to iu sato*: in the town of Ōhira, district of Shimotsuga, Tochigi.

**501** 'Took up a heavy staff' *Yama ōko wo* [5, 1b] *torite*.

**502** 'Patron of Buddha' *Dan'etsu*: from the Sanscrit, *dānapati*, an alms-giver, or one who escapes the karma of poverty by bestowing charity (see note 257).

**503** 'Above this village' *Kono sato no* [5, 2a] *ue*.

**504** Oyama: see Introduction.

**505** 'Baptism' *Kanjō*: A ritual administered to priests of the Shingon sect. It involves inauguration or consecration by sprinkling or pouring water on the head.

**506** Koshi: denoting the Hokuriku area, or the modern prefectures of Niigata, Toyama, Ishikawa, and Fukui. Here, the Eiheiji temple, one of the two leading institutions of the Sōtō sect, is located.

**507** 'It was useless – the boy finally died' *Tsui ni munashiku* [5, 2b] *narinu*.

**508** 'Now you can see why' *Saru yue no* [5, 3a] *arite*.

**509** 'A lady in waiting to the King of Ch'u,' etc. *So-ō no kyūjin*, etc.: cf. *Wu tsa tsu*, 5, 15b–16a, following the section that Akinari used for his introductory passage to 'The Caldron of Kibitsu.' The moth is fearful because of its associations in Chinese literature with the idea of death.

**510** 'Took his Zen rod' *Zen jō wo* [5, 4b] *mote*: a rod, usually about two feet in length made of hard wood, bamboo, or reed, with a ball of softer substance on the end, used by a Zen priest during practice in meditation to chastise sleepy disciples.

**511** Ma Shu-mou: an evil official who served the despotic first emperor of the Sui dynasty and was charged with the responsibility of building the Grand Canal. Eventually he was stricken with a rare disease. In order to cure the illness he drank lamb's blood, but after once tasting human flesh he became addicted to it. He fulfilled his craving for it in the manner that Akinari relates. Mentioned in *Wu tsa tsu*, 5, 7a.

**512** 'His constant piety' *Tsune no gyō-* [5, 5a] *toku*.

**513** 'Sinful path' *Meiro*: a Buddhist term defined as the 'path of delusion' and identified with the Sanscrit *māyā*, meaning 'magic,' or 'supernatural power.'

**514** 'A slothful mind creates a monster, a rigorous one enjoys the fruit of the Buddha' *Kokoro yuruseba yōma to nari, osamuru toki wa Bukka wo uru*: A Tendai Buddhist saying derived from a 6th century Chinese commentary on the Lotus Sutra (see Introduction).

**515** 'Withdrawing to his room' *Fushido ni irinu* [5, 5b].

**516** 'Towering gate was smothered with brambles and thorns,' etc. *Rōmon wa ubara oi-kakari*, etc.: cf. *Ritakugo hiten chūgi suikoden*, 6, 1a–2b; see also, ch. 6, of the 120 ch. version of *Water Margin*, *I pai erh shih hui te Shui hu* (Shanghai: Commercial Press, 1959), I, 97. The equivalent passage in Buck, *All Men Are Brothers*, I, 107 (from the 70 ch. version) does not reveal the full extent of Akinari's indebtedness.

**517** 'Hour of the monkey' *Saru*: about 3.30 to 5.30 p.m.

**518** 'Food' *Tokiryō*: Japanese gloss with the Chinese characters meaning literally, 'abstainence supplies,' a Buddhist name for the meal eaten before noon, after which one abstains from food; cf. the English 'breakfast.'

**519** Michinoku: or, Mutsu, part of the modern prefectures of Fukushima, Miyagi, Iwate, and Aomori, where during the middle ages a number of Zen temples, especially of the Sōtō sect, were being built (see note 15).

**520** 'To go back now' *Sato ni* [5, 6a] *kudaran*.

**521** 'Half-past the hour of the rat' *Ne hitotsu*: around midnight.

**522** 'The garden' *Niwa wo* [5, 6b].

**523** 'Your condition is disgraceful' *Asamashi* [5, 7a] *to mo*.

**524** Verse: from the *Ch'eng tao k'e* (Japanese, *Shōdōka*; Songs of Experience), comp. Yung Chia (665–713), a Chinese Buddhist priest of the T'ang dynasty. See also the *nō* play, *Yoroboshi*, where the answer is, 'The green mountains that fill my eyes / Only exist within my heart,' in NKBT, vol. 40, p. 411; and Nippon Gakujutsu Shinkokai, ed., *Japanese Noh Drama: Ten Plays Selected and Translated* . . ., III (Tokyo: Nippon Gakujutsu Shinkōkai, 1960), 109–10.

**525** 'Whether the monk was living or dead' *Nao sō ga* [5, 7b] *sei shi*.

**526** 'Godless Month' *Kaminazuki*: see note 25.

**527** 'Every sign marked' *Ika-* [5, 8a] *sama ni mo*.

**528** 'Dew drenched him as though autumn rains were falling' *Tsuyu wa shigure-mekite furi-koboretaru ni*: cf. *The Tale of Genji*, p. 319; and NKBT, vol. 15, p. 155, where Genji, after his return from exile at Suma and Akashi pays a nocturnal visit to Princess Suyetsumu, who lives in neglect and isolation at the Hitachi Palace (see also notes 222 and 384).

**529** 'Impossible to tell which way the path led' *Mitsu no michi sae wakara-ṛaru*: literally, 'three paths,' the number conventionally found in a Chinese or Japanese garden. See *The Tale of Genji*, p. 314; and NKBT, vol. 15, pp. 147, 454, n. 176.

**530** 'As frost that meets the morning sun' *Kōri no asahi ni au ga gotoku* [5, 8b].

**531** 'Founder' *Shoso*: the first patriarch of the Zen sect, Bodhidharma (d. AD 528).

**532** 'Shingon sect' *Misshū*: literally, 'the esoteric sect,' introduced into Japan by Kūkai.

**533** Sōtō: (Chinese, Ts'ao T'ung) one of the two branches of the Zen sect. Based on the teachings of the Sixth Patriarch, Hui Neng (Enō, in Japanese, 638–713), as preserved by his disciple, Ts'ao Chi on Mt T'ung (therefore, Ts'ao T'ung, or in Japanese, Sōtō), and introduced into Japan by Dōgen (1200–53). Along with the Eiheiji, in Fukui Prefecture, the Sōjiji, in Yokohama, is the most important temple of this sect.

## 9  *Wealth and Poverty*

**534** Mutsu: another name for Michinoku (see notes 15 and 519).

**535** Gamō Ujisato: (1556–95) one of the most brilliant military leaders of his day. He was descended from a distinguished family and baptised as a Christian. He served both Nobunaga and Hideyoshi, and the former gave him one of his daughters in marriage. Fearing his skill and bravery, Hideyoshi transferred him to Wakamatsu Castle, in the Aizu area of Fukushima, and in the end had him poisoned.

**536** Oka Sanai: This name, or its variation, Okano Sanai, appears in several anecdotal sources of the early modern period, most notably in the *Okinagusa*, comp. Kamisawa Sadamoto (1710–95). Here Sanai's wealth, bravery, service to the Gamō family, and the behaviour mentioned in the opening passage of the tale are recorded. See the text in Nihon zuihitsu taisei, 3rd Ser., vol. 11 (Tokyo: Nihon Zuihitsu Taisei Kankōkai, 1931), pp. 367–8.

**537** 'East of the barrier' *Kan no higashi*: east of the checkpoint between Hakone and Odawara on the Tōkaidō Post Road.

**538** 'Indecorously in one detail' *Katawa na-* [5, 9a] *ru koto ari*.

**539** 'Jewel from the Kunlun Mountain' *Konzan no tama*: in ancient China, the name of a legendary peak of fabulous height, which produced rich jewels. It is mentioned in such texts as the *Liu tzu hsin lun* and the *Lü shih ch'un ch'iu*.

540 'A T'ang-hsi or Mo-yang blade' *Tōkei Bokuyō no tsurugi*: wood-block, *tsuruki*; swords produced in these places are mentioned in ancient Chinese texts, such as the *Chan kuo ts'e* and *Huai nan tzu*.

541 'Of a man of humble position' *Iyashiki mi no* [5, 9b].

542 *Ryō*: a measure of gold. Many gold coins were manufactured in Japan around the end of the middle ages, and it is hard to determine their purity and weight. Akinari may have had in mind the ten-*ryō* coins known as Tenshō *ōban*, which were minted in 1588. Typical examples have been weighed at 44.1 *momme* (5.843 oz.) and analysed as being 7.384 parts gold to 2.616 parts of silver.

543 'In gratitude' *Ureshisa ni* [5, 10a].

544 'The rich need not be haughty' *Tomite ogoranu*: cf. the Confucian *Analects*, Legge, *The Chinese Classics*, I, 144.

545 'Wealthy men are always stingy and almost invariably stupid' *Tomeru mono wa kanarazu kadamashi, tomeru mono wa ōku oroka nari*: cf. *Wu tsa tsu*, 5, 7a–9b, for Hsieh's discussion of wealth and poverty, which had considerable influence on Akinari's views.

546 'Shih Ch'ung of Chin and Wang Yüan-pao of T'ang' *Shin no Sekisō Tō no Ōgenhō*: cf. ibid., pp. 7b, 8a. The biography of Shih Ch'ung (d. AD 300) may be found in the dynastic history, *Chin shu, ch*. 33. Shih was a man of vast wealth, who owned 'thirty-eight water wheels and eight hundred slaves.' But in the end his riches were confiscated, and he and his family were executed.

547 'Affluent men of old,' etc. *Inishie tomeru hito*, etc.: cf. *Wu tsa tsu*, 5, 7a–b.

548 'When the Grand Duke Wang was enfeoffed in Ch'i,' etc. *Ryobō Sei ni hō-zerarete*, etc.: at the beginning of the Chou dynasty, in China. The land was damp, brackish, and sparsely populated, but he developed trade and industry and soon made the state one of the most prosperous in China. See Watson, trans., *Records of the Grand Historian of China, by Ssu-ma Ch'ien* (New York: Columbia University Press, 1961), II, 478.

549 'Kuan Chung nine times called conferences of the feudal lords,' etc. *Kanchū kokonotabi shokō wo awasete*, etc.: in China, in the state of Ch'i, under the reign of Duke Huan (685–643 BC). It was not he but his ruler, Duke Huan, who summoned the other feudal lords for conferences, but owing to Kuan's policies the state remained rich and powerful for three centuries. Cf. ibid., 478–9.

550 'Men such as Fan Li, Tzu-kung, and Po Kuei' *Hanrei, Shiko, Hakkei ga tomogara*: Fan Li, along with Chi-jan, advised King Kou-ch'ien of Yüeh (496–465 BC) how to build a strong state. Later, he decided to apply the wisdom for himself, and he went to T'ao, where as a merchant he became a wealthy man known as Lord Chu. Fan Li's exploits are also sung in the nō play, *Funa-Benkei*.

Tzu-kung was a wealthy disciple of Confucius.

Po Kuei was a famous Chinese merchant during the time of Marquis Wen of Wei (403–387 BC). See ibid., 481–3.

**551** 'Worked for profit' *Ri wo* [5, 10b] *ōte.*

**552** 'Ssu-ma Ch'ien wrote of these men in his "Biographies of the Money-Lenders"' *Kore-ra no hito wa tsuranete Kashokuden wo shirushi haberu*: Ssu-ma Chien (135-ca. 93 BC), famous Chinese historian and author of the *Shih chi* (Records of the Grand Historian). See ibid.

**553** 'Later scholars contemptuously reproached him' *Sō iu tokoro iyashi to te, nochi no hakase fude wo kisōte soshiru*: Commercial activity was supposed to be vulgar, and a proper historian ought not to have praised people who practiced it. Such criticism may be found in Pan Ku's biography of Ssu-ma Ch'ien in the *Han shu* and also in the commentary of a late-Ming edition of the *Shih chi*, entitled *Shih chi p'ing lin* (Japanese, *Shiki hyōrin*), which was frequently reprinted in Japan and probably read by Akinari. See Gotō Tanji, 'Chūgoku no tenseki to Ugetsu monogatari,' *Kokugo kokubun*, 21, no. 11 (1952), 28.

**554** 'Without a steady livelihood no man can feel satisfied' *Tsune no nariwai naki wa tsune no kokoro nashi*: reflecting *The Book of Mencius*; cf. de Bary, *Sources of Chinese Tradition*, p. 107.

**555** 'A man with a thousand weights of gold does not die in the market place' *Sen kin no ko wa ichi ni shisezu*: cf. 'A family with a thousand catties of gold may stand side by side with the lord of a city,' Watson, *Records*, II, 499.

**556** 'The rich man and the king enjoy the same pleasures' *Fūki no hito wa ōsha to tanoshimi wo onajū su*: cf. ibid.

**557** 'Fish are plentiful in deep pools, and animals abundant on great mountains' *Fuchi fukakereba uo yoku asobi, yama nagakereba kemono yoku sodatsu*: also found in 'The Biographies of the Money Lenders.'

**558** 'Cheerful though poor' *Mazushū shite tanoshimu*: cf. the *Analects*. Confucius admitted that a poor man that does not flatter his betters or a rich man who is not proud may be praiseworthy. But he pointed out that one 'who, though poor, is yet cheerful,' or one, 'who though rich, loves the rules of propriety,' is even superior. Legge, *Chinese Classics*, I, 144.

**559** 'Maiming people' *Hito wo sokonai* [5, 11a].

**560** 'Appreciate your giving me a full reply' *Tsubara ni shimesase tamae* [5, 11b].

**561** 'Give complete loyalty to their lord' *Kimi ni chū naru kagi-* [5, 12a] *ri wo tsukushi.*

**562** 'Yen-tzu, who scarcely knew the taste of a single gourd' *Ganshi ga ichi hyō no ajiwai wo mo shirazu*: cf. the *Analects*, where it is said that in spite of his living in a mean and narrow lane and having only a single gourd dish to drink from, he continued to enjoy life. Legge, *Chinese Classics*, I, 188.

**563** 'Virtuous acts and good deeds performed in this world' *Genze no intoku zenkō* [5, 12b].

**564** 'By what sort of karma' *Ika naru mukui no naseru ni ya* [5, 13a]: *mukui*, more literally, 'retribution.'

**565** 'His ancestors received it, and his descendants preserved it' *Sōbyō kore wo ukete shison kore wo tamotsu*: cf. *The Doctrine of the Mean*, Legge, *Chinese Classics*, I, 398–9.

**566** 'The principles of earth' *Kuni no ri wo* [5, 14b]: *Kuni*; Japanese *kana* gloss with the Chinese character for 'earth' or 'land.' An alternative translation might be 'the benefits to the nation,' cf. *Wu tsa tsu*, 5, 7b.

**567** 'Bestows his largess' *Megumi* [5, 15a] *hodokoshi*.

**568** 'When they found it they took it, but when they could not get it they stopped seeking' *Motomete yō areba motome, yō nakuba motomezu*: wood-block, *motomesu*; cf. the *Analects*, Legge, *Chinese Classics*, I, 198.

**569** 'I do not depend on a permanent master' *Tanomi to suru nushi mo sadamarazu*; cf. Watson, *Records*, II, 499.

**570** 'When you think I've gathered' *Atsumaru ka to su-* [5, 15b] *reba*.

**571** 'Like water flowing downward' *Mizu no hikuki kata ni katabuku ga gotoshi*: wood-block, *katafuku*; cf. Watson, *Records*, II, 477.

**572** Mt T'ai: In Shantung Province, one of the most famous peaks in China. It appears often in classical and popular literature.

**573** 'Gentleman' *Kunshi*: used in the Chinese sense of a person who has the vision to see beyond personal profit and material interest to the broader needs of the state and mankind. See de Bary, *Sources of Chinese Tradition*, pp. 20–1.

**574** 'Four Seas . . . Five Provinces and the Seven Marches' *Shikai . . . goki shichidō*: The five provinces that make up the area around the capital and the seven large administrative units into which the rest of the country was divided in ancient times, or in other words, the entire nation. An expression found in early Chinese classics, 'The Four Seas' meant the whole world.

**575** 'Here and there,' etc. *Ochi-kochi ni hiso-* [5, 16a] *mi kakure*.

**576** Shingen: Takeda Shingen (1521–73); lord of the province of Kai (Yamanashi Prefecture), he strove to increase the productivity of the land and to improve the welfare of the people in order to strengthen his domains and expand his power. He died of illness while campaigning against Oda Nobunaga.

**577** Nobunaga: Oda Nobunaga (1534–82), who gained renown following his victory over Imagawa Yoshimoto in 1560 at Okehazama. Eventually he deposed the last Ashikaga shogun, winning control of the area around Kyoto. He was assassinated in 1582 by Akechi Mitsuhide.

**578** Kenshin: Uesugi Kenshin (1530–78); master of the present-day prefectures of Ishikawa, Toyama, and Niigata, he struggled for power against his perennial rivals, Takeda Shingen and the Hōjō family of Odawara.

**579** 'Nobunaga possessed outstanding skill' *Nobunaga no* [5, 16b] *kiryō hito ni suguretaredomo*.

**580** Shibata: Shibata Katsuie (1522–83), retainer of Nobunaga. Later he tried to block Hideyoshi's rise to power, but he failed and was forced to commit suicide.

**581** Niwa: Niwa Nagahide (1535–85), who served both Nobunaga and Hideyoshi.

**582** Hashiba: a surname Hideyoshi used at one point during his meteoric rise from nameless peasant stock to the leadership of the nation. The name Hashiba was made up of the characters for *bata*, in Shibata (also pronounced *hashi*), and *wa*, in Niwa (also pronounced *ba*).

**583** 'Rarely live longer than three years' *Inochi wazuka-ni mitose wo sugizu*; cf. *Wu tsa tsu*, 9, 3a.

**584** 'In every household they will sing "The Dance of the Thousand Autumns"' *Ko-ko ni Sen-* [5, 17a] *shūraku wo utawan: Senshūraku*, a composition of *gagaku*, or court music, by Minamoto no Yoriyoshi. First performed in 1069, it is still used on such occasions as the enthronement of the emperor. It symbolises peace and prosperity.

**585** 'Ming grass of Yao' *Gyōmei*: an auspicious plant said to have flourished in China during the reign of the sage emperor Yao. From the new moon on the 1st, to the full moon on the 15th day of each lunar month it put forth a leaf, after which it lost one daily until the moon grew dark.

**586** 'The hundred names could depend on their home' *Hyaku sei ie ni yoru*: i.e., 'home,' is written with the same character as that for *ie* in Tokugawa *Ie*yasu's name. Therefore, the spirit proclaims that Ieyasu will lead the nation to an era of peace, just as did the sage kings of China in days of old.

# APPENDIX 1

## Imperial Succession in the Twelfth Century

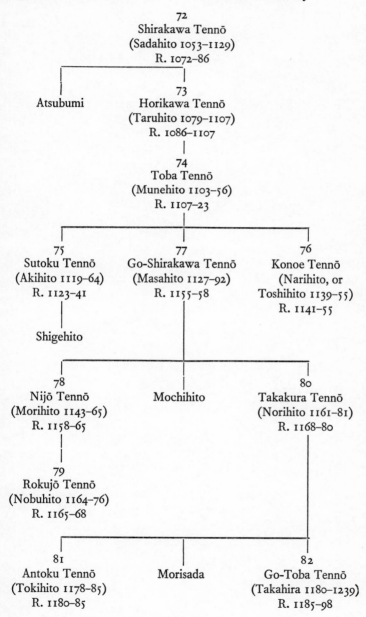

72
Shirakawa Tennō
(Sadahito 1053–1129)
R. 1072–86

Atsubumi

73
Horikawa Tennō
(Taruhito 1079–1107)
R. 1086–1107

74
Toba Tennō
(Munehito 1103–56)
R. 1107–23

75
Sutoku Tennō
(Akihito 1119–64)
R. 1123–41

Shigehito

77
Go-Shirakawa Tennō
(Masahito 1127–92)
R. 1155–58

76
Konoe Tennō
(Narihito, or
Toshihito 1139–55)
R. 1141–55

78
Nijō Tennō
(Morihito 1143–65)
R. 1158–65

Mochihito

80
Takakura Tennō
(Norihito 1161–81)
R. 1168–80

79
Rokujō Tennō
(Nobuhito 1164–76)
R. 1165–68

81
Antoku Tennō
(Tokihito 1178–85)
R. 1180–85

Morisada

82
Go-Toba Tennō
(Takahira 1180–1239)
R. 1185–98

# APPENDIX 2

## Alphabetical Index to the First Line of Verses Translated in the Text and Notes

### 1 *English*

## 2  *Japanese*

28  *Sari-tomo to* ('I have wept in sorrow'), p. 129.
29  *Sasurōru* ('As I wander'), n. 16.
30  *Sato wa arete* ('The place is desolate'), n. 237.
31  *Sumiyoshi to* ('It's a good place to live'), n. 219.
32  *Tamadare no* ('Though it may have shone'), n. 331.
33  *Tamaginu* ('Silk and finery'), n. 332.
34  *Tori ga naku* ('Where the cock crows'), n. 246.
35  *Tori no ne mo* ('Even a bird's call'), p. 142 and p. 147.
36  *Toshi mo henu* ('Year after year has passed'), n. 460.
37  *Tsuki ya aranu* ('The moon is not the same'), n. 239.
38  *Wasuretemo* ('In case you forget'), p. 145.
39  *Yoki hito no* ('When the good men of old'), n. 465.
40  *Yoshi ya kimi* ('Even though, My Lord'), p. 107.

**APPENDIX 3** *(Opposite)*

# APPENDIX 4

## Japanese Literary Sources: Alphabetical List of Selected Titles

| TITLE | GENRE | DATE OF COMPILATION OR PUBLICATION | POSSIBLE INFLUENCE OR INDEBTEDNESS |
|---|---|---|---|
| *Chikubujima* Dōjōji | *Nō* play Same | (Unk.) (late 15 C.–early 16 C.?) | 'Carp,' poetic description of Lake Biwa. 'Lust,' names of persons and places, element of plot. |
| *Endō tsugan* Fūgashū *Genji monogatari* | *Ukiyo-zōshi* *Waka* Anthology Heian novel | (1715) (1344–46) (ca. 1020) | 'Blue Hood,' idea of fondling corpses. 'Bird,' verse no. 1778 quoted. Elements of plot, style, and diction from chs. 'Kiritsubo,' 'Yugao,' 'Murasaki,' 'Aoi,' 'Suma,' 'Akashi,' 'Palace in the Tangled Woods,' 'Wind in the Pine Trees,' 'Tamakatsura,' 'Butterflies,' 'Wakana,' and 'Writing Practice,' primarily in 'Caldron' and 'Lust.' |
| *Goshūishū* Hanabusa zōshi | *Waka* Anthology *Yomihon* | (1086) (1748) | 'House,' poetic diction from verse no. 656. Elements of plot, style, and diction in 'White Peak,' 'Chrysanthemum,' 'House,' and 'Caldron.' |

| TITLE | DATE OF COMPILATION OR PUBLICATION | GENRE | POSSIBLE INFLUENCE OR INDEBTEDNESS |
|---|---|---|---|
| Hoan taikōki | (1625) | Military Chronicle | 'Bird,' details of Hideyoshi and Hidetsugu's conflict. |
| Hōgen monogatari | (ca. 1220) | Military Chronicle | Historical details in 'White Peak.' |
| Honchō jinja kō | (ca. 1650) | Shinto Institutions | Ceremony of boiling water in 'Caldron.' |
| Intoku taiheiki | (1712) | Military Chronicle | Historical details in 'Chrysanthemum.' |
| Ise monogatari | (ca. 940) | Heian poem-tale | Elements of plot and diction in 'White Peak,' 'Chrysanthemum,' 'Caldron,' and 'Lust.' |
| Kaidan tonoi bukuro | (1768) | Yomihon | Episode involving Hidetsugu's ghost in 'Bird'; meditating to exorcise a demon in 'Blue Hood.' |
| Kamakura ōzōshi | (15th C.) | Military Chronicle | Warfare in 'House.' |
| Kinuta | (early 15th C.?) | Nō play | Tone of reunion of man and wife in 'House.' |
| Kojiki | (712) | History; Mythology | Diction in 'Bird' and 'Lust.' |
| Kokinshū | (ca. 905) | Waka Anthology | Verse no. 867 in 'White Peak,' nos. 248, 387, 536, 747, 917, 947 in 'House'; no. 193 in 'Caldron'; nos. 248, 1009 in 'Lust.' |
| Kokon chomonshū | (1254) | Setsuwa | Names and legend in 'Carp.' |
| Konjaku monogatari | (after 1120) | Same | Dead wife returns to living husband in 'House'; man dies and comes back to life, in 'Carp'; death of a beloved woman, in 'Caldron'; fondling a corpse, in 'Blue Hood.' |
| Man'yōshū | (ca. 759) | Waka Anthology | Verse nos. 16, 27, 29–31, 36, 44, 52–3, 149, 199, 238, 242, 265, 273, 315, 336, 370, 419, 431–3, 503, 646, 804, 884, 1073, 1167, 1178, 1179, 1182, 1187, 1495, 1691, 1807–8, 2256, |

| TITLE | GENRE | DATE OF COMPILATION OR PUBLICATION | POSSIBLE INFLUENCE OR INDEBTEDNESS |
|---|---|---|---|
| | | | 2985, 3270, 3371, 3386, 3387, 3680, 3724, 3833, 3880, 3883, 4141, 4293, extending to all tales except 'Wealth.' |
| *Matsuyama tengu* | *Nō* play | (unk.) | Structural similarities to 'White Peak.' |
| *Miyako-dori tsumakoi-bue* | *Ukiyo-zōshi* | (1734) | Metaphorical expression in 'Blue Hood.' |
| *Nihon ryōiki* | *Setsuwa* | (8th C.) | 'Caldron,' idea of hair and scalp remaining, also, demon mutilates human being. |
| *Nihon shoki* (or *Nihongi*) | History; Mythology | (720) | Diction in 'Bird,' 'Caldron,' and 'Lust'; also Shinto ritual, elements of plot in 'Caldron.' |
| *Okinagusa* | *Zuihitsu* | (after ca. 1750) | 'Wealth and Poverty,' historical details about Oka Sanai. |
| *Otogi bōko* | *Kanazōshi* | (1666) | Diction in preface; elements of diction and plot in 'Thickets' (both texts reflecting the Chinese source, *Ch'ien teng hsin hua*), esp. idea of forsaken wife who as ghost after death returns to husband; also influence in 'Bird,' 'Caldron,' and 'Wealth.' |
| *Sangoku denki* | *Setsuwa* | (ca. 1431) | 'Bird,' legends about Kūkai. |
| *Sankashū* | *Waka* Anthology | (ca. 13th C.) | Three verses in 'White Peak.' Diction in 'Carp.' |
| *Senjūshō* | *Setsuwa* | (late 12th or 13th C.?) | Opening passage in 'White Peak.' |
| *Senzaishū* | *Waka* Anthology | (1188?) | Poetic diction, 'Carp,' resembles verse no. 461. |
| *Shigeshige-yawa* | *Yomihon* | (1766) | Traces of style, diction, plot, and narrative technique in 'House,' 'Bird,' and 'Caldron.' |
| *Shinchokusenshū* | *Waka* Anthology | (1234?) | Poetic diction, 'Chrysanthemum,' resembles verse no. 202. |

| TITLE | GENRE | DATE OF COMPILATION OR PUBLICATION | POSSIBLE INFLUENCE OR INDEBTEDNESS |
| --- | --- | --- | --- |
| *Shinkokinshū* | Same | (1206) | Same, 'Lust,' resembles no. 1142. |
| *Shinshūishū* | Same | (1364) | Same, 'Chrysanthemum,' no. 189; 'Lust,' no.289. |
| *Shinzokukokinshū* | Same | (1439) | Same, 'Carp,' no. 460. |
| *Shiramine-dera engi* | Temple Record | (1406) | Account of Saigyō's meeting ghost of Sutoku, 'White Peak.' |
| *Shokukokinshū* | *Waka* Anthology | (1265) | Poetic diction, 'Carp,' resembles verse no. 641. |
| *Shokushūishū* | Same | (1278?) | Same, no. 463. |
| *Taiheiki* | Military Chronicle | (ca. 1370) | 'White Peak,' Sutoku becomes a *tengu* king (from *kan* 27); 'Bird,' setting and manifestation of spirits (*kan* 25). |
| *Taikōki* | (See under *Hoan* . . .) | | |
| *Taionki* | Memoirs | (1702) | 'Bird,' physical description of Satomura Jōha. |
| *Tsurezuregusa* | *Zuihitsu* | (1229–31) | Association of spirits with deserted houses in 'House' and others; mention of rites for summoning the dead, 'Caldron'; description of hard work to little avail, 'Wealth'; also general style and diction. |
| *Uji shūi monogatari* | *Setsuwa* | (ca. 1215 ?) | 'Blue Hood,' plot element, the priest's sucking flesh and licking bones of the now-dead boy he loved. |
| *Yashima* | Nō play | (early 15th C.?) | 'Bird,' ghost of dead warrior summoned back to Hell, taking leave of moral witness. |

# APPENDIX 5

## Chinese Literary Sources: Alphabetical List of Titles Mentioned in the Introduction and the Notes

| TITLE | SINO-JAPANESE READING | DYNASTY OF COMPILATION |
|---|---|---|
| *Cheng tao k'o* | *Shōdōka* | T'ang |
| *Ch'ien teng hsin hua* | *Sentō shinwa* | Ming |
| *Ching shih t'ung yen* | *Keisei tsūgen* | Ming |
| *Hsiao ching* | *Kōkyō* | Former Han |
| *Hsing shih heng yen* | *Seise kōgen* | Ming |
| *Hsün Tzu* | *Junshi* | Chou |
| *Huai-Nan Tzu* | *Enanji* | Former Han |
| *Ku chin hsiao shuo* | *Kokin shōsetsu* | Ming |
| *Li chi* | *Raiki* | Chou |
| *Lieh Tzu* | *Resshi* | Chou |
| *Meng Tzu* | *Mōshi* | Chou |
| *Shih chi* | *Shiki* | Former Han |
| *Shih shuo hsin yü* | *Sesetsu shingo* | Sung (Six Dynasties) |
| *Shu yen ku shih ta ch'uan* | *Shogen koji daizen* | Sung |
| *Shui hu chuan* | *Suikoden* | Ming |
| *T'ai p'ing kuang chi* | *Taihei kōki* | Sung |
| *Ti Wang shih chi* | *Teiō seiki* | Chin |
| *Wen hsüan* | *Monzen* | Liang |
| *Wu tsa tsu* | *Gozasso* | Ming |

# APPENDIX 6

## Seven Representative Tokugawa Collections of Tales of the Supernatural that Preceded *Ugetsu monogatari*

*Otogi-bōko* (The Storyteller's Servant). 13 *kan*. *Kanazōshi*. Comp. Asai Ryoi. Kyoto: Akitaya Heizaemon, 1666. Rpt. in *Kaii shōsetsu-shū*. Tokyo: Kokumin Tosho, 1927–29. 'Kindai Nihon bungaku taikei,' vol. 13.

*Inu hariko* (The Papier-Mâché Dog). 7 *kan*. *Kanazōshi*. Comp. Asai Ryoi. Kyoto: Hayashi Kyūbei and Fushimiya Tōuemon, 1692. Sequel to the above. Also rpt. in *Kaii shōsetsu-shū*.

*Otogi atsu-keshō* (The Storyteller in Heavy Make-Up). 5 *kan*. *Ukiyo-zōshi*. Comp. Nakao Morioki. Kyoto, 1734. One of the fifteen tales in this collection was adapted by Lafcadio Hearn under the title 'The Story of Miminashi Hōichi.' See 'Akamagaseki-dome no yūki.' Rpt. in *Tokugawa bungei ruijū*. Tokyo: Kokusho Kankōkai, 1914–15, vol. 4.

*Otogi utsubo-zaru* (The Storyteller's Monkey Quiver). 5 *kan*. *Ukiyo-zōshi*. Comp. Mashida Kōwa. Edo, 1740. Also rpt. in *Tokugawa bungei ruijū*, vol. 4.

*Hanabusa-zōshi* (Tales of Elegance). 5 *kan*. *Yomihon*. Comp. Tsuga Teishō. Edo: Nishimura Genroku and Osaka: Kashiwabaraya Seiuemon and Kawachiya Hachibei, 1749. Rpt. in *Kaidan meisaku-shū*. Tokyo: Nihon Meicho Zenshū Kankōkai, 1927. 'Nihon meicho zenshū,' vol. 10.

*Shigeshige yawa* (Tales of Splendour). *Yomihon*. 5 *kan*. Comp. Tsuga Teishō. Edo: Nishimura Genroku and Osaka: Kashiwabara Seiuemon and Kikuya Sōbei, 1766. Sequel to the above. Also rpt. in '*Kaidan meisaku-shū*.'

*Kaidan tonoi bukuro* (Overnight Bag: Tales of Marvel). 5 *kan*. *Yomihon*. Comp. Ōe Bumpa. Kyoto: 1768. No modern editions available. Woodblock texts preserved in Kyoto University, Waseda University, and elsewhere.

# SELECT BIBLIOGRAPHY

1  *Texts in Japanese Consulted for the Present Edition*

A  Wood-block Edition:
*Kinko kidan ugetsu monogatari.* Kyoto and Osaka: Umemura Hambei and Nomura Chōbei, 1776. 5 *kan.* A photographic reproduction of the copy formerly owned by Mizutani Futō was the primary text. (Nakamura Hiroyasu, ed. *Ugetsu monogatari.* Tokyo: Bunka Shobō, 1967.) The title slip for *kan* 5 carries calligraphy by Tomioka Tessai. Copies of the wood-block edition in the libraries of Kyoto University, The National Diet Library, and the Tenri Central Library were also consulted.
B  Moveable Type Editions and Commentaries:
Nakamura Yukihiko, ed. 'Ugetsu monogatari.' In *Ueda Akinari-shū.* Tokyo: Iwanami Shoten, 1959. 'Nihon koten bungaku taikei,' vol. 54.
Shigetomo Ki, ed. *Ugetsu monogatari hyōshaku.* 1957; rpt. Tokyo: Meiji Shoin, 1959.
Suzuki Toshinari, ed. *Shinchū ugetsu monogatari hyōshaku.* 1916; rpt. Tokyo: Seibundō, 1929.
Uzuki Hiroshi, ed. *Ugetsu monogatari hyōshaku.* Tokyo: Kadokawa Shoten, 1969.

2  *Translations into European Languages*

Allen, Lewis. '"The Chrysanthemum Vow," from the Ugetsu Monogatari (1776) by Ueda Akinari.' *Durham University Journal,* N.S. 28, 2 (1967), 108–16.
Boháčková, Libuše. *Vypraveni za mesice a deste.* Prague: Odeon, 1971. Illus. Ludmila Jirinocova.
Blacker, Carmen and W. E. Skillend. 'Muo no rigyo (The Dream Carp).' Ed. F. T. Daniels. *Selections from Japanese Literature (12th to 19th Centuries).* London: Lund Humphries, 1959, pp. 91–103, 164–71.
Hamada, Kengi. *Tales of Moonlight and Rain: Japanese Gothic Tales by Uyeda Akinari.* Tokyo: University of Tokyo Press, 1971.
Hani, Kjoko and Maria Holti. *Esö ės hold nesei.* Budapest: Europa, 1964. (Not seen.)
Hansey, Alf. 'The Blue Hood.' *The Young East,* 2, 9 (1927), 314–9.
Hearn, Lafcadio. 'A Promise Kept,' 'The Story of Kogi.' *The Writings of Lafcadio Hearn.* Boston: Houghton Mifflin, 1922. X, 193–8, 230–7.
Sakai, Kazuya. *Cuentos de illuvia y de luna: traducción del original japonés.* Mexico City: Ediciones Era, 1969.

Saunders, Dale. '*Ugetsu Monogatari*,' or Tales of Moonlight and Rain. *Monumenta Nipponica*, 21 (1966), 171–95.

Seitz, Don C., ed. 'The Carp in a Dream.' In *Monogatari: Tales from Old and New Japan*. New York: G. P. Putnam's Sons, 1924, pp. 106–12.

Sieffert, René. *Contes de pluie et de lune (Ugetsu Monogatari): Traduction et commentaires*. Paris: Gallimard, 1956.

Ueda, Makoto. 'A Blue Hood.' *San Francisco Review*, 1, 4 (1960), 42–7.

Whitehouse, Wilfred and M. A. Matsumoto. '*Ugetsu Monogatari*: Tales of a Clouded Moon.' *Monumenta Nipponica*, 1, 1 (1938), 242–58; 1, 2 (1938), 257–75; 4, 1 (1941), 166–91.

Zolbrod, Leon M. '*Shiramine* (White Peak), from *Ugetsu Monogatari* (Tales of Moonlight and Rain), by Ueda Akinari (1734–1809).' *Literature East and West*, 11 (1967), 402–14.

## 3 *Japanese Secondary Sources*

Asano Sampei. *Akinari zen kashū to sono kenkyū*. Tokyo: Ōfūsha, 1969.
     ed. *Kōchū harusame monogatari*. Tokyo: Ōfūsha, 1971.

Fujii Otoō, ed. *Akinari ibun*. 1919; rpt. Tokyo: Shūbunkan, 1929.
     *Edo bungaku kenkyū*. Kyoto: Naigai Shuppan, 1922.
     *Kinsei shōsetsu kenkyū*. Osaka: Akitaya, 1947.

Iwahashi Koyata and Fujii Otoō, ed. *Ueda Akinari zenshū*. 1917; rpt. Tokyo: Kokusho Kankō-kai, 1923. 2 vols.

Kuwabara Shigeo, ed. *Ueda Akinari: Kaii yūkei no bungaku arui wa monogatari no hokkyoku*. Tokyo: Shichōsha, 1972.

Maruyama Sueo. 'Ueda Akinari kankei shomoku gainen.' *Koten kenkyū*, 4, 2 (1939), 76–86; no. 3, 95–104; no. 4, 180–93. Exhaustive bibliography of research on Akinari. Supplemented by that in Uzuki, ed., *Ugetsu monogatari hyōshaku*, pp. 713–27. (See 'Texts in Japanese,' above.)
     ed. *Ueda Akinari-shū*. Tokyo: Koten Bunko, 1951. 2 vols.

Morita Kirō. *Ueda Akinari*. Tokyo: Kinokuniya Shoten, 1970. 'Kinokuniya shinsho.'

Moriyama Shigeo. 'Ueda Akinari.' *Iwanami kōza: Nihon bungaku-shi*, Fascicule 8. Tokyo: Iwanami Shoten, 1958.

Nakamura Yukihiko, ed. *Akinari*. Tokyo: Kadokawa Shoten, 1956. 'Nihon koten kanshō kōza,' vol. 24.

Nihon Bungaku Kenkyū Shiryō Kankō-kai, ed. *Akinari*. Tokyo: Yōseidō, 1972.

Ōba Shunsuke. *Akinari no tenkanshō to dēmon*. Tokyo: Ashi Shobō, 1969.

Sakai Kōichi. *Ueda Akinari*. Kyoto: San'ichi Shobō, 1959.

Satō Haruo. *Ueda Akinari*. Tokyo: Tōgensha, 1964.

Shigetomo Ki. *Ugetsu monogatari no kenkyū*. Tokyo: Ōyaesu Shuppan 1946.

Takada Mamoru. *Ueda Akinari kenkyū* josetsu. Tokyo: Nara Shobō, 1968.
*Ueda Akinari nempu kōsetsu.* Tokyo: Meizendō Shoten, 1964.
Takizawa Bakin. *Kinsei mono-no-hon Edo sakusha burui.* (comp. 1833–35)
Kimura Miyogo, ed. Nara: Privately published, 1971.
*Kiryo manroku.* (comp 1802) In *Nikki kikō-shū.* Tokyo: Yūhōdō Shoten,
1913–15. 'Yūhōdō bunko.'
Tenri Giyarari, ed. *Akinari (1734–1809): Exhibition at Tenri Gallery.*
Tenri: Tenri Jihōsha, 1973.
Tenri Toshokan, ed. *Tenri Toshokan-ʐō: Ueda Akinari kankei shiryō
mokuroku.* Tenri: Tenri Jihōsha, 1973.
Tsujimori Shūei. *Ueda Akinari no shōgai.* Tokyo: Yūkōsha, 1942.
Ueda Akinari, comp. *Man'yōshū miyasu hosei.* Osaka: Katsuragi Chōbei,
1809.
Yamaguchi Takeshi. *Edo bungaku kenkyū.* Tokyo: Tōkyōdō, 1933.
    ed. *Kaidan meisaku-shū.* Tokyo: Nihon Meicho Kankōkai, 1927. 'Nihon
meicho zenshū,' vol. 10.


4 *Western Secondary Sources*

Araki, James T. 'A Critical Approach to the *Ugetsu monogatari.' Monumenta
Nipponica*, 22 (1967), 49–64.
Aston, William, trans. *Nihongi: Chronicles of Japan from the Earliest Times
to AD 697.* 1896; rpt. London: Allen & Unwin, 1956.
Bishop, John Lyman. *The Colloquial Short Story in China: A Study of the
San-Yen Collections.* Cambridge: Harvard University Press, 1956.
Boháčková, Libuše. *Ueda Akinari Ugecu monogatari: Roʐbor sbírky a
jednotlivých povídek a jejich motivických prvků.* Ph.D. thesis. Prague:
Charles University, 1966–67.
Chambers, Anthony. '*Hankai:* A Translation from *Harusame monogatari* by
Ueda Akinari.' *Monumenta Nipponica*, 25 (1970), 371–406.
Giles, Lionel, trans. *Taoist Teachings from the Book of Lieh Tʐu.* 1912; rpt.
London: John Murray, 1947.
Humbertclaude, Pierre. 'Essai sur la vie et l'oeuvre de Ueda Akinari.'
*Monumenta Nipponica*, 3 (1940), 98–119; 4 (1941), 102–23, 128–38; 5 (1942),
52–85.
Keene, Donald, trans. *Essays in Idleness: The Tsureʐuregusa of Kenkō.* New
York: Columbia University Press, 1967.
    *Landscapes and Portraits: Appreciations of Japanese Culture.* Tokyo:
Kodansha International, 1971.
Legge, James. *The Chinese Classics: With a Translation, Critical and
Exegetical Notes, Prolegomena and Copious Indexes.* 1861–72; rpt. Hong
Kong: Hong Kong University Press, 1961.
Levy, Howard Seymour, ed. and trans. *Warm-Soft Village: Chinese Stories,*

*Sketches and Essays*. Tokyo: Dai Nippon Insatsu, 1964.

Lin Yutang. *Famous Chinese Short Stories*. New York: John Day, 1952.

Miller, Roy Andrew. *The Japanese Language*. Chicago: The University of Chicago Press, 1967.

Morris, Ivan, trans. *The Pillow Book of Sei Shōnagon*. New York: Columbia University Press, 1967.

—— *The World of the Shining Prince*. London: Oxford University Press, 1964.

Nihon Gakujutsu Shinkōkai, ed. *One Thousand Poems from the Man'yōshū*. 1940; rpt. New York: Columbia University Press, 1965.

Tsunoda, Ryusaku, et al. *Sources of Japanese Tradition*. New York: Columbia University Press, 1959.

Ueda, Makoto. *Literary and Art Theories in Japan*. Cleveland: The Press of Western Reserve University, 1967.

Waley, Arthur, trans. *The Book of Songs*. London: Allen & Unwin, 1937.

—— trans. *The Tale of Genji*. 1925–33; rpt. London: Allen & Unwin, 1965.

—— *The Temple and Other Poems, with an Introductory Essay on Early Chinese Poetry*. London: Allen & Unwin, 1923.

Watson, Burton, trans. *Records of the Grand Historian of China, by Ssu-ma Ch'ien*. New York: Columbia University Press, 1961.

Wilson, William R. *Hōgen monogatari: Tale of the Disorder in Hōgen Translated with Annotations and an Essay*. Tokyo: Sophia University, 1971.

Young, Blake Morgan. '"Hankai," A Tale from the Harusame Monogatari by Ueda Akinari (1734–1809).' *Harvard Journal of Asiatic Studies*, 32 (1972), 140–207.

Zolbrod, Leon M. *Takizawa Bakin*. New York: Twayne, 1967. 'Twayne's World Authors Series,' vol. 20.